MW01253408

MAPes MONDe Editore

NIGHT OF THE SILENT DRUMS

by John Lorenzo Anderson

NIGHT OF THE SILENT DRUMS
First illustrated Virgin Island edition
Published by MAPes MONDe Editore
a division of MAPes MONDe, Ltd.

© 1992 COPYRIGHT to the illustrated edition
MAPes MONDe Editore, TORTOLA, ROME, ST. THOMAS
No portion of this book may be reproduced
without written permission
The story content of this novel belongs to John L. Anderson © 1975
First published by CHARLES SCRIBNER'S SONS, New York, 1975

ISBN 0-926330-06-3

TO MY WIFE

Adrienne Adams
WHO WAS RIGHT THERE

ALL THE WAY

This narrative concerns the island of St. Jan in the Danish West Indies in the years 1733-34. In 1917 the United States purchased the Danish West Indies and they became the Virgin Islands of the U.S.A. The name of St. Jan was then translated to St. John. The other main islands in the group are St. Thomas and Ste. Croix (now spelled "St." Croix).

The events in this book took place, as nearly as I have been able to determine to my satisfaction, as described here, and all of the names are the names of real people who existed in the times and places in which they appear. The fiction lies in the links that are missing in the source material that I studied; and these I have filled in, from hints in the material, with my imagination.

The interested reader will find a glossary and an alphabetical list of the principal characters at the back of the book.

J.L.A.

N.B. WORDS IN SMALL CAPS MAY BE FOUND IN THE GLOSSARY

William Blake, ca 1790, Allegory of Europe supported by Africa and America, MAPes
MONDe Collection

INTRODUCTION

The slave rebellion of 1733-1734 on St. John in the Danish West Indies is an important chapter in the history of the Virgin Islands and the Antilles. Among the various books which cover this episode, none is more extensive and factual than the *Night of the Silent Drums,* published in 1975 by John L. Anderson.

The author chose to recount this remarkable story as a colorful patchwork of personal perspective of the many actors on all sides of the story, together with their cultural backgrounds. No doubt, he felt that the strong passions and the incredible violence in this story could only be understood today by recreating the personalities of the main actors and the flavor of the Danish Islands in the early 18th century. Perhaps, the author felt also that by including many diverse and opposing subjective views, he might achieve objectivity, a very difficult feat two and a half centuries after the fact. Because of its recreative style and because of the lack of references, this book has been classified heretofore as fiction. It is quite clear, however, to those who have investigated the primary sources that John L. Anderson has based his book on a careful study of Danish archival materials, particularly Governor Gardelin's correspondence, the Pierre J. Pannet report, and the transcripts of the slave interrogations. In fact, the fifteen letters published in Part Five are authentic and unretouched.

This is not to suggest that this book is free of bias. As expected from the natural bias of the archival materials and the author's own biases, his brush strokes are generally finer for Europeans than for Africans. *Night of the Silent Drum* is a well-told, fascinating story and is closer to the truth than anything which has been printed on this subject to date.

Dr. Aimery Caron, St. Thomas,
University of the Virgin Islands

EDITOR'S NOTE

This novel accurately reports what is known of the St. John slave rebellion in 1733. Every character is a real person who lived and is recorded in the archives. This is, of course, the story as told by those who wrote the records of the day. The record from the African slaves' point of view is missing. In history one accepts what has survived, but this natural omission is not to be lost sight of. Pierre Dockès in his work *Medieval Slavery and Liberation* makes this point several times:

> All we know is that what has come to our notice by way of a master's pen ...
>
> For some writers 'brigandage' is a word to cover all of this. This is the interpretation that today's historians have placed on the words of yesterday's ruling class, as though one were to view the 'terrorist' of the wartime resistance in France through the eyes of the Vichy government, ... or the Polish 'hooligans' through the eyes of the Gomulka regime ...
>
> ... source material—the raw stuff of history—is sorely lacking in this regard. The sources which the historian ordinarily works are produced by the master or their clerks and executioners, their retainers of one sort or another. The pen was not wielded by Spartacus, still less by some unknown slave or dependant peasant risen in open—or more frequently silent—struggle against his master."

Readers intrigued by what the African rebels' point of view might have been have at last such a record made accessible by the anthropologist Richard Price. He has now published the oral traditions of maroon communities in works such as *Alibi's World*. In some sense the Suriname maroons could be the survivors in St. John, had the maroon community there persisted.

HISTORICAL PREFACE

The historian Waldemar Westegaard, in The Danish West Indies, 1671-1917, *sums up the events on St. John in ten pages and sets the situation in a wide historical context. For the benefit of the reader this material is presented here as a preface to this edition. Recently, various studies published by Dr. Caron and Dr. Highfield of the University of the Virgin Islands have amplified our detailed knowledge of the events of 1733 and demonstrate how accurately John Anderson has based his novel on the events of history.*

Insurrection among its slaves has always been considered the most terrible experience that a slave-holding society could suffer. Whether in Rome with its slave risings, in Sicily or on the Italian peninsula, in Virginia with Nat Turner, or in a sugar colony in the West Indies, the prospect of a general servile uprising has equally alarmed the ruling class. It was during the first governorship of John Lorentz in 1691, a year after the first serious insurrection reported in the English colony of Jamaica, that clearly defined rumors of a negro plot against the whites are first heard. During those early years, when the greater number of the slaves on St. Thomas were native Africans, it is not strange that threats should have been breathed against the governor's life and that planters and Company officials alike were constantly on the lookout for conspiracies among the slaves. Cruelty on the part of an individual planter was likely to be rewarded by his slaves running away. Planters and officials must have realized the economic advantages of good treatment of so valuable a part of their plantation investment as their slaves. It was likely to require something more than individual cases of cruelty to bring about actual insurrection.

The most persistent motive that led to general unrest among the slaves was lack of food. When months of drought ruined the crops of maize, sweet potatoes, and other foods which the negroes were expected to raise for their own sustenance, the planters were obliged to buy provisions from outside sources if they were to save their negroes' lives and prevent them from rising against their masters. In 1725-1726 the drought was unusually severe and protracted. A number of the planters let their slaves starve to death; others gave them extra holidays, with the natural result that the blacks stole right and left and became exceedingly difficult to manage. Since open resistance to the whites was the worst of crimes, it is not surprising to find recorded in the Company's books for 1726 that seventeen slaves distributed among thirteen planters had been executed and were debited to the community at a price of about 120 rigsdalers each. The planters secured the equivalent for their losses in fresh slaves from the next incoming Guinea cargo.[1]

In the time that elapsed between the War of the Spanish Succession and 1733, when the first serious rebellion began in the Danish islands, the Northern War had brought the activities of the Company almost to a standstill. Besides this the money stringency in the commercial world following the collapse of John Law's Mississippi Company made the revival of trade in the West Indies very slow. The Company had managed nevertheless to assist a group of planters in occupying the small, mountainous, but fertile island of St. John. St. Thomas reached its maximum slave population and its maximum number of plantations during its government by the Company, about 1725. St. John's plantations had risen from thirty-nine in 1720-1721 to eighty-seven plantations containing a slave population of 677 in 1728. By 1733 there were one hundred and nine plantations with one thousand and eighty-seven slaves on St. John. In other words, there had been an increase of sixty per cent in the number of slaves during those five years, but of only twenty-five per cent in the number of plantations. Clearly St. John was rapidly forging ahead as a sugar island. St. Thomas, on the other hand, had begun to decline as a plantation colony; much of its ground had been under cultivation for half a century. Many of its planters, as the census lists show, secured plantations on St. John which they managed by means of hired overseers, they themselves remaining on St. Thomas. The difficulty so often experienced by planters in securing honest and capable managers (*Mesterknegte*) intensified the dangers of absentee landlordism. It was not always possible for all the plantation owners to keep their plantations supplied with white overseers despite the Company's threats of fines and confiscation.

The uprising of the slaves on St. John began late in November, 1733. During the spring and summer preceding there had been a long period of drought, followed in July by a destructive hurricane which had inflicted considerable damage upon the already suffering crops as well as upon buildings and shipping. A plague of insects had destroyed many of the products of the islands, and the negroes were threatened with famine. Another storm in the early winter was especially severe on the maize crop on which the negroes largely depended for their food. In order to check the disorders among slaves which such a succession of disasters naturally encouraged, Philip Gardelin, who had risen from the posts of bookkeeper and merchant for the Company at St. Thomas to the position of governor, issued on September 5, 1733, a mandate whose terrible severity reflects the prevailing tension between master and slave.[2]

Governor Gardelin's mandate provided that leaders of runaways should be pinched thrice with red-hot irons and then hanged. A negro found guilty of conspiracy was to lose a leg, unless the owner requested lightening the sentence to one hundred fifty lashes and the loss of the negro's ears. Slaves failing to report a plot of which they had knowledge were to be branded in the forehead and to receive one hundred lashes besides. Informers of negro plots could secure cash premiums and have their names kept secret. Runaways caught within a week were to be punished with one hundred fifty lashes; those of three months' standing were to lose a leg; if they remained away for six months, it would cost them their lives. Thievery, and assistance of thieves and runaways, were to be punished by whipping and branding. A negro raising his hand against a white man must be pinched three times with a hot iron; whether he should be hanged or merely lose a hand was left to the discretion of his accuser. The testimony of a reputable white man against a negro ordinarily sufficed; in case of doubt the negro might be submitted to torture. A negro meeting a white man on the road was to stand aside until the latter had passed him. The carrying of sticks or knives, witchcraft among negroes, attempts to poison, dances, feasts and music, loitering in the village after drumbeat, all were provided against. Free negroes implicated in runaway plots or found to have encouraged thievery were to be deprived of liberty and property, and after receiving a flogging, to be banished from the land. This mandate with its nineteen paragraphs was to be proclaimed to the beat of drum three times each year. Thus did the authorities attempt to strike terror into the hearts of the restless, half-famished negro population.

On Monday afternoon, November 23, 1733, a very badly frightened soldier and some panic-stricken refugees from St. John appeared in the fort at St. Thomas harbor and poured into the ears of the astonished governor and his council a most fearful tale. Early that morning twelve or fourteen of the company's negroes had come up the path on the mountainside to the fort overlooking Coral Bay on St. John, each of them with an armful of wood. When the sentinel shouted, "Who is there?" he received the answer, "Negroes with wood," and opened the door. Rushing inside, the negroes pulled sugarcane knives (*Kapmesser*) out from the wood and murdered the soldier on the spot. Meantime other negroes had assembled and together they rushed in upon the sleeping corporal and his six soldiers, killing all but one (John Gabriel) who in the early twilight managed to save himself by crawling under a bed, and later escaped through the bush and down to a canoe by the seashore. With the garrison out of the way the negroes proceeded to raise the flag and fire three shots from the cannon at the fort. This was the signal for a general slaughter on all the plantations on the island.

The ranking magistrate on St. John, John Reimert Soedtmann, and his stepdaughter were among the first victims of that fateful day. A band of negroes, including some of Soedtmann's own, routed them both out and put them to death in the early morning. Soedtmann's wife was saved by the circumstance of her being on a visit to St. Thomas. Roaming about from plantation to plantation in that dim tropic dawn they slaughtered such whites as they could find, planters and overseers, women and children. As the bloody work proceeded, the band increased their numbers. The Company's and Soedtmann's negroes were joined by others;[3] and by the middle of the afternoon a body of eighty desperate blacks, half of them with flintlocks or pistols, the rest with cane-knives and other murderous weapons, were ready to attack those whites that remained. Though murder was rife, its course did not run absolutely without control. One Cornelius Bödger, the surgeon in St. John, and his two young stepsons were saved, the former because of his medical skill, the latter because the rebels hoped to make these boys their servants. Someone's intercession at the last moment saved the life of a former overseer of the Company who accepted with alacrity the invitation of the rebels to leave the island.[4]

The surviving planters, with such negroes as remained faithful, had in the meantime collected at Peter Deurloo's plantation on the northwest corner of the island. The approach to "Deurloo's Bay" was easily guarded, and the fugitive planters were within fairly easy reach of St. Thomas. While the St. Thomas officials and planters were making such preparations for their relief as they could, a small band of whites[5] under the leadership of Captain of militia John von Beverhoudt[6] and Lieutenant John Charles, together with a score or more of their best negroes, were hastening with feverish activity to prepare for the rebel onslaught. The women and children were quickly transported to nearby islets. A number of the planters on the south side and on the west end of the island were warned by friendly slaves in time to permit them to join the men at Deurloo's or to seek safety in their canoes.

The negroes had met some resistance from a planter in "Caneel" Bay.[7] They finally drove him off and stopped to plunder his plantation; consequently they did not descend the mountain path toward Deurloo's plantation until 3 o'clock in the afternoon. When they came they found themselves confronted by the few cannon with which the plantation was furnished. Fearing to face the cannon with their charges of ball, they betook themselves to the bush, from which they emerged at intervals to fire blindly and clumsily at their erstwhile masters. Had they rushed their opponents at the start the negroes might at the expense of a few lives have mastered the plantation and captured its defenders. Instead they kept up their desultory firing during the greater part of the night and resumed it the following morning with scarcely any loss to the whites. The arrival of the news at St. Thomas had paralyzed all. Wives trembled for their husbands, mothers for their children. Governor Gardelin shared the general consternation. It was not until former Governor Moth appealed to Gardelin not to abandon the children of his government to the barbarity of their heathen slaves that a boat with sixteen or eighteen soldiers, led by a sergeant and a corporal, was provisioned with food and ammunition and sent to the relief of the St. John planters. Several creole slaves with guns accompanied the party.

The arrival of the reinforcements which were commanded by William Barens, a well-to-do Dutch planter of St. Thomas, put new heart into the besieged party. Further reinforcements, consisting largely of negroes belonging to the Company and to planters on St. Thomas, enabled the planters to retake the fort and disperse the negroes to the woods. Urged on by the Company's officials, the soldiers and planters on St. John began a war of extermination. For a time the negroes managed to use the Suhm plantation as their rendezvous, but before the Christmas season they had been pretty effectually scattered over the island. Attempts by various stratagems to capture any considerable number of them failed. A white planter, one William Vessup, who had murdered a neighbor some months before and whom the authorities had failed to apprehend, was given to understand that his assistance in the slave-hunt would be welcomed by the government. The negroes proved too wary to permit themselves to fall into the trap he prepared for them. Their shortage of ammunition had even led them to offer Vessup ten negroes if he would get them as many barrels of powder. Enough negroes were killed or captured, however, to cause Governor Gardelin to express the fear that the decaying bodies of the dead rebels might bring a seventh misfortune—the plague—upon the stricken colony. The planter Peter Pannet states in his account of December 4 that thirty-two rebels had actually been executed, and that others were being tried.

The fear that the rebellion might spread to St. Thomas and Tortola not only roused the St. Thomas planters to contribute some of their slaves to the hunt on the sister island, but led their English neighbors to lend a helping hand. With many of their plantations ravaged, their crops neglected or destroyed, their cattle running wild or furnishing food for rebel slaves, it is small wonder that the St. John planters asked the Company to bear a substantial share of the burden of putting down the trouble and even requested that they should be exempted from taxes for a term of years. After nearly ten weeks of vain effort a certain Captain Tallard of an English man-of-war visiting Tortola sent sixty men to St. John to join in the pursuit; but an ambush in the night resulted in the wounding of four English sailors and the consequent withdrawal of the English forces. On February 17, that is, not long after this disappointment, the St. John planters again appealed for assistance from the English. On Sunday, March 7, another English captain, John Maddox, came from St. Kitts and landed on the island with about fifty volunteers, though his entire party was reported to Governor Gardelin as consisting of seventy men. A carefully worded contract was drawn up specifying with precision the duties of both parties and enumerating the rewards to be given for slaves captured. The attorney for the government, "fiscal" Ditlof Nicholas Friis, was sent to St. John to see that the contract was adhered to. Such elaborate precautions proved quite unnecessary. After a vain and wearying search Captain Maddox suddenly came upon the rebels on the eleventh day (March 18), but he was taken by surprise, for the negroes killed three of his men and wounded five others without any loss to them, so far as could be ascertained. Maddox's men stood not upon the order of their going; they fled at once and left the island on the following day.

Stratagems, attempts at poisoning, and the armed forces of Danes and English had failed alike to dislodge or exterminate the desperate slaves. In the extremity of their despair the Danish colonists turned to the French on Martinique. A French boat was lying in the harbor, and three or four days after Maddox's departure, the French skipper set sail for Martinique with the Company's bookkeeper, John Horn, on board. Horn's instructions permitted him to offer the French four-fifths of the remaining rebels—(their numbers were estimated at a hundred men and women)—if they could catch them. Twenty of the worst ones were to be handed over to the Company, evidently for exemplary punishment. The St. Thomas government pledged itself to furnish provisions for anywhere from one to two hundred men. Its envoy was provided with a fund of 600 rigsdalers to be expended as Horn saw fit.

When two French barks anchored in St. Thomas harbor on the morning of April 23 with the bookkeeper John Horn and two hundred and twenty creoles and experienced officers on board, the oft-disappointed colonists began to see their hopes revive. With renewed energy and resolution the governor and the inhabitants set to work to insure the success of this final effort. With a splendid enthusiasm the French had offered, wrote Governor Gardelin to John Beverhoudt on St. John, to send as many as six hundred men to the assistance of the Danes. The planters contributed seventy-four West Indian negroes to assist in the chase, though the governor had asked for a hundred and fifteen.

Why the French should respond so joyfully it would be rather difficult to explain were it not for certain European conditions. France was preparing to take up the cause of Stanislas Leszczynski, father-in-law of Louis XV, in his attempt to secure the Polish throne. France, which had scarcely recovered from the collapse of the Mississippi Bubble, was in serious need of money. She was also anxious for Denmark's neutrality in the coming War of the Polish Succession. In this extremity a shrewd director of the Danish company turned the trick by offering the French envoy 750,000 *livres* for the island of St. Croix, with Denmark's neutrality thrown in. But the news of the transfer and of Denmark's friend-ship reached the French islands through their home government considerably before the directors at Copenhagen got ready to send a ship to St. Thomas. Nor do the French from Martinique appear to have divulged to the Danish authorities at St. Thomas the mainsprings of their zeal. To the distressed planters and Company it was the fact of assistance and not its motives that mattered.

On the day following their arrival the French under their commander Longueville were promptly dispatched to St. John. The Danish governor lost no time in sending on planks for the soldiers' barracks and fresh meat for food. Crown attorney Friis was ordered to St. John to take charge of the negroes as they were captured. He was to try and judge half of those caught and the others were to be sent to St. Thomas for trial. The French commandant was to preside over the drumhead court-martial when it should be called, but a Danish representative was to be present. A force of twenty-five or thirty Danes under Lieutenant Fröling was got together and sent over to work in conjunction with the French.

Within three or four days of their arrival the French forces were encamped and ready for their grim labors. Only five days before the arrival of the French on St. John, a party of about forty rebels had made a fierce attack, lasting an hour and a half, upon the burghers who were encamped on Deurloo's plantation. They managed to set the supply magazine on fire, but suffered a loss of three killed and six badly wounded. From April 29 when they met their first party of rebels to May 27 when they returned to St. Thomas, the French force clung tenaciously to the heels of their quarry until they were unable to find the trace of a single live rebel. During the first three weeks they had to march up hill and down dale, through bush and bramble in an almost continual downpour of rain. By working in shifts they completely wore out the energies of the rebels, some of whom in lack of guns had armed themselves with bows and arrows. On May 9 they learned that the negroes were assembled on a certain point or small peninsula of land. The band escaped, but a wounded boy showed the French where eleven rebels lay in the bush, dead by their own act. A week later eight rebels gave themselves up in the hope of averting the captured rebel's fate. Two more were killed with a single shot, and two were found murdered. Of the rest there was no trace until May 24, when a report came in that twenty-four dead rebels had been found on an outjutting point of land in an unsuspected place, with their muskets broken. They were reported as having lain there for perhaps a fortnight.

The Danish officials in their reports to the directors could not praise highly enough the courage of the French on the field and their uniform courtesy everywhere. "The fatigues that the French have undergone," wrote the governor in his report to his masters, "from the first day that they came to St. John cannot be adequately described. . . . The obligations that we are under to the French officers merits a far greater reward than we are able to give them. The commandant himself marched with his men for four days through forests and valleys, up steep mountain-sides, and in a continuous slush and rain, with no roof above him but the sky. Next to God, they [the officers], because of their tireless effort, deserve the credit for the present peace. Their bravery and persistence and the cheerfulness with which they encouraged their men, who began very early to tire from their strenuous efforts, will we trust be properly rewarded in high places. . . ."

On their arrival at St. Thomas on May 27 Commandant Longueville and his officers and men were shown every attention and courtesy. An offer of 5,000 "French guldens" was politely refused by the French officer. After five days of celebration the French, accompanied by John Horn, embarked for Martinique. There, in turn, the Danes were treated by the French officials with marked cordiality and deference.

This happy outcome, happy so far as the whites were concerned, was marred by a bitter quarrel between the local government and the planters, each side trying to blame the other for the uprising with a view to being relieved of part of the expense. But the end of the rebellion was not quite at hand; for early in August—two months after the French had left—the report came in that a party of fourteen negroes and negresses, led by one Prince[8] was still at large, though without firearms. To avoid an expensive "maroon hunt" Theodore Ottingen, an officer who had taken part in the suppression of the rebellion since its beginning, managed on promise of pardon to lure the fifteen remaining rebels to their former owners' plantations. On the pretext that they would have to be appraised, every one of them was seized at a given signal on the morning of August 25 and brought to St. Thomas. Prince was not among them, for he had—fortunately for himself—been beheaded, and his head was a trophy in Ottingen's baggage. Of these fifteen rebels four "died" in prison before they could be brought to trial, four were condemned to be worked to death on the St. Croix fortifications, and the rest were done to death in various ways "such as they deserved because of their gruesome deeds," as the official letter has it.

With this piece of treachery, as it would be called in this age, a success for which the responsible officer received high praise from his superiors and a lieutenancy on St. Croix, the insurrection of 1733-1734 on St. John came to an end. Besides those killed in conflict and those belonging to the Company, twenty-seven negroes were estimated to have been tried and executed. A list made out in February, 1734, just before Maddox's ill-fated attempt, showed one hundred forty-six negro men and women implicated in rebellion at that time.

When the time for stock-taking came, it was found that planters were entitled to remuneration for thirty slaves that had been condemned to death or to work in irons, and for six others—two belonging to St. John and four to St. Thomas planters. These six had been killed while fighting for their owners. Of ninety-two plantations listed by Theodore Ottingen probably late in 1734 or in 1735, forty-eight were recorded as having suffered damage, forty-four as having escaped it. Of the former, thirty were being cultivated when the report was made; of the latter, thirty-two were being cultivated. On forty-one plantations, valuable buildings had been partly or wholly burned down by the rebels. The money loss was estimated, according to Höst, at 7,905 rigsdalers, a considerable sum for so small an island. As to loss of life by the white population, probably not a fourth of the whites were killed by the negroes. But this human hurricane had been far more devastating than any sent out from Nature's workshop, for it had not only destroyed men and their labor of years, but hardened their hearts and greatly delayed the prospect for more normal and human relations between master and slave in the Danish islands.[9]

NOTES TO THE PREFACE

1 *N. J. for 1726* (June 29). This may represent the slaves executed since 1723, as the planters were requested in 1725 to send in lists of slaves who had been condemned to death or severe punishment since that date. Cf. *Martfeldt MSS.*, Vol. I, "*Placater for St. Thomas*" (1684-1744).

2 The governor and council reported two ships, thirteen barks, two schooners, and two two-masted boats, many canoes, sloops, and ships' boats to have been washed ashore and practically destroyed. *Martfeldt MSS.*, Vol. VI, 227 et seq. (July 28, 1733). In the report (*Generalbrev*) sent by the St. Thomas government to the Directors on June 18, 1733, it is stated that because of the drought, the Company's plantation on St. John yielded only sixty-two hhd. of sugar, where one hundred and fifty hhd. had been expected. *B. & D., 1732-34.*

3 Among the others were the negroes of former Governor Suhm, of town-judge Lorentz Hendricksen and of Pieter Kröyer. *Gardelin MSS.* (November 23, 1733); cf. *Martfeldt MSS.*, III, "*Om Rebellionen paa St. John.*"

4 This was Dennis (or *Dines*) Silvan. He fled to Tortola, the English island lying within sight of St. John.

5 P. J. Pannet in his *Relation* dated December 4 (*Werlauff MSS.*, No. 22, Royal Libr., Copenhagen) gives the number at Deurloo's as about seventeen whites and twenty negroes, while the Company's officials in their letter to the Directors of January 5, 1734 (*Martfeldt MSS.*, III), give forty whites and about twenty-five negroes as the number of those on the defensive against the rebels.

6 Also spelled Bewerhoudt, Beverhout, Beverhoudt. Among the other white inhabitants at Deurloo's plantation were John Runnels, Timothy Turner (*Thörner*), William Zytzema, and Peter Sörensen. *Gardelin MSS.* (November 23, 1733.)

7 "Caneel" means cinnamon and refers to one of the Cinnamon Bays where John Jansen lived with his wife on a cotton plantation belonging to his mother which was 3000 x 1500 feet in size. Three

"capable" slaves and four children constituted his labor outfit in 1733. *L. L., St. J., 1733.*

8   A negro belonging to Madame Elizabeth Runnels.

9   (Ed.) The opposite might be argued. In spite of local feelings, national public attention was aroused by this violent class conflict. The islands were moved to Danish rule from Company rule in 1754. The rule of Law eventually encompassed the African population as a solution to such struggle.

PART ONE

April 31, 1733

The Planter's House, MAPes MONDe Collection

I

IN the hush before this moonlit tropic dawn not even the GECKO stirs.

Nature seems to hold her breath and wait to see which of her creatures will shatter the stillness, and unfailingly it is the bantam cock perched in MESTER Bodger's MAMPOO tree. Blatantly he lets out his shriek that starts a cock-crow chain running through the countryside and introduces a fresh morning with its joys and terrors.

In the slave quarters of PLANTAGES from here to the other end of the island the BUSSALS and old-line field slaves, astir under the insistent reveille of the TUTU and the threat of the lash, breathe the sweet ocean air and dread the sweat and fear and hatred of this, another inevitable day.

A master, almost any master of BUSSAL slaves, startled out of sleep in the darkness of his hammock-bed by their hubbub and the admonishing shouts of the BOMBAS, must shudder as always in this first instant awake. His heart starts up, thrumming like a wild bird, cold flesh creeps along his neck and he thinks "Oh, God, the time has come! They surmise their strength!" Then reading his reprieve in the blessed everyday quality of the sounds, he subsides gratefully upon his pillow with the unpleasant prickle of drying perspiration on his brow, and prepares himself to arise and beat down another day.

The red-brown bantam in MESTER Bodger's MAMPOO tree is conscious only of an irresistible compulsion. He preens himself and cocks one flat, staring eye westward toward the height and length of St. Jan that points toward St. Thomas, as the first flush of morning insinuates itself across the horizon to color a cloud. He stretches his neck, flaps his wings, and once more screams.

A puff of the dawn-stilled trade wind stirs a prattle in the dry

pods of the drought-stricken WOMAN'S-TONGUE TREES and the morning
of April 31, 1733, is under way on the island of St. Jan in the Danish
West Indies among the Virgin Islands.

II

MESTER BODGER, Cornelius Frandsen Bodger, CHIRURGEON and
physician officially to the Danish West India and Guinea Company's St. Jan plantation and unofficially to the whole island,
yielded at last to the insistence of the bantam cock and stirred
heavily in his bed. The cock, as always when the moon was bright,
had squalled at intervals throughout the night, but now Dr. Bodger
knew in his bones that it was time for the dawn.

He had been dreaming of his wife, but then he came awake and
knew again that she was long since dead.

He supposed he would never lose the pang he felt whenever he
thought of having been unable to save her while he and the boys
had survived without even falling ill.

Staring at the ceiling, he let his mind take up where it had really
never left off of late, trying to find reasons for the waves of death
that swept over the islands from time to time. If they were connected with the drought, what was the connection? Sickness and
death on the Danish islands during the first two years of the drought
had not shown much deviation from the usual. If anything, there
had been less sickness than in recent years of normal rainfall.

The "Krankenzeit" as it was called—in German because the
person so to label it was a German-speaking pastor—the sickness
time started as always approximately with the "Julekuling," the
"Christmas breeze," the cool dry wind of the Antilles winter. People
would start to shiver and be unable to stop, and a terrible fever
would be upon them, and they would die. There was nothing
Bodger or any other physician could do about it, in spite of all the
pills and powders and phials that could be had from Europe; in
spite, too, of the incantations of the officially prohibited witch

doctors, and even of the wizardry of the weed women with their concoctions from the islands' plants.

MESTER Bodger sighed deeply and rolled himself to a sitting position on the side of the bed, which he used in preference to the usual hammock.

This much accomplished, he sat marshalling his forces for the next move. He heaved himself up and went barefoot in his night-shirt across to the east window, where he came to rest with his elbows on the cool stone sill.

(He was fond of saying, for a laugh, "It is not true what the English say, that practice makes perfect. All my life I have practiced getting up in the morning, and *still* I do not do it well.")

The hooting of the conch-shell TUTU had sounded on the Suhm and Sødtmann PLANTAGES to the east and west of him, and now Bodger could hear the usual hubbub of the field slaves starting toward their work under the harsh shouts and whip-cracks of the BOMBAS.

He could hear the sounds of his own servants stirring about in their quarters a little way up the skirt of Buscagie Hill.

In the dawn's kindling red gleam the MESTER's square, ruddy face was reflected as he glanced into his dead wife's mirror in the corner beside him. This light made his head seem to cast a glow like that of a live coal, and his hair, short-cropped, was as a patch of white ash forming on the surface. The scar that parted his hair in a fairly natural manner but marred his forehead and left eyebrow could still catch his eye as a memento of the horror of the slave ship. The smallpox scars, trademark of the Indies, he had long since ceased to see.

His arms and shoulders showed firm and chunky, his hands blunt, strong. His chest was barreled. He was not a large man, yet he was not small. It was as if material for a taller man had been forced into the skin of a man of medium height.

He stretched himself, his joints cracking, yawned enormously with an exaggerated rattle in his throat, gathered a handful of the front of his nightshirt and, scouring his chest with it, chuckled softly.

That early morning chuckle was in itself indicative. Cornelius Frandsen Bodger, perhaps best of all the men on this island, could greet the new day, any new day, without dread. He was neither oppressor nor oppressed. No man had a valid reason to hate or fear him, for he had no competitor here and was, so far as he could know, a threat to no one, even his slaves.

It was in this moment, before the day had had its chance to seize him, that he saw and appreciated the monstrous joke he had played upon himself. How did he find himself in this situation, here at one of the ends of the earth? He had wanted to study at Oxford, in England. Son of Frands Nielsen BØDKER, English-oriented physician of KJØBENHAVN, and related to the great German-oriented Johannes Gottlieb de Bötticher, physician of Helsingør and KJØBEN-HAVN, he had a natural bent toward healing. The art and science of medicine, he well knew, were in his time little advanced beyond the practice of barbering, despite the resounding fight for dignity put up by physicians.

As a young man looking forward to a career in medicine, he had seen himself as a man of future importance, pedestaled with honors, healing the illustrious sick, sought by the great, revered by the common.

But the urge to wander had interfered. He had gone to sea, often in English ships, and changed the spelling of his name to fit the pronunciation given it by Englishmen who saw it written down. Led on and on always to just one more strange and distant land, he had found the Oxford dream forever being postponed.

He did take along aboard ship whatever books he could find that would give him the use of other men's experience and thinking.

He had fallen naturally into the job of assistant ship's doctor on one of his voyages, through the death of the physician on board. From there, with gathering experience, it was only a step to becoming a ship's doctor in his own right.

Then, almost killed on the voyage to St. Thomas aboard a slave ship, and beguiled by the suave climate of these Danish dots in the Indies, he had been glad to stay ashore for a while. His assistant aboard ship had been only too happy to step into his shoes there and choose a crony as his own assistant. Ignorance of medicine and its practice had little bearing; it was what one was called that counted. One learned to ply a trade aboard ship, as in the Indies, by plying it, and sometimes by defending the job against all comers.

Bodger had been under the impression that he owned land for a PLANTAGE on St. Thomas. An uncle had been given a piece of the island in 1675 by Governor Iversen, on a contract that required him to pay yearly, to the Company or its chief representative on the island, one capon and one hen, for so long as he should live. He had not lived long enough to pay enough capons and hens to justify ownership of the land, and when Cornelius arrived to claim it nearly a half-century later, he found that someone else had legal title to it.

Cornelius was then persuaded, in view of his experience, to take up medical service in the Company, with the rank of sergeant. Transferred later to St. Jan, he had got the undeserved reputation of "the sergeant who married money" by taking to wife, in 1731, Susanna, the widow of Johannes Minnebeck. The widow did own a paltry PLANTAGE on East End peninsula that Johannes Minnebeck left her at his death, but she gave it to her stepson, Johannes, Junior, sired in an earlier Minnebeck marriage, and went with Bodger to live on his PLANTAGE, which he had legitimately bought from former governor Moth, and had almost finished paying for, in Coral Bay.

Here he was, then, MESTER Cornelius Frandsen BØDKER, more commonly called Bodger, amateur planter as well as the Company physician on St. Jan, sitting in middle age on this little island, which looked as though it were one of the peaks of many flooded mountains. He was surrounded by fugitives, renegades, remittance men, fortune-hunters—the dregs of Europe, it sometimes seemed—and overwhelmingly by Negro slaves, some of them bitter and most of them hopeless.

Each man chooses what he wants; this was his firm belief. Everyone does what he really wishes to do, if only by refraining from doing what he more fervently wishes not to do. So this was probably what he really wanted: to be a man of importance in a microcosm, microcosmically honored, free to indulge his everlasting woolgathering and endless curiosity without being too heavily burdened with the necessity to compete, to battle for existence, self-aggrandizement, and eminence.

Even as Bodger's chuckle echoed softly in the semi-stone-walled room, he found himself idly wondering where the boys, his step-sons, Hans and Peter, had got to. There was neither sign nor sound of them, and it was not likely that they would be in bed or so quiet as this when there was light in the sky. Perhaps they had slipped off early to pick whelks along the rocky shore of the bay by the day's first light. That was slaves' work, but it was one of the boys' great pleasures, as was eating the resulting potage prepared by Finkil, the cook, as only he could do it.

As the light grew, Bodger pulled on his loose-fitting linen clothing and his sandal shoes, and stepped outside. Scattering the self-important bantam cock and his harem and chicklets, he walked along the dusty clay path around to the western side of the house.

From here he could watch the morning's first sunlight pick out the top of Bourdeaux's Mountain, which towered above the other side of the bay, and the nearly two-thousand-acre amphitheatre, most of which comprised the West India Company's St. Jan PLAN-TAGE.

The flood of light caught the top of VÆRN Hill, a conical eminence not far from the southeast corner of Bodger's house. Atop the hill, gleaming in the silvering glow, sat Frederiksværn, a loose-stone breastworks surrounding its mean little buildings. Bodger could hear Soldier Tiil's reveille on the drums there—a bit late, he thought.

Up the valley to the west another cone-shaped hill, much smaller than VÆRN Hill, rose above the uneven floor of the broad plain of the Company PLANTAGE. On its top stood the Company's unfinished master house, a two-story shell of red Dutch brick.

In the roofed caverns of the low wings of this building lived Svend Børgesen, MESTERKNEGT of the PLANTAGE, and his assistant Jan Frederik August, with their body slaves, male and female, and children. The house slaves lived in their little compound to the rear and came into the caverns to do their daily work. The kitchen slaves were in the cookhouse, also in the rear.

The huts of the field and windmill slaves clustered about the foot of the hill, and above them to the southwest loomed the great unfinished stone windmill tower, set to catch the trade wind as it swept up the slot between Buscagie and VÆRN hills.

Now the morning splendor reached the floor of the valley on the far side. A great bay of land this was, with here and there the low mound of a hill to save it from monotony, and bounded on three sides by the mountains, on the southwest by Coral Harbor, the relatively imperturbable inner waters of Coral Bay. Here in the usually moister lowlands were the Company's cotton fields that should be green now with spring showers but stood burnt to a russet brown.

As the morning trade wind began to strengthen, it brought the odor of dusty fields without actually stirring up any dust as yet.

The Company's storehouse buildings, at the foot of the mountain near the harbor, shone now in their whitewashed brightness.

The PLANTAGE next door to Bodger's on the west, between him and the Company holdings, was that of the magistrate for St. Jan, Herre Johannes Reimert Sødtmann. The Sødtmann establishment was more imposing by far than Bodger's, as befitted the highest representative of king and Company on the island, and stepson-in-law of the new governor of the Danish West Indies.

Bodger was pleased to have such neighbors as the Sødtmanns.

Their young daughter, Helena, though, was a problem to him. Every time he thought of her his heart would start thudding uncomfortably. This always made him feel guilty and foolish.

On the other side of Bodger, eastward along the track that led to Franske Strausche Quarter, French Bush, the East End peninsula, lay the large PLANTAGE of Henrich Suhm, absentee owner, previous governor.

Bodger could hear, now, borne on the freshening breeze from the northeast, the sullen sounds of Suhm's BUSSALS as they worked in the upper BARCAD; like Sødtmann's, they were terracing in preparation for the end of the drought. They had started at dawn, on empty stomachs, and would eat their breakfast, brought to them in the field by children, when the sun was climbing. They would pause at high noon, according to the custom, and go to their quarters. There they would prepare their own midday meal and rest while the sun was at its highest. Then at one-thirty they would return to the fields.

Before sundown they would stop work on the terracing and forage for grass, all dry now, and for whatever green leaves of any kind could be found, but preferably GENIP, and take them back to the slave quarters to be fed to the half-starved donkeys and goats. Then, at sundown, they ate the third meal of the day, prepared by themselves in their quarters.

All three meals would be the same for Suhm's BUSSALS, just now when it was impossible for them to grow or raise anything for themselves: mouldy, rejected bread from St. Thomas, baked with the weevils still in the flour; and rotten PEKELVLEES—salt pork, lamb, or mutton—from Holland or Iceland, or stinking POORJACK from Ireland or New England, out of whatever barrels had been rejected by the merchants and the Company because their contents were not fit to eat and therefore could not be sold at a profit for the nourishment of free men.

The food was grudgingly given in the name of the owner, purely to keep the slaves alive. The master was not obliged to give the slave any food at all, but only to furnish a small plot of ground in which the slave could grow his own fruits and vegetables to supplement the chickens and pigs and goats he could raise or acquire by some means from other slaves. But the drought had put an end to the growing of fruits and vegetables, and almost to the raising of chickens, pigs, and goats.

III

On this April 31, 1733, the angriest place, by far, on St. Jan was that Suhm PLANTAGE.

In 1732, with the unprecedented arrival at St. Thomas of two

Danish slave ships within five months, Suhm, then governor of the Danish West Indies, comprising St. Thomas and St. Jan, had snapped up twenty-five BUSSALS to send to his undeveloped St. Jan PLANTAGE.

These newly arrived slave cargoes had had in them something that had seldom been seen in these islands since the abortive attempt to enslave Carib Indians in the early days of the St. Thomas colony.

It was customary for slaves coming in from Africa to be docile. Generally they had been slaves at home, born in slavery, bred for it by a long line of ACCUSTOMED SLAVES, aided, when they did not reproduce fast enough for the purposes of trade, by their African masters.

The arrival of *HAABET Galley* and, four months later, *GREVINDEN AF LAURVIGEN*, had brought a jolting change. First had disembarked a few of the expected shuffling, resigned, ACCUSTOMED SLAVES, looking unusually haggard, while behind them aboard ship all was bedlam.

Then had come ashore—not shuffling, but struggling in leg-irons and chains, cursing in their African tongues—the new breed of slave.

These were Aquambos and Aminas. The two tribes were warriors, hunters, high-living noblemen, the cream of Africa, slave *holders,* not slaves—and implacable enemies of each other.

Aquambos and Aminas arriving in chains together, emaciated, ravaged by whips and hunger and the sicknesses of the ship's stinking hold, but still superb specimens of bodily and facial beauty and strength; still able to fight, they fought not each other, but their common captors.

Such noble slaves had arrived occasionally in the past, waylaid in some personal African vendetta, but those who had not been subdued and integrated into the slave population had either been killed in the struggle to subdue them or committed suicide when put to women's work in the fields.

But the arrival of this sort of slave in such numbers—how had it come about?

Accra, the Danish enclave on the Slave Coast of Africa, was running out of slaves, and the Danish ships, not being free to pick up cargo anywhere but at the Danish FACTORY there, had had to shop up and down the African coast, staying offshore and bargaining as best they could. Finding next to no cargo in this way, they had had to press hard upon the tribal chieftains with whom they had contracts at Accra. These chieftains, having bound themselves to deliver a certain number of "PIÈCES," were ambushing each other's war and hunting parties and turning their captives over to the slave FACTORY at Accra.

And so here in the slave pen on St. Thomas, enslaved but not by any means slaves, stood African royalty and nobility, constituted royal and noble by the selfsame process of many generations of heritage as were the royal families of the Kingdom of Denmark and Norway, or those of England, and France.

Good hard rum, the only currency now demanded for slaves along the coast of Africa, had already been paid. The value must not be lost. These noble slaves would have to be beaten into submission. Once trained, it was assumed, they should make extraordinarily good workmen, for they had superb bodies, nourished all their lives by plenty of the best food in Africa, and strengthened by constant athletic contests and martial training when there was no foe to fight and no need for hunting.

It was considered worth the trouble of training them, for the tamer would presumably end up with the finest slaves—and the finest studs for producing more slaves—in the West Indies.

Suhm's purchases, when sent up to his St. Jan PLANTAGE, would have to be placed in charge of someone capable of handling them. Perhaps a FREE NEGRO would be best, if a suitable one could be found to take the job. That was the trouble with FREE NEGROES—one could not order them to change their occupations according to one's wishes.

Mingo Tamarin would be ideal. Founder and head of the FREE NEGRO Corps, big, tough, accustomed to fighting other Negroes, keeping order among them, Mingo Tamarin would be the perfect MESTERKNEGT to see to the taming and training of these new slaves.

Slaves preparing cassava bread, Dantj Print Collection, Florence, Italy

But Mingo Tamarin did not have to do this, and he did not wish to go to the relative wilderness of St. Jan when he liked the capital island and his prestige there so much, and so he simply refused the job.

The final choice fell upon Jens Andersen, a white man, a Dane, who was nearing the end of his period of servitude as a SERVING, an indentured worker, for one of the Dutch planters of St. Thomas.

In the early days of the Danish colony on St. Thomas, the Danes, who detested the idea of slavery and yet wanted to compete in the New World with the other European nations, hit upon the idea of emptying the jails of Denmark and Norway. They brought the prisoners, both male and female, to St. Thomas, to let them work out their sentences. The men became laborers on the plantations. The women, officially household workers, unofficially were whores, thought by the male population to be badly needed, and child-bearers, who really were badly needed if the colony were to survive.

It had turned out that Scandinavian men could not live long, working under the tropical sun, eating the local foods, and drinking the local liquids. Women, yes, since their labors were largely indoors and in bed, and their eating and drinking habits less excessive than men's, could and did survive in greater numbers, but without solving the problem of labor for the fields.

Eventually the Danes, of necessity in the West Indian slave economy, turned reluctantly to slavery, but the precedent of white indentured labor had been established. Prisoners in Denmark and Norway might, if they wished, become SERVINGER, indentured workers, in the Danish islands, with long sentences automatically reduced to six years, after which time the workers were free. For a man under a life sentence, this could be a very appealing alternative.

Unfortunately the indentured man would generally have been much better off staying in prison. Even if he lived through the years of his indenture, which was unlikely, he would emerge so scarred that he would never be a whole, sane man again: for the indentured

William Blake, ca 1790, from a painting by Stedman, ca 1775, Mingo Tamarind was probably not quite as grand as this portrait of the celebrated Granman Quancy (see Richard Price's *Alibi's World* for a fascinating account of this remarkable man and the account of his missing ear as confirmed by this etching), MAPes MONDe Collection

man was lower than a slave.

Unless the plantation owner or businessman who contracted to let the indentured man work six years for him for precisely nothing liked and trusted him enough to let him work in his house or his business—and how many convicted criminals could be so lucky as that?—he had to work in the fields with the slaves, naked like them when his clothes wore out or otherwise disappeared, and sleep in the compound, on a mat on the ground, without covering. Every hour of every day he was an object of contempt, for the lowest Negro slave felt himself to be, and was, his superior. Any slave could, and would, point out to him that the master had paid good liquor for him, the Negro, whereas the white laborer was completely without monetary value. The result was that the indentured man took the brunt of everything from everyone of every hue of skin and station in life.

Once in a while it would happen that such a man was tough enough, lucky enough to survive through his six years of hell. Then suddenly he could take whatever job he could find, don the clothing that the master was required to give him, put on a hat, eat decent food, take a woman, and call himself a man. If by then he had not become so depraved that his life was virtually destroyed, he had a fair chance of success.

Such a man was Jens Andersen. A convicted murderer from Borreby, in Denmark, he was so befouled by his life, so utterly embittered by his six years of slavery, so icy in his hatred of Negroes for the way they had treated him, and yet strangely so forgiving of the white men for their treatment of him, that he was the ideal MESTERKNEGT for Suhm's St. Jan PLANTAGE. What made him perfect was the fact that the noble slaves whom it would be his job to beat into submission on St. Jan island would not know that until recently he himself had been, on St. Thomas island, the lowest kind of slave—a white slave.

Thus Jens Andersen, unknown on St. Jan, virtually unrecognizable in any case in his SUCKERDONS clothing after six years of nakedness in the sun, became the MESTERKNEGT of the Suhm PLAN-

TAGE on St. Jan, with four brutal BOMBAS, purchased at bribery prices from St. Thomas planters, to help him.

His greatest problem with the new BUSSALS—their willingness to commit suicide rather than do woman's work in the fields—had been a surprise. One of the best-known facts about Negroes was that they did not commit suicide, no matter how badly they might be treated, and among the spiritless, habituated slaves this was true.

These new slaves were different. They had simply refused to work, accustomed as they were to make war and hunt while the work was done by slaves and women. When forced, they had tried to kill themselves with the tools they were supposed to be using. Some, cut off from this avenue of escape, had tried to die by refusing to eat or drink. They were sustained by the knowledge, according to their tribal teachings, that their spirits would leave their self-killed bodies and reappear in newborn noblemen at home in Africa.

It had been an ugly, hand-to-hand battle to keep them alive, but eventually, using combinations of violence and surcease, starvation and choice foods, thirst and water and even KJELTUM (first-class rum), Andersen and his bloodthirsty BOMBAS had got most of them into a routine of eating, sleeping, and going sullenly to the BARCADS with tools in their hands. But the only real work was still done by the old-order, trusty, ACCUSTOMED SLAVES, who were terrified of the BUSSALS and hated them—understandably, for the BUSSALS treated them with contempt.

On this morning of April 31, 1733, on Suhm's PLANTAGE at Coral Bay, the tooting of the TUTU was a hollow sound, for the night had been made heinous by the BUSSALS. Some of them had broken their chains and the chains of others as soon as the compound was asleep, and neither the BOMBAS' whips nor Jens Andersen's TSCHICKEFELL and firearms had been able to stop six of them from dashing off in the darkness into the bush, hotly pursued by the number two BOMBA, Clæs.

Jens Andersen had not been disposed to risk his life in pursuit. He had only to report the escape to Magistrate Sødtmann, on the Company's account, for the tax record; to two planters, who would be asked to swear to affidavits if the slaves were never recaptured and their escape became a tax matter; and to Dr. Bodger, to be transmitted by runner to the Civil Guard, which had no member in Coral Bay. The Civil Guard was theoretically but hopelessly expected by the Company to mount periodical MARON hunts.

Andersen could smile at the thought of the MARON hunt. When the order for it came, the Civil Guard of St. Jan would duly meet, discuss the weather and other mutual problems, have a drink, ride out to a cool, shady spot, have another drink and some lunch brought along by body slaves, and have a nice afternoon nap, with the insects kept off by the body slaves waving leafy branches over their masters. They would then ride home to report no results, since St. Jan, unlike St. Thomas, was still largely covered by forest and bush, where a thousand MARONS could effectively hide if they wished to risk dying of hunger and thirst.

This morning, noting that under-BOMBA Clæs had not returned from pursuing the MARONS, Jens Andersen put him down as a MARON too and, after checking the situation in the BARCADS under the remaining BOMBAS, set out on horseback down the road to protect himself by making his reports.

IV

As Dr. Bodger continued to watch the advance of the morning sunlight, it edged across the plain toward him from the Company warehouses. At last it reached him and his modest cotton plantation nestling against the northeastern hills beside Konge Vej, King Road, that soon became the rocky, plunging, climbing, lunging trail to East End.

Not until he was bathed in the sun's quick warmth did Bodger give his attention to the morning need to urinate. Even this claimed his attention. He experimented like a small boy with various angles against the stone storehouse wall to regulate or eliminate splash. He admired the beauty of the sparkling amber color of the stream.

He even noted with interest the shadow he cast in the low-slanting rays from the sun that made him a giant along the ground, tied by a wavering, vaguely translucent rope to the great slab that was the shadow of the building.

The odor that arose was interesting to him too, as always; he tried to analyze it in terms of what he had eaten and drunk the night before, ever in search of clues to what goes on inside the human body.

For some reason he thought of Suhm's MESTERKNEGT Jens Andersen, and in the next instant saw him approaching on horseback along the road from the east.

The MESTERKNEGT flourished his TSCHICKEFELL as he rode, flicking off dormant buds or anything else that struck his fancy, even the heads of small lizards stalking the island's insects. He carried the long whip always, practiced with it incessantly, and boasted that he could extinguish a candle's flame with it at ten paces without upsetting the candle. He kept the leather oiled and the tip smooth and sharp. Ingeniously bound into the leather at intervals were tiny scoops of metal that excised bits of flesh from anyone being flogged. This whip was the terror of every slave within its domain, and made Jens Andersen a man who walked alone even among free men.

He came now in the clothing and hat of unbleached SUCKERDONS that his slave women kept spotless for him. As a sign of respect that Bodger noted with some contempt, he coiled the TSCHICKEFELL and carried it so in his sun-blackened hand. His blue eyes squinted to slits from six years' custom in the sun, he held his uncontrollably twitching mouth in a slant, as if he meant to cross out his bony face, so dark from the sun that his bleached white eyelashes were silhouetted against the tan.

As he approached he spoke, without greeting, in Southwest-Sjælland Danish: "I have to report that last night six BUSSALS went MARON in spite of all we could do, and with them went under-BOMBA Clæs."

Bodger nodded, and involuntarily said softly, "Clæs! Oh, God, poor Clæs . . ."

Jens Andersen saluted with his coiled TSCHICKEFELL, raised the slant of his mouth ever so slightly, and passed on in the direction of Magistrate Sødtmann's house.

Bodger now busied himself with his parched flower garden, which he would let no one tend but himself. He would send the runner to Civil Guard Captain van Bewerhoudt after breakfast.

Helena Hissing, Sødtmann's wondrously beautiful stepdaughter, walked down the road from the Sødtmann home where Jens Andersen had gone. At such an early hour, no protection from the sun was needed. She shook her yellow hair in the magic morning light and plumped her arms against her sides.

When she was younger, Helena had had a charming way of looking deep, almost searchingly, into the eyes of anyone approaching or being approached by her. Bodger had adored this in her. But over the last year or so she had acquired the disconcerting habit of glancing first at a man's genital area and only then looking into his eyes. It was like the flicker of an eyelash, a tiny flash of lightning, but it was always there, that apparently uncontrollable glance. Bodger had seen it now and then in full-grown women, but in this youngster—only three months past eleven years of age—he found it less than lovable, a little shocking.

This morning, as she approached, Bodger, aware of her, suffered the usual lurch of his heart. He was down on his knees watching a lizard egg hatch. As he glanced up to welcome her, he saw that disquieting flicker of her eyes, and then she looked at the object of his attention before turning a questioning gaze upon his face.

"Lizard egg," he said, indicating the little white pellet that was agitating itself upon the ground. "Hatching. I was piling some leaves about this caladium, to keep it from dying, and I accidentally raked this egg out into the sunlight. It must have been about to hatch, for the warmth of the sun set it to wriggling almost at once. It is the first time I have ever had a chance to watch such a hatching."

"Oh, I love lizards," she said softly. "They make good pets, especially the females."

Quadroon Slave, *Perry, from a painting by Stedman, ca 1775,* MAPes MONDe Collection

"They make more than that," Bodger said. "If I mistake not, they prevent you from being eaten alive by insects on this island. Have you ever noticed how many thousand insects they eat every day, and how many millions of them there are?"

"Well, yes, now you mention it . . ."

"Have you any idea, then, how many insects the lizards eat every day, for your protection?"

"I have not that many numbers in my head," she said, smiling. "I simply cannot imagine."

"That, I suppose, is what I wanted you to say."

Suddenly, under their gaze, the wobbling little white shell opened wide.

A tiny, perfect ANOLE unfolded itself before their eyes—and the red ants attacked it before it could even begin to dry.

Helena gasped. "Oh! Don't let them!" She made shooing motions with her hands.

Bodger looked at her calmly. "Why not?"

"But the little baby! Poor thing!"

"The ants," Bodger said, "are perishing for food and moisture."

"But the lizard—you said yourself that if it were not for them!"

"It is the way of nature," Bodger murmured. He watched in fascination.

"Man," he said, almost absently thinking aloud, "is ordinarily so helpless under the beautiful and merciless sky. Yet in a situation like this he is all-powerful. He can reach out his hand and save the tortured creature, at least for the time being. With a negligible effort he can prevent the ants from devouring or maiming it, give it a chance to develop into a full-grown lizard."

"Then do it," Helena cried, "do it, before it is too late!"

"Or," Bodger continued, "he can maintain the detached, scientific point of view of the perhaps superior individual, watch and see what happens and how it happens. He can let nature have its way."

"Oh, cruel!" Helena said, moving impulsively to brush the ants away.

Bodger took hold of her arm. "Let nature have its way."

William Blake, ca 1790, from a painting by Stedman, ca 1775, Planter, MAPes MONDe Collection

The ants tore at the tiny lizard from all sides, and as it writhed Helena took up a twig.

"Kill it, then," she said. "I will kill it!"

Before he could stop her—and he did not really try—she pressed the twig's end upon the lizard's head and quickly crushed out its life.

"That too," Bodger said, "is in a way a working of nature!" Helena sighed, looked away across the bay, bade Dr. Bodger good morning, and went back toward her home, kicking at the dust with her pretty feet and watching it drift away and settle on the dead and dying roadside plants.

Looking about, Bodger noticed the mast of the Company GALLIOT waving gently beside the Company dock a few hundred English yards to the west, in the safe nook of Coral Harbor. The boat must have sailed up overnight from Christiansfort at TAPPUS on St. Thomas; with a good breeze it had doubtless arrived deep in the night. Someone was just then leaving the dock and turning at a jog-trot up the gentle slope toward Konge Vej.

Bodger could see that this was no slave coming, but a FREE NEGRO, distinguishable by his round white linen cap and floppy white clothing. The man broke from his trot into a run as soon as he was near enough to see Bodger standing by his house.

It was the ever-smiling FREE NEGRO Christian Alexander, blacksmith, skipper of the GALLIOT when needed, who arrived panting and laughing. He always either giggled or laughed when he arrived in the presence of a White. Whether he giggled or laughed, and what gradation of either he produced, depended upon how he felt about the White in question; in the case of a group of Whites he always managed to strike a most extraordinary average.

Arriving now in Bodger's presence he appeared to be in a state of near-hysteria, gasping with the intensity of his laughter.

Bodger, having known him for all of his years of freedom, took the merriment as the compliment it was, and smiled broadly in greeting.

"MORRUK, CABÉ."

"MORRUK, MESTA!" Alexander replied, bobbing happily with all his powerful frame.

Bodger took the piece of paper Alexander handed him. It was an unofficial letter from Governor Gardelin, in the governor's handwriting. If it had been official, it would have been written by a scribe and sealed with the Company seal.

Bodger opened it. It said simply, in Danish:

"Kindly obey my order of one week ago. Come down at once with Alexander. I have need of you."

Bodger smiled. At least Gardelin was kind enough not to write an official note, which would have had to be entered in the record and eventually sent, in copies, to KJØBENHAVN.

Bodger looked at Alexander quizzically.

"What are your orders?" he asked, continuing in the CREOLE patois.

"To return with you as soon as you wake, MESTA," Alexander said merrily.

Bodger looked at the puffy trade wind clouds to judge the breeze outside the bay. He squinted at the distant waters beyond the point and saw them beginning to hustle and to show white tops and mares' tails in the quickening wind.

"It looks like a three-hour breeze," he said.

"A three-hour breeze it is, MESTA, a good running three-hour breeze for true! If it build we can slip down to Christiansfort in even less time—two hours and a half, perhaps. Tee-hee!"

Bodger automatically took into account the rule of slave, FREE NEGRO, and FREE MAN alike: tell a white man always what he wants to hear. He ticked off an adjustment in his mind, and said:

"Then we are in no hurry, are we? Let us have some breakfast!"

V

FREDERIKSVÆRN sat on its cone hill which formed a peninsula that jutted like a swollen uvula into the great dragon-jaws of Coral Bay on St. Jan, southeastward from Dr. Bodger's house.

26

Only from the firing steps of this fortification was any view to be seen from inside, for the breastworks of loose stones had no aperture but the barred doorway on the west.

In the middle of the enclosure stood the commandant's house, a stone building five windows long and four wide, according to the specifications, roofed with cedar shingles from North America. Added to it like a wart was a cubicle for the second in command.

The building was used only fitfully these days. Both Lieutenant Frøling and Corporal Høg were mainly occupied with furthering their private designs elsewhere on the island, Høg running the PLANTAGE across the harbor that he was about to acquire by marrying the widow Schacht, and Frøling developing the PLANTAGE he had married on the high ground between Water and Waterlemon bays, and including Water Bay, on the north side, out of sight from the VÆRN, behind Northside Mountain.

Next to the commandant's house in the VÆRN was the powder house, windowless, built of brick, and next to that, athwart the entrance gate, the so called corps-de-garde, a mud-and-wattle structure roofed with sugarcane blades, where the five common soldiers slept and guarded the entrance.

Peeping over the encircling pile of stones from masonry firing steps were four cannons, one commanding each of the major directions-west up the Company plantation and along the Bourdeaux range, east toward East End, north along the shore of Hurricane Hole, and south toward the open bay.

Three of the cannons were eight-pounders and one a sixteen-pounder. The smaller ones covered the land area. The greatest menace, from day to day, lay inland, where the population of slaves vastly outnumbered the people who owned or managed them. The range, reaching only to the summits of the heights that dominate the bay, was relatively short, requiring only eight-pound guns.

The danger from the sea was negligible. Englishmen with their warships were such an overwhelming force that they were not even to be feared, and pirates were by now generally in the same category, for the time had come when they had to be big enough to corrupt high officials and the commanders of warships to survive.

Slave Woman, *J. Holloway, from a painting by Stedman, ca 1775*, MAPes MONDe Collection

The sea approach was theoretically covered by a "water battery" on an exposed shelf below the VÆRN to the south. It had six cannons, two each of six-, eight-, and twelve-pounders, rusting away unused because of the neglect of the water approach. Their carriages were broken, and all parts were in sorry need of repair.

Still, in common sense, the sea approach had to be covered, but the sixteen-pound cannon that pointed in that direction from the southern firing platform of the VÆRN went unused except for firing salutes.

Surrounding the loose-stone breastworks of the VÆRN, which could be climbed by any agile person, was a wide cactus hedge so thick and hostile that not even a goat would willingly endure the pain of penetrating it, and the only gap in it was a path leading to the bottleri and doorway.

Below the hedge the hill was covered with second-growth bush; the construction of the PLANTAGE had not progressed far enough for the terracing and planting of cane rattoons on these slopes.

There were no provisions for servants inside the VÆRN, for no slave was theoretically even permitted within the walls. For this reason, the brick oven and the bottleri—combination kitchen, mess, commissary, and bar—were located in the normal lee of the VÆRN outside the entrance, under a cane-blade thatch. The thatch was supported by four plump, naked-looking, reddish-pink-barked TURPENTINE TREES that had started as posts and had taken root, as expected.

The slaves who manned the outdoor kitchen were not permitted to live in or beside it, but slept in huts at the foot of the hill, some four hundred twenty-five vertical feet below, on the peninsula that jutted into the harbor.

At dawn on this day, these slaves had already climbed the hill without the prodding of any MESTERKNEGT and were at work preparing the day's food. Sam Maria, the baker, whose name was a corruption of the Portuguese Santa Maria, betraying his origin as a man accustomed all his life to slavery in Latin Africa, had fired up the oven and was mixing dough for the day's bread in the early light.

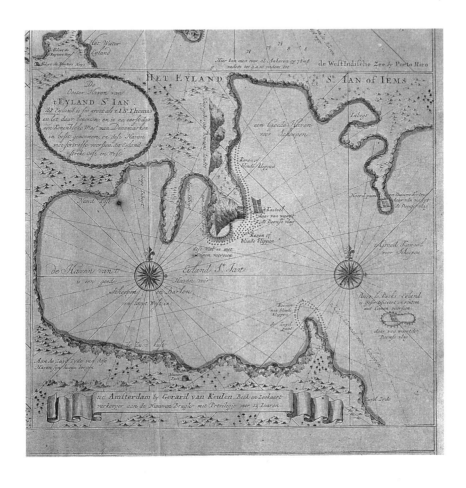

Detail of Coral Bay Harbor, St John, *Gerard van Keulen, 1719,* Amsterdam, MAPes
MONDe Collection

Willy, the cook, was another ACCUSTOMED SLAVE, brought from one of the English islands. He knew what the soldiers liked, and made it his business whenever possible to have it for them. This morning he was frying POTFISH as a special treat. He had seen to the hauling of the woven-vine FISHPOT himself only a short time ago, in the morning's earliest light, and had brought the catch up the hill with him, his long legs dangling almost to the ground as he rode ludicrously on the very tail bone of his little donkey.

He would serve the fish with boiled yams and Guinea peppers, as the soldiers liked it best. Normally he would have grown the peppers himself and served them green, but that was impossible in the drought. Now he had only dried ones, so he stewed them a bit to soften them. Not only did the men love the peppers, which were blistering hot in the mouth, but they believed they needed them to ward off disease and constipation.

The bearers, Adam and Anthoni, were already finished with the first morning's labor and sat waiting on the ground for their breakfast. They were asleep, their heads clasped between their knees and their arms locked about their naked legs. Seen so, they looked like twins.

They had carried, slung on a pole between them, a large skin of water all the way from the well behind the bay near the Company storehouses a mile and a half, English, from the VÆRN. The skin of water, semi-brackish in this drought, would serve the garrison, the kitchen, and the slaves for ablutions, cooking, and, for the lower slaves only, drinking supply for one-third of the day. There would be another trip before the sun became too hot, and another in the early evening. If more water should be needed for any unusual purposes, other trips would have to be made.

All buildings here had crude gutters, with wooden run-offs leading to hogsheads, and a good rain would release the water bearers for other labors. These days the staves of the hogsheads had shrunk until daylight showed between them. Much of the next rainfall would be wasted in swelling the wood so that the hogsheads could hold water again.

The soldiers were sleeping late. They had stayed up till all hours the night before, playing klaverash, the card game, new to the islands, that was the current favorite. No night guard had been posted, for there was no sense of uneasiness and no one in authority was likely to drop in unexpectedly.

Willy's breakfast preparations were right on time and approaching the proper point for serving. Although he felt secure in the appreciation of the men of the garrison, he did not feel free to call them to breakfast; he was supposed to have it ready when they appeared.

He did feel free to sing, and that might bring the men alive. Starting softly on a lament for his pet kitchen KAKKATESS, caught and eaten by the kitchen cat, he let the crescendo swell gradually. As the refrain became apparent, Sam Maria joined in. The water bearers awoke and took up the chorus, and soon an eerie, elemental keening song was pulsing in the hilltop air.

The reaction from the corps-de-garde was slow to come, but it came in time with good-natured curses in Danish and shouts of "SNO DE MUN!" and "RUS EN VRE!" in SLAVE TALK, but when Talencam's voice suddenly reverted to Danish, "JEG LUGTER FISK!" there was a scramble to get up, for the odor of frying fish in the morning meant more than sleep, which would be made up in the heat of the day.

Soon the bar on the heavy wooden door was lifted inside and Talencam appeared, followed by Knudsen, Lind, and Callundborg. All were blond but Callundborg, who was a "black Dane," dark of hair and swarthy of face. And all were pock-marked like almost everyone still alive in the islands.

Over his shoulder Talencam called, in a mixture of Danish and the everyday CREOLE of the islands, "Hey, Tiil, better bang that drum for Høg, man, before we all end up arse-in-pincers!"

"Oh, God, yes!" came Tiil's muffled voice, and soon from the southwest firing step, so that there would be no doubt of Corporal Høg's hearing it across the harbor, sounded the loud clatter of the reveille drumming.

VI

O<small>NE</small> of the happiest of the large plantations on St. Jan on April 31, 1733, was Bewerhoudtsberg.

The conch-shell T<small>UTU</small> sounded at four o'clock, S<small>LAVE TIME</small>, the arbitrary instant when Cockney Harry Hawkins, the M<small>ESTERKNEGT</small> decided that this was the moment of dawn. The T<small>UTU</small> here was somehow not the sound of doom, but had a touch of gaiety in it, born of the African insistence upon rhythm.

The sounds of forty-six slaves coming alive, without a lash crackling to hurry and intimidate them, were family sounds. The M<small>ESTERKNEGT</small> did not even bother to shout, and there was no B<small>OMBA</small> not one slave driver on this huge P<small>LANTAGE</small>. The moans of grandparents, the laughter of children bouncing on their parents' stomachs, the wails of some being spanked for bouncing too hard, the babble of the day beginning mingled with the cackling of hens, crowing of cocks, blatting of goats, curdled maa-ing of the oddly naked tropical sheep, and the wailing of the ruminant kids sounding like little children wanting their breakfast—these were normally the sounds at dawn in the slave quarters of Bewerhoudtsberg.

All of the forty-six slaves but two, Cesar and Café, were C<small>REOLES</small>, P<small>LANTAGE</small>-born. They were jealously guarded by both master and mistress from all harm that could be warded off.

A sign of a happy P<small>LANTAGE</small> was the horde of laughing, squealing children, all of them living with their parents, most of whom had taken the trouble to get married. No child here had been taken from his parents and sold to this estate.

The P<small>LANTAGE</small> was homesteaded in 1721 with the aid of these same slaves or in some cases their parents, and some others who had by now died. The land was cleared by them, rid of stones by them and, where terracing would help, terraced by them. The houses, both stone and wattle, were built by some or others of them;

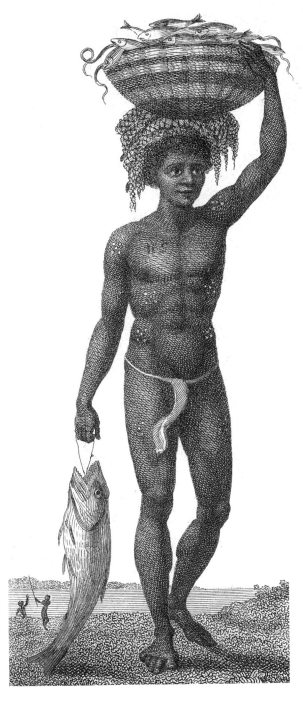

William Blake, ca 1790, from a painting by Stedman, ca 1775, Fisherman, MAPes MONDe Collection

the BARCADS marked out and fenced with stone and dug and rowed and planted by them, the harvests taken in and sugared, or ginned and baled, by them. This was their place, and they felt at home here.

Only one female, Café, was a foreigner, from Hispaniola, CAFÉ-CON-LECHE in color, a wetnurse purchased in defiance of the law off a passing boat in 1731. This woman, a fountain of milk for the children of the master, was a stranger to the home slaves, ignored by her from day to day; and yet, with her Spanish fire and her love of violent dancing, she could take charge of them en masse any night she cared to come out from behind her sullen, retiring front and respond to the wild, gay beating of a drum—for drumming and dancing were permitted here on Saturday nights and nights of festival. Male slaves, disdaining Café in the day, slunk near her in the night like dogs drawn to a bitch in heat. Without fail she mocked them loudly, spat upon them, and laughed.

The other foreigner, Cesar, had an easier time. Although he happened to be off the same slave ship as Suhm's first ten and one HALF BUSSALS—ten adults and one child between twelve and sixteen years old—and therefore a BUSSAL himself, he was an ACCUSTOMED SLAVE from the Aquambo king's own household, thrown into the pot to fill out that king's contract at the last minute. It had taken him a very short time to become a devoted lackey, aiming at a soft berth as a house slave, a long step up out of the field-slave compound.

Any PLANTAGE was in a sense the shadow of its owner, and the owner of Bewerhoudtsberg was Johannes, nicknamed Jannis, van Bewerhoudt. Jannis, Captain of the island's Civil Guard, was by nature a laughing man, a man on horseback, galloping. Before coming to St. Jan he had reversed the usual West Indies process by outliving a wife. Sara May, on Tortola, had given him children fecundly, but only one daughter and one son had survived the baptism of fevers to which all islanders were subject.

The daughter, Susanna, already was a widow at twenty-five, mistress-in-absentia of the neighboring PLANTAGE that her adoring husband, Isaac Runnels, had named for her as he built it, when she was still a child too young to wed. Susannaberg, despite Jannis van

Bewerhoudt's imploring his favorite daughter to stay on St. Jan, with or near him, was left in the hands of a MESTERKNEGT Cousin Jannis Runnels.

Susanna's brother, Daniel, aged twenty-two, was now gaining experience by managing Bewerhoudtsberg PLANTAGE under his father's tutelage.

On St. Thomas, after the family had been evicted from Tortola by the English taking over the island, the mother of Susanna and Daniel had died, and Jannis had deeply mourned her.

Jannis had then chosen St. Jan, where he would have no taxes to pay, for a second PLANTAGE. He found all of the choice bays already taken, but that was all right. No seaman, he was really more interested in the highland interior.

He had staked out for himself a huge area in the island's elevated central valley straddling the shallow GUT before it fell sharply away to drain into Fish Bay. But, having a St. Thomas PLANTAGE to run, he was for a long time helpless to go ahead with his plan to make a PLANTAGE on St. Jan.

The Danish West India and Guinea Company, not the Danish crown, was sole owner and ruler of the Danish West Indies. On becoming firmly lord and master of St. Jan in 1716, the Company kept pressing angrily for the established inhabitants to take out land grants for their property so that they would start paying taxes seven years later, according to the terms the Company was giving to all comers.

Finally, in 1720, by threatening to issue grants of the old-timers' lands to persons of its own choice and send troops to oust the old-timers as squatters, the Company had forced stubborn pioneers to apply for grants to their own property.

Jannis van Bewerhoudt then had scrambled to apply for his future mile-square PLANTAGE in the central valley, even though it meant that he had to have the sugar works built and operating and paying taxes seven years after the date on the grant that came from KJØBENHAVN. Other Tortola refugees had hastened to legalize their acquisitions on St. Jan.

Dour old Pietter Duurloo, seaman and St. Thomas planter, had finally, reluctantly, applied for the right to pay taxes on his great PLANTAGE in Fortune Bay, which he had renamed Klein Caneel, Little Cinnamon, lying west-northwest of Bewerhoudtsberg.

Until Pietter Duurloo's sturdy, no-nonsense daughter Maria grew up, there had been no one Jannis van Bewerhoudt wished to marry, and he had been satisfied to live in concubinage with his children's slave nursemaid. The only two surviving fruits of those years of waiting for Maria were in his and Maria's household now—twin, dark-skinned sixteen-year-old daughters, Sara, in memory of his first wife, and Anna, for her slave mother, now long since dead.

By 1720, Maria Duurloo, dark and plain, but worshipfully in love and ready and waiting, was at last old enough for decent marriage, and with the regularity of a clock striking six she gave him children—first three sons in a row, and then three daughters. Incredibly, all six of them, from Johannes Junior, now aged twelve, to Elisabeth, aged one, had survived.

On this morning of April 31, 1733, Jannis van Bewerhoudt, restless as always, had awakened early and, being subject to a degree of moon-madness, had gone off on horseback for a gallop along Konge Vej in the brilliant pre-dawn moonlight.

Coming home now at dawn, he stayed on Konge Vej, turning right at Adrian's estate instead of taking the road leading to Bellevue and Rendezvous Bay that ran straight ahead down the GUT and through his PLANTAGE. He wanted to check on his daughter Susanna's PLANTAGE, as he did every morning and evening. The master of the field slaves, a cousin of Susanna's deceased husband, had a PLANTAGE and family of his own and was not always on hand to keep an eye on things. Of course, there was not much to worry about; Susanna's slaves were all trusted and appeared interested in her welfare—at any rate, in the absence of a master or orders of any kind, they were accustomed to carry on, doing the things that obviously needed doing, and even teaching the new BUSSAL, Prince, how to be a slave.

Slowing his horse to a walk as Konge Vej turned to skirt his east BARCAD, Jannis found himself thinking how death had stilled the élan of this island in the seventeen years since the Danes had taken

Susanaburg and Adrian Plantation, St. John, F. von Scholten, 1833, Marine and Craft Museum, Krønborg Castle, Elsinør, Denmark

firm hold of it. This morning he had galloped all the way to the point where Konge Vej dwindled to a donkey path at Mamey Peak, and back, and he realized that every PLANTAGE he had passed— Vlach's, where he had turned back; the Magenses' Rustenburg and Adventure; the Delicats' Katrinaberg and, until recently, Jochumsdahl; Adrian Runnels's imposing PLANTAGE right here behind him; and his own daughter's ahead of him there, not to mention the great majority of the others all over the island—as owned by a widow or orphans, most being in the hands of MESTERKNEGTS or, in some cases, illegally, trusty slaves.

Jannis rounded the northeast corner of his PLANTAGE where the dawn was destroying the deep moon-shadow beneath the grove of exotic mangoes. The ground here had been wet through all the years he had known this island, and even now it was moist enough to make this one of the few green spots. The busy JACK-SPANIARD WASPS and endless flies were stirring into life in the growing light, buzzing, ready to go back to work.

The feet of Jannis's horse counted softly by twos in the dust. Jannis looked at his east BARCAD as the land fell away down a wide ravine toward the GUT. Only here, inheriting some of the age-old moisture in which the mango trees stood, was there anything green for his slaves to eat; everything else down the whole ravine was parched. A hundred and more garden plots were there, for his slaves and Susanna's grew their vegetables here as a rule, but almost all were curled and brown in the growing light.

In his mind Jannis could see them vividly as they ought to be, crowded with the plants that produced the islands' favorite food for slaves' and masters' families alike—banana trees, ragged-leafed in the wind; TANIA, large-leafed and handsome in its kinship to caladium; chick-pea, CALELU vine, GJAMBO, INDIAN CORN, GUINEA CORN, yams, Guinea pepper, SALOP . . . This would be the ideal ground for cotton, but the people must eat.

With a feeling of despair, Jannis looked at the sky—clear, with tantalizing trade wind clouds drifting, shrinking in size, some of them vanishing, as they passed over the dry land, giving rise among many planters to a certainty of God's curse upon them.

Food for all those hungry, childlike, trusting mouths, he thought. The slaves were willing to grow their own, according to the custom. Indeed, they preferred it, for then they could suit themselves. When they could not, they knew that the master was all-powerful—he would find food for them. But it was not so simple as that; the salt meat from Ireland, the salt cod from New England, and pickled Iceland lamb were in short supply now, everywhere in the islands, and terribly expensive as a result. The blessed sea surrounding the island was the only salvation. The seaside planters had trusty fishermen and fortunately for Jannis, his father, as he called Pietter Duurloo, eight years his senior, was now living on his PLANTAGE down below and supplied enough fish to keep Bewerhoudtsberg's slaves alive.

At the crossroads Jannis turned right to Susannaberg, and as he crested the ridge he could see the bearer slaves from his PLANTAGE thudding down the GUT into Hawksnest Bay, ignoring the switch-backs that crossed and recrossed it to make a safe grade for the wagons. The slaves went down the worn path among the rocks of the GUT and the terraces of withered cane curved outward from their feet along the flanks of the plunging ridges like the ribs of a wrecked ship.

Out beyond the rocks at the mouth of the bay below he could see Duurloo's fishermen coming in from the fish-rich shelves of Kukkelusse Cay nestling behind Lewanger Cay across the sound. With a feeling of thankfulness and relief he could see that the boat lay low in the water.

Jannis did not ride into the compound, but cocked an ear to test the usualness of the morning sounds as the slaves went to their tasks. Then he turned his horse back toward the crossroad and Bewerhoudtsberg.

Entering his own PLANTAGE, he rode down the wide draw through the browned pastureland that extended up over the plateau to his right. He left the road and took the path up the slope to the corral that dominated the complex, opening to the pasture at the top and to the HORSE MILL and living quarters below.

Most of the cows, pigs, sheep, and goats had had to be eaten for lack of feed for them, and those that remained were kept in the stone-walled corral to huddle with the donkeys, horses, and mules, subsisting on whatever green leaves, palatable or not, and browned GUINEA GRASS could be brought long distances by the slaves. Starving dogs and cats, staring uncomprehending out of big eyes, vomited from eating too many lizards.

Next to the corral stood the round HORSE MILL where the land fell away to give the proper slope so that gravity could carry the cane juice from the rollers down through the various processes to its resting-places, as molasses and MUSCOVADO in hogsheads in the storehouse, and KILL-DEVIL rum in the distillery that used up all of the kettle-skimmings, spoiled or dirty sugar and other unsalable by-products of the sugaring process.

In a good season the sugaring would still be going on now, but seeing and smelling and hearing and tasting it all would have to be in Jannis's mind's eye and nose and ear and palate until happier times returned with the rains.

Jannis left his horse with a slave in the corral to be rubbed down, noted that smoke and the proper sounds were coming from the distillery below the sugar houses, and strode through the stone gateway and down the shank of the slope away from the HORSE MILL toward his house that was carefully placed to windward of the sugar-mill stink. A two-story building of stone and Flensborg brick, with above-ground cellars for storage and house slaves, an outside staircase, Dutch-tile roof and floors of tile, even upstairs, on a mortar base laid on close-set West Indies cedar poles, this small-and-cramped-roomed structure housed Jannis and Maria, nine of his ten offspring, seven house slaves and ten body slaves, not including Café, the baby's nursemaid, who came in daily from the slave compound. It was new, only this year fully completed so that he could with pride move his wife and family from his St. Thomas PLANTAGE to occupy it in comfort.

His shout of "Ho for breakfast!" roused only silence from the family but titters from the house slaves who were preparing the food in the outdoor kitchen under a tight thatch of cane blades. On down to the slave quarters he went.

Jannis took some pride in the fact that his slaves were clothed, if they wished to be. Nakedness was generally the mark of the KAMINA the field slave. Most planters provided the field slave with nothing at all until something became necessary to keep him alive and in some manner productive.

Jannis van Bewerhoudt was unusual. A dusky-skinned CREOLE, he had in him a nagging sense of the basic dignity of anything human. It was impossible for him to treat a slave, or to hire a MESTERKNEGT who would treat him, as a beast.

This was a trait that he had in common with very few of the CREOLE planters. On St. Jan, of the large planters only his daughter Susanna, his father-in-law Pietter Duurloo, the "KILL-DEVIL Widows" above Little Cruz Bay, and Daniel Jansen's redoubtable widow in Caneel Bay were with him in this. Otherwise, only the Danes straight from Denmark—Dr. Bodger, for example—were in that company, and these were the Danes that Jannis van Bewerhoudt liked.

Thus it was that even the KAMINA slaves at Bewerhoudtsberg were clothed according to their wishes. Jannis regularly bought from Emanuel Vass, on St. Thomas, bolts of coarse-wool blue PENISTONE from England, unbleached SUCKERDONS or MOLLE-MOLLE from East Asia, and Flemish cloth in which cotton bales were wrapped. From these the slaves could cut according to their needs, for covering on chilly nights as well as clothing. The ACCUSTOMED SLAVES had among them women who had the art of sewing and would make clothes for all their kind; the field slaves generally would drape themselves with lengths of the cloth only when they needed it for warmth, laying them aside, carefully folded, when they worked. What pieces of cloth they used for their witchcraft, which was not very interesting to Jannis, and beyond his comprehension, they were welcome also to take.

No one ever expected to see a field slave properly clothed; therefore no one but a new arrival from the north ever looked twice at a naked slave, male or female. Yet a CREOLE, free or slave, was as prudish as a Puritan, regarding the human skin as a disgrace, and referring to the sexual manifestations of the human body as "the

shame," "your shame," "my shame," never, ever, to be exposed—
the difference being that a KAMINA slave was not a human being,
and therefore his skin not a disgrace and his sexual parts not a
shame to see. No man thought of clothing his dog or donkey.

Even Jannis van Bewerhoudt did not notice the nakedness of
workers in the field, but he did unfailingly notice the pregnancy of
a female KAMINA slave and always insisted that she take plenty of
time off from work to stay in her hut, before and after the delivery
of a child. The general custom was quite different. Since field
slaves were not human, they were therefore animals, and a female,
when her time came to have a child, simply had it, like any other
animal, and resumed her field work as soon as she was physically
able, which was very soon when a lash was ready always to hurry
her.

Nor did Jannis van Bewerhoudt follow the general custom of
breeding slaves himself when the slaves failed to reproduce fast
enough to provide a fresh supply. He took his sex enthusiastically,
as everyone knew, but only for pleasure and convenience, and with
girls who not only aroused his desire but responded to it with
pleasure.

The breeding of new slaves, even among the KAMINA workers,
somehow took care of itself on his plantation. He was not sure why,
but he hoped it was because his slaves were happier than most. One
of the good reasons, besides economy, for denying the field slaves
clothing was, as everyone knew, the need that nakedness imposed
on them to snuggle close together on their straw mats in the chilly
darkness before dawn. The snuggling could be depended on, as a
rule, to arouse a certain amount of sexual desire and result in some
new slaves without cost. But miserably treated, unhappy slaves—
this could be noted by observing the various PLANTAGES, and Jannis
and Bodger had often discussed it—simply did not reproduce
themselves, whereas the better-treated, happier ones often did, and
apparently in direct proportion to the relative heartlessness and
heartfulness of their treatment.

Jannis would have liked very much to free his slaves. It would
have made him feel like a king to be able to do such a thing. Yet

ANIMAL-POWERED SUGAR MILL

A -Solid Wooden Scaffold, B-Mill Table Hollowed out of a Solid Log Covered with Lead, C-Three Rollers: Each a Metal Cylinder, D-Opening in Mill Table to Permit Changing Pivots and Grill, E-Openings to Tighten or Loosen Roller Tension, F-Other Opening to Lock upper Pivot, G-The Gear Teeth on the upper Rollers, H -Mast extended from Central Roller, I-Upper Mast Brace, K-Mill Arms to attach to the Motor Force, L-Wooden Roof Beam, M-Covered Canal carrying the Juice of the Crushed Cane.
Geografia Americana, Livorno 1763, MAPes MONDe Collection

what would he then do? Until everyone else did likewise, it would be impossible for a man to make a living here, and even in that case he wondered how it would be. The only alternative was to go away to Europe, but Jannis felt that he was not equipped to make his way among the pure-white strangers there.

The field slaves were at work by now extending the cane BARCADS higher up the slope beyond the cotton pieces to the northeast in preparation for the return of rain. They would have their breakfast brought to them in the field by small boys, along with water, after they had worked a while and needed a break. Breakfast this morning would have to be POORJACK alone, for there was nothing else to be had. This would make for great thirst as the sun climbed high, but there was perhaps enough water to assuage it. By noon there would be fresh fish.

After looking closely up and down the row of huts, Jannis stood and sniffed the air for offensive odors. He would not permit the odor of any sort of offal to persist long after dawn. All odorous material, either actual or potential, must be buried in the cotton piece, where the ground was soft and digging easy. Jannis would not permit the burial of it in the garden plots, as some did, for Bodger, odd one though he might be, had noticed and managed long ago to prove to Jannis that the well-known griping in the guts, which griped many poor souls into their graves, was more common by far on PLANTAGES that used nightsoil for garden fertilizer than even on those that just let it lie and endured the stench and flies it bred.

There was no use inspecting the rain barrels, for they were as dry as on the day the cooper put them together. Normally that would have been Jannis's next act. Because of Bodger, he would not permit rain barrels to be left open. They must be covered with cloth, tightly bound or with a hoop dropped over it to keep it in place. Bodger had long ago noted, and duly recorded the statistics, that on the PLANTAGES where the rain barrels were open and as a result so jammed with mosquito larvae that a man could, if he were so minded, dip out a strainer full of them in all stages of development and cook them in a stew—on those PLANTAGES the incidence of fevers and deaths was far higher than on, for instance, his own, where mosquitoes were no longer permitted to breed in the rain barrels.

Perhaps most interesting of all was the fact that among the richer planters, every member of whose family had extra body slaves whose duty it was to stay at the side of master or mistress and, among other things, keep mosquitoes away during sleep, the incidence of some of the fevers was almost nil, while among the field slaves on the same PLANTAGE it might be high.

Jannis van Bewerhoudt could well wish that it were necessary to inspect the rain barrels. A great deal of his labor force these days had to be used to haul and carry water laboriously the long, steep way from the sea and to use his KILL-DEVIL works to distill the salt water into enough potable liquid to keep his people and animals alive.

Planters who would not or could not do this had an even worse problem. They had to pray that a Puerto Rican boat would heave-to offshore with water for sale, and they had to pay well for the precious stuff, with the result that the only living creatures on their PLANTAGES were human beings, the necessary horses and mules, and a few chickens and pigs to eat the garbage and manure, and once in a while some dehydrated, emaciated goats. Whenever a brief shower scurried tantalizingly across the island, there was such a scrambling on St. Jan to catch every possible drop of it that masters and slaves alike became human beings together, and even animals looked at the sky.

A number of springs on the island were still wet, but because the water from them was badly needed by their owners, they were guarded day and night by armed sentries. The three springs that were trickling enough that one could purchase water from them were so far away from Bewerhoudtsberg as to make the hauling either impracticable or impossible.

The accursed Spanish water was often so dirty that a man had to let it settle for a whole day before he could bring himself to drink it if he could wait so long. The cost of the stuff was enough to make a man swoon. These days, the damned Spaniards were charging a

PIECE OF EIGHT per tubful. A tubful was as much as a Negro could carry on his head, and the smart planter trained his biggest, best, and strongest slaves to be water bearers when needed. To the Spaniards from Puerto Rico this made sense, and far from resenting the huge loads of water that a slave like Jannis's giant Cesar could and did carry away from their boats, they showed open contempt for such bearers as could not head-carry a full tub up a hill without spilling a drop.

All contacts between slaves and these Spanish devils had to be watched with a hawk's eye, for the Spaniards always had more in mind than selling water—they were after slaves without cost. At the slightest opportunity they would pass the word they managed it somehow across the formidable language barrier—that slaves escaping to Puerto Rico would be taken into the Catholic church, educated and, after working for a year, given their freedom. It was devilish and indecent, Jannis declared, and he was outraged. But he had to admire its cleverness, for it worked; every KAMINA slave who heard of it believed it. Now and then a slave would, if he could not get hold of a boat—and if he could swim, which most could not—simply jump into the sea and start swimming in the direction of Puerto Rico.

Water, water, Jannis thought as he cocked an ear toward the new BARCADS to the southeast. It had got so a man hesitated to urinate or spit, so precious was the moisture.

The sounds coming from the distant field slaves were normal; they were chanting some sort of happily heathenish song to keep time with hoes and the heaving of stones into place for terracing. Jannis would go after breakfast and check on the progress of the work.

Like that of the slaves his breakfast was POORJACK, but with a special horseradish sauce that Maria had learned from the governor's fabled cook, Paris, and had taught her cook how to make. It was not that the field slaves were not welcome to the same sauce on their POORJACK, it was simply that it would require dishes. Food served in the fields had to be eaten with the hands, without dishes, and it was the custom to serve breakfast and lunch in the fields on

Mulino da zucchero

Sugar Mill, ca 1733, MAPes MONDe Collection

working days, now that the slaves could produce no food of their own to cook.

Maria and the children—Anna and Sara, the dark twins, aged sixteen; Johannes, twelve, Pieter, ten, Lucas, seven, all wearing the pallor of the MESTIZO; Neltje and Gertrud, five and three, blossoming miraculously with white Nordic curls and china-blue eyes; and Elisabeth, pallid, going on two—waited submissively for the master in the pole-ceilinged dining room on the house's ground level near the cook shed.

Maria was not pregnant. For the first time in thirteen years she had a child more than a year and a half old without being gravid with the next one. But Alma, her body slave, was pregnant; and Anniche, the youngest, prettiest slave girl in the cook shed outside giggled without looking up when the master passed through on the way to the dining room. He smiled and glanced at the familiar curve of her carelessly draped hip, as he pulled up his chair and sat down at the table.

"My wife is staring at her plate this morning," he said. Gretje brought in the food.

Maria flushed under the CREOLE gray-brown of her cheeks. "It was a beautiful night," she said, "a restless night."

They spoke in the CREOLE tongue.

"Ah, yes," he said, "the bright, bright moon."

"It was light enough, almost, to read the future by," she said "and the wind was so strong it made the hammocks swing."

He laughed. "An empty hammock will swing in the wind," he ventured with conscious bluntness. She had been cool to him of late. Cold. A wife had no such rights.

"Café was singing yesterday morning," she persisted. "Café, who never sings."

"Ah, coffee is a noble drink," he exclaimed. "and that reminds me: Lieven Kierwing is raising coffee down in that GUT of his, even in this drought. I have the selfsame conditions down this GUT just above the waterfall. *WATERFALL!*" he shouted. "*What is that?*"

The children, listening raptly, laughed more boisterously than was necessary.

"I can't remember!" Jannis Junior, said, and all laughed again.

Maria was eating quietly. "Guantje is happy this morning," she said.

Jannis took the short cut. "The Bible commands a man to sow his seed on fertile ground, not on stone. I don't recall the exact words, but you ask the preacher, ask Grønnewald what the Bible says about that."

Maria's eyes were closed over her plate and her chewing was suspended for the moment.

"Speaking of Grønnewald," Jannis said, "when does he come again to teach the children their letters and numbers?"

"Yesterday and before yesterday," Maria said, "but he is not well."

"It is barely an English mile," he said.

"He is an old man," she said.

"Then let them go to him. Cesar can escort them. Nothing can happen to them with Cesar guarding them."

"Very well," she said.

"Is it true what I hear—that Grønnewald is teaching slaves to read?"

"He wishes them to know the Bible."

"But he must know the law," he said.

"Does anyone talk to him of the law? Does anyone try to stop him? No."

By now the sun was staring at the field slaves and their water-and-breakfast break was due. The slave kitchen in the compound by the GUT had already sent out the youngsters with their welcome burden to the new BARCADS as Jannis started in that direction.

Suddenly from the BARCADS came screams of children. The chanting of the KAMINA workers ceased as if chopped off by an ax. Then after a moment of complete stillness, a frantic babbling began.

Jannis jumped and ran toward the sounds.

When he came into sight of the BARCAD, he saw Harry Hawkins, the MESTERKNEGT, kneeling near the edge of the bush, clutching to him protectively two naked, hysterical slave children. Two others were hiding in terror among the clump of field slaves.

Hawkins was staring angrily into the bush while trying to calm the children. The field slaves huddled, chattering noisily, a hundred yards away.

Jannis hurried to Hawkins.

"Wᴀ ᴋᴀ ʜᴀ ᴘʟᴀᴛs?" he demanded sharply in the Dutch Cʀᴇᴏʟᴇ patois.

"Mᴀʀᴏɴ," Hawkins said. His lean Cockney jaw was tense as he let the children go and stood up. "Vɪᴇʀ ᴀ ᴅɪ, ʜᴏᴘᴘᴏ ᴅɪ ʙᴜsᴋɪ ʏᴛ, ɢʀᴇʙɪ ᴅɪ ꜰʀᴏᴋᴏ ᴇɴ ᴡᴀʜᴛᴀʜ ᴅɪ ᴋɪɴᴛ ᴅᴇᴍ ᴋᴀ ᴅʀᴀʜ ᴅᴇʜ."

Oh, God, Jannis thought. What is happening on this island, when children cannot carry food and water to the fields without being ambushed by ᴍᴀʀᴏɴs in broad daylight?

"Ju ka kig di?" he asked. "Did you see them?"

"Ja, mi heer. Yes, sir."

"Do you know them?"

"No, sir. Looked like Amina ʙᴜssᴀʟs, sir."

"No doubt," Jannis said. "and looking out of the bush and seeing the children with food and water was too much for them." He shook his head slowly. "Trouble, man," he said. "Trouble on this island. Send to warn Adrian's ᴍᴇsᴛᴇʀᴋɴᴇɢᴛ to watch for them. I'll see to getting more food and water, and I'll bring out a gun to you. Your people here are frightened. See you explain to them that these ᴍᴀʀᴏɴ ʙᴜssᴀʟs mean them no harm." Jannis was one planter who never wore his sword except for dress or Civil Guard duty, but now he went and put it on, and it would be a long time before he took it off again.

VII

Pʜɪʟɪᴘ Gᴀʀᴅᴇʟɪɴ was a young bachelor brewer at Christianshavn in Denmark when the lure of the Indies hit him as a result of labor trouble and a girl who, because he was so fat, laughed when he mooed at her. He reasoned that in the Indies a man would wield whatever power was given him without having to take any back talk from workers. As for girls, a pox on them—a man would be better off without them.

He sold his brewery and signed on to go to St. Thomas as bookkeeper for that branch of the Danish West India and Guinea Company.

The back of his neck was barely tanned before a St. Thomas CREOLE widow, Barbara Pedersdatter, acquired him, fat and all. She gave him a pallid child, who promptly died. Having proved that he could sire a son, he then explained to her that all he really needed was a companion, which she admirably was.

Her grown children and stepchildren by other men were children enough for him, especially when they were males, and her daughters grew up to have husbands, and he loved them all and referred to them, loudly and proudly, as his sons. For two of them, Johannes Reimert Sødtmann, a son-in-law of his wife, and Peder Krøyer, her stepson, he found jobs in the Company when they grew up.

When his wife died in 1731 he became convinced that he too was dying. He took an avid interest in every sickness that St. Thomians were heir to, and had each one, vicariously. He hounded the Company doctors for whatever pills they had for whatever ills, meanwhile begging the directors in Denmark by every ship to send someone out to take his place and let him go home to die in peace.

Unfortunately, as Dr. Bodger loved to point out, he would have to die in order to get a replacement; the directors were far too grateful to any man from home who managed to stay alive on St. Thomas to be willing to go to the trouble and expense of replacing him.

Bodger also liked to expound his theory that Gardelin stayed alive because he was a brewer, and so detested both rum and water. When Gardelin first came out to St. Thomas he brought along hogsheads of his own beer, and when that had rejoined Mother Earth, as Bodger put it, he was panic-stricken. He abhorred the local MABY beer, could rarely get any beer from home, or even the ingredients for brewing it. No one in a position to authorize such shipments was impressed with his need for it when the cargo space

This idyllic view of St. John shows a provisions garden with papaya, bananas, pumpkins, corn, sweet potatoes, cassava and sugarcane. Karen Fog Olwig calls attention to this in her book (*Vestinderne,* Skarv, 1980, Holte, Denmark), *Friz Melby, 1850,* MAPes MONDe Collection

was required for more important things, including—as he noted with noisy anger—sugar candy for the sweet tooth of the St. Thomas masses, made from the MUSCOVADO sugar so laboriously shipped from St. Thomas to KJØBENHAVN. When he did manage to get a shipment of beer sent out, it was always subject to the most extraordinary leakage en route—whole hogsheads would arrive empty, with the blank-faced crew completely ignorant as to what might have happened to cause such a thing.

So Gardelin brewed himself a beer the like of which was never tasted, using local substitutes for the malt and hops that he could not often import, and causing an occasional unnerving explosion or fountain of foam.

When asked why drinking beer instead of water should keep Gardelin alive, Bodger could not answer. He could only note, when someone from the north lived on year after year, that in every case there was something unusual about his drinking and eating habits.

Gardelin turned out to be a more effective merchant than bookkeeper, and eventually he was appointed Chief Merchant, with his friend and housemate, Johan Horn, as Chief Bookkeeper.

While begging to go home, he made a record as Chief Merchant that impressed the directors so much that they ignored his letters. When it became apparent that Governor Suhm was a rascal, the directors, without waiting to ask Gardelin's consent, sent out a letter to St. Thomas appointing Gardelin in his place. Gardelin took this as a messianic sign, and ceased to request retirement.

Traditionally, promoted from Chief Merchant or Chief Bookkeeper, a governor was expected to continue in that position while acting as governor. Gardelin, promoted in the face of his eagerness to go home, proposed to be the ruler, the lawgiver, and the supreme military commander, and at once divested himself of all other duties.

He appointed as Chief Merchant Johan Horn, who was to keep his job as Chief Bookkeeper as well. Being second in command, Horn was automatically Vice-Commandant of St. Thomas and Commandant—in absentia—of St. Jan.

It had recently been said of Horn by the "Gammel Englander,"

The Old Englishman on St. Jan, who was a renegade actor: "He has a grimace for a face, lies for eyes, noes for a nose, arse-cheeks for face-cheeks, fears for ears, whips for lips, dung for a tongue, and to all who know him it seems strange that he has but one horn for a name." This description had promptly been memorized by everyone in the islands who was familiar with the English language, with the exception of Commander Horn himself, who wondered aloud what all the laughing was about.

On the head of Jacob Schønnemann, an old Africa hand not yet caught in any provable misfeasance, Gardelin placed the hat of Treasurer, in addition to the two he already wore: Government Secretary and Chief Magistrate of the Common Council Court.

In his letter of acceptance to the directors, Gardelin explained this as a prudent precautionary measure—in case anything should happen to him, his subordinates would be better able to carry on, being habituated in the various aspects of government.

As a widowed Chief Merchant he shared with perennial bachelor Johan Horn an unpretentious house belonging to the Company. (Indeed, he took care to describe it as dilapidated in correspondence with the directors.) It was located not far from the fort and near the TAPHOUSE that gave TAPPUS its name.

As governor he refused to move into the sumptuous governor's mansion, insisting on continuing to live simply. He sold the mansion to a rich planter and ordered most of its extraordinary complement of servants rented out or put to work at various jobs on the Company PLANTAGES. He kept Paris, the cook. Paris, whose name was known everywhere in the Caribbean and in parts of Europe, a slave who could speak to any man—as often as not in his listener's own language—without servility, was a chef so superb that Gardelin's juices could not resist him despite a determination to show the directors a shining example of penuriousness and regard for the Company's interests.

In writing of his economies to the directors he did mention that he planned to move into the fort as soon as he could have rooms prepared. He did not bring up the fact that the proposed quarters would be in the King's bastion—the southeast, reserved theoretically for the King because it was in every way the most pleasant—and that they would consist of a sumptuous apartment with gilt-leather walls—refurbished from a seventeenth-century occupancy—and princely furnishings. He pointed out that it was fitting that, as military commandant, he should live in the fort, and that as governor he would there be available to more people. He proposed eventually to move the entire Secret Council—comprising, in addition to himself, Johan Horn and Jacob Schønnemann—into the fort, so that the Council might function more smoothly under his baton.

Besides Paris, Gardelin and Horn had, at Company expense, the customary two body slaves each, one for the day and one for the night, to act as valets and keep the master fanned when it was hot, and untroubled by flies in the daytime and mosquitoes and other intruders at night. In addition, the little Company house had only the usual crew of house slaves, all belonging to the Company—housekeepers, laundresses, kitchen helpers, porters, and footmen—in sufficient numbers that none had to work very hard.

On the morning of April 31, 1733, Gardelin relaxed over his bodily functions after breakfast. His body slave, Æro, waited patiently outside the privy, ready to whisk him clean.

The whisk that Æro held consisted of horse-tail bristles lashed to the end of a polished mahogany rod embossed in gold with Gardelin's monogram. The use of this instrument was a hateful thing to Gardelin. When the time came he had to let Æro into the privy, bend in an uncomfortable position, panting, with his fat belly pressed against his thighs, while Æro, astonishingly deft, flicked away the odious residue as Gardelin gravely held his genitals high out of harm's way. This was a procedure that a homeland Dane like Gardelin would never be able to take for granted, but which he could not omit here without losing face in a community where no upper-class person was supposed to condescend to perform even such an intimate service for himself.

Later Æro shaved him carefully, as Bodger, when stationed at Christiansfort, had taught him to do. It had taken Gardelin some time to be willing to bare his throat to a slave with a razor in hand, but Bodger had persuaded him by alternately jeering and lecturing.

As he was preparing for his bath, Gardelin heard the honor guard coming to perform the daily symbolic early morning ritual of the key to the fort. He barely had time to lunge into his tunic, with Æro's help, buckle on his sword, and hang the ceremonial key from the sword belt.

When the guard faced the house with a booming of drums and stamping of feet, Gardelin took the salute standing in the window, naked below his tunic, with only his finery and the hilt of his sword showing above the sill. Solemnly he handed the ceremonial key out the window and received it back again after the sergeant had gone through the motions of unlocking a massive door with it.

Horn, on his way to the office, stood erect in the dooryard to receive his portion of the honors, a wide-swinging military salute returned by him in proper style, and the guard then turned on its collective heel and marched back to the fort, by-passing Secretary Schønnemann's house because the Secretary, who had been ill for weeks, could not bear the noise of the ritual.

No one could enjoy a laugh at Gardelin's discomfiture, for none but Æro and Gardelin knew what had happened, and Æro would never think of laughing, even in the slave quarters at the end of the day, for he himself caught in the same situation, would have behaved in exactly the same way without thinking twice about it.

By the time Gardelin was bathed and clothed, his official day had begun. The line was already forming outside his door. The amanuensis had arrived to take down his words for the day, and with him, Inspector Jens Thrane, also an interpreter-translator, who would help Gardelin to deal with the many languages that would be spoken, and translate into written Dutch the things that concerned Dutch planters and shippers.

First in line was a West Indies hybrid named abraham Rosetti. A cast-off outside mulatto son of an upper-class German, von Roslein, who had Latinized the name for prestige, Rosetti had heard that Gardelin, to get some desperately needed cash for salaries, had sold the Company barque at a fancy price to a passing New Englander who had lost his ship. He had come, he explained, to ask Gardelin how the Company could get along without a BARQUE.

"It cannot," Gardelin said. "I will buy yours cheap."

"It is not for sale," Rosetti said, going into hiding behind the bargaining veil that all traders carry with them.

"Then it is for lease, or you would not be here," Gardelin said, "and of course I have been expecting you to show up. You are standing in a long, long line, and I must tell you that you have not the chance of a fly in a roomful of lizards. I hope you will not take up too much of my time this morning, for I am very busy, as you can see."

There followed a full hour of the market-place dickering that they both enjoyed enormously, and in the end Gardelin, who had no other ship in mind, and none offered, agreed to pay, on the Company's account, the trifling sum of ten RIGSDALERS a month for lease of the BARQUE, including the salary of Rosetti, as skipper, and the crew.

Both Gardelin and Rosetti knew that the skipper would make his real money transporting non-Company goods and passengers when sailing on Company business. Rosetti had bought—stolen, the former owner said—the BARQUE from a cornered Englishman who called her *The Sweet Tooth,* and that name it retained.

With Rosetti disposed of, Gardelin turned to other matters for the rest of the morning, sweating profusely, and drinking his substitute beer and dealing with things as fast as they came up.

An Englishman, Captain St. Lo of the British man-o'-war *Experiment,* at anchor outside the harbor, eventually arrived in what to his officers he loudly called The Presence.

Gardelin, using his confident but execrable English, and with the help of the two clerks, apologized for having to receive him in such an unprepossessing office, explaining that he was waiting for his new apartment to be completed.

With studied politeness, St. Lo assured him that his house was charming, and stated his business. He came in the name of Captain Toller, who had been summoned to England to commission a new ship of the line and bring her out here for duty in the West Indies. Captain Toller had a friend, an Englishman, a planter on the west end of the French island of Ste. Croix, who was badly in need of slaves.

"It is for this reason," he continued parenthetically, speaking slowly and distinctly, "you understand, that I could not bring my ship into harbor and exchange salutes in the proper manner, and have our visit properly recorded, since I am here only as a favor to Captain Toller, and not as officer of a ship in His Majesty's navy."

"Yes, I understand." Gardelin said, after consultation with his two clerks. "Very good. But you ask for slaves?"

"Yes, sir. To be sent to his friend at Sainte Croix."

Gardelin made it plain that slaves were the life-blood of the islands. There never were enough slaves.

"But you are suffering from a long drought, are you not?"

"We are, God help us."

"And there is no work for your slaves to do."

"It will rain," Gardelin said, with the help of the clerks. "God will bring us rain."

"Meanwhile," St. Lo said, "there are arrangements that can be made, there are sums of money . . ."

Gardelin halted him with a raised hand and consulted the clerks. Then he spoke, through Thrane when in need of help.

"There are arrangements, as you have said. How many men are you on board your ship?"

"I have a full complement."

Gardelin explained that on St. Jan there were a number of slaves that had run off into the bush. If the captain cared to use his full complement, whatever that might be, to beat the bush and round up these MARONS, Gardelin was certain that arrangements could be made for the friend on Ste. Croix to purchase as many of them as he might wish.

St. Lo protested that it was obviously impossible to use His Majesty's ship and seamen in such a private enterprise.

Gardelin told him that if he should ever change his mind he should make the change known to him. He requested that he pass along the information to Captain Toller as well.

Before leaving, Captain St. Lo said, "at the dock, during the formalities, I noted a date placed on the papers by your dock master. Now, what is today's date on this island?"

"Thirty-first April," Gardelin said with a slight archness of manner, "seventeen hundred thirty-three."

"But how can that be? No such date is possible. And even if it were, still, by my good English reckoning it is the nineteenth of April."

"You jest, of course," Gardelin said with an air of patience. "You are aware that Denmark, along with the rest of Europe, long ago adopted the Gregorian calendar."

"Yes, and I am surprised at you. Such popish nonsense, why would good Protestant Danes adopt it? We English have better sense!"

"It may well be," Gardelin said quietly.

"But even so, what of this thirty-first April? I am curious. By your popish reckoning it is the thirtieth of April."

"Officially, by my order, this day is the thirty-first April," Gardelin said with a small smile.

"Well, by all that's holy! You are more powerful aboard this island than a captain is aboard his ship, and believe me, aboard his ship a captain is virtually a god!"

"That is true," Gardelin said.

"But what is the reason for such an order? Surely you must permit me to be curious!"

"Last year," Gardelin said, "was a leap year. But we are so isolated here—and without calendars as a rule—that none of the clerks remembered the fact when it came to the twenty-ninth of February. As a result, all business on that day was recorded as having taken place on March first. The error was not discovered until after copies of all documents had been sent to Kjøbenhavn and it was too late to make any changes."

"Well, damme!" St. Lo exclaimed, with a look of combined delight and contempt. "But why was the month of February this year not given twenty-nine days in recompense?"

"Again, I fear no one thought of it," Gardelin said. "Finally, in this month the omission was pointed out to me and I issued the order to make April a thirty-one-day month for this year only."

Through the window Gardelin spied Cornelius Frandsen Bodger coming along the street past the TAPHOUSE. He stood up abruptly, making the Englishman feel dismissed, and St. Lo departed in good grace.

When Bodger came into the room, Gardelin had sent away everyone but his body slave and was standing, one eyebrow arched high and ferociously, a stubby finger pointing accusingly at the doorway.

"BØDKER!" he roared. That was the correct Danish name, and Danes insisted on calling him by it. "Nelli BØDKER! I could have your head for this, you know. Ignoring my orders to come down here! Knowing how you would feel, I put off issuing the order until a week ago and you ignore me! Who do you think you are?"

"Good morning, Your Excellency," Bodger said blandly. "I have had no opportunity to congratulate you upon your elevation to the governorship. Congratulations, sir!" He made a friendly sign of greeting to Æro, who smiled.

"You had a chance to come a week ago and congratulate me," Gardelin said accusingly.

"Much sickness on St. Jan," Bodger said. "Not so much, I pride myself, among the Company slaves, but the inhabitants of the island are sorely tried with sickness, and both Castan and Papillaut, who have some knowledge with which to help them—both of them are ill with the FLUX."

"That is sad. But you are not paid to serve the inhabitants of the island, but only the Company officials and slaves."

"True," Bodger said, "Yet a man must have a heart."

"I have a heart, man, but I also have a duty. Our MESTER here on St. Thomas is dead . . ."

"Dr. Clausen is dead? I thought only ill!" Bodger cried.

". . . and Hans Liebig, who was promoted to take his place, is gravely ill, and the Company slaves are dying like flies. The sickhouse behind the fort is overflowing onto the water battery and you can smell it across the bay. The gravediggers in the slave cemetery work night and day digging trenches—I tell you, it's like a plague."

"Well, that is worse than St. Jan, I must say," Bodger said. "But you are looking well, I must also say."

"Looking well!" Gardelin shouted. "I have been sick for years and no one will help me." He sighed deeply. "Come, Nelli, I need you badly here. You are now the Company CHIRURGEON and physician on St. Thomas."

"Oh, no!" Bodger protested.

"Oh, yes! With a rise in salary. That is my order. Do I have to put it in writing?"

"But my PLANTAGE—I cannot just leave it sitting there."

"Sell it."

"To whom?"

"My son."

"Which son? Everyone is your son!"

"Reimert."

"Reimert Sødtmann? How can he buy it? He is in debt up to his hair line!"

"He is selling Frederiksdal, on the north side, to Moth. That will get him out of debt to the Company, and then some."

"So this whole thing is a plot to add my plantation to Reimert Sødtmann's!" Bodger exclaimed with mock anger. "You are using your powers as governor to force me to sell my PLANTAGE to your so-called son—what are you going to get out of this?"

Gardelin ignored the insult with a wave of the hand. "Sell it back to Moth, then."

"I shall!" Bodger exclaimed with cheerful malice. "Then he can sell it to your son at a profit."

"Good," Gardelin said. "So you agree to stay here and sell out on St. Jan."

"Oh, God, what have I said! You caught me off guard!" Gardelin laughed and made a motion of delight.

"Man, it is good," he said, "to talk honest KJØBENHAVN Danish after all the idiotic accents and languages I have to listen to around here!"

"I have heard no KJØBENHAVN Danish," Bodger said. "You are a Christianshavner."

"The difference is how many hundred ELLS?"

"The difference cannot be measured in ELLS."

"True, I daresay. But let us be serious. You knew me when I was only a bookkeeper here. Now, through no choice of my own, I am governor, and you are subject to my orders. It is no pleasure for me to force you to move back to TAPPUS, but I have desperate need of you here."

"Of course," Bodger said quietly. "I understand."

Gardelin sent Æro to tell Paris that there would be an extra mouth for MIDDAG, then turned to Bodger. "You will take MIDDAG with me, and after nap time I wish you to look after MESTER Liebig and see how it is with the sick slaves."

"Very well—but I shall not need the nap. On St. Jan only the rich indulge in such luxury, and no one is rich but Pietter Duurloo, and he never sleeps."

"By the way, where is your body slave?" Gardelin asked.

"I do not wear one," Bodger said.

"Oh, nonsense. Be serious. On St. Jan you maybe can dispense with one, but here in town you will lose face. You know that. A physician must have the people's respect, and a Company man must have it most of all."

"Sorry. It is against my principles."

"Damn it, man," Gardelin said testily, "I cannot permit you to go about without a body slave. You might as well go naked! and your wig. Where is your wig? It is not considered decent to go about with a mere hat, in town. Take one of my wigs, and one of my house slaves to look after you."

"Thank you, but no. However, I did bring along Christian to assist me in whatever work I might have to do, and he can walk with me if that will make the Company feel better. He is waiting for me on the dock."

"Christian?"

"Christian Sost."

"Oh, yes. I know of him. But walk with you? He is your slave! You mean walk behind you. Have you been out there in the country so long that I have to instruct you when you come to town?"

"He will walk with me," Bodger repeated.

⌡

VIII

OF the large PLANTAGES on St. Jan, that day or any other, the most bitter and hopeless was that of the Coop family on the south shore.

The Coops—Cornelius, who had recently died, and his brother Joachim, called Jochum—were rich, old-time Caribbean-Dutch immigrants to St. Thomas who now owned large PLANTAGES there and four houses in the TAPPUS complex of six villages.

Their St. Jan holdings comprised the entire area from Grootpan Bay to Nanny Point, excepting the salt pond and Ram's Head peninsula, which belonged to the Company. In addition, their land grants included the full southern face of the thousand-foot hill behind that peninsula and these landmarks.

The wretched buildings were set on a low, breeze-swept height behind the salt pond. The estate, called Concordia by the Coops and Discordia by others, was absentee-owned and run by a Cockney renegade MESTERKNEGT who managed always to keep his name from being written down, but when he was not called SCHIJTKOP, which he never seemed to mind, he was called KIDDLE, a name he had acquired in years as a net-fisherman in the old country.

The twenty slaves that KIDDLE herded through their daily work of preparing the land for the raising of cane and cotton were a sorry, sickly lot. Old-line, ACCUSTOMED SLAVES of the type that elsewhere, when well treated, were generally bright and cheerful in their work, these were as spiritless and mangy as starving dogs. In the past three years, eight of their fellows had died of disease, starvation, or KIDDLE's cruelty; four had had the spirit to escape to Puerto Rico, another had stolen a canoe and disappeared, and a fourteenth had rebelled against KIDDLE's whip and been hanged for his pains on the savannah on St. Thomas. And in January of this year, one named Mina because he was an Amina nobleman had committed suicide with a sharpened stick, secure in the knowledge that his spirit would reappear in Guinea and be reborn in the body of a noble child.

The wonder, to the islanders, was that the absentee Coops did not summon KIDDLE to town and call him to account for the loss of those thousands of RIGSDALERS of investment—fifteen grown slaves were worth two thousand and more RIGSDALERS in the market, depending on their condition and demonstrated capabilities—not to mention the production of wealth lost by the loss or stilling of their bodies. But St. Jan had come to be considered a charnelhouse by many on St. Thomas, and when KIDDLE sent in his reports of death or escape, they were always accepted by the wealthy, easy-going Coops as inevitable.

Of the twenty Coop slaves who remained alive on St. Jan, thirteen were listed by the tax collector as "capable" adults, although Margritha was this morning praying audibly to her DJAMBI-gods for death, and was perhaps not far from it, back in her hut after the bestial night that KIDDLE had put her through, for it had been her turn again in the torture chamber of his perverted bed.

Three more of the Coop slaves were MANQUERONS, incapable of doing more than light chores. Two of them had been mutilated, one with the loss of a leg for trying to run away and being caught at it, one with the loss of an arm that had been caught in the cane crusher at the Company sugar mill on St. Thomas years before—the MESTERKNEGT had had to be quick to use the ax that hung handy for this very purpose, and chop off his arm before the entire slave should be pulled into the inexorable machinery. The third MANQUE-RON, a woman, was slowly being eaten away, her limbs being reduced to useless stubs by a mystery which no one could explain and which left her feeling otherwise perfectly well.

The remainder of the slave roster was filled out by a fourteen-year-old boy, a twelve-year-old, another aged six, and a five-year-old girl-children, variously hued, of women in the compound.

Of all the adult slaves, only Hans had some spirit left, perhaps because Bandje, his mother, had always managed to slip some extra food into his mouth when he was a growing boy. He was young, and quick with the cutlass in the bush and GUINEA GRASS, always able to find whelks for the pot, along the black-wet rocks of the shore. He never spoke in the presence of a white man unless required to under the threat of the lash, yet when he did speak, he was not sullen, but merely quiet, with eyes averted, looking to the distance until required to focus on the white man's face, at which times he was able to make them totally devoid of expression.

Pietter, the only other adult slave who went with his head up, was no longer young. He walked with a double limp that gave his steps a shoveling motion, but he could nevertheless carry tremendous loads, whether on his head, on his shoulders, or in his arms, and he seemed to enjoy doing so.

No TUTU sounded here, but only the growl of KIDDLE, and the grubby compound came creaking to life in the dawn.

KIDDLE was tired and languid after his night's exertion and would go back to bed as soon as he had eaten the POORJACK-and-pepper that the MANQUERONS were silently preparing over the smoking fire.

He ate with gasping, sucking sounds, and then said, yawning, "Orders for the day. Hans, Popo, Guantje, go to the west BARCAD and terrace for cane, as yesterday. Pietter, take the children, pick salt. The rest, find green for the donkeys and goats."

The adult slaves went slowly to their tasks. The children ran ahead of Pietter down toward the salt pond, their bare feet pounding in the rocky red dirt of the path, to try to surprise a land crab away from its hole. Their scrawny naked bodies twisted to dodge the grasping underbrush as the sun glinted over the watery horizon and caught the purple highlights on their skin.

This salt-picking expedition was thievery, and of course Pietter knew it, but he could hardly have been expected to care.

In this long, windy drought, the salt pond had come to perfection. KIDDLE was stealing the Company's salt and hoarding it in hogsheads against the time when for years on end there would be enough rain to prevent the pond from fulfilling itself. Then there would come a shortage of salt, and KIDDLE would supply it at an inflated price.

Oddly, it never seemed to occur to people that they could use seawater in cooking, and even evaporate it in shallow pans, or boil it dry in kettles, for sprinkling-salt.

Pietter put the children to work picking salt while he went into the bush to break off branches with many fine twigs and stick them into the mud at the bottom of the mile-round shallow pond. All over the bottom were similar branches, sticking up, coated with salt. The wind, gusting across the water, whipped up a spray that caught and crystallized on the twigs. All along the shore the foam that stood in bubbles and froth had crystallized on the stones and debris that lay there, and large areas of the very shallow places were solid white, sheets of salt-crust on the mucky bottom. The water itself, not blue as was the sea, looked reddishly dirty with its burden of mineral, but at every opportunity of exposure to evaporation in the air it was blinding white in the sun. Replenished by occasional violent storms smashing seawater over the barrier beaches on either side, and perhaps, too, by seepage in nature's effort to keep the water level the same as outside, the pond lay there through the ages, alternately evaporating, thickening, concentrating its mineral content, and being diluted by rainfall, which at the same time would dissolve the crystallized salt.

The children picked the crystals off the coated twigs, avoiding splashing in the water because the salt was strong for their skin.

From the bush fringing the pond came the rrr*ow*rr of a cat. Pietter and the children stood transfixed, for any slave would know that this was no cat, but a fellow slave, a MARON, a runaway living in the bush.

The children stood staring, but Pietter turned his back on the sound and appeared to hold his breath.

Now came the shape of whispered words, cavernous in sound, out of the bush. The language would be incomprehensible to Pietter or any other OLD-LINE SLAVE, whose only speech was the CREOLE slave-talk patter.

Pietter knew at once that this was a pure African language, spoken by one of the BUSSALS from the slave ship last year, all of them, to the ACCUSTOMED SLAVE, strange creatures of anger and violence, to be feared.

The voice in the bush switched to SLAVE TALK, but spoken by a novice in it.

"*Wa ju mesta?*"

"Hem le slæp," Pietter whispered, shaking with fear.

"*Wah-tah,*" the voice said with urgency. "Wahtah fo trik!"

All of the little pockets of rainwater in the rocks of the mountains that would in normal weather be waiting, cool under coatings of green tropical slime, to be exposed and sipped by the thirsty were long since dried up, along with all unguarded natural springs. A slave who chose in these drought times to lay his life on the line and be a hunted animal rather than work for the hated master had to bludgeon water, super-precious water kept under guard and lock, out of any situation he could create with loyal slaves. Sometimes there was a woman who would sneak it to him, along with purloined bits of food and the solace of sex deep in the night, on the fringes of the compound, or in the compound itself, whence he would silently steal away before the sounding of the tutu, and no slave would dare betray him. But some of the bussal marons had been so violent in captivity that no woman, in spite of the attraction violent men have always had for many women, ever became attached to them before their escape—and this voice in the bush, Pietter knew, belonged to one of these.

Food the maron could somehow manage alone. A land crab, pounced upon in the moonlight and eaten raw. Fish, caught by throwing poisonous stinkwood into a quiet sea pool, would float to the surface.

In the drought there were no fruits in the bush, but there were occasional wizened kitchen gardens that could be raided in the night for tania, gjambo, calelu, or a sugarapple or soursop fruit to ripen in the bush.

"Wahtah, mon!" The voice in the bush had lost its drawl; it was sharp and desperate.

Pietter ventured an angry gesture. "Me no ha wahtah," he growled fearfully.

When the voice threatened to kill him and drink his blood if necessary, Pietter sent one of the children scampering with a message to the kitchen manquerons that Pietter was dying of thirst at the salt pond and must have some liquid. He was not to mention the MARON, for fear the MESTERKNEGT might hear.

While the boy was gone, Pietter made a move to leave the spot, but the voice held him hostage there, and he stood, trembling and speechless, waiting.

at last the boy came back with the leftovers of KIDDLE's rum. There was no water to be had until the MESTER awoke, for he had it under lock and key.

But the rum, with its mite of comfort, would be more welcome to the MARON than water ever could be.

Pietter set the pot on the ground near the invisible presence. The voice curtly ordered him and the children away—they must not see the face of the MARON stranger.

Obediently Pietter and the trembling, moon-eyed children walked up the path and waited for a signal to come back. No signal ever came, and after a long wait Pietter ventured fearfully down the path.

The pot was not where he had left it.

Softly he called out, asking for it back.

Silence from the bush.

Pietter begged for the pot.

The voice told him to get more rum.

But, Pietter insisted piteously, he could not get any more.

Then forget the pot, the voice told him.

Pietter wailed, and tears started from his eyes. But, he cried, he had to return the pot. It would be bad enough to have taken the KJELTUM for the MANQUERONS would never admit to the MESTERKNEGT that they had given it to him.

He heard a chuckling from the bush.

"But, man," Pietter cried, "this will mean a heavy LUSSING for me."

The laughter rose slightly in pitch and slowly faded away in the distance. Pietter could hear the MARON's stumblings among the bush vines; he had been too thirsty and had swallowed the rum too fast.

Pietter called the children, and with them went back to gathering salt crystals in crocks to be carried up the hill on their heads. He swallowed twice and faced up to the prospect of the sure LUSSING, perhaps up to fifty lashes, that he would have to take from KIDDLE's TSCHICKEFELL with sealed lips and surrounded by sealed lips, all by himself in a hopeless heap on the hard ground of the slave compound.

IX

AT this time, there were four African princes serving as slaves on St. Jan, at least fifty lesser noblemen, and one African king.

Most planters insisted upon robbing their BUSSALS immediately of their African names, in an attempt to divest them of their identity and individuality. Accordingly, the king, Bolombo, was renamed Clæs, and was nowhere called Bolombo, except among the most recent BUSSALS, who knew his name.

But there was a certain satisfaction in having royalty for slaves. It was obvious to anyone that it should make the ordinary slave more content with his lot if he knew that these men, from among the mighty of Africa, were here after all only slaves like him, and so Clæs was permitted to be known as King Clæs.

For the same reason, all four of the princes, although deprived of their African names, were called Prince, and nothing else. One of them belonged on Magistrate Sødtmann's PLANTAGE in Coral Bay; Susanna Runnels, daughter of Jannis van Bewerhoudt, owned one on her Susannaberg PLANTAGE; John Charles, The Old Englishman, had one on his subsistence PLANTAGE high above Little Cruz Bay; and the Company itself, on its vast Coral Bay PLANTAGE, held the last.

Two of these, for reasons best known to themselves, had quickly adapted to their new situation. Susanna's Prince was content to work for her while learning the ways of the New World, even when she had left the island. John Charles's Prince came prepared to accept the idea of the supremacy of the white race and was willing to admire Mr. Charles for being a white man, and to learn to work for him ungrudgingly, for the present. Both of these princes had hopes, and were given good reason to expect, that they would be able to buy their freedom and become important men in the community, holding slaves of their own as in Africa, and becoming rich in the New World. They regarded themselves as realists, perhaps without being able to put the thought into words; they were willing to work their way up in the white man's world, for which they had somehow conceived a certain admiration.

Sødtmann's and the Company's Princes were realists of another kind. They managed to master their anger to the extent of avoiding the whip while biding their time for whatever opportunity might arise.

King Clæs, Bolombo, was the first-born of the Number One Wife of a king of the Adampe nation, which held sway along the Gold Coast and hinterland to the east of Accra. This fact alone did not necessarily mark him for succession to his father, but it happened also that his father took a fancy to him, and after that it remained only for him to stay alive long enough to be king.

This he managed to do, spending his youth learning the princely arts of hunting and war, singing and dancing in the magnificent ceremonial celebrations. Only highborn males were permitted to engage in these activities; their followers were mere flunkies and battlefield servants, not permitted to do battle with either animal or man, except in an extreme case, to save the life or dignity of a nobleman. Nor were the followers permitted to take part in any of the ceremonies of dancing and incantation. They were, however, required to observe and applaud.

This was the atmosphere in which Bolombo was king.

All kings who hold the reins themselves are practical men. King Bolombo had been a practical man as a king; King Clæs was a practical man as a slave. He understood the system in which he was trapped, and his chances in it. Like all men of power, he had a respect for power, and the power here was white. It was a long road back to Africa, and he knew he would never travel it. He did not have it in him to be a wild man or, for long, a slave. There were stepping stones out of his present situation, and those he would tread. Thus he had rapidly learned PLANTAGE ways and within months of his sale to a master he had become an under-BOMBA assistant to a BOMBA whose grandfather had been an ACCUSTOMED SLAVE and who knew no other way of life than submission to the white man's will and the imposition of it on fellow slaves.

King Clæs as a BOMBA was strong and tough, and had an end in view.

And in his mind he had the bitter memory of how he came to be here.

As young Adampe royalty he had learned from the example of his rapacious Amina neighbors the value of war, not for conquest, not any longer for heads to use as trophies and excuses for ceremonial dances and festivals, but purely and coldly to capture men from neighboring tribes and sell them—for rum, a form of power—to the slave traders along the coast.

It was on one of his trips to the coast, with two of his favorite wives and a convoy of noble warriors, to transport his latest collection of captives to the Danish fort at Accra that he found himself ambushed by an overwhelming force of Aquambo warriors. After a wild battle, Bolombo's warriors had been bested, and not only Bolombo's captives, but he himself and his two wives had been taken. The Aquambo prince, leader of the war party, had personally disarmed and held Bolombo, laughing in his ear and burning his likeness into Bolombo's memory.

And as Bolombo's men had run away into the bush, he had cursed them and shouted after them:

"This man, remember him! This man, of all the men in the world, must live to kiss the slaver's hand! See to it! *See—to—it!*"

X

AT the PLANTAGE of the magistrate, Johannes Reimert Sødtmann, in Coral Bay, all was serene when Jens Andersen approached after making his report to Dr. Bodger. The greathouse and all the other

PLANTAGE buildings on the slope above the road still stood in the shadow of Buscagie Hill, although breakfast had been served to everyone but the twenty-odd KAMINA slaves in the cotton BARCADS.

Sødtmann's house aspired to take all of the island's meager laurels for splendor. Built of fine-grained yellow Flensborg brick, it was roofed with highest-quality tiles from Amsterdam. It was furnished, like none this side of St. Thomas, with pieces made with marvelous KJØBENHAVN craftsmanship out of mahogany, West Indies cedar, and red and yellow Brazilwood, sent "home" specially for the purpose. Besides being beautiful, they were, as MESTER Bodger put it, not eminently suited to the digestive tracts of wood-eating ants.

Judge Sødtmann lived here with his wife, Birgitta, her pubescent daughter, Helena Hissing, fathered in an earlier marriage, and her ten-month-old child Thomas, third and so-far-successful attempt to keep alive a son of this seven-year-old marriage to Sødtmann.

The slaves that Sødtmann brought to St. Jan were mostly BUSSALS, but they were tightly ruled by one who was no BUSSAL at all, but a man of mixed breed whose father, a planter of white and Carib Indian blood in the islands to windward, had sold him and his slave mother down islands to different traders to get rid of their knowing faces.

This white-Indian-Negro BOMBA was named Junio, called Juni. The family admired his control over the field slaves and the way he seemed to make them like it.

Juni, with the craggy Caribbean carve of his face, and the slight slant of eye, showed nothing to the master class but careful cheerfulness, deference, and total obedience, and he demanded that the slaves under his hand all behave so. The look in his eyes was rarely seen by any but a slave, for his gaze, in any but a slave's presence, lay along the ground and off to one side or another.

With Juni on the job, a MESTERKNEGT was superfluous. The overseer required by law was made unnecessary by Sødtmann's presence.

Different, yet astonishingly the same, was the chief of the Sødtmann household slaves, Asarconssong, called Asari. A household slave of one of the Amina noblemen captured by a vengeful Aquambo, Asari was no Amina, but a MALAGASY who wandered far from home and was captured and converted capriciously into a eunuch for the benefit of the Amina master's wives, as the Amina had heard was the custom in some far-off lands. A eunuch was, for reasons that no one could explain, said to be sexually inexhaustible, and thus able to keep a harem happy when the master found it inconvenient or impossible to make his proper rounds.

Sødtmann, seeing Asari naked on the slave block and feeling sorry for him, as well as being impressed by his straight black MALAGASY hair and his chiseled handsomeness, had bought him at a greatly reduced price because of his inability to reproduce himself. He had proved so clever and quick that he had from the start been exempted from work in the BARCADS, where, it was thought, he would quickly have been destroyed by his fellow slaves because of his infirmity. The obvious place for him was in the house, where he soon climbed to the position of majordomo.

In demeanor, Asari very much resembled Juni, and the only white person at whom he ever looked straight, like a human being, was Helena, Sødtmann's adored and adoring stepdaughter.

Helena, born at the very beginning of the year 1722 when her mother was married to a man named Andreas Hissing, was known throughout the two islands, by name if not by face. People had been known to make daylong pilgrimages just to look at her. Even on the French island of Ste. Croix was Helena Hissing known by reputation. She was as irresistible to the eyes as the moon is to the tides of the sea.

She was not the only perfect Nordic blonde in the islands, protected from babyhood, to her nose and toes and fingertips, from extended exposure to the rays of the sun, but she was unique among them, and nearly unique among all inhabitants of the islands, in that she had on her skin not a blemish, not a pockmark, not the mark of any disease or accident.

Her eyes were shining blue, and her lashes like rays of sunlight. Her lips were healthy pink, and she had early learned to bite them covertly, behind a handkerchief, on pretext of sopping up perspiration from the peach-downed pores above and below them, so that they would shine red at the right moments.

Her beauty was a misfortune, some—all of them women—said, for it was bound to turn her head and spoil her life.

An even greater misfortune—and wiser heads even among the men agreed to this—was the fact that she was maturing too soon and much too rapidly, and this was making her behave sometimes in odd, unhealthful-looking ways.

John Charles, her legal guardian since her father's death, summed it up to his own satisfaction with a characteristic couplet:

> "Adult or child, yon brimming miss
> Is old enough to concupisce."

Ever since Birgitta had married Sødtmann, when Helena was five years old, the child had adored him in ways that were touching and sweet. But now she was fawning on him, clinging to him in unnatural ways sometimes, subtly brushing her too-full-blown breasts against him until, flushing uncomfortably, Sødtmann would have to break away from her, push her firmly, sometimes rudely, aside, and tell her to leave him alone. Not once, though, had anyone ever heard him tell her why she must not behave so, and her insouciant mother, in whose presence such scenes never took place, was never quite made aware that she needed to be told such things. Helena's nature was becoming moody, secretive, sometimes sullen and pouting.

She stood now on the west gallery of the house, watching the morning sun possess Coral Bay, when Jens Andersen rode up, requesting recognition and the right to approach the house, according to the island custom.

"BINNE!" he shouted in the CREOLE language from Konge Vej, below the house.

"BUITE," she said. The way she said it, it was an invitation for him to *stay* outside, and she tossed her yellow-white curls like a filly and went inside.

"Lena, don't run away," he cried in Danish. "I only want to see your father."

Anyone looking at him now would scarcely have recognized Jens Andersen. His mouth was almost straight, his whip-arm hung limp, and his eyes were lighted like lamps.

"Tell him," she said from the shadowed interior.

"Can't you send your body slave to notify him?"

"My body has no slave."

Her stepfather's voice sounded sharply from deeper within the house: "What's that you're saying, Helena?"

"Oh, Papa," she said, her voice changing. "Herre Suhm's MESTER-KNEGT is outside, asking to see you."

"So early!" He walked from his chamber toward the gallery. "And what was that you were shouting about your body?" he demanded crossly. "You sounded like a . . . hmm."

"A joke, Papa. Like a what?" she asked, following his slender, dark-Dane figure with her eyes as he crossed toward the daylight.

He looked back at her. "Don't make jokes with Jens Andersen," he said quietly. "Come, man!" he called brusquely to Jens. "What business can you have here so early in the morning?"

Andersen approached. "Sir, I have to report that six more KAMINA BUSSALS went MARON in the night, in spite of all we could do, and my under-BOMBA King Clæs, on the pretext of pursuing them, ran away, too."

Sødtmann lowered his voice. "This is growing serious. Go into my office, I'll be right down."

Birgitta, blonde and plump, pockmarked and open-faced, came to the gallery.

"What is it, KJÆRESTE?" she asked.

"Jens Andersen. He has to make depositions to notify me and Bodger and two planters of some MARONS. Regulations." He hurried down.

Left in the anteroom to the gallery, Helena looked up to see Asari staring full-eyed at her like a child, as he never failed to do when he had a private chance. He stood in his livery that was so out of place at this end-of-the-earth, looking handsome and sad.

Helena stuck out her tongue at him. He smiled faintly and turned away to his morning duties. She went out of the room, dreamily down the stairs and down the slope into the morning sunlight, turning east along the dusty road toward Dr. Bodger's house.

XI

ON the northeast side of St. Jan, where the island begins to lose the modicum of moisture enjoyed by the lee of the heights of Tortola and the raising of crops becomes more uncertain than on the north and northwest, lies the shallow bay named for its original occupant, an Englishman, John Brown.

In Brown's Bay, protected from seas and currents alike, the water is so warm and quiet that weeds grow happily on the bottom and even the thinnest-blooded slave from the hottest part of Africa could splash and bathe with pleasure. Because there is seldom any pounding of surf, the beach never had the joy of sand, but was only stones and shells and scraps of coral, blackened by sun and salt.

In this bay, close by the shore at its western end, lived Peder Krøyer, who had married the place, as his detractors liked to say. His young wife, Marianne Thoma, had grown up here. Her father, Jacob Thoma, was an old sea dog from Tortola, son and grandson of sea dogs, descended from the revered sea captain in whose honor the island of St. Thomas was named for his patron saint.

The Thoma PLANTAGE, being merely the pied-à-terre of a seafaring man, had never in his years amounted to anything except as a residence. Peder Krøyer proposed to make a living off it, but could not yet afford the expense of setting up a sugar establishment. He was content to raise cotton for the time being, if it should ever rain again, so he bought the eastern end of the flat land behind the bay from Michel Hendrichsen, his wife's uncle by marriage. The Hendrichsens, an old couple who had raised six children, went on living there, with their MESTERKNEGT and seven slaves eking out a subsistence with cotton on the hill land that was left.

Krøyer sold the westernmost of the old Thoma houses and the hill land behind it to his neighbor on the west, a young CREOLE

Dutchman, Gabriel van Stell.

Gabriel and his wife, Neltje Delicat, and their small son left Gabriel's stepmother's house on the hill above and moved in as the Krøyers' close neighbors, since they were also close friends and all pretty much of an age together. Marianne, Peder Krøyer's wife, was still lissom and darkly lovely, although five months pregnant with her bridal child.

Peder, with a MESTERKNEGT, a Tortola mulatto named Charles Hill, and twenty slaves, two of them children and two of them decrepit old men who could not do much but had grown old in service, was building a respectable estate. He badly needed more slaves to expand his PLANTAGE rapidly and be ready for the rains that must soon come, please God.

All of his field slaves were off the three slave ships that had arrived in the past two years, and he was appalled by their anger and violence under the whip of the MESTERKNEGT when he compared them with his gentle household slaves. One, called Christian, took out his anger in being a hopeless drunkard, and on the PLANTAGE somehow always managed to get his hands on quantities of KILL-DEVIL rum. To be dried out, Christian had finally had to be shut up in The Trunk, the dank, stinking, dreaded hell-hole for miscreant slaves deep in the entrails of Christiansfort on St. Thomas, and he was still there after several months.

Gabriel van Stell, like Peder Krøyer aged twenty-five, having bought Peder's hill land and wishing to build an eventual sugar estate, bought half of his own ancestral land, contiguous on the west, from his twice-widowed stepmother. She lived on her St. Thomas PLANTAGE and used the St. Jan place nowadays as an occasional retreat from the summer's heat.

Gabriel's three unwilling slaves, one of them an Amina bought off GREVINDEN AF LAURVIGEN on her 1732 voyage, were not enough help for his project here in Brown's Bay. He would just have to make do, acting as his own MESTERKNEGT until the next slave ship. When he could acquire more slaves, it would be worth his while to hire a MESTERKNEGT.

Keeping under control the one Amina slave he had was hard

work for him, and with a pretty young wife and three-year-old Gabriel III, it was a comfort to be living within a hundred feet of Peder Krøyer. His two household slaves, although not Aminas, were rather surly, having been brought to this earth's-end from St. Thomas, where life had been much more interesting for them. The Amina, whom Gabriel called Japhit, was so violent that he had to work in irons, his steps hobbled by ankle irons connected to each other and to the ankle chain. It would be better, Gabriel felt, when some companion workers could be bought for him.

Up the GUT behind the flatland lived the Huguenot Frenchman, Pierre Castan, and Marianne's sister Elisabeth. They had a two-year-old daughter, Agethe, and Elisabeth was recovering from the birth of a son just one week before. She had already named him Jacob Thoma Castan, after her father, although it would be some time before he could be baptized and christened.

Castan, a doctor of sorts who knew how to bleed patients and pull aching teeth, raised such cotton as he could on the hill, the north side of Buscagie Hill. In spite of being partially deaf, he acted as his own MESTERKNEGT and he was a cruel man with slaves. For this reason, although they had what John Charles called their leechery in common, Bodger could not bring himself to associate very closely with him.

One of Castan's slaves was King Clæs's second wife, whom Castan had for some reason named Judicia. Peder Krøyer had bought her and three other women, now called Alette, Sara, and Suplica, out of the cargo of GREVINDEN AF LAURVIGEN last year, but when the contract date came for him to deliver the necessary cotton in payment, he had been unable to make the full delivery and had sold the women to Castan for a profit of two bales of cotton on each slave.

Castan preferred female slaves, because by working them in both bed and fields he could produce with them a double crop of profit. He had already achieved two new slave children, and another was on the way. Unfortunately he had to whip these particular women bloody and insensible before they could be made to do the night work when he demanded it of them, and because they were Adampe and Aquambo princesses they were really unfamiliar with field work. So the KAMINA women had to be driven to their daytime work as well.

It seemed to many people who knew him that Castan enjoyed whipping women in particular, and seemed to like to stir up good reasons for doing it. Oddly, his partial deafness was largely to the higher tones, the tones of most women's voices.

There were some compensations to working for Castan. He had a fetish for keeping his slaves well-fed and as healthy as possible, much as a cattleman might take pride in the sleekness of his beasts. The result was that all ten of his slaves, when not disfigured with sores from the whip and discounting the tribal markings cut into their skin, were beautiful to look at, both female and male, of whom he had two like oxen, to do the really heavy work.

The other living beings on this side of the hills were on the PLANTAGE of Cornelius Stallart, who was dead. Even his widow was dead, along with her second husband, and the place was owned by the Stallart children, who were being cared for on St. Thomas by relatives. The PLANTAGE, which was the next one west of Gabriel van Stell's stepmother's, normally tried to grow cotton on rolling high ground, with some thirty slaves under the gun, sword, and lash of a Tortola Englishman, William Eason, who had his own small PLANTAGE overlooking the Stallart place. In his house he kept for pay, in tiny, cramped quarters, four old people, two men and two women, with a Negro woman to take care of them. Castan, with his limited medical knowledge, was the physician for this, the nearest thing to an old-people's home that St. Jan could boast.

The only air of vitality in the Brown's Bay area was in Brown's Bay itself, where Peder Krøyer strove to build a paying PLANTAGE.

Krøyer's able-bodied slaves, excepting four old-line household and garden slaves and their two children, were all BUSSALS. These were all off *HAABET Galley,* the same stinking, wallowing death ship that had brought King Clæs and his wives to St. Thomas. Furthermore, the males were—all but two, named Accra and Josje—Adampes, former subjects and retainers of Bolombo, King Clæs.

Of all the Adampes, Krøyer had left only one with her rightful name, because he liked the sound of it and could remember it, and because he liked the looks of her. Breffu was her name. Her long-shanked legs, her marvelous mound, which she kept carefully covered with a small, clean loincloth, her splendid abdominal muscles, rippling as she moved with incredible grace, her strong, firm breasts that kept their shape even when she worked, bent over, in the BARCADS, and when she ran merely rode like coconuts floating in a choppy sea, her cheekbones, strong in a strong face, all contributed to her magnificence. The tribal and status symbols carved into the skin of her forehead and belly, far from disfiguring her, served only to enhance the stunning effect.

Breffu was the only slave woman who ever roused desire in Peder Krøyer, but he never availed himself of his prerogative of visiting her, not because he was recently wed and in love with his wife, not because Breffu was the wife of the slave he had named Christian, and had been his wife in Africa, and Christian was a wild bull of a man. There was something so royal in her body and bearing that he was intimidated, touched with doubt of himself, even when in the startling flash of her eyes, like a mirror catching the sun in passing, there was a tiny sign of invitation mixed with her anger, frustration, and haughtiness.

The other BUSSALS Krøyer had named Accra, Aera, Bastian, Jacob, Martha, Mingo, Josje, and Picaro.

Of the household slaves, only one was in any way remarkable. Santje, an old-line ACCUSTOMED SLAVE bought from a Dutch estate, was a creature of endless sentimentality who spent a great deal of her time either moping or unaccountably weeping.

But on this oddly dated morning in 1733, Santje was smiling, not weeping, when she brought breakfast to her young mistress, who had slept very late. Marianne smiled too as the mass of Santje advanced like a juggernaut into the room, her brown toes darting at every step from under the voluminous Dutch skirt she loved to wear.

"MISSIE SA JEAT!" she said.

Marianne impulsively felt moved to say thanks for what was her due from a slave, and said, "Danki, Santi," affectionately.

Santje's smile was destroyed; she burst into tears.

Marianne brought her up sharply and made her set down the tray.

"What are the tears for?" she demanded, continuing in the CREOLE patois.

"Missie is so kind!"

"Oh, nonsense! Then what was the smile for?"

"My child is here. My child whom I have not seen for long months."

"Cotje? From Sødtmann's? What is he doing here?"

"He brought some messages for the master." Although it was against the Danish custom to split up a slave family against its will, in the course of liquidating the estate of a dead Dutchman, Santje had been separated from her husband and son and daughter. Marianne knew of this and of Santje's sorrow over it, and she said to Santje:

"Bring Cotje to me."

She had never seen Santje's child. She aimed her eyes at a point in the doorway three feet off the floor, only to have them assaulted by the sight of a great hulking figure that shuffled in, staring desperately at the floor and darting anxious glances backward under his armpits at the doorway.

"Santje!" Marianne did not cover her astonishment. "This is your child?"

"My child, Missie."

"That you have been crying over since you came here?"

"My child, Missie." Marianne spoke to Cotje. "You bring messages?"

Cotje brought from behind his massive back a pudgy hand that clutched two papers, which he dared not hand to her.

Marianne knew that the writing would be in Danish, which she could not read. Besides, the messages were not for her and could be of no interest to her.

"Give them to the master," she said.

"Master is not here," Santje said.

"But where is he? He left me alone here?" Marianne cried in sudden panic, although she knew no reason why she should be

SUGAR PLANTATION

1-Great House, 2-Slave Cabins, 3-The Savana or pasture, 4-Land planted to Sugar Cane, 5-Water Driven Sugarmill, 6-Sugar House, 7-Mill waste called Bagasse, 8-Place to purge the Sugar. Geografia Americana, Livorno, 1763, MAPes MONDe Collection

afraid.

"Mr. Hill is on guard outside," Santje said. "Master heard gun-shot signal from Konge Vej and had to ride fast, fast."

Fear grew at the base of Marianne's throat, but she refused to show it. She knew that the gunshot signal, three shots, fired as rapidly as they could be got off and passed from PLANTAGE to PLANTAGE, was a call to the Civil Guard meaning trouble. The planter passed on the signal, then was supposed to ride toward the sound of the gun, tracing the source of the signal from PLANTAGE to PLANTAGE until he reached the scene of the emergency.

Marianne had heard no shots fired by her husband, so she knew that Brown's Bay was the end of the chain of signals, and she, sleeping late, and on her pillow inside the stone house, had not heard the distant shots.

"If Mr. Hill is guarding the house, who is watching the KAMINA slaves?" she asked.

"Mr. Hill. He brought them in from the BARCAD."

"MESTER van Stell—is he gone too?"

"Yes, Missie."

"Who is guarding his Japhit?"

"Mr. Hill, Missie."

"Good. Let me see the messages.

Santje took the papers from Cotje and handed them to her. They were indeed written in Danish. One was a legal-looking document, and the other was a personal note. On both of them she recognized the words "MARON" and "King Clæs."

She took the papers to Charles Hill, the MESTERKNEGT a wiry, tough little man, who stood, gun in hand, back to the house, face to the KAMINA slaves who sat sullenly, uncomprehending, on the ground.

"Read you Danish?" she asked in English, without greeting.

"But very little, Mistress," Hill said.

She thrust the papers at him, and he held them just below eye level, facing the KAMINA slaves, so that he could see both them and the papers.

"One," he said, "is a law paper, a swear paper by Jens Andersen that do seem to say, now let us see, six, yes, six of Suhm's BUSSALS

William Blake, ca 1790, from a painting by Stedman, ca 1775 Whipping, MAPes MONDe
Collection

do be gone MARON this very night past, and King Clæs, yes, as clear as a sunrise, King Clæs it says, with them."

"The other one?"

"Well, ah. Some of the words do be like English, after a fashion. But, ah. Even so, I have not the sense of it. But I be that sure it would say this is a dangerous matter, be on your guard, and the like. Think ye?"

"Yes," Marianne said.

She sent Santje next door for Neltje van Stell and her dusky little son Gabriel III, whom Marianne adored while waiting for her own child. The two young women spent the day huddled in Marianne's house behind the protective back of Charles Hill and his weapons.

Not until mid-afternoon did Peder and Gabriel return home, relieving the tension and sending the slaves back to work.

Peder was furious. "That idiot, Barnds," he said. "Just like his father, shoots first and then looks."

"What Barnds?" Marianne asked.

"Herman. MESTERKNEGT for Elisabeth Runnels—you know, Adrian's, up next to Captain van Bewerhoudt. Father is William. Big man on St. Thomas and owns half the south side of St. Jan, plus a big boat. Disinherited the boy, Herman."

"Oh, yes. But what happened?"

"Well, some MARONS jumped out of the bush at van Bewerhoudt's and when Barnds was notified of it he lost his head. He fired the signal, instead of just being on guard. Says he thought we could capture them."

"Well?"

"Anyone in his right mind knows that you can't catch these MARONS in the bush. You couldn't even catch me in the bush if I were in that situation. The only thing we can do is starve them out—see to it that they get no food or drink from any PLANTAGE. One good thing about this accursed drought is that MARONS can't live in the bush without help from slaves on the PLANTAGES."

It was almost sundown when a clamor broke out among the KAMINA slaves working in the BARCAD, and Peder rushed to see what the trouble was. He saw the slaves lying on the ground, crying

"Bolombo! Bolombo!" and Charles Hill staring transfixed at the bush, pointing his gun.

Looking closely, Peder could see, half-merging with the darkness of the shadows in the bush, the superb figure of a pure African male, standing stock still. Peering more closely Peder could see the burning gaze of a pair of great dark eyes under brows like promontories of finely wrought ebony.

The man's whole body, from his forehead and temples to his toes, was decorated with the symbols of his tribe and his royalty.

"Step forward!" Peder said sharply in SLAVE TALK, clutching his sword.

The figure emerged from the bush, naked. His gaze continued to sizzle the very air, and he was completely silent.

"Who are you?" Peder demanded, although he knew that this was King Clæs. He had long since, in Accra, learned more than a smattering of the languages there.

"Bolombo! Bolombo!" cried the KAMINA slaves, lying still on their faces.

Peder suddenly remembered that these, his slaves, were formerly the subjects of this man. When King Clæs nodded and spoke in his native tongue some majestic syllables including "Bolombo," meaning "I am Bolombo, the king," and when Peder heard the marvelous voice issuing from the throat and resonating in the wide cavities of the African's skull, he would have been less than human if he had not been impressed.

But Peder, like all masters, was able to rescue himself from any possible weakness by remembering what every old-timer had always said: these African noblemen, however majestic in manner and sound, were actually majestic only in their own estimation; behind the outward majesty, born of the habit of being right through might, there lay only a vast emptiness and vacuity, an inability to master any idea larger than a pin-head, or any skill beyond the customary hunting and singing and dancing and making war and children, without being patiently taught, slowly and painfully.

Thus Clæs, a king standing at the edge of a forest surveying his people and domain, became to Peder the animal that the master class had no choice but to consider him if it would retain its sanity. Peder, holding the power to coerce him, was able to bark at him, "Take your place on the ground!" and force him to do it.

He ordered Charles Hill to take the slaves into the compound, and when they were gone, he turned to King Clæs.

"Now why come you here?" he demanded, roughly. He was puzzled, for King Clæs had not been in the bush even one full day, and was not forced to give himself up.

"I come to make palaver."

"But I do not have to palaver with you," Peder said. "You are my prisoner, and you shall be returned to your master's PLANTAGE. And where are the other six MARONS that went with you?"

"I know not, Master. They did not go with me."

"You have remained alone?"

"Yes, Master."

"I repeat, why are you here to palaver with me?"

"I would stay here," King Clæs said. "I would be your BOMBA."

Peder Krøyer did badly need more slaves, and King Clæs, if willing, would be the finest possible BOMBA since these slaves were his subjects, and he could easily control them. Peder was strongly tempted to use his connection with the magistrate of the island and the governor of both islands to arrange to keep King Clæs and pay for him. He would, of course, have to turn him over to Reimert Sødtmann as a captured MARON, but he could easily get him off with a few lashes and obtain permission to take him on as BOMBA pending settlement of the matter.

"But why my BOMBA?" he asked. "I can understand you might not wish to work for Jens Andersen, but why come you here?"

"My Number Two Wife you bought. My Number One Wife is on the other island."

"But I sold your wife to Monsieur Castan. Did you not know that?"

"I knew that."

"Speak to me with respect!"

King Clæs hesitated only a second.

"Yes, Master," he said.

"Then why come you to me and not to Monsieur Castan?"

King Clæs looked at him for a moment as one man looks at another. "Master know why."

Peder Krøyer was caught off guard. This was flattery of a sort, for King Clæs was saying to him that Monsieur Castan was known among the slaves to be a cruel master, and he, Peder Krøyer, was known to be otherwise. At that moment King Clæs became Peder Krøyer's trusted BOMBA but it was not until Peder had put him up for the night, under guard, and had eaten and slept an hour, and waked with King Clæs on his mind, that Krøyer knew it.

He could tell himself that King Clæs had run away from the cruelty of Jens Andersen, not because he wished to be a MARON and live in the bush, but because he wished to be near his wife and working as BOMBA for a kind master, Peder Krøyer.

It did not necessarily ever occur to Krøyer, until perhaps the last moment of his life, that the matter might have been not quite so simple as that, or might possibly have been a great deal simpler.

PART TWO

To the Brink

I

Cornelius Frandsen Bodger stayed in Gardelin's unfinished apartment in Christiansfort pending the preparation of a place for him elsewhere. With him stayed Christian Sost, his slave and unofficial assistant.

It was considered all right for Christian Sost to stay in the same apartment with his master. After all, a body slave—and Christian Sost was taken by the casual observer for Bodger's body slave—would spend the nights in the same room with his master, but public opinion made impossible his sitting or walking beside him. So strongly did people feel about this that if the two walked along the street together they sometimes had stones and other objects thrown at them covertly, and once in a while a jar of slops emptied on them from an upstairs window.

Bodger's reaction was not anger, but sorrow and frustration, for he wished he could understand the way the minds of the perpetrators worked, since he noted that, oddly enough, the casters of stones and throwers of slops appeared to be slaves. True, masters, seeing the two men walking shoulder to shoulder would hmph and harrumph sometimes, and even speak sharply to Christian in passing, but the really angry people seemed to be privileged slaves—household, shop, boat, artisan, and the like—and their anger seemed to be aimed at Bodger and Christian equally.

Christian wished to solve the problem in the simplest way, by walking a couple of steps behind. Bodger would not hear of it, and was willing to take the consequences. He wished only that he could get out of this town atmosphere. He yearned to get back to the relative simplicity of the country, where life was more basic and, it seemed to him, people more real.

Christian Sost, of course, was no ordinary slave. As his name indicated, since he was not named by Danes for a Danish king, he was a Christian, and that, in itself, was strictly against the rules. However, when a slave was already a Christian, there was obviously no help for it.

Sost had been a Christian before he was a slave. As a young man he had made his way to France from the Congo, somehow escaping servitude, probably because he could look a Frenchman in the eye and speak his language.

In France, an oddity but not an outcast among white people, he had got an education and taken up the Protestant faith at a time when that was still permitted in France by the Edict of Nantes.

He had even journeyed to England, where he learned the English language. Through the kindness of an English physician who employed him for years, he even learned the rudiments of English medicine, which was very different from the Continental. But Englishmen were not so tolerant of him as were the French, and so eventually he went back to France. Then he returned to the Congo, where he proposed to use his knowledge of medicine to help his fellow tribesmen. He made himself into an African witch doctor, for he had talents in that direction, and without that he would have been unable to gain anyone's confidence. He simply tempered the medicine-man mystique with knowledge and applied as well the genuine benefits of bush herb medicine, which everyone recognized.

He fell at last into the clutches of a raiding party from a predatory tribe and was sold to a passing Danish slaver on the coast for shipment to St. Thomas.

Bodger got him cheap because the auctioneer was not impressed with his physique, which was wizened, nor with the qualities of his mind, which he simply did not display as he stood naked and wretched on the auction block.

Bodger had not the slightest idea what he was getting. It was his habit to attend auctions and buy what he could afford of the sick and dying on whom no one would bid. It made sense to him, being a doctor, to buy the unfit and try to bring them back to health. It was fortunate that such slaves did not cost much, for he was not a man of means.

Slave carrying on head 100 lb weight to which she is shackled as to a semimobile tether, *Bartolozzi, from a painting by Stedman,* MAPes MONDe Collection

On the other hand, he did not consider himself a saint. He lived in a slave society and economy. He could not subsist decently on his miserable salary of ten RIGSDALERS a month, even with the perquisites that went with it, and so it was necessary for him to have a PLANTAGE. That meant slaves.

Still, he saw no reason why a slave should always be an embittered, lost soul. Bodger fully intended to grant his slaves freedom as soon as he could bring them to the point where they could compete among FREE NEGROES and make their way satisfactorily. They all knew this; he made them know it as soon as he put them to work. Every slave he owned knew that he was not yet ready for freedom in this society, had not been with Bodger long enough to have become sufficiently well trained to be able to make his way as an artisan.

Christian Sost quite simply did not wish his freedom yet. If he went on his own he would have great difficulty making his way. He was not yet sufficiently familiar with the bush herbs of the islands and their proper uses, for they were different from those of the Congo. If he stayed with Bodger as a slave, he could study the local medicine and learn, assisted by Bodger, to combine them with what he and Bodger knew of conventional medicine.

It was a realistic relationship that was accepted on St. Jan; but on St. Thomas, among strangers and familiars, slave and free, whose minds were tuned to a different fiddle, it was difficult for both of them.

After three days of TAPPUS, Bodger came to Governor Gardelin and stood solid in the doorway when his turn came.

"I wish to be free of this duty," he said.

Gardelin dismissed the scribe with a wave of his hand. "Oh, nonsense, man. Come in and close the door before you disgrace me with that wigless porcupine head of yours! Sit down, sit down. I have here somewhere a long list of things to upbraid you with."

"Well, good," Bodger growled. "That should get me back to St. Jan."

"Without a job?"

"Read me your list," Bodger said.

"Well. First, I am told that you have ordered that all water and food given to the slaves in the sickhouse shall be boiled first. Now, what nonsense is this? Do you not realize how much time and labor this will consume—and for what?"

"Read on," Bodger said.

"I am told that you have ordered the water barrels of the sickhouse and the smithy provided with cloth covers in case it should rain and mosquitoes should be tempted to inhabit them. Our seamstresses have better things to do than hemstitching for rain barrels."

"Read on," Bodger said.

"I am told that you walk the streets with your slave shamelessly at your side, bringing disgrace upon yourself and the Company that employs you."

"Read on."

"Now, I will not read on until you answer me some of these complaints."

"As for the boiled water and cooked food," Bodger said, "those have been my practices on St. Jan for some time, since I noticed that Englishmen and the like, and women who spend their days tittering in the kitchens and getting their liquids by tasting cooking pots and sipping tea while spreading gossip in the afternoons— these Englishmen with their passion for tea and toddy, and these women—and you, guzzling that filthy beer of yours—simply do not die as others do. At least, they do not die of the same diseases, and they invariably live far longer, on the average, than other people do. Now, the thing that tea and toddy and boiling pots have in common is heat. I agree that we cannot be serving our sick slaves tea and toddy—they would spit it out if we did until thirst changed their attitude—but we can serve them boiled water, and on St. Jan we do, and on St. Jan the sickhouse is empty a good deal of the time since I began requiring the cooks and MESTERKNEGTS on the Company PLANTAGE to serve only cooked food and boiled water, even in the BARCADS. I admit to you that I know not why this is. I hope some day to find out. I know not what heat has to do with it, but I have lately noticed, by the accident of the impossibility of serving hot food and drink in the distant BARCADS because it is cold by the time it gets there, that it matters not if it be cold, so long as it be boiled first, for the health of the slaves, now that they are working in the far BARCADS, has not changed. There is still a great deal of sickness and death on St. Jan, but among the Company slaves, health is improved."

"Hm," Gardelin said, "that was quite an oration."

"It is not ended yet. Now, there is a thing here in town that is different from my situation in the country, and defeats me in my purpose here. You see, being a hater of filthy odors, I began some time ago requiring that all of the nightsoil on my PLANTAGE be buried each morning—mind you, not the manure of the cattle, which is impossible to control and has a rather pleasant odor in any case, but that of the humans only, the meat-eaters, which smells so foul. Almost immediately I began noting a decline in certain illnesses on my PLANTAGE, and you know me—I am a great one for putting two and two together . . ."

". . . and getting five," Gardelin interposed.

". . . and getting sometimes, fortunately, far more than five, as you shall see. In conversation with Captain van Bewerhoudt I discovered that he too was filled with disgust by the human odors, and I told him of my new rule. He adopted it, with precisely the same results. Now he has adopted my other rules, about boiled water and cooked food and covered water barrels. On his PLANTAGE, as on mine and the Company's of St. Jan, several of the most tiresome, and some of the most dangerous, diseases have virtually disappeared."

"I applaud," Gardelin said, applauding.

"Now," Bodger continued, "here in town, unlike on a PLANTAGE, it is impossible for me to control such matters, because of the multiplicity of people owning small properties, and their proximity to each other. In other words, I can require certain health regulations on Company property, but I cannot require the general public, which is right next door, to comply. Therefore, I obviously am unable to succeed here as on St. Jan, unless you, who have the power to do it, institute and enforce similar rules for the whole

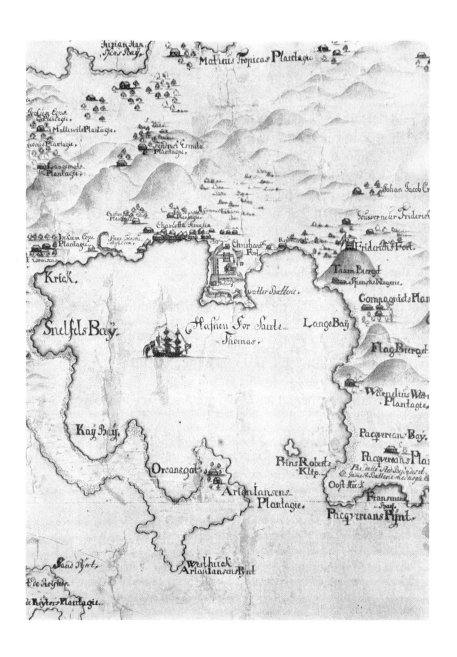

Harbor, St. Thomas, 1730. Charlotte Amalia was one of six Villages on the bay. Marine and Craft Museum, Krønborg Castle, Elsinør, Denmark

community."

"Come, now!" Gardelin cried, "what kind of fool do you take me for? How do you think I can speak of such things to the Secret Council and write of them to the directors in KJØBENHAVN? They would declare me insane."

"Then do not expect me to make much improvement in the health of the Company slaves and officials here. And send me back to St. Jan and my PLANTAGE, for I cannot subsist in town on what you propose to pay me—and furthermore, I do not like it here!"

"Nonsense, man. I shall see to it that you starve not."

"That is hardly my objective."

"And what about this rain-barrel thing?"

"You want another oration?"

"No. Not if it is another of your hare-brained theories. Spare me. But also spare me the thought of ordering clothing made for the barrels, for I have to explain much things, have to get them ordered by the entire Secret Council, not just by myself alone."

"I shall see to it myself, if it rain enough while I am still here to fill the barrels."

"Oh, you will be here. I have sold your PLANTAGE and slaves back to Herre Moth."

"You have WHAT?" Bodger thundered, leaping to his feet.

"Oh, well, of course the formalities require your signature, but I've got you a very advantageous price . . ."

"Perhaps you know that it is a very advantageous PLANTAGE, located right alongside Reimo's under the protection of Frederiksværn and near to one of the finest harbors in the Antilles—and I do not wish to sell it."

"I think you do."

"And even if I should be willing to stay in TAPPUS a while, to try out some of my theories, my slaves are not for sale."

"Why, man, there is where your greatest profit lies."

"My—slaves—are—not—for—sale."

"For rent, then?"

Bodger looked at him out of his blue eyes and considered for a moment. "For rent, eh? But there is only one man I would rent them to."

"Who? Now I'm curious. Who?"

"Jannis van Bewerhoudt."

"Hmph. That wild, pig-headed Dutchman!"

"When I talk to him he comes close to knowing what I am talking about."

"Well, rent him your slaves. You will stay here, then, without making such a fuss?"

"I think not."

"And you will sell the PLANTAGE to Seigneur Moth? He has already ordered it resurveyed, you know. You can hardly say no to a man as important as Moth, a nobleman, the son of one of the directors of the Company, personal friend of His Majesty the King, once governor of the islands, who quit not because he had to but because he wanted to . . ."

"Well, we can talk about that some time. I am, I admit, not the land-owning type."

"I must get over to Saint Jan," Gardelin said. "I love that stupid little island—it is so beautiful, and it has some of my favorite people on it."

"You have it pretty well stocked with your sons," Bodger gibed.

"Yes," Gardelin said, unruffled, "and I love them and their families. Yet I never seem able to go and see them. I'll manage it one of these days. I'll make it a business trip. There are some things that need straightening out at the Company PLANTAGE. What is going on there?"

"What do you mean?"

"Well, Dennis Sylvan . . ."

"Sullivan."

"Sullivan, in charge of the sugaring—now what do you suppose that Irish rascal has been up to?" Gardelin mused. "Have you really no idea at all?"

"No more than you. The sugar cookhouse is far from being my province. But I have heard, as have you, that some of the Company's cook-pots have been disappearing in the direction of Tortola, and that simultaneously Sullivan has seemed more prosperous."

"And I have had to send masons, whom I badly need to finish

my apartment in the fort, up to St. Jan to repair the boilinghouse."

"It is well to get it repaired," Bodger said, "for there is still sugar to be made on the Company PLANTAGE. The sugar will be somewhat dark because so late, but still it will be salable. The Company PLANTAGE is the only one on St. Jan where there is any sugar or anything else to be made—because it is so vast that what would amount to scraps on a small PLANTAGE manages on a huge one to add up to a crop of sorts."

"Where is most of it growing still?"

"Up in the Company GUT coming down off Bourdeaux's Mountain—below the spring and the wet-weather waterfall. There is still some moisture there, enough to make cane. In normal times there is too much for anything but cotton. Changing the subject, I wonder why you permit this ridiculous situation where a man has to switch from cane to the poor man's crop of cotton when it rains a lot in any growing season, when there is cane in the East Indies that will grow high-quality sugar in moist lowlands. Why can you not have the Company send a ship and bring a load of it here for rattoons?"

"I have heard some speak of this cane. You are sure of its existence?"

"I have seen it."

"It is interesting. I shall see what I can do. But I do not 'have' the Company do anything. It takes years to get an ordinary thing like a shipment of quills, and ink powder, and paper for the scribes and bookkeepers—and calendars . . ."

"That reminds me, I need some paper. I must send in an order for medical supplies."

"I shall find you some," Gardelin said. He sighed. "You have no idea how desperately we need paper. And uniforms! Self-respecting uniforms to sell to the soldiers! You would think that The Powers would care enough about the Danish face to send some out; but the only way we can get new uniforms is to bring soldiers in them, and there are no soldiers to bring!"

Bodger laughed.

"And pastors, to take care of our spiritual needs—when they finally do send pastors, they send drunkards! Why, do you know

Fort Christian in 1730 was still home to the Governor and to the Lutheran Church as well as the lockup: the land to the left had been filled between 1701 and 1733, probably with fill from the Polyberg road cut and garbage: a shallow lagoon was formed wich was filled by 1780s: Norre Gade was the original shore line. Marine and Craft Museum. Krønborg Castle, Elsinør, Denmark

that I—I!—have to officiate at the services in Christi Kirke in the fort as often as not because the pastor is drunk?"

"Oh, now," Bodger said, grinning, "you know very well you enjoy that—you fancy yourself as a preacher."

Gardelin raised a protesting hand. "At least I have a sense of sin. This terrible drought that is threatening to destroy us all—I believe it is God's punishment for our sins, including the sin of slavery."

"It is an easy assumption, and I wish it were that simple," Bodger said, "but I must point out to you that on the islands where the mountains are much higher than here, there is no drought, although there is shameless slavery."

"Ah," Gardelin cried, "but on those islands God finds other ways to punish. The snakes, for instance, the infernal snakes that crawl everywhere in those islands."

"Then," Bodger said, "consider the fact that it is precisely the slaves in our islands on whom the punishment of the drought falls most heavily."

"Why, how do you see that? The Company, and the private planters—curse them, but they are a necessity to the Company— are losing money every day, and stand to be destroyed if this keeps up—and on St. Jan it is even worse than on St. Thomas."

"Your Excellency," Bodger said with exaggerated protocol, "you embarrass me. Here you have been talking about sin, and now suddenly you pretend that financial reverses are the wages of sin."

"Oh . . . well . . . I mean . . ."

"You know as well as I do that the master of slaves passes on to the slaves as much as possible of the drought suffering, in the form of food that is so spoiled that it is cheap and no one but a desperately hungry slave will eat it; in the form of a shortage of water, which a master will not tolerate for himself or his family; in the form of hard labor under the glaring sun of the drought; in the . . ."

"Yes," Gardelin interrupted, with a touch of remorse, "I see what you mean. The weight of drought suffering is bound to fall more heavily on the oppressed than on the oppressor. I don't know what I can do about it, though . . ."

"Nor do I," Bodger said. "But the newly imported slaves seem to have some ideas on the subject."

Gardelin nodded. "I know. The crop coming in lately is a different matter. They are not really slaves." He sighed. "This is the cross we are bearing now, and we may very well find ourselves crucified on it. And," he added in a lowered voice, "do not let it be heard outside of this room, but I have to say that in my heart I cannot blame the hot-headed nobility among the new slaves. In their place, I should feel just as they do. That does not change my responsibility in the matter."

Bodger was by now looking at him with eyes slightly widened. "I have to say to you, Your Excellency," he said, still humorously, but without an edge to his voice, "that in my opinion you are not all bad!"

"Of course I am all bad," Gardelin said testily. "And I am confused. My position in the world depends on slavery. The lives of the people I love most depend on slavery. Huge investments for which I am responsible depend on it. Slavery is the foundation on which our whole civilization out here rests. And a great many of the slaves seem to like it that way, to love being looked after, not having to worry about tomorrow—having none of the responsibilities and troubles of a man on his own. Yet in my heart I cannot believe that it is right for one man or one people to enslave another."

"I tend to forgive you for the moment." Bodger said. A knock sounded at the door.

It was the scribe, and he had an urgent message. The skipper of a North American ship newly arrived in harbor had just come ashore with news that he had overtaken and passed a Danish slave ship three days out of St. Thomas on his run down from the African Gold Coast.

"Ah!" Gardelin cried. "That would be *Laarburg Galley!* A new ship. This is her first voyage. She left Kjøbenhavn almost a year ago for the slave coast, and of late we have been thinking often of her, fearing she was lost."

"But what would take her so long—nearly a year?"

"Oh, she is an experiment. According to the information I have from the Company, the fort at Accra—Christiansborg—has in

Fort Christian and the town of Charlotte Amalia, 1733. Two running streams are shown at the center; between them is the Queen's Quarter; to the left, the King's Quarter and to the right, the Crown prince's Quarter. These stream beds exist today at both ends of Main Street as the large guts at Garden Street and Guttets Gade, near Market Square. Marine and Craft Museum, Krønborg Castle, Elsinør, Denmark

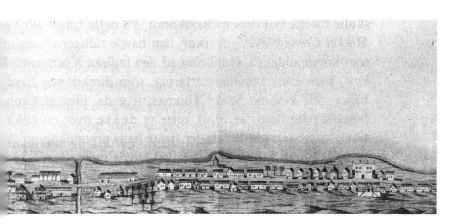

recent years been unable to function properly as a slave FACTORY—
the area is running out of slaves, for one thing, and for another, the
native population attacked it last year, viciously attacked it, mind
you, because it was no longer dispensing large quantities of rum to
the local tribes—and how could it, when they were no longer
bringing in enough slaves? But anyhow, because we now have no
reliable source of slaves at Accra, *Laarburg Galley* was sent last
year to cruise the coast of Africa, even as far south as Cape de Lupe
González, if necessary to go that far, asking for slaves and shopping
the whole coast, as an experiment to see if it may pay to sell
Christiansborg and secure our slaves in future by means of floating
slave factories."

Gardelin was so excited that Bodger could only say, "Oh."

"Forgive me, now," Gardelin said briskly, "but I have much to
do, to prepare for the arrival of the ship. And you, Nelli BØDKER,
you now have no choice but to stay here. With the arrival of the
slave ship, you will have your hands full, and we shall have to
scrape up some assistants for you. Do get yourself prepared, man,
and now excuse me."

Bodger, leaving the house, could hear Gardelin issuing orders
right and left, and at the same time dictating a letter to be sent by
special courier boat to Svend Børgesen at the Company's St. Jan
plantation, ordering him to halt all work involving slaves that were
experienced in caulking and otherwise refitting ships, and send
such slaves down forthwith to St. Thomas.

II

THE magistrate's court on St. Jan was in informal session, at
Reimert Sødtmann's PLANTAGE instead of at the VÆRN. There was no
scribe to take down the proceedings, and no witnesses had been
called from among the planters or, as was the custom, hired by the
planters from among the soldiers at the VÆRN because they spoke
Danish.

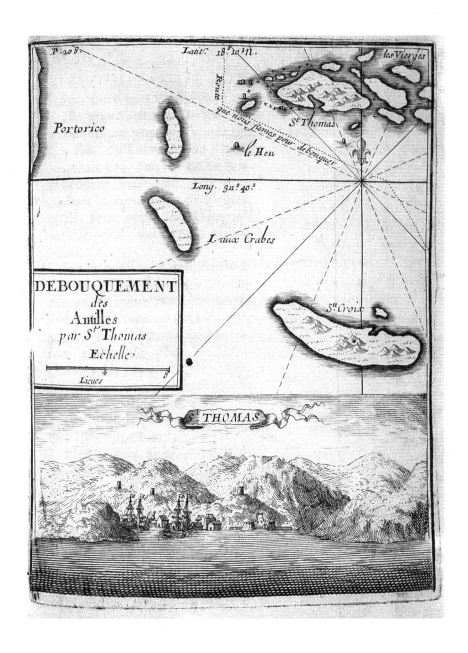

Map and sketch of St. Thomas from a French ship, *Froger, 1697*, MAPes MONDe Collection

Judge Sødtmann sat to hold court at the massive table in his mansion's dining room. He gave the impression, as always, of trying not to look as important as he felt. His dark, up-and-outward-slanting eyebrows and the black hair-peak above his low forehead all pointed commandingly at his nose, which when the observer obeyed the command and looked at it, was a disappointment, being subtly too small, too short, vaguely porcine.

Peder Krøyer, earnest tower of a young man, had brought King Clæs in, as he was bound to do as captor of a MARON.

"This way, I can in all truth back up your statement that you brought King Clæs in for judgment," Judge Sødtmann was saying to Peder, "and that you made arrangements to take him home as your BOMBA after he had his punishment, pending purchase settlement. And it would not make sense to mutilate a good BOMBA as you have said, therefore the punishment shall be"—he looked at King Clæs, who, not comprehending the Danish words, stood like a statue, staring into the unseeable distance—"some twenty lashes, to make him—and, incidentally, my slaves, who shall watch—remember that a MARON, even a king, must come to justice."

"It is well—I suppose," Krøyer said doubtfully. "But tell your executioner to go easy. I do not wish King Clæs hurt. He could be the best slave on the island."

"He will have to be hurt, for the sake of my slaves. They will know if the LUSSING be not genuine. Besides, as you know, the executioner is one of mine."

The court's judgment and sentence were quickly handed down, and the participants and attendants moved outdoors to the JUSTICE POST.

The executioner, Bawa, a massive, frog-eyed slave, was for rent as a butcher throughout the island. His eyes, in spite of their bulging prominence, showed not a glint of expression, but around the corners of his mouth there were hints of pleasure as he was handed the official whip and twirled it in the dust, as if to warm it up.

Sødtmann was eyeing King Clæs thoughtfully where he stood on the elevated brick and stone platform that held the JUSTICE POST. He was not yet trussed up to the post.

"Perhaps," Sødtmann said, "it would be as well not to give him a regular LUSSING. That would merely be pain, and might make the audience feel sympathy, since he is a king. Perhaps it would be best to humiliate him. He seems overly proud and haughty. That, in front of his fellow slaves, could be a more serious punishment."

"Whatever you say," Krøyer said.

The KAMINA slaves were brought in from the BARCADS, where they were topping the dried-up cotton stalks to encourage new sprouting when the rains came. They stood stolidly, massed by the BOMBA and MESTERKNEGT in front of the JUSTICE POST. The household slaves were summoned to the scene, tittering expectantly, for the pleasure of watching a BUSSAL being punished.

When all were stilled by a raised hand, Sødtmann began by notifying King Clæs, in SLAVE TALK, that he was to be punished for going MARON.

King Clæs made no reply.

"They tell me," Sødtmann said, "that you are a king." King Clæs said nothing.

"Are you then a king?" Sødtmann demanded sharply, and Bawa flourished his whip to suggest a reply.

"I am Bolombo," King Clæs said. The baby-talk slave dialect "*Me bin Bolombo*" sounded degrading in his mouth.

"You are Bolombo," Sødtmann said, using the form of speech for addressing children. "And as Bolombo the king, what work are you accustomed to do?"

There was no reply. Indeed, King Clæs had probably not understood the question.

"Mostly you sing and dance, do you not?"

The other BUSSALS made little sounds showing that they understood the words. King Clæs gave no sign of understanding.

"Then suppose you sing and dance for us," Sødtmann said. King Clæs stood silent and still. The house slaves giggled.

The KAMINA slaves made breathing sounds.

Sødtmann signaled to Bawa, who gestured with the whip and spoke spittingly to King Clæs in a slave-coast dialect that he could understand. Bolombo betrayed his understanding with a subtle flicker in the eyes, but he stood still.

Helena Hissing came onto the gallery of the house above. Birgitta, her mother, followed.

The assemblage below seemed now to hold its breath.

Sødtmann nodded almost imperceptibly to Bawa, and the whip cracked playfully about the ankles of Bolombo, who stood still.

Juni the BOMBA stood in the forefront of his charges. His eyes were open and his gaze was raised level for all to see.

The executioner swung the whip expertly so that it curled about Bolombo's ankles and left a mark on the skin. There was no response.

Some of the household slaves cried, "Sing! Dance!" and Sødtmann nodded at them approvingly.

Bawa now raised welts on Bolombo's ankles; then with the tip of the whip he drew spots of blood, then made long raw slashes on the calves.

At each swing of the whip a little gasp was heard from somewhere among the watchers, but Bolombo's feet remained still. Although an involuntary wince would sometimes travel through the musculature of his belly and thighs, no part of his face so much as twitched.

Helena Hissing went back inside the house.

Judge Sødtmann by now showed the beginnings of embarrassment. When finally King Clæs's blood was pooling about his motionless feet, Sødtmann was shaking his head.

"Reimo!" Krøyer pleaded softly. Sødtmann put a stop to the losing game. Everyone in the assemblage looked embarrassed, even the BUSSALS.

Sødtmann now ordered a regular LUSSING of twenty lashes, and Bawa trussed King Clæs with his wrists bound high on the elevated JUSTICE POST. Then sounded the twenty lashes, one by one, accompanied by involuntary grunts from many throats, and welts rising on King Clæs's back.

The crowd was dismissed and King Clæs taken down. Krøyer made as if to apologize, then thought better of it, and took him home to Brown's Bay. He would not let the executioner rub salt and Spanish pepper into the bleeding wounds as he felt he was entitled by custom to do, and as was prescribed by custom to hasten healing. Krøyer, wincing with pain at the thought of it, preferred to find another way, at home, to hasten healing. The weed-woman's big loblolly leaves would do it without adding to the pain.

III

Laarburg Galley was no galley, but a frigate, newly wrought in 1732 for the West Indies and Guinea trade. She was designed to carry passengers and cargo. If the cargo happened to be slaves, as on this her maiden voyage, she carried greater ballast to steady her, and above the ballast the sides of her hold had cleats on which rested extra decks for slaves. The decks were just far enough apart vertically that a man could not sit up, but must remain prone or propped on his elbows.

Straight athwart the main deck of the ship and extending out over the water on either side, the ship's carpenters had erected a plank wall so tightly constructed on the forward side that not a fingernail could be inserted into a crack far enough to make it possible for a man to climb it.

In the middle of this wall was a strong door, recessed from the forward side so as to offer no finger-hold, and strongly locked on the after side. Whenever a member of the ship's company had to pass through this door and perform any work on the forward deck, he was massively guarded by "the fort," a platform atop the wall, crowded with guns and men.

The forward deck and the slave decks in the hold beneath it were for the use of the male captives. Every day, all of the slaves in this hold were brought on deck, chained together by ankle irons and wrist irons. The hold was then cleaned of its accumulation of filth by the ship's slaves, and "perfumed," as the orders read, by burning gunpowder. Then half the captives would be returned to the hold so that the other half might have room to lie down on deck for the day, with their connecting chains fastened forward and aft. The next day the rest would have their turn on deck.

The slave women and children were segregated in the after part of the hold at night and abaft "the fort" on deck in the daytime. They were not chained, and were treated with as much other consideration as they showed that they could support without disorder. At night many of them, women and sobbing girls and boys, supplied considerable comfort to some of the seamen.

When the ship ran before the wind the slave holds were ventilated by a sail hung above them, aft, in such a way that the following breeze was turned downward. The theory was that the breeze would flow through the holds and emerge, forward, to join the odors from the pigsty in being carried away. The ventilating sail had the further virtue of adding slightly to the forward motion of the ship, downwind.

The weekly allowance of food for each slave was one-half pound of salt pork, a half-FIRKIN of dried beans, a half-FIRKIN of groats, one-sixth FIRKIN of GUINEA CORN, a quarter-pint of KILL-DEVIL rum, an eighth-pound of tobacco and a pipe to smoke it in, as well as palm oil in all gruel, totaling an eighth-pint. Guinea peppers, because replaceable ashore, were used generously along the coast. Six bushels of them per hundred slaves were to be distributed over the whole voyage from the last African port to St. Thomas.

The weekly allowance was split up thus: on Sunday, salt pork, beans, groats, and a pipe of tobacco; Monday, beans, groats, and rum; Tuesday, beans, groats, and tobacco; Wednesday, beans, groats, and rum; Thursday, salt pork, beans, groats, and rum; Friday, beans, groats, and tobacco; Saturday, GUINEA CORN twice, and rum.

In the event of a good wind and a fast voyage, the daily allowance would be increased, toward the end, to the greatest possible extent, in order to fatten the cargo and save fattening time at St. Thomas.

The water boys and oarsmen (for *Laarburg Galley* was a galley to the extent that in the HORSE LATITUDES she was propelled day after day by oarsmen, while everyone on board whistled for a breeze), slaves all, had a special barrel of rum, which they were supposed to make last the whole voyage; success had never in history crowned such efforts, as Peter From, Assistant Ship's Doctor, sententiously observed.

The pigsty was in the bow so that the odors would blow away in all situations but an anchorage without moorings or a tight tack into the wind. It was stocked with enough pigs to eat the slops, their progeny to be eaten on the voyage by the captain and officers. The sows and boars would be left at St. Thomas as breeding stock. They slid and tripped, squealing and grunting, on the deck that everlastingly lifted and fell away beneath them.

Also on deck, along with hay to feed them, were two milk cows destined for plantation life on St. Thomas. They were able to stand, and barely to lie down, in narrow, individual stalls that rubbed the hair off their sides as they swayed to the motion of the ship. In rough weather they wore rope body-halters that were belayed fore and aft and on each side tightly enough to keep the animals from crashing into the planks of the stalls. The milking was done, with some difficulty, from outside the stalls through the spaces between the planks. The calves took their share, as often as not, lying down, being unable to stand in rough weather.

Chickens and guineas were tied aboard with endlessly tangled strings to eat the cows' manure and the table scraps and tickle the captain's and officers' palates when required.

Large, flat boxes of good Danish earth occupied whatever spaces could be spared amidships and on the after deck, protected from the salt spray in rough weather by high, removable walls of wood and canvas. In them grew beets, parsley, cress, chicory, lettuce, and radishes, under armed guard day and night.

In storage were beer barrels, one for each man for the voyage, all soon empty; rum casks sufficient to provide a quarter-pint per man per day of the projected voyage; casks and bottles of Madeira, Amontillado, whisky, brandywine, and other necessities for the captain and officers, enough for an extra year's voyage, for it would be foolish to take chances.

Captain Andreas Hammer carried a Latin Sea Pass, signed 4 April 1732 by King Christian VI at Frederiksberg Castle for a fee

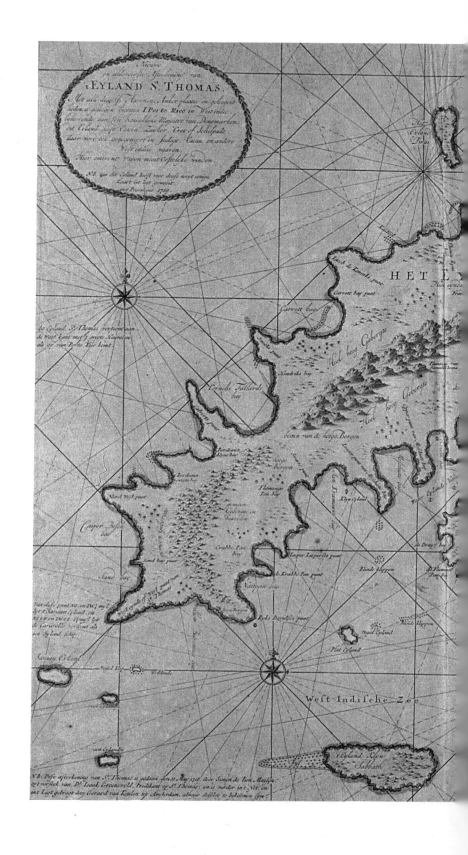

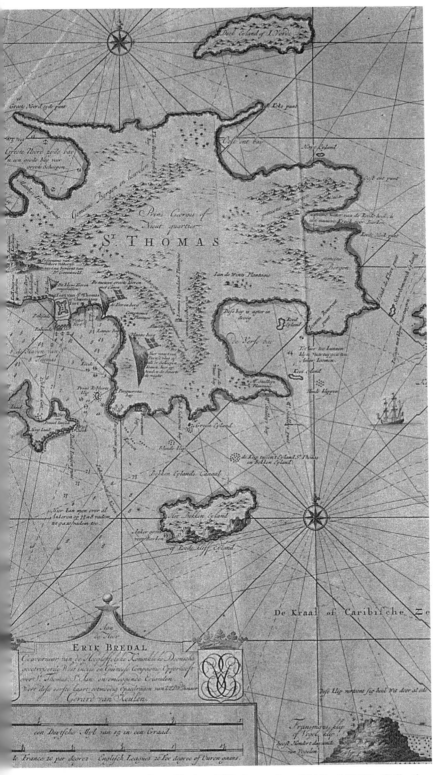

Map. St. Thomas, *Gerard van Keulen, 1719,* Amsterdam, MAPes MONDe Collection

of four RIGSDALERS placed, without the king's having to touch it, in the royal treasury.

Nos Christianus Sextus, Dei Gratia Rex Danæ Norvegiæ Vandalorum Gothorumque; Dux Slesvici, Holsatiæ, Stormariæ, Ditmarsiæ; Comes in Oldenburg & Delmenhorst; Omnibus et Singulis quibus hæ Nostræ Salvi Conductus Literæ exhibibuntur . . .

It served notice on the world that the King authorized this voyage from KJøBENHAVN along the west coast of Africa and to St. Thomas in the West Indies for the purpose of purchasing slaves along said coast and transporting them for sale to said St. Thomas, that he would much appreciate it if the ship were left alone to go about its business, and would deem it a considerable affront if his royal wishes were ignored.

The trip along the African coast was leisurely, covering the summer, fall, and winter, in an effort to establish good contacts with tribal chieftains for use on possible future trips. On board was Merchant Andreas Willumsen, an old Africa hand who knew what he was doing.

Willumsen tried to buy a certain percentage of Senegals and Congos because they were handsome, intelligent, educable, and made the finest house servants when trained, and therefore would bring high prices from wealthy St. Thomians; the Congos tended to be downright beautiful, both men and women, and they had a marvelous sense of humor, which was a great comfort in a slave.

Mokkos, Willumsen tried to avoid, save for the women. Male Mokkos he knew to be turbulent, stubborn, and given to suicide when confronted with field labor, which was all they were good for in his book; still, if you could get a Mokko to work, you had a good hard worker, and the women of that tribe were the equals, in the field, of most men.

He tried especially to avoid buying any Mandingos. The Mandingo country, he knew, was so rich in soil and rainfall that food was everywhere for the taking, and no Mandingo had any concept of what it was to work or hunt, or even, strangely enough, to do

Stoore Fridericks Borg

FROM THE COMPANY'S RECORDS: *Haabet Galley*, Danish registry, Capt A.H. Hammer, brought a cargo to St. Thomas, July 1729, of 63 men, 45 women, 14 boys, and 4 girls—total 126 (of 126 out of Guinea); cost to company wholesale 70 rigsdalers, cost to planters 120 rigsdalers. Danish slave ships and fort on the Guinea Coast of Africa ca1733, MAPes MONDe Collection

much carousing. The result was that they were indolent by their very nature, and of no use except in sit-down jobs, such as watch-men and, if trained in the process, boilinghouse bosses.

Nevertheless, Willumsen found that he had to take what was offered if he wanted to be sure anything would be offered on the next voyage, and so he ended up with a few Mandingos and Mokkos on board.

Some of the captives actually seemed relieved to be going to a new life. Their lands were laid waste, they said, by civil wars dedicated to capturing men to sell to the slavers; a man could never get a night's sleep because no sooner had he closed his eyes than he might find himself with a new fight on his hands.

The shopping along the coast was not very good, for other nations had the sources of supply tied up. Willumsen finally had to order the ship to Fort Christiansborg, at Accra, where he would have to get whatever slave cargo he could, whether desirable or not.

The strife among the patrician tribes in Guinea had been unusually bitter, and waiting for Laarburg Galley was a surprising collection of future PIÈCES DES INDES, mostly undesirable noblemen, enough to fill out the cargo. Willumsen had no choice but to take them.

Waiting with others in the slave pen was Aquashi, a prince of the Aquambo nation.

Aquashi had enjoyed being a prince. It was a life of indolence and action. Pampered as a son of a king, he had liked to make war and love, to hunt, to fight in the athletic contests of the tribe, to sing and dance himself into insensibility in tribal rites and celebrations.

The most exciting exploit of his life had been to take part in a bold and brazen Aquambo attack the previous year on this very fort at Accra. The object of the attackers was to emphasize their displeasure with the Danes for not providing enough rum. Of course they had been repelled by the defenders of the fort, but it had been a heady experience for Aquashi, daring to attack the white man in his own lair; and the news of this had not been slow to reach, and impress, the Aquambos' enemy neighbors, the Aminas and Adampes.

He had long since learned the value of rum, not only in making him feel grander than he was, but also in buying the women and weapons, cattle and slaves that constituted the power he wanted.

He had also learned from his father, who had a contract with the slavers, of the enormous amount of rum to be earned from these slavers by delivering a man to them, and it had occurred to him that men might be obtained in the course of making war on his favorite enemies, the Adampes.

Drunk on his father's rum, Aquashi had taken a large party of his fighting men into Adampe country and ambushed a small caravan that was escorting a group of military captives for sale to the slave traders. While his men rounded up as many as possible of the members of the caravan, including its captives and two of its leader's wives, Aquashi personally had disarmed and held the leader, laughing in his ear as his war party chased fleeing warriors into the bush.

His prisoner had turned out to be a young Adampe king, and ringing in Aquashi's memory were the king's words, shouted after his bested warriors in Adampe words that Aquambo Prince Aquashi could easily understand:

"This man, remember him! This man, of all men in the world, must live to kiss the slaver's hand. See to it! *See—to—it!*"

They had seen to it.

The Evil Eye was on that maiden voyage of *Laarburg Galley*. This was obvious to everyone on board by the time the ship sailed from Accra for St. Thomas.

Captain Hammer was dead of a fever contracted in Guinea, and First Mate Lorens Jager was captain now.

Captain Jager was in a hurry to get away from the accursed port of Accra. Accordingly he brought aboard a few slaves who were ill, because he needed them to fill out the cargo. He was sure that, once away, the sick would get well—the ship's doctor concurred in this opinion—and the run down to St. Thomas would go as planned.

The ship sailed with a near-full cargo of slaves, four hundred and forty-three, and an incomplete crew.

Health on board did indeed improve, once the ship was away from the coast, and by the time she put in to the Cape Verde Islands to fill the water casks and otherwise bring the ship's provisions up to scratch for the long, uninterrupted voyage to St. Thomas, there was hardly enough illness to keep Dr. Schlevoigt and Peter From properly busy.

But in Praia sickness was raging. So many slaves had died that the merchants refused to accept any payment but slaves, and so for water and other supplies the ship had to part with two of its PIÈCES DES INDES.

It must have been the water, everyone agreed later, although what could be wrong with water? It looked and smelled all right. Its taste was not pleasant but who could expect pleasant-tasting water at sea? At any rate, not long after leaving the Cape Verdes, such a wave of sickness and death swept over the ship that slaves and crew alike were soon dying like trapped animals. The slave hold could not be cleaned, for the ship's slaves, those who were not dead, were too ill to be put to work. Most of the BUSSAL slaves themselves were eventually too ill to be brought on deck. The stench that drifted along with the ship was itself enough to make a well man vomit. Each day, for a while, the few who could operate the ship had to throw overboard twenty, thirty, one day more than fifty bodies. Then no one would go into the slave hold to take out the dead, and the captain had to shoot a seaman in order to force his sick fellows to do the dreadful job, to avoid the horror of putrefaction on top of the horror of excretions. The captain himself had his turn at the sickness, but survived. The mate died. The doctors themselves were fearfully ill, and the third assistant had to be thrown overboard at last.

When the sickness had run its course, one hundred and ninety-nine of the slave cargo were dead, and the crew of the ship was reduced to below the level of necessity. The survivors gradually recovered.

The drastic reduction in the number of people on board, and the fact that for many days no one could eat anything, created a plethora of food. For the rest of the six-week voyage the rations of everyone, slave and free alike, were more generous than the allotments called for, and everyone gained back his weight.

The passage through the HORSE LATITUDES was painfully slow, for lack of enough men to man the oars, until the stronger BUSSALS in the hold were put to the oars, under guns. Then the ship's inching speed increased somewhat in spite of the BUSSALS' clumsy and unwilling rowing.

Toward the end of the voyage, food was lavished upon the slaves in the hold and they were fattening, although still weak from their illness and idleness.

Three of the children were still ill—a boy of eight and a girl and boy, twins, aged fifteen. All of them had lost their parents on the voyage. It was thought that because of their grief and terror at finding themselves orphaned they were unable to get well. The eight-year-old was barely alive, and it was hard to find anyone on board who cared very much, for the awful voyage was nearing its end.

It was just dawn when St. Jan was sighted, and the sighting was the signal to start preparing for arrival at St. Thomas.

The barge, all freshly painted, was hoisted off its seat on deck and hung over the side, ready for dropping into the water. Balls were taken out of the cannons and the cannons blown off. The flag and jack were hoisted.

Passing Coral Bay in the early light the fresh-blown cannons were loaded with powder and a salute to the VÆRN was fired. There was a delay before the VÆRN managed a reply. The delay was duly noted, to be reported to the commandant at Christiansfort, for it seemed obvious that the garrison at the VÆRN had been sound asleep, and had been awakened by the ship's salute.

At eight glass *Laarburg Galley* dropped anchor at St. Thomas, in five and a half fathoms. She fired nine cannon shots for Christiansfort, then three, then seven, and received seven in return. The roar of the cannons, with the echoes ricocheting among the hills, was a fearful and stirring thing.

The whole population of all the villages along the bay and of all the PLANTAGES in the hills overlooking it was out to watch.

It took all day to put the ship to bed, send the few sick ashore, take on clean water and fresh meat, and receive the governor aboard.

The population was outraged to learn that the ship's ballast was bricks, not water. It was recalled that at times when all cisterns and rain barrels were overflowing, ballast always seemed to turn out to be water instead of badly needed bricks.

Only Gardelin was pleased to have the bricks, for now the work on the fort could continue uninterrupted.

Bodger was brought on board to inspect the cargo. It was agreed that the slaves who had survived the plague on board could do without a fattening period; indeed, in view of the shortage of food at St. Thomas, any undue delay in selling the cargo might well result in their loss of weight.

Accordingly, it was determined that the slave auction should take place on the following Tuesday, allowing five days for advertising, preparations, and viewing.

Gardelin hurried ashore to prepare the campaign. Bodger went with him, drawn to the sick children who had been placed in the little room attached to the slave pen off the dock.

The twins were not yet able to take nourishment, but there was life in their bodies, and their eyes, big and full of fear, were open. Bodger could not communicate with them, but his voice and touch were gentle, and they stared out at him with a lessening of fear.

The eight-year-old was unconscious, lying in his own filth. Bodger cleaned him up and spoke to him gently, trying to pierce his coma with a feeling of reassurance that might bring him back through it.

Feverish activity was everywhere. Even activities that had nothing to do with the slave ship or her cargo were speeded up. The field slaves in the country caught the fever and increased the tempo of their working chants and the accompanying action with their tools.

The poster scribes were put to work preparing placards advertising the auction. The first placards must be got off to St. Jan without delay, along with runners to spread the word throughout that island.

FROM THE COMPANY'S RECORDS: *Haabet Galley*, Danish Registry, Capt A.H. Hammer, came to St. Thomas, Feb.1731, to sell 21 men, 29 women, 5 boys, total of 55 out of Guinea; cost to company wholesale 70 rigsdalers, cost to planters 120 rigsdalers. MAPes MONDe Collection

Early next morning, Friday, before the populace was up, the BUSSAL cargo was brought ashore, for it was not seemly that the general public should see the merchandise until it had been looked over, sorted out, and prepared for sale. The area around the iron-barred slave pen would not be open to the public until Monday, the official viewing day.

The water in the harbor was glassy in an early morning calm, and the ship could be warped in to the dock alongside the weigh-master's office and made fast, with four-inch hawsers for bumpers between the ship and the dock. Thus no gangway was used, in order to prevent what had happened at the unloading of the last slave ship, when the unruly part of the cargo had jumped off the gangway, chains and all, and managed to drown a good part of its number before dock slaves could be got overboard to haul their chains within reach of grappling-hooks. The limp BUSSALs had been rolled over barrels in order to get the water out of their lungs and bring some of them back to the life they no longer valued.

This time no chances were taken. The unruly ones were brought off one at a time, in chains, by teams of dock slaves, and padlocked to the bars of the slave pen. The women and children, and the more docile of the males, were escorted in and allowed to group them-selves as they pleased when the iron gate was closed and locked.

The tribal markings of each BUSSAL, if he bore any, were noted. If he wore none, his tribe was identified in some other manner by old Africa hands. An ACCUSTOMED SLAVE of that tribal origin would be sent for to talk to him in his own language, in order to make him feel at home.

These ambassadors were ex-BUSSALs who had made the adjustment to the white man's world. They would come to the slave pen wearing decent clothing. It was their job to allay the fears of the newcomers, assure them that they had come into a good thing, that it was much better here than in Africa, where the climate was too hot and humid to be borne and there was no future but incessant tribal wars and early death. Here a slave might one day become a man, his own man, and take his place in the world of profit and power.

This ploy did have a considerable effect in calming the BUSSALs.

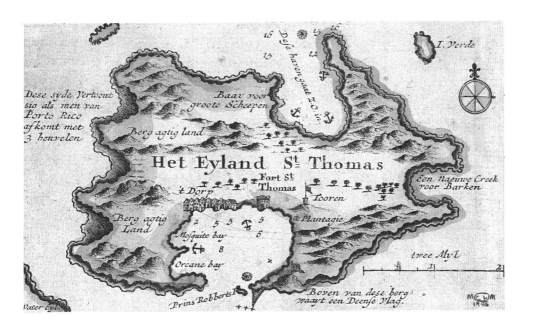

Map of St. Thomas, *Johannes van Keven, 1684,* Amsterdam, MAPes MONDe Collection

Hearing their own language spoken in this strange place by a fellow tribesman who was not naked brought a startling reaction from some of the newcomers. Once in a while, the ambassador and the BUSSAL turned out to have known each other at home, or even to be relatives.

Gradually little knots of fellow tribesmen formed. If the difficult BUSSALS joined in with this friendliness, their padlocks were removed and they were free to move about. If they showed a good adjustment, their chains were removed entirely.

Treats were served to the tribal groupings—sweets, cakes, rum. A feeling of GEMÜTLICHKEIT was devoutly courted.

If, through all this, a BUSSAL remained sullenly chained to the bars, all hope for a good price for him was abandoned by viewing time on Monday, and the sadists among the prospective buyers knew which PIÈCES DES INDES they were going to bid on and take home at bargain prices.

Prince Aquashi was one who remained sullenly chained to the bars. He would not join the assembly of Aquambos, the largest on the floor, even though it contained former friends. He would not talk to any Aquambo ambassador, but spat upon them as he had seen Moslems do to those they despised.

The placards went up, advertising the auction. In Danish, Dutch, German, French, and English, they were posted at Mme. Oligh's TAPHOUSE in TAPPUS, and The KILL-DEVIL Widows' corner on St. Jan, and at other public places on the two islands.

Just arrived from the Coast of Guinea in the Frigate *Laarburg Galley,* Capt. Jager Commander,
A Cargo of Prime Gold Coast and Other

SLAVES

Which will he exposed to sale, on Tuesday next, the 12th of May, at 9 o'clock forenoon at the Warehouse of the Danish West India & Guinea Company by the Company Dock

The same day the public's attention was loudly called to the event by the crier, accompanied by the drummers from the fort, with the booming and rattling of their drums. On Sunday, Pastor Thambsen in Christi Kirke read the notice in German and Danish at the sacred services.

On Monday, the BUSSALS in the slave pen were anointed with oil to make them shine. Then the prospective bidders were permitted to inspect the merchandise through the iron bars and make up their minds which items they would bid on and how much they would be willing to bid. It was difficult, sometimes, in the excitement of the auction, not to be carried away and find oneself bidding beyond common sense.

By now the St. Jan buyers or their agents were in town, competing for places to spend the night and adding to the growing air of excitement.

Before the sale, the Company took for itself the forty BUSSALS it judged to be best. The forty were herded, with cracking whips, to the Company smithy, across the inlet to the pond, near the shore to the east of the fort, where the smith's forge could most conveniently heat the branding-iron. Soon from the smithy wafted the odor of burnt flesh and screams of outrage, and when the BUSSALS emerged they bore, among their tribal markings, the Company brand, fiery and blistered, on their left thighs, with Dr. Bodger in angry attendance in case needed.

When Bodger returned to the slave pen he found that no one remained in chains.

Prince Aquashi sat alone on the floor, staring into space. He would not respond to Bodger or anyone else.

The sick ones, a huge man who was too weak to stand, the twin boy and girl, and the eight-year-old boy, still in a coma, were in the little dispensary, where Bodger stopped from time to time. The remaining one hundred and ninety-seven, plus those who were under the taxable age of twelve, and so were not counted even as fractions, stood or lay about on the floor.

Occasionally one was ordered to stand up and walk about so he or she could be seen. Often the adults would ignore the order, which would then be enforced by the dock slaves at a signal from the auctioneer.

Willumsen, who was in charge of the sale, ruled that the sick man should be sold, but the sick children should be kept back. The twins, who according to his records were just under sixteen years old, would be kept till they were well, at which time they could be sold for sixteen, the official age of adulthood. Being young and good-looking, they would bring high adult prices from some rich house-holder who would wish to train them for specialized duties. The eight-year-old would not live, and so would not be offered for sale.

Bodger protested that he would take the child, salable or not; but the mule-headed Willumsen, having made a decision, would not change it for anyone. He would not give the child away, and obviously he could not sell a corpse.

Bodger believed in the healing power of the human voice, properly applied, and spent time talking and singing softly to the child, in Danish, hoping to reach him, wherever he might be, not with the incomprehensible words, but with an assurance that someone was there, caring. He rubbed the emaciated little body with rum in which were soaking crushed cinnamon-bay leaves from Bourdeaux's Mountain, a thing he had learned from Christian Sost.

No one was permitted in the slave pen after dark, even doctors, and Bodger had to bow again to Willumsen's firm decisions and leave.

In the morning he found the sick child lying with eyes open, staring blankly at the ceiling. When Bodger spoke to him, the child moved his eyes enough to look at him, then turned his face away. Bodger touched him with his warm hands and cleaned up the night's mess.

The town awoke to a carnival air. Booths were set up to sell food and drink and sugar candy, and trinkets from near and far. The ship had brought money for salaries. Most of the soldiers and clerks owed the Company more than the amount of their back salaries, and this money went into the till. The higher clerks came off with some cash over and above their debts. The sailors had brought coins, Danish, Dutch, French, and German; PIECES OF EIGHT, shilling-pieces, PIASTRES, centimes, centavos, from one whole side of the world, and these were circulating throughout the town with exhilarating effect.

The nondescript orchestra with its nondescript instruments got together and did its practicing by playing in public. Drummers paraded up and down, drowning out the cries of commerce. All the bells in the fort and the town rang all the time, and the tolling of the hours was lost in the uproar.

The crowd was sprinkled with bright colors from the Far East. Every East India Company ship that came this way brought bales of sarongs in dazzling colors, for they were irresistible in the islands, especially to FREE SLAVES and FREE NEGROES. They were worn by male and female alike, the men wearing trousers under them and the women, as often as not, a net bodice that, with the bright sarongs, made their rich-colored skin a delight to behold. As a result, the carnival air this day was a pleasure to the eye, as well as a din to the ear and an affront to the sense of smell, as the streets and passages among the beautiful stone warehouses teemed with crowds under the brilliant sun.

At noon, the auction had not yet begun, for the auctioneer, gauging the air with his expert ears and eyes, had not yet felt that the town was ripe and reckless enough.

By one, four hours late, the pitch was right, and the first PIÈCE DES INDES was taken from the cage and placed on the block for all to see. The bedlam subsided, and the item of sale raised his chin and displayed his nakedness and let his eyes betray his bewilderment.

The bidding was reckless indeed, for the shortage of slaves was acute. The St. Jan bidders were hopelessly outclassed by the rich St. Thomians, who simply had their way with most of the items placed on the block, committing themselves for as much as two hundred RIGSDALERS per PIÈCE for some.

The day wore on. The auctioneer's voice began to rasp. The crowding spectators cheered or booed every hap and mishap, yelled their approval of well-proportioned female flesh; shouted obscenities even though these bodies were officially not human; cried out with high-pitched feminine squeals at the oil-polished, long-flanked male lines and pendant parts, for adult nakedness was not tolerated in town except on the part of slaves being auctioned.

In case a whole family had been captured together and had survived the deadly voyage, it was offered and sold together. If children had a mother but no surviving father, they were sold with the mother; if they were motherless, but their father had survived, they were sold away from the father, on the theory that a father does not make a good mother. Completely orphaned as well as merely motherless children, even though they might have brothers and sisters, were sold individually if no one wanted them all, for it was not considered important to keep siblings together.

The BUSSALS from the block, some haughty, some bewildered, some frightened, were taken in hand invariably by trusty slaves under the barking voices of master and MESTERKNEGT placed in boats, if destined for the outbays, in carts if destined for the hills, and walked or carried home if—motherless children always—destined for the town, some in chains if obstreperous, but most in hands varying from rough to tender.

It was a show that would not have its counterpart until the next slave ship, and one that none would have missed for anything short of the threat of death. All segments of the population, slave and free, black and white, were engaged in the jubilee.

POORJACK St. Jan came away with only twenty-seven whole PIÈCES, two halves, and seventeen underage children. The twenty-seven included every one of the undesirable angry ones who had to be chained at last.

The agent for Estate Adrian near Bewerhoudtsberg bought four adults, including Prince Aquashi, raising the number of African princes on St. Jan to five.

Gabriel van Stell took three adult males back to Brown's Bay. Along with them, as a favor to the Company and Peder Krøyer, he took Christian, the drunkard, who had been shut up in The Trunk for so long that the Company, tired of feeding him, now pronounced him sufficiently dried out to go home. Soon after he arrived in Brown's Bay, Christian demanded rum of one of the

FROM THE COMPANY'S RECORDS: *Countess of Larwig*, Danish registry, Capt. Cornelius Bagge, arrived with enslaved men and women at St. Thomas, in June 1732. It carried 120 captives out of Guinea and arrived with 115 (102 reported in sound condition at time of sale); cost to company 80 rigsdalers, cost to planters 100-150 rigsdalers.*William Blake, ca 1790, from a painting by Stedman, ca 1775*, Group of Africans, as imported to be sold as slaves, MAPes MONDe Collection

MANQUERON house slaves, stabbed him when he said no, took the rum and ran away into the bush.

At the auction a dozen or more PIÈCES were left unsold. No one would have them. Cornelius Bodger bought the sick mastodon of a man, whom he felt he had to call Goliath, and an orphaned thirteen-year-old girl whom nobody else would touch because she could not stop screaming. He had no idea what he would do with them, since he no longer had a PLANTAGE, but he could not see them go into other hands. He had permission, for the time being, to keep them with the sick children at Company expense in the little dispensary while doing the Company's work.

IV

RAM'S HEAD peninsula, on St. Jan's south side, named in the seventeenth century by English sailors, is a mile-long finger pointing straight at the midriff of Ste. Croix, forty miles to the south. The sea and wind seem to resent its abruptness, and even in their more relaxed moods they worry it testily. On any normal day they claw at it, and in rough weather they are in a froth of fury.

The tip of the peninsula is a promontory ending in a creased, irregular cliff and in an indentation of this cliff plainly visible from the sea at a certain angle, nestles a ram's head, in what The Old Englishman, John Charles, liked to call a baaa relief. The head is slightly cocked, its nose a few feet above the rubble beach, its horns reaching to the top of the cliff as perfect as such a picture in nature's own stone can be.

Above the ram's head stands a flat eminence of stone, with the irregularities filled in with the eons' collection of humus. It is decorated here and there with Turk's-head cactus and antlers of frangipani thrust out about its edges two hundred feet above the white foam of the blue sea that crashes and soars there on a southeast wind that can come unhindered from the Gold Coast of Africa.

FROM THE COMPANY'S RECORDS:
Crown Prince Christian, Danish registry, Captain Andrea Veröe arrived in St. Thomas, July 1718, with a captive cargo of 104 men, 38 women, 19 boys, 3 girls, total 164 (36 men, 7 women, 5 boys, 4 girls or a total 52 captives had died on the voyage); cost to the company per person was 50 rigsdalers, cost to the planters 120 rigsdalers.

In 1731, portrait statues were made in Canton, China, of three Danish officers on the same ship, the *Crown Prince Christian*: top, Captain Michael Tønder, Viceadmiral; lower right, Pieter Van Hurk, Supercargo for the Dansk Asiatic Co.; and, lower left, Joachim Severin Bonsach, Supercargo. Marine and Craft Museum, Krønborg Castle, Elsinør, Denmark

In the rocky saddle behind the point, on the precipitous side facing the prevailing winds and seas, are slashed a series of fierce gashes in the stone, where softer stone has washed and weathered out from between upthrust layers of harder rock. These gashes plunge right down to the level of the sea's fury and are an open invitation to death. The wind there screeches a warning under brilliant blue and sunny skies, and will happily trick the unwary into over-bracing against a capricious gust, only to throw himself headlong down the jaws of a gash when suddenly for an instant there is no wind to lean against.

At the foot of the promontory a small bat cave yawns with its chin in the foam, and among the rocks lies a litter of flotsam from the South Atlantic Ocean.

On the lee side of the hills, in 1733, stood the remains of a forest of LIGNUM VITÆ, fustic, West Indies cedar, both red and white, and other useful trees, mixed with the tropical kin of the weed trees that clutter every wild hardwood stand.

These patches of forest still served as a source of tall, straight masts, as well as booms and spars, for Company ships and others whose masters cared to anchor in warm Salt Pond Bay and pilfer them.

On the windward side, toward Africa, these hills had their trees stunted and twisted and splayed low by the same incessant winds that threw up the spray to make salt in the salt pond behind the outflung shell-and-stone, flotsam-and-jetsam windward beach of the isthmus.

The entire peninsula, outside of the patches of woodland in the protected stretches, was a forest of cactus-towering organ cactus and uncountable thousands of Turk's-heads. Stored in these cactuses, even after two years and more of shriveling drought, was a little water. A thirsty man had but to take his cane knife and peel off the thorns. There in the sponge of the pulp was moisture to soften his thirst, and available only for the chewing. It made a feeling like dust in the throat, but it was moisture.

At this time of the year the Turk's-heads were bearing a reduced crop of pleasing fruit, mildly sweet-and-acid little red-pink morsels

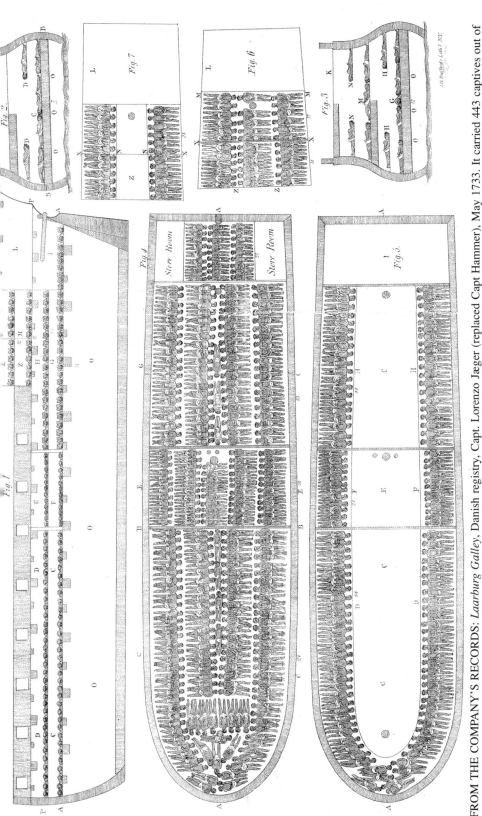

FROM THE COMPANY'S RECORDS: *Laarburg Galley*, Danish registry, Capt. Lorenzo Jæger (replaced Capt Hammer), May 1733. It carried 443 captives out of Guinea of whom 242 survived (124 men, 64 women, 26 boys, 28 girls);199 died of dysentery and two were sold to the Portuguese. The ship made an overall profit of 69.5 percent from the survivors; cost to company 70 rigsdalers, cost to planters 120-150 rigsdalers, MAPes MONDe Collection

that squeezed themselves out of the Turk's turban one at a time and stood there, each with a tiny handle to hold it by, begging to be picked off and eaten so that the microscopic seeds might be spread far afield, wherever the eater might choose to defecate.

Because of the cactus, the sheltering woods, the abundance of fish, conch, turtle, and langusta in the water, and whelks on the rocks at the water's edge, Ram's Head peninsula was a sensible place for MARON slaves to live. From its heights they could see the details of every approach by road, path, or sea, from far off. And so, in the peninsula's sheltered spots, these nights, could be seen from far away the fires of MARONS cooking, in sea water, in purloined pots, these sea foods and the meat of emaciated goats and pigs found wild in the bush during the day.

There was no need for concealment. Only a large force of men could corner the MARONS here, and no large force of men was either available or willing to undertake the arduous task.

These MARONS were free, their life a scrabble for existence, but free; and the ultimate means of escape lay just up the slope, where wind and sea and deep-gashed rock constantly extended their invitation to death.

At the western end of the rubble beach of Brown's Bay, four miles due north of Ram's Head across hills, valleys, Coral Bay, and Buscagie Hill, six laborious miles by road and path, rises a steep little hill.

At the foot of this hill young Gabriel van Stell and Neltje and their child lived in the stone house that Gabriel had bought from Peder Krøyer along with a strip of land. On its uphill side the house was built right into the slope. It was located a mere hundred feet from Krøyer's house, and so near to the sea that salt spray would sprinkle it if heavy seas could get into Brown's Bay.

The little house that the van Stells had moved out of stood up above, on a shelf of this same hill, facing Tortola, a mere giant's stone's throw away across the hustling waters of the Virgins' Gangway. The house was wooden on a stone foundation, and shingled with wood. Gabriel had left it scantily furnished for his stepmother's occasional use, with her body slave and house slaves.

The seaward side of this precipitous hill, exposed to the unceasing drying winds from the east, was forested, like Ram's Head, with cactus, and although Gabriel had left no water in the hogsheads under the roof's MONKEY-POD GUTTERS, he had left the hogsheads themselves, and any little squall of rain, useless though it might be to plants, would deposit in them a little water for cooking or drinking.

Here a small company of MARONS took up residence.

It was a precarious existence, but the MARONS could get some food from the sea, from the bush, and from fellow slaves who had not gone MARON and whom they could intimidate into stealing food for them or sharing what they had.

Gabriel knew they were up there, and so did Krøyer; but they could not go after them alone. They could only check the chains and padlocks on their boats and report the MARONS. One day perhaps a MARON hunt would be mounted that would be massive enough to dislodge them. Even a massive approach, unless it came at them from all sides of the hill at once, could not corner them, and there was always the sea on the precipitous side. In the minds of most of them the sea meant death, but it also meant Tortola and the bare possibility of Puerto Rico to the few who might make it, and in a choice between capture by MARON hunters and a chance at Puerto Rico, the shark-infested sea would win.

Facing northwest and stretching nearly a mile along Konge Vej where it climbed to its highest point in the mountains after it ceased to be a road and became a donkey path was the PLANTAGE of William Vessuup, a St. Thomian. Its northwestern boundary comprised the entire waterfront of Maho Bay.

Vessuup, through the efforts of a MESTERKNEGT and as many slaves as he could spare from his St. Thomas PLANTAGE, had for years been clearing, terracing, and planting the two GUTS with cane, and raising cotton and coconuts in the lowlands. He had built a HORSE MILL on a shelf high up the mountain, where the earliest terraces were, and planned another at the bottom, in the slot where the master house would be.

Near the HORSE MILL, MESTERKNEGT and slaves had lived and grown their garden vegetables on terraces on the north slope that fell away from the house.

But all this lay deserted now, and the wild tamarind, MARAN, KASHA, and CATCH-AND-KEEP were rapidly taking over the cleared spaces, for Vessuup had committed murder on St. Thomas and had fled to Tortola.

Vessuup's drinking companions, his brother-in-law, a Dutchman named Hans Pietter Dooris, and an opportunist renegade named John Robinson, apparently thought they would have trouble proving their own innocence in the face of the governor's wrath, so they went along with Vessuup to Tortola, deserting their St. Jan PLANTAGES.

The Vessuup PLANTAGE offered shelter; water and mosquito larvæ in the deserted barrels at the ends of the troughs of split MONKEY-POD trees that hung under the drip of the roofs; food in the deserted gardens of the slaves and the chickens and guinea fowl and pigs and goats that had had to be abandoned and had gone wild; and even some clothing, left behind by the artisan slaves and MESTERKNEGT in their haste.

Here lived MARON slaves in comfort, convenience, and indolence, and no one tried to come and get them.

The MARON slaves had slaves of their own, snatched in the dark of night from crowded slave compounds about the island—ACCUSTOMED SLAVES, some of whom would rather have been working for their lawful masters than for this violent African royalty; and some of whom cared not for whom they worked, if they had to work.

The shortage of women, though, was a problem. Some of the BUSSALS who had run away were women, but they were few. Some of the trusty slaves who had been kidnapped to serve the BUSSALS were women, but they were simply unable to do all that was required of them, and it was necessary to beat them frequently. There had to be some concentrated effort to get women.

It was in response to this need that a leader of sorts arose: Kanta, an Amina who had at first adapted superficially to the slave life and attained the position of under-BOMBA on the Company's PLANTAGE in

Coral Bay, but who finally had decamped.

Kanta, in doing something about the shortage of women, was not thinking of himself as a leader; he was thinking of himself as Kanta, a former Amina nobleman who needed the comfort of a woman and who had heard the grapevine discussions concerning a light-skinned Spanish slave named Café at Bewerhoudtsberg. He simply went to Bewerhoudtsberg to get Café for himself, not for the community good.

She was easy enough to find, and he went in the night and lifted her from the KABÆN on which she slept. She fought him, at first, and the commotion was fearful at Bewerhoudtsberg. Then he must have ceased to be such a stranger, for she grew quiet and ran like a deer beside him along Konge Vej through the night, and grunting and gasping on their heels in the darkness came the mighty bull of a slave, the moonstruck Cesar, with his cane knife.

V

WHEN the wind blows out of the northern quarter at a certain angle and velocity, small boats anchored in Little Cruz Bay, at the western extremity of St. Jan, fall into a state of confusion. Accustomed to face smartly into the trade wind that normally funnels through the cut in the hills, they become like a leaderless group of foxhounds without a spoor to follow. John Solomon's ridge to the north and the little peninsula jutting out into the bay do odd things to a north wind by the time it reaches the surface of the waters. The boats, caught in swirls of wind and teased by subtle currents and eddies around their hulls, lash uncertainly about on their tethers, now facing each other from far apart, now touching. Their dinghies, hanging off the parent sterns when there are persons aboard, wag like the tails of sleeping dogs.

Sailing into Little Cruz Bay, reaching on a north wind, and coming up to an anchorage, works out sometimes to an exercise in exasperation.

It was that for Skipper Rosetti and *The Sweet Tooth* at noon on the twentieth of May, 1733. Heeling happily, with the sea chattering against her windward bilge, *The Sweet Tooth* scurried past Meeren Cay, The Bitch, the flat, tufted sandbar resting on a bed of rocks well outside the bay. Skipper Rosetti had to put in to Little Cruz Bay to drop off his passengers, MESTER Bodger, soldier Jan Gabriel, and slave Christian Sost.

As soon as she came under the point and lost the steady wind, *The Sweet Tooth* began to act affronted. She coasted a bit, and flapped her sails. Then her sails went aback at one moment and at the next almost knocked the boat down, when a strong gust caught her broadside.

Skipper Rosetti, dark and mustached, wizened as a sun-dried piece of leather, cursed and took her hard alee, scrambling to avoid a jibe, for another boat was close to windward. Then he had hastily to haul in the mainsheet and start sailing, for the wind changed again. Reaching the lee of Hendrich Petersen's rocky little peninsula, he was once more almost knocked down by an errant gust. Finally he managed to come up with a neat flourish and cast out his anchor, too close to someone else. From shore and other boats came shouted curses and ridicule, some jocular and some tentatively angry.

The Sweet Tooth hung there, thrashing about like a skittish, haltered colt, and Rosetti shouted insults at his tormentors as he put over a dinghy and sent one of his boat slaves to row the passengers ashore.

They were met on the strand by the old Basque, Francis Gonsel, owner of the waterfront. Bodger introduced the newcomer, Jan Gabriel, using the CREOLE language, and asked for three horses.

"TRE KABAJ?" Gonsel repeated.

"Tre," Bodger said.

"JU SLAAF SA RIE?" he asked incredulously, gesturing toward Christian Sost. A slave, when accompanying his master on the road, was supposed to run alongside or behind the master's horse.

"HEM SA RIE," Bodger said firmly.

Gonsel shook his head with a slow, exaggerated motion. He explained that he had only one horse, could probably get a mule and a donkey from Robben de Cléry and Jannca Girard, but they were not at home.

"And why did you not have Rosetti take the three of you on around to Coral Bay? Why make the hard ride overland?"

"Well, for one thing, I bear letters from the governor to Lieutenant Charles and Captain van Bewerhoudt—and that gives me a good opportunity to pay them a visit."

"Oh," Gonsel said.

"Also," Bodger continued, "I wish to show the island to our newcomer here, young Jan Gabriel, and acquaint him with its interior."

Gonsel nodded. "I see. Well, Robben and Jannca both know you well. I'm sure there is no need to ask. I go to see what I can find."

"Many thanks." Bodger said.

Preying on Bodger's mind were the sick, frightened, orphaned slave children. He kept wishing he had been more firm in his demands to be allowed to take them under his wing and make them well instead of leaving them with the inexperienced and callous young Peter From of *Laarburg Galley.*

Gonsel brought a horse, a mule, and a donkey, saddled and bridled. Bodger promised, with thanks, to send them back early in the morning.

The three travelers set out up the rocky wagon-road that was Konge Vej, leading up the GUT and over the hills to Coral Bay more than eight rugged English road miles away, nearly a whole Danish mile. Christian Sost rode the donkey, saying that he was the lightest and had the shortest legs; Jan Gabriel, stocky, Nordic-blond, and grinning, rode the mule; and Bodger, the bag-of-bones horse.

On a shelf near the top of the climb up the GUT where a road turned off to run southward down Guinea GUT, there stood the nearest thing to a tavern that could be found on St. Jan, a refreshment stand serving the two local grades of rum, KILL-DEVIL the raw and KJELTUM the double-distilled, to revive and encourage travelers going up and cheer those going down.

Here all public notices were posted and were eventually seen, before the blazing afternoon sun rendered them illegible, or the rain rendered them pulp, or the wind tore them off and blew them away, by perhaps three percent of the island's inhabitants; but the three percent sufficed to start the word-of-mouth tide that would spread the message, with dwindling accuracy, throughout the island.

Bodger had a notice that he had to post. It was from the governor, written in Danish and rewritten in Dutch by scribes, and it had eighteen parts. There was nowhere near enough room for it on the board, so Bodger simply tacked it there as best he could and let it hang, flapping, to be read through by exactly no one, he knew very well.

The proclamation went exhaustively into the matter of MARONS, which were increasing alarmingly in number, set up penalties for various categories of MARON, ordered intensive MARON-hunting, set up new rules for the governing of slaves, and reorganized the Civil Guard, effective May 30, with Civil Guard officers named for the various sections of the island. The name of the new Civil Guard officer for the Coral Bay area was Cornelius Frandsen BØDKER.

The refreshment stand was here because this turn-off was also the entrance to the KILL-DEVIL works, located on the line between twin PLANTAGES two or three hundred yards away from Konge Vej on the brow of the ridge above Guinea GUT.

The properties belonged to "The KILL-DEVIL Widows," two elderly sisters, the Mesdames Elisabeth van Bewerhoudt and Anna Matheusen, called Mathias.

The widows were a no-nonsense pair who knew how to browbeat the tax assessor and to run their PLANTAGES and business without the help of any man, but they were required by law to have, at least on paper, a man in charge of their slaves, and that man was the "French Spaniard," Francis Gonsel, on an informal basis.

Bodger told the slave girl at the refreshment stand to say hello to the mistresses and apologize for his not stopping to visit because of lack of time, and the three travelers went on their way.

They soon turned right to the modest stone residence, on the brow of the ridge looking down the GUT of The Old Englishman, John Charles, called Jannis on this Dutch-CREOLE island.

They found him already well started on his afternoon drinking, propped up in his mahogany bed—at this elevation, with the trade wind howling through the house, one did not need a hammock for cool sleeping—grinning beneath his flowing white moustaches, crinkling his waxy old English cheeks, and shouting happily at them.

John Charles was scion of a British family of some importance that felt proud when he distinguished himself as a cannoneer fighting King George's endless battles, but later felt disgraced when he insisted on becoming an actor, traveling about with a vagrant troupe, spouting Shakespeare.

When John finally began to attract some attention as an actor, his family shipped him out of England and soon he was playing the real-life part of a remittance man on far-off Tortola in the West

Cruz Bay, *F. Melby, 1850*, MAPes MONDe
Collection

Indies, where one of his cousins was a planter. Gradually the remittances stopped coming, and John Charles was on his own and impecunious. He had the happy faculty of making people like him, with his posturings and spoutings, and somehow his fellow man saw to it that he did not want.

When the Dutch pre-empted much of the land on Tortola, he found that he liked Dutchmen better than Englishmen, considering them less stuffy. The Dutchmen liked him, and he easily learned their language. When the English finally reasserted their claim on Tortola and drove the Dutchmen off to St. Thomas, John Charles left, too.

He took up land on St. Thomas, but when the time came to start paying taxes on it he could not pay, having not the slightest idea how to operate a PLANTAGE at a profit. After a decent waiting period, the Danes, who bore him no ill will, evicted him from his property but gave him a consolation prize of this relatively worthless PLAN-TAGE high on a ridge of St. Jan.

Here he sat in his old age, loved by everyone, including his slaves. A wife, Rachel, looked after him with the help of three slaves.

To give him the feeling that he had something to do, a governor had appointed him lieutenant of the Civil Guard, in charge of the entire northern half of the island, from Maho Bay to Coral Bay, responsible to Captain Jannis van Bewerhoudt. He was so far removed from the field of his authority and from the physical ability to gallop around and attend to its business that everyone knew it was purely an honorary appointment.

"What fools these mortals be," he shouted as his three visitors came in the door, "that they trudge these hot, dusty roads when they might be in bed! Nelli Bodger! I had thought we had lost thee from this isle of blood and joy! Pray, what do you here?"

Bodger shook both of his outstretched hands happily. He felt at home with Charles's English.

"But what takes you to bed, in the broad light of day?"

"The bottle, man! Think you my wife? She is not here. She visits with The KILL-DEVIL Widows down there, prattling with them like a WOMAN'S-TONGUE TREE.”

"Ah, I am glad you are well. Now I must present to you a young soldier, Jan Gabriel, of Lübeck, who is assigned to the VÆRN in Coral Bay, and whom I am introducing to the island on the way."

"Good! And which of our languages doth he mouth?" Bodger laughed. "The one you mouth not, I fear."

"Danish!" Charles shouted. "Oh, God! A barbarous tongue. Why, even their king admits still that he is king of the Vandals and Goths as well! But welcome, Dane, e'en though thou know not what I say to thee."

Jan bowed, uncomprehending, and smiled.

"I lived," Bodger continued, "for three weeks in Christiansfort, and Jan and I found that we had much to say to one another despite our differing ages. I shall be glad to have him nearby, at the VÆRN, for how often is there one to whom one can talk, and in one's own language?"

"Sit, man, sit, and have a drink. You too, young Gabriel, and where's your horn? And Christian, come, man, you are in the company of friends—be not shy."

His lap dog occupied one of the chairs, and Charles shouted at him, "Out, damned Spot! Out, I say!" and chased him off.

"Spot!" Bodger said, laughing. "But he hath not a spot upon him."

"Oh, I named him so, that I might say to him, 'Out, damned Spot!' on the proper occasions. Since it was not the melancholy Dane who said that, you would mayhap not understand."

"Mr. Charles, your wits are beyond mine. But I must not linger long. I have to hand you the governor's latest proclamation, whose tenor you will perceive. And I have to report to you that you now have three assistants to do your Civil Guard work for you. And I have to report that one of these unfortunates is myself—it is a part of the price of my permission to return to St. Jan that I accept leadership of the Civil Guard in Coral Bay—leadership, hah! I am to *be* the Civil Guard in Coral Bay, since there are no private planters there, but only Company and Company officials. That makes me responsible to your command, Sir." He saluted humorously. "And I must tell you, my Lieutenant, that it would be difficult to find a more ridiculous job for me than Officer of the Civil Guard; but I had no choice—there is nothing that I would not have promised in order to escape TAPPUS and get back to St. Jan."

"But," Charles said, neglecting his Shakespearean role, "your PLANTAGE is sold, I hear, by Seigneur Moth to Judge Sødtmann. Traded, rather, for Sødtmann's PLANTAGE beside Vessuup, on the north side—and I hear that he has already dubbed it Frederiksdal, in honor of himself and his namesake kings of Denmark! So what shall you do for a PLANTAGE?"

"Rent mine back," Bodger said. "My salary will pay the rent and my PLANTAGE will provide my living. I am to be paid for the property in sugar over the next three years, and I can sell that, or trade it . . ."

"Or buy thyself a wife," Charles suggested.

"This sort of sugar is the wrong currency for that," Bodger said, smiling. "But now we must be on our way, I fear. I am bound to see Captain Jannis, and then we must on to Coral Bay as we may."

"It saddens me to see you go, but if go you must, then be off with you!"

He accompanied them to the door and waved them farewell as they rode on toward Bewerhoudtsberg.

Across the little valley to the right as they rounded the shoulder of the mountain lived an old man, a truly old man for this island. He was Isack Grønnewald, the Dutch Reformed Church preacher without a pulpit. He went from PLANTAGE to PLANTAGE, visiting his parishioners, trying to help them with their spiritual problems and, above all, trying to educate their children in both letters and religion.

As a child he had learned to fear horses, and so he walked wherever he went.

He held services at a different PLANTAGE each Sunday, so that his flock would all have the treat of occasionally not having to travel to meeting. When there was a wedding, a funeral, a baptism, he went to the PLANTAGE involved and performed the necessary rites. He ministered as best he could to the French Huguenots as well as the Dutch Reformed. The only parts of the island he could not serve were the far north, northeast, and East End—he was just too old to walk so far, and the people there would not make the great effort required to come to him.

He taught not only the children of planters, but the children of slaves, the bright ones who were interested, and the grown slaves themselves if they showed such leanings. He did this in open and outspoken contempt of the law, and no one had ever threatened him.

He was mindful of the peculiarly desperate situation of the St. Jan slaves caused by the fact that there was no town on the island. On other islands, the towns provided opportunities for the ambitious slave to pull himself up out of the mire, make contact with sophisticated people who might help him. Above all, a town offered the opportunity to sell things made or grown in spare time, so that a slave might save up the money to purchase himself and gain his freedom. Many slave owners were humane enough to go along with this practice, although most were not above charging a slave several times his actual cash value.

On St. Jan, only the slave who belonged to a benevolent St. Thomian whose St. Jan PLANTAGE was secondary had, generally speaking, any hope of rising above his bondage. If good enough and bright enough, he might attract the attention of the owner and be transferred to the St. Thomas PLANTAGE or town house and whole new horizons. This tended to make the ambitious St. Jan slave either more servile or more uncontrollably angry than his St. Thomas counterpart, and the hopeless and resigned more sodden.

Grønnewald, like Bodger, would not hold any man in slavery who wished his freedom and was demonstrably capable of sustaining it, and he was genuinely interested in finding ways to help any slave.

Education was the obvious and happy way in which he could be useful. He was capable of teaching in English and French, as well as Danish and Dutch, and he tailored the language to the need. Rotund and cheerful, he told children and slaves about God in such imaginative terms that he managed to capture their interest with ease.

Preacher Grønnewald was a realist and a good man, and Bodger wished he could take the time to ride the half-mile in to visit him, but the sun showed a third of the afternoon gone, and he had to press on, for traveling down Konge Hill's tortuous donkey track at night, even by the light of tonight's half-moon, would be perilous.

Christian Sost kept lagging behind wherever there was bush in sight, peering at it and occasionally tying his donkey and darting into the undergrowth to emerge with leaves, twigs, or roots which he stuffed into the cloth bag he always carried when away from home.

At the Susannaberg crossroad, the travelers turned right into Bewerhoudtsberg, and found Jannis van Bewerhoudt in an unaccustomed state of agitation.

"Nelli Bodger!" Jannis cried. "Apparition! Spectre! We thought we had lost you!"

Bodger finished off the introductions and the delivery of Gardelin's orders and proclamation, and swore his jocular fealty to his superior officer in the Civil Guard, Captain van Bewerhoudt.

Then he explained that he had got his freedom to return to St. Jan when *Laarburg Galley* brought a young ship's doctor named Peter From, who was willing to stay ashore. Bodger had been able to convince Gardelin that he was needed more urgently on St. Jan than on St. Thomas, and had to make only one real concession—taking on the Civil Guard duty.

"Well," Jannis said, "we can only be glad to have you back. But you may be required to take the Civil Guard duty to heart, as shall all the rest of us. This MARON situation is growing serious. Last night one of my most needed slaves vanished—Café, of whom I would never have expected it—the milk cow on whom my baby depended, as did two of my slaves' babies as well. And after her went Cesar, by far my best male slave, a tower of strength and dependability—I always thought. And I am informed that the Company's under-BOMBA Frang? Frank? has been missing for some time. I know not what we are coming to."

Bodger's head was cocked.

"You said the Company's under-BOMBA? The MESTERKNEGT calls

him Frank? Kanta is his name."

"You know him?"

"How well do I know him!"

"I see that this proclamation has to do with MARONS," van Bewerhoudt said. "I fear it is one proclamation I shall have to take
seriously, for the sake of the island as well as myself. BUSSALS keep
dropping off into the bush nearly every day. How they can survive
in this drought, and why they wish to try, I have no idea. So gird
yourself my friend. You are now an officer of the law!—or will be
in a few days."

Bodger grimaced. "Well," he said, "if you hand me a weapon to
be used on slaves, let it be made of common sense and not of
wrath."

Jannis threw him an odd look, then relaxed. "But come! Refreshments for the weary travelers!"

Now Bodger paid a price for his regard for Christian Sost. It was
natural for Christian to be largely left out of this conversation, along
with Jan Gabriel, because of the language difficulties, but Christian
was left also outside the house.

Bodger knew that, up to a point, on this PLANTAGE the family
slaves and the family were one community. The children all grew
up together; van Bewerhoudt liked the fact that, until it was time
to start their formal education, his children spoke the slave patois
better than Dutch, and he made hardly any distinction between his
little ones and the slave children with whom they played—until it
was time to come to bed or meals, and then only his children were
permitted to enter the house.

When van Bewerhoudt now included only Bodger and Jan
Gabriel in his gesture of invitation to enter and stepped in front of
Christian to exclude him, Bodger was not surprised. Glancing back,
he found Christian trying to catch his eye. Christian's signal plainly
begged Bodger to make nothing of it, and Christian called out, in
English, "MESTER, there are some herbs growing along the GUT
farther down that I would like to investigate."

Bodger decided that Christian's way was the intelligent one, in
view of the complexities involved, but the episode colored his

feeling toward van Bewerhoudt.

The visit soon developed into a council of war.

"There is going to have to be a MARON hunt," Jannis said, "in spite of the enormous difficulties. The days of holding picnics and taking naps are at an end. You, MESTER Bodger, will have to act in accordance with the governor's order."

"Zondenloon," Bodger said.

"Wages of sin?" Jannis repeated, puzzled. "What sin?"

"The sin of accepting the appointment in order to obtain something I wanted. I think Gardelin may be smarter than I thought. Knowing how impractical I am in many ways, from his point of view, he has confronted me with—hah! ensnared me in! the facts of life; and he was able to pull it off because, with his bird's-eye view, he could see better than I what he was involving me in."

"In any case," van Bewerhoudt said drily, "you are duly appointed and have duly accepted, and you will duly serve until relieved of the duty by the governor."

"Yes, sir," Bodger replied meekly.

"I shall have to consult with Lieutenant Charles, and we shall have to set a date. Lieutenant Charles, as your immediate superior officer, will notify you far enough ahead, MESTER Bodger."

The talk drifted to the more usual topics of the weather and health until Bodger stepped outside to see the elevation of the sun and announced that he must be on his way.

Christian was ready, the animals watered, and the leave-taking was nearly the same as it would have been if the matter of the relationship between masters and slaves had never come up.

The ride up the shallow valley through Adrian Runnels's widow's estate was in silence, each man thinking his own thoughts.

Beyond Katrinaberg there was a thicket of mango trees and other fruits surrounding a spring that could now be no more than a damp spot, and after they passed this point they heard drumming behind them.

It was not the sound of military drums, but of a hollowed log being played on with sticks of dense, heavy LIGNUM VITÆ or BULLET-TREE wood.

The travelers halted dead in their tracks, listening.

"Talking drum," Christian Sost said.

"Sending a message?" Bodger asked.

Christian nodded.

"Can you read it?"

"Let us listen," Christian said.

In a few moments the sound came again. The hollow wood varied in thickness, so that the drummer could change the pitch of the sounds he made to imitate, in the uncanny African way, the modulation of the human voice. The sounds were far more penetrating than any voice and could pierce jungles and top the hills. They rattled and tripped, and galloped and jumped—and spoke in African tongues for African ears.

They stopped, and now, from far away, ahead, a talking drum spoke in reply.

Then there was silence.

"Do you understand it?" Bodger asked.

"Remember I am Congo," Christian said. "My traditions are different from the Amina and Aquambo. But let me listen if it sounds again."

"Those are MARON messages," Bodger said to Jan Gabriel in Danish. "That sort of drumming is strictly forbidden. Only the dancing and singing drums are permitted anywhere here, and then only on certain occasions and by certain planters with the permission of the government."

"But why?" Jan Gabriel asked.

"Messages that cannot be read by white men are the ideal way to further a plot against the white man."

"Of course. How stupid of me. I really have not yet left Lübeck!"

"Let us push onward, then," Bodger said in English for Christian.

Konge Vej skirted the southern base of the hump of MAKOMBI's lesser peak, following the land-grant boundary lines, and dipped down to run between the absentee-owned Rustenburg and Adventure estates. From MAKOMBI's bouldered, tree-furred summit, nearby, came the rumble of a talking drum.

Christian Sost listened, and again to the answer when it came from Mamey Peak, far ahead.

"I was not certain," he said, "but I believe it to have to do with you, sir."

"With me!" Bodger was astounded.

"I believe it to have to do with you."

"But you know not what?"

"I believe it merely tells of your presence, sir."

"And should my blood be running cold?"

"I believe it should not, sir."

"Well, that is a comfort!"

As they passed between Rustenburg and Adventure, the twin PLANTAGES that opened up the whole sweep of the vast GUT leading down to Rif's Bay, the entire slave population had turned out to stand in a knot and watch the travelers pass.

The MESTERKNEGT Joris James, came running to ask what the drumming was all about.

"I know not," was all Bodger could say.

"Well, it fair give me the gripes!" James said, and walked away, shaking his head.

From nearby came, scuttling crab-like on spidery legs, the hunchback Cesar Singal, so called after his Senegal tribe to distinguish him from the hundreds of other slaves named Cesar.

He was an outcast among his fellow slaves, not from contempt but from fear. His strange form and manner of moving convinced them that he had magic powers that he could wield over them if he chose, and indeed he did, since they believed so strongly, and he knew it.

Cesar Singal had a better mind than most of his possible masters or mistresses, and yet in spite of this was an inexhaustible worker, cheerful and willing, fully aware that his chances in life had been destroyed by the misfortune of his misshapen body. But no master or mistress who could bear the sight of him, including Doctor Bodger, could have him in the house because of the fear he inspired in the other slaves.

Here on the Magens PLANTAGES he worked alone and generally unsupervised in the fields whenever he felt like it, with wide space left between him and the others. He went fully clothed among the naked, in clothes he made for himself out of whatever came his way. Someone was always willing to give him cloth.

He knew the island as a bee knows its valley, and like a bee he roamed the labyrinth of hidden paths that laced the bush from one end to the other. He was a natural ally for Christian Sost, who could have used him to great advantage for gathering herbs, for he knew every valuable plant and where it grew best. Bodger often wished he could buy him and give him his head, but he could not have his household constantly disrupted by the ignorant terror he inspired.

Cesar Singal came forward now, bowing, bobbing, smiling, to express his pleasure at seeing the doctor and to note that he was expected.

Bodger greeted him affectionately. The phalanx of naked, watching slaves muttered among themselves and, as if conducted by a ballet master, recoiled a step in unison at the sight of the two men of magic, the white Dakta and the spidery little slave, speaking to each other like close friends.

They could communicate only in SLAVE TALK or French, and Christian Sost could join in.

"You were expecting me?" Bodger asked.

"Yes, MESTER. The drums, you know."

"What do they say?"

"Only that you come, and how far away you are."

"From where?"

"From the MARON encampment up there." Cesar motioned toward the heights ahead.

"And for what is this?"

"I know not," Cesar said. "But you need have no fear, MESTER."

"Then we shall have to see," Bodger said, waving good-by.

At the HORSE MILL of the Vlach PLANTAGE, the three travelers started the labored climb up Mamey Peak, because Konge Vej, becoming at this point a switchbacked donkey trail, insisted on slavishly following the property lines of the land.

They climbed past the Vlach slave quarters and master compound. Here too the slaves were anticipating their coming, and staring at them as they passed, and here too the MESTERKNEGT Hendrich Jochumsen, expressed his apprehension.

Near the crest of Mamey Peak a delegation waited, unconcealed, patient, firm.

Some wore odd pieces of a MESTERKNEGT's wardrobe; the rest were naked. Some stood in tall dignity, arms folded, like Indian sentries; others lolled upon the ground or sat on rocks beside the road. Some glared balefully, some looked at the ground, with occasional glances up; and some toyed uncertainly with their facial expressions and ended looking apologetic, in the main.

They all held cutting weapons in their hands—cane knives, bill-hooks, sharpened hoes, axes.

Bodger knew that these were MARONS, but not one of them had a face that was familiar to him.

Of the three travelers, only Jan Gabriel was armed, with a wheel-lock worn on a sling on his back and a heavy Christian V sword at his waist. Bodger never carried even so much as a sword, for he never felt unsafe anywhere.

Jan brought his wheel-lock to the ready, after flipping open the pan to check on the condition of the powder, from pure habit. Bodger admonished him in low tones and he replaced the gun on his back.

The animals came to a stop at the solid wall of MARONS. The travelers looked in silence.

The MARON leader, a lank giant with fan-shaped tribal markings starting between his eyes and intricate designs carved into his belly, looked at Bodger and said, "Mesta. Dakta. JU SA KOM." He gestured with his cane knife in the direction of Vessuup's HORSE MILL.

"JU DA KEN MI," Bodger said.

"JU SA KOM," the MARON repeated, gesturing impatiently with his cane knife and ignoring Bodger's comment.

"All know you, MESTER," Christian said. "Whether you have seen them or not—and even if they have never seen you—they know you."

"What do they want of me?"

"Someone is dying, I believe. I have heard the men in back . . ."

Perhaps this can represent Christian Sost. It may represent Anton, a St. Thomas slave taken to Denmark by his master. There he met Count von Zinzendorf and several of the Moravian Brethren, who were in Copenhagen for the coronation of Christian VI in 1731. This chance meeting led to the sending of two Moravian brothers in 1732 to St. Thomas, which was the first Protestant mission to the slaves in the New World. Original drawing, MAPes MONDe Collection

"It is for that, then? They wish my help?"

"Yes, MESTER. They know you as a healer."

"I am a fool." Bodger said bitterly.

"I take you not, sir—your meaning."

"My dilemma, see you not . . .?"

"Dilemma. It is a word I know not."

"I am an officer of the law—or shall be soon. I let myself make the bargain. I am in duty bound to fight these MARONS."

"We are in no position to fight them, MESTER," Christian said quietly.

"JU SA KOM," the MARON repeated once again, more impatiently. He gestured imperiously, and Bodger followed him down the Vessuup PLANTAGE road that went off to the left. Down along the crest of the razor-back ridge pointing toward Maho Bay below, with terraced cane pieces falling away to right and left, the road plunged for a quarter-mile until it came onto a nearly level verandah of ground on which stood the PLANTAGE buildings.

Bodger had never been here before. Vessuup was not a man he had known.

The entire operation clung to this slender ridge and was visible to almost the whole of the north side of the island—and from it the north side was equally visible. Bodger, in his quick glance, saw at once that it was a marvelous hiding place for the rebels, in plain sight of everyone, for it could not be surrounded by stealth so long as anyone there had his eyes open.

Behind Bodger rode Jan Gabriel and Christian Sost, followed by the rest of the MARONS.

On the floor of the front room of the house they found a MARON, unconscious, but breathing still, lying in a grisly welter of caked and clotted blood. His head, face, and arms had been badly chopped, and he had been stabbed twice through the chest. He was lying on his side, an arm flung over his head.

From a far corner Bodger heard a moan.

There, propped half-upright in the angle of the walls where she had fallen, lay a young coffee-colored woman with blood from a head wound draped like a tattered shawl over neck and shoulders and staining the wall. One of her breasts had been slashed open, and around her were drying streams that were a mingle of bright blood and incipient milk, froth tinged pink in bloodied streaks. She lay limp, palms up, staring with large glazing eyes.

"Van Bewerhoudt's Café!" Bodger exclaimed. "It must be she. God help her. It is at times like this, Christian, that I feel like praying—like clasping to myself everything that my reason tells me is not so!"

"I will pray, sir," Christian said.

"But first," Bodger said, "please find some fire and get the linen shirt off that man in the doorway—you can manage some way of explaining—and boil it for me—boil two, if you can find two. Find some water, even salt water."

Christian looked puzzled for a moment, and Bodger said impatiently, "You know my reason for boiling the cloth—if the inside of a man deserves boiled water, perhaps—who knows?—his outside deserves boiled cloth when it is hurt. I have not enough bandages in my bag here; I did not anticipate such a need . . ."

Christian went to order the fire uncovered and water put to boil.

Bodger, followed by two of the BUSSALS who were silently watching, hurried two hundred yards to the bush to find a loblolly tree, with its large analgesic leaves; most estates had at least one, planted nearby, for medicinal purposes. He could not find one, and looked for other herbs.

He found not one that was useful in this situation; he would have to use his blue vitriol and MALAGUETTE, and he had not nearly enough for such massive wounds.

The shirts were aboil on the fire, and he sent Christian to try his luck, with his greater knowledge of the bush.

"Bring something styptic, too, if you can find it. The bleeding has clotted and dried, but in cleaning it off I may start it again. Never mind if what you find is painful, for this man will not feel it. The woman is less seriously injured, and perhaps we can clean her without hurting her too much."

He lifted a steaming shirt out of the pot with a stick and draped it over a boulder. He poured some of the boiling water into a pan and sloshed it to cool it a bit. He tore a piece of boiled cloth from a shirt and started cleaning the back wounds of the unconscious man. The bleeding began again in one of them, and Bodger felt that this was encouraging. He used what little styptic powder he had with him, applied blue vitriol and, placing one of the boiled shirts on a straw sleeping pad he found in the next room, rolled the man over on his back onto it.

Now he recognized the BUSSAL's face but he was no BUSSAL; he was by now an ACCUSTOMED SLAVE.

It was Kanta, called Frank by the Company's MESTERKNEGTS, and Bodger suddenly felt the scar across his scalp and forehead throbbing as he stared at him.

Back in the days when Henrich Suhm was factor at the Danish Fort Christiansborg at Accra in Guinea, Cornelius Bodger let himself be so unwise as to sign on as ship's doctor aboard a slaver bound for St. Thomas.

It was, by some miracle, not an especially unhealthful voyage as slave-ship voyages went, and Bodger's charges, being in relatively good health, were correspondingly lively.

One item in the cargo, named Kanta, was particularly impatient of his chains and kept hurting himself trying to get out of them. Bodger, in repeatedly stopping the bleeding and treating the sores, became well acquainted with him.

Kanta had been an entrepreneur of sorts, ever a starter, never an ender, as the saying went, with an unquestioning self-confidence. The acquisition of a tool made him automatically an expert in its use, just as to some the mere ownership of a musical instrument would be deemed to convey the ability to stand up and give a concert with it.

He had achieved his slave status because a woman he wanted, and therefore felt free to take, happened to belong to someone who had the power to have him picked up and sold into slavery.

He readily saw himself as captain of the slave ship, although he had never been aboard a ship before. He noted the things that had to be done to run a ship, and none of them, he felt, was anything that he himself could not do.

It was easy to communicate with Kanta, or at least to listen to him, for, having a need to make himself heard, he had picked up a smattering of a number of tongues in circulating about in Guinea. But he also had an ability to work in secret, as began to be apparent one day when Bodger was talking to him.

He raised his arms above his head to show Bodger a sore that he said was developing in his armpit, and brought down his shackles across Bodger's head with all his strength.

During the weeks of recovering from the wound and the ensuing infection, across his scalp and forehead, Bodger learned, from Kanta himself, who was perfectly friendly, what had happened and what it was all about.

Kanta had developed a plot to take over the ship, with the help of his fellow slaves, and sail it on to the New World, where, having replaced his fellows in their chains, he would sell them and the ship's company and be rich.

He started by taking Bodger as a hostage, with the idea of forcing the seamen to remove his chains and turn over the ship to him.

The seamen on the "fort" atop the wall dared not shoot Kanta for fear of hitting Bodger, but they shot down the slaves that knotted as closely about Kanta as their chains would permit, and then, pointing a pægel, a small swivel-cannon, directly at Kanta's head, they demanded that he surrender Bodger's limp form.

Kanta would never have held his fire to spare a hostage. It never occurred to him that the threat might be a bluff. Meekly he surrendered Bodger to the seamen.

The captain of the ship put off executing Kanta until Bodger should be able to watch the act of vengeance, and so Kanta was never executed, for Bodger talked the captain out of wasting a slave unnecessarily.

The Company took Kanta for its own use, and sent him to St. Jan because he was untrained. There he came under the hand of an old-line, loyal BOMBA who liked him and gradually converted him into an under-BOMBA; but Kanta never lost his delusion of omnipotence.

VI

MESTER BODGER was tired but unable to rest. He had passed the night without a tittle of sleep, and would not sleep properly again until he had settled his mind.

Even the dawn, battleground between gold and silver, with both surrendering in the end to blue, could not beguile him. A guest in his own house that was no longer his, but with his own servants that were still his, he dispatched the borrowed mounts to Little Cruz Bay. Then he saw to the comfort of his overnight guest, and at breakfast spoke seriously to him.

"Jan Gabriel, I am sorry I brought you with me, for now I have involved you in a problem that need not have been yours. Your duty at this point differs from what I see mine to be, and there is nothing that I can say to you about it."

Jan Gabriel, the fair young Lübecker with the Cupid's-bow mouth, looked at his plate and toyed with his food.

"MESTER," he said, "I am my brother's keeper. I feel I must be that. In these islands there is some confusion as to who my brother is. Until it be made clear to me who he is, I shall have to decide for myself. Whereupon it becomes a very simple matter: my brother is he for whom I have a brotherly feeling."

Bodger sighed. "That is the best summary of my own train of thought that I have ever heard even in my own head. It leaves us with the same point of view, but not necessarily with the same brothers."

The drum-reveille was sounding at the VÆRN on the hill above. "That banging drum reminds me that you have to report for duty," Bodger said. "When you are ready I will show you how to go up to the VÆRN, for I must be about my day."

"Please let me not take your time," Gabriel said. "Just show me from here, if you will."

"Very well. There, along the road, to the left, you will find an upright stone with DVC chiseled on the side facing the hill where you can see the VÆRN up there, and HMM on this side. DVC is of course the Danish West India Company, and right there by that stone the path up to the VÆRN goes off."

"Many thanks," Gabriel said.

They parted, and Bodger sent a servant to find his two stepsons.

The boys came running, and leapt upon him in greeting. Hans and Peter Minnebeck, aged ten and twelve, two deeply tanned but white little Dutchmen, speaking their stepfather's Danish on top of the CREOLE patois, these children had been with him for two-and-a-half years. They were the only children he had, for their mother, after delivering him a stillborn child, had been barren until her death.

"You were asleep when I came home last night," he said. "I am glad to see you. Now, I must go straight back to TAPPUS today. Would you like to go with me?"

He stilled their happy shouts. "I may need you to help me a bit. And in any case, a trip to town will do you good. But first, run to the Company dock and attract Lambrecht's attention. Tell him, whatever he is doing today, I will pay him more—hmm, within reason, of course—than he can make doing it, if he will take us down to town today and bring us back tomorrow, with some others. Done?"

"Done!" the boys shouted, and were off at a sprint.

Bodger followed them up the road and went to catch Judge Sødtmann at his breakfast.

"Reimo, do not get up, nor disturb the ladies. Just let me sit and talk to you."

"Welcome, Nelli. I knew you were there. My servants told me you came past in the night."

"Will you rent me my PLANTAGE? I must go back to town today, and when I return I shall probably be a simple planter—oh a physician, of course, for private hire, but not the Company CHIRUR-GEON."

"Now, what is this?" Sødtmann demanded in a friendly manner.

"First you come sneaking in, overland, by night, and move into my house down the road that has your furniture and family and slaves in it. And here in the dim dawn you tell me you are rushing back to town, without telling me why you left there, and you wish to rent a PLANTAGE before you go."

"If I return a planter," Bodger said, "I'll explain everything. If I am still the Company CHIRURGEON when I return, I shall explain nothing at all. In either case, I shall need a PLANTAGE. Will you rent me mine, and for how much?"

"Yes, and for ten percent of your crops. Fair enough?"

"Fair enough, and more than fair!" Bodger exclaimed. "And I shall need some help in the BARCADS. In view of the uncertainty of my position, I must put the PLANTAGE into more intensive production. You are doing less and less with yours—may I also rent some of your workers—say five?"

"Well, yes, as a matter of fact. I was planning to sell some. Let me see, there is Cinadi—and Adu, Asjanje, Aba—female, a good worker—and Sépuse. At the going rate. Satisfactory?"

"Satisfactory and done!"

"But what happens—excuse me if I make a guess from the expression on your face!—if you land in jail?"

"Oh," Bodger said, momentarily nonplused. "Well. In that case, you will come and get me out, so that you may collect your ten percent!"

"Now, Nelli BØDKER!" Gardelin cried. "I thought I was rid of you!"

"Perhaps you shall be," Bodger said. "May I sit? I shoot best from a sitting position."

"Shoot? Sit, then, and shoot! What ails you?"

Bodger sighed. "Where to begin? I sat here in this chair and let myself be cajoled into making commitments that I cannot sustain."

"Oh, come down off that horse and walk alongside me!"

Bodger grinned, and flounced in his chair. "I wanted to get back to St. Jan and away from this Bedlam, and you played on that and made me promise to be a Civil Guard officer. But that is only the

Firing the furnaces, Dantj Print Collection, Florence, Italy

beginning of it!"

"Very well, so you do not wish to be the Coral Bay Civil Guard officer. Who else is there that can do it? No one else is located in Coral Bay. Reimo Sødtmann cannot be a Civil Guard officer, for he is the judge. Lieutenant Frøling and his soldiers cannot do it, for they are soldiers. No one else but MESTERKNEGTS and widows and children and slaves lives there, and MESTERKNEGTS and widows and children and slaves cannot be Civil Guard officers!"

"No Civil Guard officer is needed there, with the VÆRN and its soldiers on hand."

"Nonsense, Nelli. Most of the MARONS on the island are runaways from Coral Bay, and it is the chief business of the Civil Guard to deal with MARONS."

"The fact remains that I am not interested in dealing with MARONS on any but medical terms."

"Now, just what do you mean by that?"

"I mean that my mission in life here is to heal people who are hurt or sick, regardless of whether they be MARONS or not."

"Hold, now! Are you saying that you propose to give medical treatment to MARONS and let them remain MARON?"

"That is what I am saying, precisely."

"But do you not know, man, that I could throw you into prison for that?"

"Now," Bodger said, "we have come to the heart of the matter."

"And high time," Gardelin said coldly. "Tell me what you are talking about."

"Yesterday, on my way across St. Jan, I found myself called upon to render medical aid to some MARONS. At the same time I found myself called upon to be a Civil Guard officer and arrest them, or try to. I chose to render medical aid according to my calling."

Gardelin stood up in his agitation, breathing audibly. "BØDKER, you place me in a very difficult position."

"That is correct, and I am sorry. I am sorry I promised to be a Civil Guard officer when I really had no intention of being any such thing—I confess that at the moment it did not occur to me that I could be told seriously to put a gun on my shoulder and go out and chase MARON slaves."

Gardelin was not even listening. "You have committed a serious crime," he said. "What am I to do with you?"

"If you are truly asking me," Bodger said, "you are to strip me—publicly, if you like, on an elevated JUSTICE POST, with the entire populace looking on and drums beating to summon the rest of the world—strip me of my commission as Civil Guard officer and send me in disgrace to St. Jan to practice medicine to the best of my limited ability."

"But, damn it, man, why should I do anything so generous as that for you?" Gardelin sat down heavily, gnawing his knuckles. He jerked off his wig and threw it into a corner, for he was sweating.

"I must of course come part-way to meet you, Nelli. I am able, and being able I am required, to put myself in your place for a moment, and I must admit that I sympathize with your point of view, but I have a huge business to run here, and I am responsible for it to the stockholders, who are the most important people in Denmark, including His Majesty himself. And being in this position, I am the law here, whether I like it or not, and at times I do not like it."

"You are thinking aloud," Bodger said, "trying to gain time."

"That is true. Now. I can see the importance of healing MARONS as well as loyal slaves," Gardelin continued, thinking out his words one at a time, "because slaves are valuable, and a MARON, when recaptured, becomes a slave again. But damn it all, I can not imagine that you would refuse to tell us the location of the MARONS!"

"Then," Bodger said drily, "may I give your imagination a hand? In this particular instance there is no secret, for everyone knows that these MARONS are living on Vessuup's PLANTAGE. I speak now of the future, and in general terms. If I answered a call to help a sick MARON and then reported the location of the MARON, how many more opportunities do you believe I should have to help sick MARONS?"

"None," Gardelin said. "Then am I to say to you, because I am soft and because I like you—and damn it all, admire you in spite of my better judgment! Am I to say to you, 'Go, my son, and heal the sick wherever you may find him. It matters not that I am governor here and am bound by my duty to throw you into jail for being a traitor to your own kind, and for flouting the law.' Am I to say that?"

"Precisely," Bodger said. "But I am not flouting the law. In your mind you have stripped me of my commission in the Civil Guard, and there is no law, outside of your mind, requiring me to report the position of any MARON."

"As a planter, you are automatically a member of the Civil Guard even though you are not an officer in it."

"Touché," Bodger said.

"And yesterday you flouted the law."

"Touché," Bodger repeated. "Now, may I save you some time? You are working yourself up to the point of telling me that I am free to practice my calling wherever it is demanded of me, but that you do not wish to know about it when it happens that I cross into the camp of the enemy to do it; that if I am caught at it you will have to treat me as a common criminal, without mercy. But you know that you cannot say all that to me, because of your position, and so you are very glad to have me say it for you. And meanwhile, you know that I am badly needed on St. Jan, and that was really your sole reason for letting me go back there."

"BØDKER," Gardelin exploded, "will you get out of here!"

"No," Bodger said. "Not yet. Something else has been keeping me awake—that sick child that Willumsen refused to let me either buy or take as a loan. Now, I wish you to order him to turn that child over to me. I have that right because I am the only person in the world who really cares whether he lives or dies. If you wish, I will buy him, by the pound as meat, or by the piece as a slave, but I am taking him home with me, and I am keeping him until he is either well or dead."

"Take him, take him," Gardelin said impatiently. "I will privately tell Willumsen to give him to you without charge, since he is worthless. Anything else?"

"No, Your Excellency. Thank you very much. Tomorrow morning I shall take along the slaves I bought."

"Very well." Gardelin signaled Æro to bring him his wig from

Boiling the cane juice down to sugar, Dantj Print Collection, Florence, Italy

the corner.

Bodger turned at the door and said quietly, "Your Excellency, I am deeply grateful to you. I was grievously in error."

Gardelin fingered his eyebrows and closely examined a paper on his desk. As Bodger left, he signed it, shook fine sand on it, and spilled the sand off onto the floor.

Jan Gabriel climbed up the looping path that led from Konge Vej to Frederiksværn at the top of Værn Hill. The morning sun was in full glare now on the hillside, and by the time Jan reached the top he was ready to add to his debt to the Company by ordering a pot of ale from the bottleri.

The garrison, at its breakfast, had watched him come, and when he arrived he was greeted formally, for none of these men had seen him before. They gathered about him, openly envious of his uniform, introduced themselves cheerfully, then waited for him to explain his visit.

"I am assigned here," he said, "to augment the garrison."

"Augment?" Tiil said. "Has war been declared on us?"

Everyone laughed, and Talencam said, "Welcome. We may cut your throat for your uniform, but outside of that, we are glad to see you."

"Thank you," Gabriel said, smiling. "And who is the commissary department here? I wish to open an account by quaffing a pot of ale."

"Oho!" Callundborg, the 'black' Dane, cried, "he's that sort! The rich type."

"The dry, hill-climbing type," Gabriel said.

"And I hope the type who has a new pack of cards in his gear," Knudsen said. "Ours is so badly worn that the queen is bleeding from all openings."

"New I would not say," Gabriel said, "but a pack of klaverash cards I do happen to have." He paused. "Ah, hmm, is there no commanding officer?"

"What rank?" Lind asked, grinning.

"Any rank," Gabriel said. "But preferably Lieutenant Frøling. I have a dispatch for him from the governor."

"Oh?" Talencam said. "Then perhaps there is a war?"

"Not to my knowledge," Gabriel said. "But I am required to deliver this into his hands personally."

"God," Tiil said, "it looks dangerous. Hold it up to the sun. Let's see if we can make out what it says."

Gabriel held it up, and the soldiers all crowded around to look, but the opacity of the paper spoiled the show.

"Where is the lieutenant?" Gabriel asked.

"Excellent question," Callundborg said. "He may possibly show up some week, if there happens to be something here he forgot to take for his PLANTAGE."

"Can we send for him?"

"For sure," Lind said. "That is what slaves are for. But do you think we should send for him? If we send for him, he will be here, and so far as I know, there is not a living soul who wishes him here—least of all the lieutenant himself."

"Governor Gardelin wishes him here," Gabriel said. "I hope it will not make you unhappy, but I am required to hand him this at the earliest possible moment, and at no other spot than within the walls of this VÆRN."

"You make it sound serious. Are you sure you know not what it says?"

"I know not, but it could be serious. The governor was looking thunderclouds when he handed it to me."

"Oh," Tiil said uneasily. "Then I suppose we ought to send Anthoni up to Water Bay to fetch him."

"I suppose we ought," Talencam agreed. "Or do you think we ought to send for Corporal Høg, in the other direction, and let him send for the lieutenant?"

"My orders say nothing of the corporal," Gabriel said. "Let us keep him out of sight as long as possible—if I am any judge of corporals."

"You are a judge of corporals," Tiil said.

VII

AFTER twelve hours of beating against a reluctant wind, Lambrecht's BARQUE was tied up at dusk at the Company dock in Coral Bay, and Bodger and his stepsons came ashore. Hans led the huge sick Goliath, who could now walk. Peter led the bewildered but no longer wailing orphaned thirteen-year-old girl; she would not be led, and wrenched her hand away, walking fearfully behind the boy.

Bodger carried the sick eight-year-old boy in his arms. The child, by tribal custom, had been named for the month of his birth, which Bodger had translated into January for his own convenience. January stared up at Bodger's face with big, wan eyes, and even when the sun shone full on his face he only winced a little and kept on staring silently.

Christian Sost came running down the road to meet them. "Trouble, MESTER," he said. "Terrible trouble."

In the Company boiling house some of the new BUSSALS had been put to work learning to be sugar-house slaves, in the charge of Dennis Sullivan. Sullivan had put them with the sugar cookers to be taught, and had left them there. They had caught the cookers, all four of them, off guard and had pushed them all, each into his own kettle, and run away with no one to stop them. The four cookers were boiled in their own pots and died before they could get out.

At the VÆRN, Lieutenant Frøling came grudgingly, a day late, to receive his letter. He read it and sent for Corporal Høg. The corporal came, and the lieutenant ordered him to place the garrison on full military rules and keep it that way.

The lieutenant then went back home to Water Bay.

On the twenty-seventh, after a week of illness, Gardelin, with renewed vigor, sent letters off in all directions. One letter, to Reimert Sødtmann, on St. Jan, appointed him guardian of his stepdaughter, Helena Hissing, because John Charles no longer wished the responsibility.

During the little family celebration of Reimert Sødtmann's appointment as guardian of Helena there was a good deal of merriment until Helena, too big for that, sat on her guardian's lap and he, having drunk a bit too much, suddenly paled up and down his thin, swarthy face, gasped, and crushed her to him so hard that her joints cracked, and she fainted.

The next day, sober as the judge he was, Reimert Sødtmann sent for Lieutenant Frøling and gave him the tongue-lashing he required, in Gardelin's name. Complaints about laxness at the VÆRN, about Frøling's inattention to duty, had long been piling up on Gardelin's desk. The growing tensions of the times, the increasing numbers of MARONS escaping into the bush, made it necessary for laxness to cease. Frøling could easily be relieved of his commission; there were plenty of sergeants waiting for promotion. From now on, he concluded, there would be constant alertness at the VÆRN, full attention of Frøling to his duties there.

The result of this was the full attention of Corporal Høg to Lieutenant Frøling's duties at the VÆRN. The lieutenant's new-wed PLANTAGE took precedence over the corporal's new-wed PLANTAGE by reason of rank; and besides, the corporal was less deeply committed, for his widow-wife's PLANTAGE was already a going thing—and the corporal wished one day to be a commissioned officer.

The lieutenant was far too deeply committed to his new venture to risk the loss of everything for the sake of a military man's pay that never came, in a Godforsaken hole where there were precious few perquisites with which to line the pockets. His only source of extra income until he could make a paying thing of the PLANTAGE was the fee he charged for hauling slaves into the VÆRN for punishment. Many St. Jan planters were pleased with him for his willingness to maim their troublesome slaves, converting them into MAN-QUERONS, tax-free slaves who could still be made to perform useful services. However, they had complained so bitterly to Gardelin about his exorbitant fees that the governor had had to limit him to two RIGSDALERS per punishment, cannily refraining from ordering him to stop making so many arrests of slaves, for so long as Frøling was happy he would not pester Gardelin for more pay.

Gardelin's orders for a MARON hunt on St. Jan were never carried out. The St. Jan planters knew things that Gardelin could not know. High-spirited Jannis van Bewerhoudt himself, captain of the Civil Guard, could not stand off and look realistically at the thousands of acres of mountain and valley woodland on St. Jan without realizing that there were not enough free men in all these islands put together to find and corner and capture any runaways who sincerely did not wish to be found and captured. Every free man knew that the bush was laced with a crisscross of paths going from everywhere to everywhere else, but no "white" man knew where they all were. So cleverly were their beginning and ending points disguised that only a sharp-eyed search could spot them, and no free man, even escorted by his body slaves, ever lingered in passing the bush or through parts of it to watch for cleverly disguised beginnings and endings of paths. Slaves, both old-line and BUSSAL, knew these paths intimately, from frequent use, but would not lead a free man to and through them, for to do it was to die, perhaps mysteriously in the night, later; and so it came about that no slave, and no freed slave, ever had the slightest idea, when asked, how to go about finding the well-worn paths through the wilderness. If they did not know, they could not be forced, even at gunpoint or the hurting end of a whip, to go and corner the MARONS in their hideouts.

The three chief hideouts, Ram's Head, Gabriel van Stell's Point, and Vessuup's PLANTAGE, were well known to everyone; but to approach them in the open was a waste of energy, without at the same time approaching them through the bush.

The MARONS remained free, and gradually other slaves escaped and joined them.

Jannis van Bewerhoudt did take seriously his responsibility to himself and his fellow planters in the matter of safety. He demanded the same protection for the western end of the island that the Company was giving its own holdings in the east, and incidentally the private planters there, with the VÆRN. Van Bewerhoudt demanded that the Company build a fort in Little Cruz Bay. He was ignored.

Then, he demanded, give him the cannons off the outworn slave ship, *HAABET Galley*, that lay abandoned in St. Thomas harbor.

He got two of them, and his father-in-law's schooner, *Elisabeth Johanne,* brought them over. He set them up on the stone-paved, stone-walled terrace of the residence of his father-in-law, Pietter Duurloo, in Klein Caneel Bay on the northwest exposure of St. Jan.

The guns, for the same reason that the guns in the VÆRN at Coral Bay did not pretend to protect against assault from outside the island, were set up to point at the slave population.

On June first, Gardelin moved into his new, leather-lined, vault-ceilinged apartment in the fort, the ultimate that he could manage in luxury, and gave a party at which he deigned to drink something besides beer, and got drunk. Everyone else got drunk as well, and for a night and a day the island of St. Thomas was without a government and defenseless.

VIII

THIS dreadful drought often seemed a willful and malevolent caprice of nature to the planters of St. Jan.

There were rain clouds in the sky in normal numbers, but nearly always at a distance. A man would stand on his PLANTAGE and watch a passing cloud dump a million gallons of life-giving water into the sea a mile or two away. In plain sight of the north and east ends of St. Jan, nearby Tortola would be drenched by a massive squall, which would then march maddeningly past St. Jan's whole north side, and out across Jost van Dyke, nine miles away—sometimes even along the chain of cays from Carval Rock, outside Trunk Bay, to Thatch Cay and St. Thomas, while St. Jan thirsted in the blazing sunlight. Or the parade of squalls would run for a whole day along the British chain of lesser cays and closely pass St. Jan's entire south side which, in winter when the sun was in the south, sat and parched in the very shadows cast by the clouds.

The annual and biennial plants withered and died. The perennials, accustomed over untold tens and hundreds of thousands of years to recurrent drought, had learned to shed their leaves, down to the barest minimum required to keep their roots from dying, and to huddle patiently thus until rescued by rainfall, just as the deciduous trees of the north waited for rescue from cold by spring's rise in temperature.

The island was brown—a tropical island more brown than the northern landscape after the January thaw, for even the evergreen cinnamon-bay tree leaves were curled up. The CHARATA—century plant—the Turk's-head cactus, the spiny cactus and all his brethren; the PINGUIN, in prickly hedges, closely clumped about most masters' homes; the frangipani, wild on the cliffs and arid rocky points; the air plants, the orchids, that preferred trees and shaded rocks to fickle soil, and the anthuria that could do with either; the sundry euphorbias, guarding their dangerous juices; all, accustomed to wait during drought and grow during rain, hoarded their dwindling water supplies, shrank slowly to wrinkled apologies for their normal selves, but never gave up, for they alone had developed matted roots at the surface of the ground that were relatively impervious to the bite of the sun—the ones on the surface could die and shade those a quarter-inch below, and so only they, of all the plants on the island, could fatten on a shower and most easily win the endurance contest with the sun.

The complete death of most of the crop and garden plants, and of unnumbered fruit and other trees, was accomplished by nothing less than what was joyfully considered a three-day rain. Rain, however, it could not properly be called; it was a mild storm that blew directly out of the east, accompanied by clouds, occasionally thick and pregnant with promise, that gave off, from time to time, nothing but the faint hiss of droplets that were not rain, while everyone, including slaves, listened and watched for the sight and sound of the full-bodied drops of lashing, splashing tropical rain.

The three-day moisture penetrated just far enough into the dry earth to bring thirsty rootlets to the surface, or just below it, by the billions—and then the clouds vanished and the sun glared, sucked up the meager moisture and killed the venturesome roots, and with them, through shock, the plants.

In the month of June, when the crop of cotton ought to be maturing, rice should be ripe in shallow ponds that were now dry, corn and yams should be growing, and next winter's cane should be burgeoning from the rattoons—in "June month" it rained every day.

At least, the casual observer would have said it rained every day. Each morning a procession of frowning squalls passed directly across the island, each one dropping a little moisture—and each one followed by a period of thirsty sunlight. The afternoons were brilliantly sunny without fail.

For a whole month the surface of the earth was actually moist enough to sprout the persistent TAN-TAN seeds that lay waiting wherever they had fallen—but as they tried to put down their necessary taproots they were unable to do so, and stood waiting, wilting.

Still, every day it showered, and the haggard hands of cactus fattened fast, but the leafy plants, rooted in dust, never got a taste of moisture; they were unable to enjoy the refreshment even through their leaves, of which they had almost none left to sustain the life balance, and so they continued to die.

The showers did put a little water into cisterns and barrels, but that was soon gone. The barrels had barely enough to swell the staves and make them watertight.

Tempers shortened, supplies of food and liquids were critically low. A few more slaves ran away, but most now preferred to let their masters take the responsibility for keeping them alive rather than take their chances in the bush; either way, the prospect was bleak.

Everyone in the islands, slave and free, was a master at conserving water. No drop that could be used twice or three times was used only once or twice. Drinking water alone was limited to one use. Rinse water was used for wash water, was used for watering food plants. The end of every chain of use was the watering of plants.

Pots, pans, and dishes were not washed at all; they could be scrubbed clean, dry, with the coarse MARAN leaves that grew wherever the soil was poor. The fat fronds of the CHARATA, AGAVE, when split open, held a juice that was cleansing and sudsy when suds were needed; the fact that it was caustic and burned tender hands had merely to be overlooked, endured.

July brought searing sun, but plenty of breeze—which desiccated the skin, the soil, the plants, while cooling them.

On the tenth of July the breeze died away. The sea, to all horizons and beyond, was like polished glass. Nature hushed herself and almost ceased to breathe.

The sultry, breathless day brought eruptions of human wrath, unaccustomed cruelties. Men fought each other and whipped their slaves over trifles, and women whined who would have scolded otherwise.

One shower passed over the island with drops as big as hailstones, and people watched in astonishment as the heavy drops caused the deep dust in the roads to splash like water; and splashing, it rose and drifted along the breeze among the hurtling raindrops as if no water were there.

By evening the clouded sky was afire, with leaping flame about the edges and long streamers of it darting overhead. Rolling, drumming thunder, distant but tumultuous, cast fear into every heart. It shook the earth, and the earth shook of itself with quakes.

The knowing whispered, "Hurricane!" and prepared to try to shut it out. The ignorant huddled in fear and waited to be told.

Boatmen hurried to secure their boats, the small ones lashed securely ashore, the larger ones hidden and multiple-moored in hurricane holes, the one in Coral Bay if they could get them there, for it was the safest.

A gentle rain began, and all night long it fell quietly on the parched earth.

By dawn there was no falling rain, no lightning, no thunder but the occasional rumble of an earth tremor, moving through from the south.

Then came the wind like something out of a mad sailor's ravings. It struck as a palpable wave of force that had to be visible, but was not. It built and built and screamed and teemed and the rain that came with it was like bullets. They whelmed and overwhelmed, the wind and rain together, and every living thing in their path was contemplating death.

People huddled wherever they could hide, locked in each other's arms or clinging to whatever seemed permanent; forgiving every sin and hurt, and praying if they knew how.

Hours and hours of this, and a few people died, a few were injured, by hurtling pieces of houses and trees.

Then came the eye of the storm, calm, innocent, a smiling Judas. The only sounds were the roar of the sea against the shores and of the wasted water tumbling down the GUTS with its brown burden of soil.

Then Judas walked away and the storm crashed in again upon the earth to drain the hearts of all creatures and numb their souls with fear.

It ended with the day, in time to catch the fattening sliver of the new moon, two days old, hovering above the western horizon in a suddenly cloudless sky, looking the other way in its impersonal loveliness.

People found places to sleep in the tangle of wetness and destruction, and animals soaked up the unaccustomed moisture and were relieved of fear.

There was not a living coal of fire on the island of St. Jan. All covered fires, even indoors, were saturated. Gunpowder was generally dry in its tight containers. Tinderboxes that had been weighted under slabs of rock indoors were dry as well. Gradually, with whittlings of outwardly wet wood, and flint and steel to spark the powder, fire and cooking and drying warmth returned to the island.

IX

In Brown's Bay the hurricane had been a thing of special terror, for the buildings of Peder Krøyer and Gabriel van Stell stood close beside the sea. Miraculously everyone had found something dependable to cling to, and when the sea came up about the houses there was enough stone to keep the people safe.

Krøyer's tender-hearted house slave, Santje, came out of the experience apparently demented. Her dementia, however seemed more benevolent than dangerous, and since she was beloved of everyone, Marianne, now seven months gone and growing lumpy about the face and clumsy, was patient with her.

Peder's BUSSALS were doing well under King Clæs as BOMBA. They did their work patiently, spent their short evenings knotted loosely together, conversing quietly in their own language. Even Breffu, now that King Clæs was there, had lost much of her regal anger and fire.

At Gabriel van Stell's house, once the hurricane mess was cleared up and the necessary repairs were made, conditions seemed remarkably good. The three Aminas Gabriel had brought home from the slave auction had had the desired effect upon Japhit, and indeed, finding him there, and having him to talk to, had had a good effect upon them. It was no longer necessary to keep Japhit in chains, even at night, and that pleased Gabriel very much.

Oddly enough, Peder Krøyer's BUSSALS seemed to benefit from the new arrivals. Although they were Adampes and Gabriel's were Aminas, their languages, since they were neighbors in Africa, were in some ways similar, and there was a good deal of camaraderie across the boundary between the two estates.

Only the known presence of the MARONS at Gabriel's mother's

place on the point above placed a damper on the feeling of well-being in the little cluster by the sea. The food consumption among the slaves had increased greatly, more so than the arrival of the new BUSSALS would seem to warrant, and Peder and Gabriel wondered if the MARONS were not perhaps being given food in the night. The BUSSALS, however, knew nothing of anything like that; they had been working especially hard, they said, and it was natural for them to eat more food. Peder and Gabriel agreed that, of course, that would make a good deal of sense.

It was Peder Krøyer's job, as Civil Guard officer for the area, to organize a posse to surround and capture the MARONS on the point above. He would very much have liked to be rid of the discomfort of having them there, but what could he do about it? There were only six free men in the entire area.

The MARONS on Gabriel van Stell's Point remained unmolested. The MARONS at Ram's Head and at Vessuup's PLANTAGE remained unmolested, and at all three points they increased greatly in number, now that there was moisture in the bush.

Saturday, July 25, was Intercession Day, Supplication Day, Hurricane Prayer Day. The intercession, the supplication, the prayer, intended to ward off hurricanes, took place with the devastation caused by the hurricane of two weeks earlier by no means cleaned up and repaired.

In the intensification of the drought a million grasshoppers had laid their eggs and died; and as it continued, more millions of them grew old or starved, relieving themselves of all their eggs before their death in a desperate bid for immortality. The drought somehow prevented hatching. For reasons that no one understood, the moisture produced by the hurricane seemed to start the incubation process in this abnormally vast accumulation of grasshopper eggs, and suddenly there appeared on the islands a sky-blackening deluge of the insects such as no one had ever seen. They ate every vestige of the leaping new green of the long-suppressed vegetation. They devoured everything that a grasshopper can eat and, in their ravening rapture, many things they cannot eat. When they had finished, and laid their eggs to provide another, later wave of grasshoppers, and died, they left the islands bare.

Someone spoke the phrase "plague of locusts," and each person hung the heavy cross of the Biblical scourge about his neck and felt it as his private curse. "Plague of locusts" reverberated in Gardelin's head, and he fell into a fearful awareness of the Old Testament face of his God. The conviction returned that the islands were being directly punished by God for their sins, and Gardelin knew in his heart that the greatest of these sins was slavery. Yet he could not forget that this whole life now depended on this sin.

Then as soon as the crop plants began once more to put out leaves and buds, a new scourge, the scourge of caterpillars, wiped them out again. Gardelin fell to his knees before his God in real anguish, certain, along with everyone else, that the scourge of famine would now be added to the list.

A British ship, Captain Goodrich in command, came into TAPPUS harbor for supplies and went aground. In helping her off the authorities discovered that the ship had smallpox aboard. Gardelin ordered the Britisher to leave the harbor at once under dread penalties if he delayed, but no one could get him off the shoal, and one of his sailors swam ashore in the night, to get away from the death ship and to visit a brothel. The sailor fell ill, and a wave of smallpox swept over the islands, infecting nearly everyone who had not previously survived the pox. Children, slave and free, died like poisoned rats.

On St. Jan it began on the PLANTAGE of the teen-age Boufferons children in the GUT above Little Cruz Bay. A trusted female slave named Abyss had been to St. Thomas to mourn the death of her slave mother, and returned to die in the Boufferons house. From her, her sixteen-year-old master, Elias Boufferons, took the disease, and he died of it.

The islands lost a heavy count of their young, especially among the slaves. The Biblical scourge of pestilence it was, everyone said, and Gardelin felt mortally sure of it.

In the long drought the people had almost forgotten about the baneful insects, the gnats and, especially in the early mornings and in the evenings and nights, the MAMPI—no-see-ums, midges—that now once more accompanied a man everywhere he went, biting him, sucking his blood, infecting him. They surrounded him always with the unwelcome music of their whining—pitched almost too high for the human ear to hear it—making it necessary for even the more lowly master to have a body slave by his side all night, keeping them and the mosquitoes off him with a whisk, if he were to get any rest. At times people almost wished for the good old days of drought.

August was a month of death, that year, and Bodger and all his confreres on both islands were haggard with the confrontation.

The MARONS in the bush paid only a token toll, for most had long since survived the pox and were immune.

King Clæs began spending his Saturday nights in the bush. By now he had made himself so trusted on Krøyer's PLANTAGE, so useful because of his control over the BUSSALS, even those of Gabriel van Stell, next door, that no one checked on his use of his free time.

KAMINA slaves worked five and a half days each week, with Saturday afternoons for cultivating their garden patches and Sundays for rest. King Clæs, being both king and BOMBA had no need to work his garden piece. He now slept all Saturday afternoons, spent Saturday nights in the bush, unbeknownst to the master class but with the full knowledge of all slaves, loyal and BUSSAL alike. On Sundays he rested in Brown's Bay and seemed to do a great deal of serious thinking, which was considered a very good sign in a BOMBA.

Peder Krøyer's wife, Marianne, gave birth to her bridal child, a boy. Governor Gardelin took ten days off from his desk and sailed up to St. Jan to combine the business of his long-postponed inspection trip with the pleasure of welcoming his "grandson" into the world.

He brought along the Lutheran pastor, promising to send him right back as soon as he had baptized the child, for the young preacher was fearful of St. Jan.

Gardelin and the Lutheran pastor spent the night at Sødtmann's, and on Sunday all of them, including Helena Hissing and the year-old baby, Thomas, set sail.

Across the bay the boat came ashore at The Haulover and was dragged across the low, sandy isthmus, with the passengers still aboard, saving the long sail out around East End. Placed in the sea again, it was sailed up the northeast to Brown's Bay.

There the preacher baptized the Krøyer baby, christening him Hans, after Peder's father, and Gardelin and the Sødtmanns, Reimert and Birgitta, solemnly and proudly assumed the responsibilities of godparents. Gabriel and Neltje van Stell were smiling onlookers, Neltje now swollen with her second child.

And while they were there the talking drums could be heard, for the first time in numbers, in the bush, originating on the point above and repeated and amplified throughout the island. At the sound the hair stirred at the back of Gardelin's head. Everyone in the baptismal party, except the babies, glanced uneasily at the rest and spoke of other things. Little Thomas Sødtmann was old enough to catch the uneasiness in the air, and wailed.

In the evening, when the guests had sailed away, Santje, the Krøyers' pleasantly demented house slave, took little Hans from his crib, clutched him desperately to her breast and ran with him out through the falling shadows of the night. Perhaps she knew where she intended to take him, but Marianne's screams brought Peder running, and he caught Santje in the cotton piece to the west, running, stumbling between the rows, panting, grunting like a wounded animal.

Krøyer held her, snatched the child away, and kicked her. He beat her as best he could in his fury with the fist of his free hand, until the bewildered little Hans began to whimper, not having learned to fear, but only to react to discomfort and the unfamiliar. Then Santje, on all fours and on her feet, stumbled off, sobbing, into the night, never to be seen again by Peder Krøyer.

The talking drums, with their quasi-human mouthings of tongues unknown to white men, followed Gardelin from the island, and MARONS on St. Thomas somehow knew of it and took their cue and made that island shudder in the night.

FLAMBÉE-STOKS were seen by night on both islands, streaking

along a skyline or through the high bush, streaming sparks and stirring up the darkness. Grass pieces, with the dead grass from the drought lying beneath the new green growth, were set afire on their windward sides to light up the sky and throw terror into law-abiding people.

Planters of both islands came to Gardelin time and again demanding that he do something about the MARONS. He demanded in turn that they do something themselves—they were the Civil Guard, theirs were the PLANTAGES that stood in danger. But, they cried, for what does the Company collect taxes, if not to protect the taxpayers from harm? The answer was that the Company was powerless to guarantee safety to anyone in this extraordinary situation. Indeed, it truly was.

One night on St. Jan at Estate Adrian, Adrian's prince, Aquashi of the Aquambo nation, vanished, not of his own volition, but seized and hauled away in the dead of night. Next morning King Clæs, badly hurt, was found lying in the cotton piece at Brown's Bay, where he had stopped crawling, trying to get home before dawn. And MESTER Bodger, when called to help Pierre Castan patch him up, was not available. He had been summoned secretly to the MARON camp at Vessuup's PLANTAGE to heal Prince Aquashi, who had been taken there, badly hurt, by MARONS. The score between King Clæs and Prince Aquashi was now settled. Perhaps the two were not friends, but they had satisfied each other in combat.

Loyal slaves were coming to their masters, complaining of being terrorized by the MARONS. DJAMBI magic was being practiced upon them, they said, hexes were being applied to them, to force them to go MARON as servants to the MARONS. They were frightened. DJAMBI dolls were being made in their images in the bush, and were being pierced and tortured, and the loyal slaves could not long bear this sort of treatment, for they would die of it. These reports were fearfully relayed to Governor Gardelin, with demands that something be done.

In that August, a new hatch of grasshoppers cleaned off the islands again, and then a new wave of caterpillars did it once more.

The dreaded famine had come to pass—among the POORJACK

planters and among the slaves, who were made dependent on their garden patches, with little relief given them by their masters, who had all they could do to feed their families.

Hunger extended into the bush, where the MARONS took more and more slaves from the PLANTAGES to enslave and send fishing and stealing food. Guns and ammunition were somehow stolen from a few PLANTAGES, and those among the MARONS who knew how to shoot straight were back at their old African pleasure of hunting—but now it was for sustenance instead of sport. They killed off every runaway or unattended pig and cow and donkey, mule, or horse on the island, and even wasted ammunition shooting at the few parrots that still swooped about the island looking for food. The planters customarily killed the parrots by the thousands, salting and pickling them in hogsheads for leisurely delectation, and had by now virtually exterminated the species in the islands.

On St. Thomas island, by September, the MARON problem had grown to alarming proportions. Everyone feared that what had happened on St. Jan would repeat itself on St. Thomas. The planters' anger at the Company, which was the government, had by now opened so wide a rift between them and the governor that Frederik Moth took a hand behind the scenes.

A proclamation addressed specifically to the St. Thomas Negroes was released on September 5 in Gardelin's name, with Gardelin forced to sign it. It set up dreadful punishments for a long list of crimes, but for some reason only one attracted wide attention among slaves: a MARON would have a leg cut off unless his owner preferred to let him off with a hundred and fifty lashes, and in slave minds this boiled down to one thing—loss of a leg.

Nothing similar was done about the situation on St. Jan for lack of knowing what would work.

Prince Aquashi did not return to Estate Adrian. He liked it at Vessuup's. When he was well enough, he simply took over the encampment from Kanta, not by force but by rank. He informed Kanta that he was welcome to stay, but Kanta preferred to leave and go to the camp at Kierwing's PLANTAGE, where most of the Amina MARONS were now living, having moved up into the hills from Ram's Head.

Gradually the three encampments were sorting themselves out by tribal origin. As time went on, this process was completed. Gabriel van Stell's Point became the Adampe headquarters, with Bolombo in charge; Vessuup's, with Prince Aquashi in charge, the Aquambo; and Kierwing's, of which Kanta soon took control, the Amina. There were hangers-on from other tribes in each encampment, and each warrior in every camp had several slaves, without regard to tribe, all either MARONS picked up in the bush and enslaved, or hapless PLANTAGE slaves kidnapped right out of their compounds at night.

X

WORD of the St. Thomas proclamation filtered through drumbeats, grapevine, layers of ignorance and misinformation, and finally reached the MARONS in the St. Jan bush in garbled and abbreviated form. As the MARONS received the message it had nothing in it concerning St. Thomas, but said simply that the Danes had issued orders that the feet, specifically, of the St. Jan MARONS were to be cut off.

The message proved incendiary.

The St. Jan MARONS rode high, making the nights hideous with drums, FLAMBÉE-STOKS, thieving raids, fired fields and buildings, and DJAMBI incantations intoned along the edges of the bush for the terror of all FREE MEN, and of all slaves who remained in their service.

To the accompaniment of the campaign of terror from the bush, the PLANTAGES were still busy replanting cane and cotton and repairing the damage to terracing and roads wrought by the hurricane.

A cloudburst in September washed out roads, terraces, and newly planted crops; repairs and replanting began again, prayerfully.

Many people began preparations to leave the islands and seek haven somewhere, anywhere, else, but most of them, being in debt to the Company and unable to satisfy their debts, could not obtain permission, and had no way of leaving without it.

September and October, traditionally fever months, lived up to the name as a new wave of death from West Indies fever swept over the islands. Jan Gabriel had his baptism of it, and survived.

Hurricane Thanksgiving Day on October 25, to give thanks for protection against hurricanes, was a sour fruit, not only because of the terrible hurricane that had come to pass, but because it was no holiday, being a Sunday, and therefore of no special use to any working person.

The St. Jan planters were swarming over Sødtmann to force the government to do something to help them against the terrorizing MARONS and the shortage of food. In spite of the sufficient rains, the food crops had not yet recovered from the successive waves of insects, that fortunately kept diminishing because of the lizards and insect-eating birds, which were by turns exuberantly fat and woefully lean.

November was a time of sweltering, of failing winds, festering clouds, mounting fears, and shortened tempers.

Early in the month, with St. Jan being frightened every night by the FLAMBÉE-STOKS and drums of the MARONS, Birgitta and Reimert Sødtmann decided that for safety Birgitta had better take the children to St. Thomas until St. Jan could be calmed. They would visit Birgitta's relatives.

Birgitta was nervous about leaving Reimert there alone. Reimert calmed her by pointing out that if there should be any trouble it would be better for him not to have women and children to worry about.

When the time came to leave the house, Helena, pouting, weeping, balked. She would not go. She would not leave her "father."

"Men min KJÆRESTE, but my dearest one"—Sødtmann's voice degenerated suddenly into a husky growl—"it is for safety. I feel safer if you are safe."

She would not go.

Sødtmann touched her lovingly and gave in to her adamant stand. Her mother could not move her, and at last went off to St. Thomas without her.

Gardelin decided that his pains of indigestion would not be worse on St. Jan, dealing with the accumulated and coordinated complaints first hand, than they were on St. Thomas, dealing with the endless clutching and clinging of hands and minds. He cleaned off his desk and sailed up to Coral Bay for a visit with his "son," Judge Sødtmann—a vacation he would make it, please God. At least it would be a change.

The earth trembled when Philip Gardelin set foot on St. Jan, and yet no white man caught a hint of any new excitement. The house slaves, for the most part hardly slaves at all, save for the technicality that they received no pay, felt the temblor and thought, said, did nothing about it.

The loyal field slaves felt it, and their blood quickened, but their faces remained blank or bland or smiling for the white man.

This Gardelin was the man the MARONS had labeled once and for all in their deepest bitterness as having said, "The St. Jan MARONS shall have their feet cut off."

The talking drums spoke, but no more than was usual of late, though perhaps more succinctly.

A council of war gathered and the leaders of the three MARON encampments were as one: Kanta for the Kierwing, Prince Aquashi for the Vessuup, Bolombo for the Gabriel van Stell group. Amina, Aquambo, Adampe. Equals in weight. Even though Kanta was not a prince, he was the leader of the Aminas.

The meeting place was the tip-top of MAKOMBI peak, the camel's higher hump, which everyone believed to be St. Jan's highest point. The spot gave a sense of commanding the entire island. The night was black, for the moon was nearly new. The men needed no clothing, despite the chill of the night at that elevation, for their blood was running hot.

The objective was limited and specific: "Kill this white man who would cut off our feet."

Kanta could do it easily.

How?

Simply run in and do it and run out.

Good. The matter was settled.

Sunday night came and the white man was still alive.

The talking drums spoke. The leaders assembled.

The white man was still alive. Why?

Kanta the all-powerful had not been able to get near hint without certainly being stopped. By day the white man was surrounded by his family and friends, at night the doors were locked and barred, and the windows blocked off with cactus and PINGUIN, and shuttered as well.

Cactus and PINGUIN can be cut.

Not fast enough, not quietly enough.

Then. . . .

The horizon expanded. "Kill the white man with all his family and friends."

There was no Sødtmann MESTERKNEGT: Sødtmann acted as his own, largely by trusting his BOMBA.

It could be done. All three of them, hiding in the slave quarters at night—the loyal slaves could be controlled with hexes and DJAMBI threats—and in the morning when the house was opened, at the right moment, springing forth. . . . Sødtmann's Juni would help, and then join them in the bush. There were others who could be made to help. It could be done.

By morning, Peder Krøyer and Gabriel van Stell were dumbfounded, frightened. King Clæs, Krøyer's superb BOMBA was gone, and with him every Adampe, Aquambo, and Amina BUSSAL, female and male, in Brown's Bay. Krøyer could not understand; he had done so much for King Clæs!

A slave who raised an outcry in the night when three hulking dark figures stole into the Sødtmann compound was dead. It was Bawa, the executioner, and a pleasurable shudder ran through many a compound at the news, which spread with a speed that was beyond all seeming possibility.

The Sødtmann estate was in an uproar, with the three hulking figures nowhere to be found.

That morning, Monday, the dead Bawa was buried at Sødtmann's and his fellows were cajoled, threatened, a few were whipped, in an effort to learn the killers' names, with no result. At Sødtmann's, the planters began descending upon Gardelin in their wrath.

That day, Christian Sost said to Dr. Bodger, "MESTER, the governor will be killed if he remain here."

"Yes," Bodger said, "I have the feeling of that. I believe it is my duty to warn him."

Warned, Gardelin blanched. "But why? Who me?" and retreated to the VÆRN. From the VÆRN he moved out, under armed guard, to make his inspections and plans. Each time he came and each time he went, the guns in the VÆRN fired the governor's nine-gun salute and the VÆRN's drums rolled, and the governor's crested yellow flag was agitated up and down on the flagpole.

Second thoughts brought a summons to Bodger.

"See here," Gardelin demanded, "how know you that my life is in danger?"

"It is a feeling I have," Bodger said.

Gardelin peered at him belligerently, suspiciously. "You have some knowledge," he accused.

"It is a feeling I have," Bodger repeated calmly.

"And what have I done to deserve this? Have you a feeling about that?"

"You are the man who proposes to cut off the feet of the St. Jan MARONS."

"Now, you know that is not true!" Gardelin flared.

"It is close to the essential truth," Bodger said. "In any case, it is not what is true but what is believed to be true that brings these little griefs."

"But you know it is not true," Gardelin insisted. "And," he added ominously, "if you have the means of knowing the feelings of these savages, you have the means of telling them that they are wrong! I command you to do it!"

"I have no means," Bodger said. "It is beyond the scope of my influence."

"I am told that you go and treat the hurts and illnesses of MARONS who summon you."

"I told you that myself. It is simple common sense. If it be impossible to decide where a line should be drawn, then no line at all may be drawn."

Gardelin lowered his head, looked at him as though peering over eyeglasses, and said, cocking his head, "Nelli Bødker, be you careful. Be you very, very careful. The ice here is extremely thin."

It was an inconclusive end to a dangerous interview, and neither man felt good about it.

The mouthings of a cat along the edges of the bush, a cooing of a mountain dove, the raucous waauk of a parrot, indistinguishable to the dulled ear from the genuine sounds. To a sharpened ear these were signals to find a way to draw near and listen to the whisper.

In Frederiksværn, on VÆRN Hill, the Company's Emanuel, known to himself and his fellows as Apinda, had learned so well to bide his time and avoid the whip that he was now a bearer in the honorable service of the fortification. He chose to wear a fairly open face and was quick in movement. The lacework of his noble tribal markings that covered his whole body was disturbed by the jarring note of the Company's brand of nearly seven months ago.

Apinda's open-faced gaiety was underscored by his trick of tightening his throat to produce, gleefully, one of the island's most raucous sounds, the squall of the parrot. This often sent even his white listeners into gales of laughter.

Another bearer was Odolo, renamed Abraham, belonging to Andreas Henningsen and rented to the Company for service at the VÆRN.

Odolo was no BUSSAL, but dated from an earlier slave ship. He was of Amina origin. His powerful, sleek body bore upon it the marks of lesser tribal nobility preceding the brands of slavery.

The original Company brand had been crossed out with a more

recent, livid X brand, and the initials AH had been burned in above it on his left thigh.

He was quick in learning the sounds of other people's tongues, but spoke with a stammer when moved by emotion, such as talking to a white man produced in any slave. His speech was punctuated with the sound "Maaaa, mmaaa," like that of a sheep, when he talked to Jan Gabriel.

Jan was the only white man who ever spoke to Odolo, except to issue an order. He soon learned his name, attracted by his intelligent face, and hoped for a chance to learn what lay behind this hesitant front—and to teach Odolo anything that he might need to know.

The VÆRN was a bustle of activity, with Gardelin a hot coal under everyone's tail. He could not carry out his threat to strip Frøling of his lieutenancy—and Frøling knew it—because he had no one he considered fit to replace him. He was determined to get a tower started and built in the middle of the VÆRN, and the bearers, including Apinda, were bringing up stones from wherever they could collect them, piling them along the inside of the redoubt's walls. The St. Jan stones, tossed into heaps, had the characteristic clink and clatter of high-fired ceramic as they struck against one another.

Apinda was being allowed inside the VÆRN for the first time by the master of all the masters himself, and he took care to look closely.

Gardelin also moved the bottleri and cook shed and eating table inside the VÆRN. Otherwise, he wanted to know, how was the garrison to eat and drink, in case of trouble, if the sources of food and drink were located outside the fortification? He had Company masons build a new bake oven inside, attached to the eastern firing step because that one would rarely be used, and the smoke and heat would bother no one.

Apinda, bringing stones, taking a short rest, going for more stones, studied everything with fascination. Soldier Tiil, noticing him, nudged Talencam and pointed with his chin, as if to say, "Touching, is it not? Like a savage set afoot in KJØBENHAVN taking it all in."

When the soldiers attended to the cannons, cleaning them, pouring in the powder and ramming home wadding-ball-wadding with military smartness, Apinda watched.

When the soldiers opened the powder house, so strongly built of yellow brick, and closed it again, Apinda saw it done, saw the key where it hung at Corporal Høg's belt with Lieutenant Frøling's permission, saw the measuring-out of the powder, saw the slow match and how it worked, and he loved to watch.

One of Suhm's slaves was Abedo, called Haly, sometimes MABY for the local beer he loved so much. He was an Aquambo of noble but not princely status. He had learned in his youth to respect and envy the white man. It was the white man, after all, who had the marvelous ships, the guns, the powder, the rum and the means of making it and transporting it across the seas. The cloth of many colors that Abedo loved to wear, the mirrors, the beads, the hundred-and-one items of trade goods, all came from the white man. It could hardly be an accident that it was he, and not the African, who had these desirable things.

Abedo, then, was not entirely surprised to find himself enslaved by the white man, especially since it had come about by his falling into debt to one of his Aquambo neighbors beyond his ability to pay. If the situation had been reversed, he would have collected the debt, if he could, by selling his neighbor to the slavers. His lack of surprise did not make him like his bondage, and he was constantly on the lookout for ways of improving his situation, obtaining his freedom and partaking eventually of his portion of the white man's prosperity.

Abedo, too, was watching, studying.

Jan Gabriel was free of duty in the evening, and went to visit Dr. Bodger, as he liked to do whenever he felt he would not be in the way. He found him treating one of his slaves, Magerman, the Thin Man, as Bodger called him, for an illness.

Bodger was holding Magerman's wrist, and when he had finished, Jan asked him why. "I saw you do the same with the wounded

William Blake, ca 1790, from a painting by Stedman, ca 1775, European private, uniformed inappropriately for the climate, MAPes MONDe Collection

MARONS," he said, "and I wondered why."

"The action of the heart can be measured in the wrist," Bodger said.

"Of the heart?"

Bodger placed his hand to his heart and signed to Jan Gabriel to do the same.

"What is that thing, knocking, knocking inside your chest?"

"My heart," Jan said.

"What is your heart?"

"It is my life, I suppose."

"But how does it work?"

"I know not, sir. How does it work?"

"I know not. I would give my soul to know," Bodger said. "An Englishman has found out something of what it does. He knows, at least, that it is not just some creature in there with its fist doubled up, pounding on the inside of your ribs, either to be let out or to remind you at every second that you are alive. It is what makes your blood move to the tips of your fingers and toes and back again—through your wrists and ankles—I know not how, exactly, but it is something like the pumps that you have seen for moving water into places where it would not by itself go."

"But, sir, these pumps are worked by human hands. What works the heart? What keeps it working?"

Bodger signed to Magerman to lie still and sleep, and led Jan Gabriel back toward the house.

"That," he said, "is to me the greatest mystery of all—what keeps the heart going, and since it seems to go by itself why does it ever stop?"

"What does it look like? Is it really in the shape of the heart that we inscribe on our love letters?"

"No. That I do know, and you would perhaps not like to know how I know."

"Oh, but yes, sir, I would."

"I have opened up the bodies of dead slaves, against all the rules, because I must know what is inside the human body—and you could do me a great deal of damage with that knowledge."

"I would not think of it," Jan said gravely. "But I feel a little ill, thinking about it. You are right, sir, I do not like to know so much. And yet I would like to know—it is said that a Negro is not the same as a white man, so how . . . ?"

Bodger snorted. "Nonsense! I assure you, I know that this is complete nonsense."

"But, sir! Sir, you cannot mean that you . . ."

Bodger nodded. "I do indeed mean that I . . ." He smiled wryly. "How am I to know if I have not the courage to find out?"

The MARON leaders conferred once more to make sure of the plans.

Sunday morning was the time for action. At dawn or before. There were ways to get into the VÆRN; and a way was prepared to get into Sødtmann's. There would be no outcries in the night this time.

XI

THE drums were still all day Saturday. Gardelin was encouraged: he had issued repeated orders to have the nonsense of drums and carousing and terrorizing cease, and he thought he had been obeyed, for they had finally ceased.

·Late Saturday afternoon a row of masts punctured the sky on the southeast horizon. The watch at the VÆRN called Gardelin's attention to them. They rose, and became the masts of a single large KOFFARDI-MAND, a merchant ship well equipped to defend itself in a fight.

No such ship was expected now from any direction.

The rapt watchers saw the great sails swelling in the southeast breeze with the light of the sinking sun full on them, heading straight down the passage between St. Jan and the Northman's island leading to St. Thomas.

Frøling's glass caught sight of the flag.

"DANNEBROG!" he yelled.

"DANNEBROG!" everyone shouted, gathering round.

It was indeed the Danish sea flag. As the ship came nearer it could be seen with the naked eye.

The garrison scurried to ready the cannon for firing salutes. Odolo was there, watching, learning. Apinda, too.

The ship came on, and Gardelin was beside himself. He should be in St. Thomas to welcome the ship, and here he was, perched atop a rock on St. Jan.

The governor's flag flew from the pole.

"Run it up and down, to catch the captain's eye. He must be told that I am here!" he shouted.

Jan Gabriel, as excited as anyone by the magnificent sight of the ship, hurried to make the governor's flag scurry up and down the pole where it hung beneath the Danish flag.

The ship continued, coming opposite the open jaws of Coral Bay.

"Catch his eye," Gardelin kept yelling. Then, "Catch his ear! Fire a salute! Do not wait for his."

The gun crew fired.

The VÆRN waited for the ship's salute, and then saw the puff of smoke from the number one gunport. As the roaring boom of the gun reached the VÆRN the second gunport puffed white smoke. The ship fired the five cannon shots allotted to St. Jan and proceeded on its way.

Gardelin ordered the garrison, in firing the return salute, to keep firing without counting the shots. The VÆRN's guns, smaller than the ship's, boomed as fast as they could be loaded and the slow match applied, and Jan Gabriel kept the governor's flag scampering up and down the pole.

"The idiots!" Gardelin shouted. "They don't know my flag when they see it!"

Suddenly, before she disappeared behind the southern point, the ship swung off, came up, stood-to and fired the governor's nine-gun salute. Someone aboard had come alive and looked up the flag in the book.

Gardelin, panting as if from a long climb, clapped on his wig and his finery, surrounded himself with his armed escort, and rode down to the bay, sending men scuttling ahead to ready his boat.

The VÆRN fired the governor's nine-gun salute, and the governor's flag continued to dance on the pole.

The ship angled her sails to the wind and began a beam reach into the bay.

When she came to anchor far outside the inner harbor and Gardelin, still panting heavily from the excitement of it all, boarded her, she turned out to be DRONNING ANNA SOPHIA, straight from the Far East.

She had sailed from KJØBENHAVN two years and more before, with a sea pass for Tranquebar—a Danish enclave on the coast of Madras, India—the Sunda Islands, and the West Indies. For eleven months she had been on her way from Tranquebar to St. Thomas, via the Cape of Good Hope, bearing Far East goods for St. Thomas and for home. She would tarry a while at St. Thomas to avoid a midwinter arrival at KJØBENHAVN on the icy Baltic Sea.

The captain, Eggers Lorentzen Holm, was a blank-faced, sepulchral man who welcomed Gardelin aboard with something like disdain, but caused the governor's nine-gun salute to be fired again, just the same, and the ship's drums to roll.

Gardelin was overwhelmed by the noise and honor. When it subsided, he explained that it would be necessary for him to accompany the ship to town in order to insure the proper welcome, and since night was no proper time to arrive at Christiansfort and receive the honors due, it would be common sense to spend the night here and arrive in St. Thomas harbor in the full light of a Sunday morning.

Captain Holm gravely agreed, and Gardelin sent the company ship EENDRAGTEN, so named because she had only one suit of sails, scooting into the sunset to prepare St. Thomas to give the ship a thunderous welcome.

In the hills and mountains of St. Jan, the MARONS, from their many vantage points, saw the ship, heard the fearful booming of the guns, and knew that this, after all, was not the night, and tomorrow's dawn was not the proper dawn.

The next morning Gardelin went aboard DRONNING ANNA SOPHIA, with his sword and Æro, his favorite body slave, and the ship sailed down to St. Thomas harbor to receive a daylong roaring, rattling, flag-waving welcome that could be heard all the way up to St. Jan's west end.

Gardelin had not thought to send messengers throughout St. Jan to calm the natural fears aroused by the unbridled cannon fire of the previous evening, but the marvelous island "grapevine" somehow had gradually taken care of all that.

Everything was changed now. The quarry had got away. The MARONS had stood on Bourdeaux's peak and Buscagie Hill, had peered over the edge of the bowl of Jakob Flat, and watched him go aboard the strange ship and sail away.

But no.

The tree was cut too nearly through. It had to fall.

That day, Sunday, the fifteenth of November, 1733, the decision was made. When the drums spoke in broad daylight, the three MARON leaders and their lieutenants came together in disappointment.

The master of all the masters has escaped.

Then kill all the masters.

Kill the white man and all his tribe. Kill every man who holds a slave. Every man, woman, and child.

Take this island for our own.

It was something to think about. There were enough MARONS to do it.

How many slavemasters on the island? Surely not more than one for each MARON.

The drums in the bush at night, like a heartbeat, quickened the pulse. The heart of the slave, even the loyal slave, leaped with excitement at the sound of it, even as perhaps his head took charge and calmed him down; the heart of the master lurched in fear, even as his head took charge and assured him that he was still the master.

That night, Sunday, November 15, the MARON leaders killed and roasted a pig at Vessuup's PLANTAGE. To help eat this pig they had sent for Samba, Pietter Duurloo's head sugar boiler, the most important, most respected slave in the western end of St. Jan. To Samba came the whisper, on his day off and he listened, and slipped away from Duurloo's PLANTAGE, and came.

There was rum for Samba, and roast pig, and sweet IGNAMES from the garden, roasted in the hot ashes; and rum again, good rum, KJELTUM not common KILL-DEVIL.

Samba was needed. Not one of the leaders had ever been west of MAKOMBI, except Prince Aquashi, and he had no influence west of Adrian. Van Bewerhoudt's mighty, lovesick Cesar was sulking somewhere in the bush. There was otherwise not one BUSSAL MARON from the western end of the island, and there were more members of the master class, black and white, in the west than in all the rest of the island together. The absentee-owned PLANTAGES were in the north, south, and east—nearly all east of Duurloo's and Bewerhoudtsberg.

It happened that all but a very few west-end slaves were old-line, loyal slaves; loyal, at least, in that none of them had run away into the bush. The very few who were BUSSALS—except for Susannaberg's and Lieutenant Charles's Princes, who did not complain—were under such tight control, working in chains or under close supervision, that they were helpless even if they heard the summons.

Samba was known by repute in every slave compound on the island. He was known too to all planters as the best sugar cooker this side of St. Thomas. The whole great Duurloo PLANTAGE revolved about Samba; his genius at the striking pot was the crucial point of the PLANTAGE's sugar production, which was far and away the best per cultivated acre on the island.

What no white man knew, and every slave knew by heart, was that Samba, behind his smile, behind his knowledge of his importance, loathed his slavery and the master class, regardless of skin color. What no slave, even Samba himself, knew was that he had a deep respect for the master class, for its ability to be the master class and enslave him. Only Samba knew that, away from his striking kettle, he was indecisive and procrastinating.

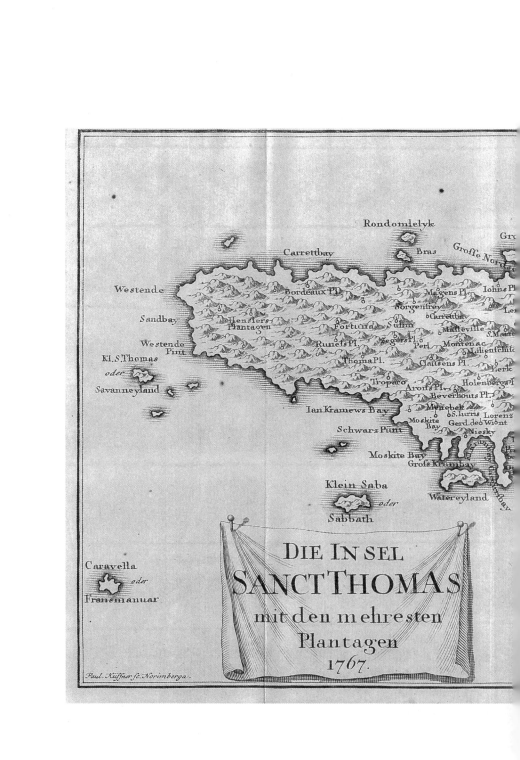

Rondomlelyk

Carrettbay

Bras

Groſſe Nord

Gr

Westende

Bordeaux Pl.

Mægens Pl.

Johns Pl

Sandbay

Henslers
Plantagen

Sorgenfrey

Carrettbay

Le

Fortuna

Suſin

Malleville

S.Mat

Westende
Punt

Runels Pl.

Tegers Pl.

Perl

Montenac

Kl. S.Thomas
oder

Thoma Pl.

Clautsens Pl.

Lilienfenie

Perk

Savanneyland

Tropaco

Arons Pl.

Holenbergs F

Beverhouts Pl.

Ian Kramews Bay

Menebek

S.Iurris Lorenz
Gerd. deo Wiont

Schwarz Punt

Moskite
Bay

Niesky

Moskite Bay

Grofs Krumbay

Klein Saba
oder

Watereyland

Sabbath

Caravella
oder
Fransmanuar

DIE IN SEL
SANCT THOMAS
mit den mehresten
Plantagen
1767.

Paul. Küffner sc. Norimberga.

Map of St. Thomas and a piece of St. John, showing existing plantations, *Paul Küffner, 1767,* Nürnberg, MAPes MONDe Collection

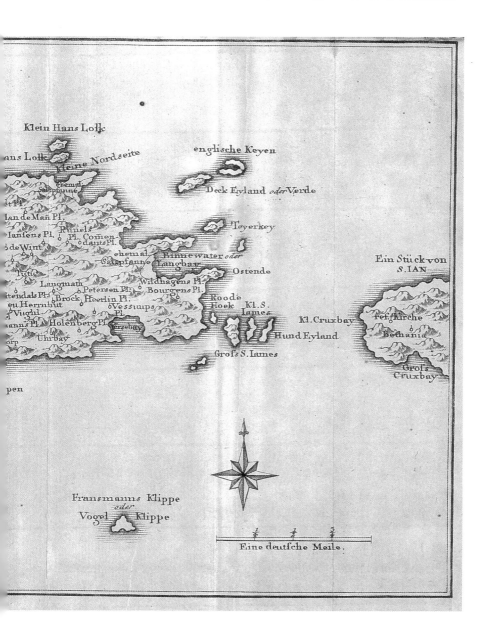

The roast pig, IGNAMES, and most of all the good rum, brought Samba into harmony with the MARON leaders. When the drumming and dancing began, he came to his feet in a heavy, shuffling, dimly remembered dance—for Samba had been away from Africa and accustomed to the white man's ways for the better part of a lifetime, having come to the West Indies as a child.

When the dancing and feasting were over, Samba had a job to do, a big job, and in a hurry. He had to choose and persuade key slaves in key locations in the west to take their cue and carry out their assignments without fail when the time came.

The cue? Three cannon shots from the VÆRN.

Listen for them, listen well. You will hear them when all of Coral Bay is ours.

Who knows how to take a fort?

Aquashi.

Prince Aquashi. He attacked a fort in Africa. He knows that the white man can be attacked like anyone else.

Kanta.

Kanta knows that attacking the fort is a simple matter.

Bolombo. He knows something that no one has thought of: a fort is only as strong as its door, and when the door is open the strength is drained away.

Why do this?

For freedom. The white man's riches. The white man's power. And vengeance.

Samba would do his best.

Quassi listened to Samba—Susannaberg's Quassi, no BUSSAL now, a long-time slave, but still an African. He had to listen when Samba spoke to him. He would find recruits to do the deeds at Susannaberg, Bewerhoudtsberg. The MESTERKNEGTS at the other PLANTAGES would be easy. The God man, the old man who teaches— harm him not. All others in the west—kill.

Samba would take care of Duurloo's.

In the north there were only the widow Jansen's two sons and a wife and baby of one of them in Caneel Bay, and Lieven and Didrik van Stell and their wives and babies at Mary Point. Outside of them, there was only a MESTERKNEGT here and there, hopelessly outnumbered by the slaves in his charge if they chose to outnumber him.

But in the north and west no one listened to Samba and Quassi. Slaves who could listen had been slaves too long. To fight the white man, to win, and then to have no white man to take the responsibility for today, tomorrow, and the years to come—no, it was too much to face.

Samba and Quassi would somehow have to do it all. They let themselves go numb, and waited. They did not, perhaps could never, explain to the leaders that the west and north were impossible in their plan.

The east was the fever spot, and the fever was running too high in Bolombo, Kanta, and Aquashi for fretting about the north and the west. Leave them to Samba. The seat of the white man's power was in the east. The focus of the MARONS' hatred was in the east, in Coral Bay.

Friday night, November 20, Odolo came into the bush. Anthoni and Adam, wide-eyed and frightened, were warned. No wood or food would be carried up to the fort-the VÆRN was thought of by the MARONS as a fort. Nothing could be cooked there.

The soldiers in the fort would be starved until the right moment came, at dawn Sunday morning.

(There was plenty of wood, as well as food, in the VÆRN, and the absence of a fresh supply was not noticed.)

Saturday night was the night.

The drums spoke and sang. The dancing began in all the MARON camps. Café danced madly at Vessuup's PLANTAGE, her left breast deep-scarred; she leapt, as only she could leap, and twirled with a dizzying Spanish feeling that intoxicated all who watched and joined her. Breffu, long-shanked, regal, the almost iridescent purple-black of her skin draped in a swag of cerise-dyed MOLLE-MOLLE from old Madame van Stell's trunk, danced gravely, as though lost in thought, atop the hill on Gabriel van Stell's point above Brown's Bay.

All night long the MARONS worked themselves into the frenzy that was necessary for the dawn attack, and by dawn they were all asleep, exhausted, drunk.

On Sunday they slept, and by Sunday night they knew what they had done, and that this was not an African hunting party but a matter of life and death.

Sunday night heard no singing, no dancing, no drumming anywhere. There was silence and through the silence ran a knowledge of the plan among the MARONS.

Working slaves all over the island, loyal through long habit, but deathly afraid of the warlike BUSSAL MARONS, knew that when the guns boomed at the VÆRN the white man everywhere, to and beyond the horizon that they could see, would die.

Not one slave gave warning. The white man had his incomprehensible ways, the warlike BUSSALS had theirs, and all these things were beyond the ken of the accustomed, working slave. Not one was willing to become involved.

Even Bodger's slaves, even Christian Sost, knowing that Bodger himself was safe, kept silent.

On Sunday night, late, Reimert Sødtmann came running in person to MESTER Bodger—he did not send a slave.

"Nelli," he said in agitation. "Lena. Come, help me with Lena. She is ill."

Bodger dressed hastily, scooped up his bag, and ran down the road with Sødtmann.

They hurried into the house together, and Bodger turned left to Helena's room.

"No, no!" Sødtmann said. "This way. I have her in—you know, my room is the coolest in the house."

Standing impassive at the turning point was Asari, the straight-haired MALAGASY, head of the household slaves, his gaze cast down along the floor to one side.

Helena was writhing like a snake in Sødtmann's bed.

"Now, my girl," Bodger said, professionally jaunty. "What is this? You can't be ill!"

"I know not . . . Oh, Papa, I am so cold!" She shivered. Her whole body shook like a shutter in the wind. "May I please have my linen wrap? It is still in the laundry shed—Lorche will know."

Sødtmann was already running out of the room on his way to the laundry shed.

"You *are* cold!" Bodger exclaimed. "Here, let me"

"No! Listen to me!" she whispered, panting. "I'm not sick—but I think I'm going to die. I think I ought to die!"

She seized both of his hands and clung to them. "I'm a bad girl!" she said, still tensely whispering.

"Oh, nonsense, child. Bad girl, indeed! You have obviously caught some . . ."

"I am not a child. Oh, but help me! Your healing hands . . ."

She pulled his hands and tried to place them on her young body. He wrenched them away.

"Lena, child!" His heart slammed at him mercilessly. "Now, my hands may be healing hands, but I must place them where my judgment tells me. Let me have your wrist."

Her pulse was racing.

"Mester, please! Papa will be here . . ."

For the first time in his life as a physician he felt that he had no control in the sickroom.

"Yes," he said. "Papa must be here."

"Mester," she panted desperately, "let me come to you—only you can understand—I must come—where can we be alone?—and if you speak of this, I shall die—I promise you faithfully and truly—I shall die!"

Suddenly he believed that she spoke the truth, that she could and would die if she made up her mind to it.

Sødtmann ran into the room with the linen wrap and tucked it tight about her.

Lena subsided onto the pillow and turned her face away. Her fists were clenched, but she made no sound.

Bodger beckoned Sødtmann out of the room.

"Reimo," he said, "bleeding and purging and fever powders are not what she needs. I have a liquid at home that I do not carry with me, for it is only for rare special cases. I will send Christian Sost

with it as fast as I can. He will show you exactly how much of it
to give her, and you must give it to her at once in that amount, and
not again until and unless this frenzy that you see now shall return
upon her."

He hurried home and said to Christian, "That relaxant that you
made from the bush herbs you found in the Company GUT—you
call it what?"

"ELLUBÈ is the bush name of it," Christian said. "I call it the mercy
tea."

"That is the one. Please do me the favor of taking a few spoonfuls
of it to Sieur Sødtmann and showing him exactly how much of it
to give to Lena at one time. The child is in a state of hysteria—I
mean literally. Did you learn, in France or England, any of the
Greek words, like HYSTERA?"

"No, MESTER," Christian said.

"I will explain to you. But first, please take the medicine to
Sødtmann."

"Yes, MESTER."

Bodger sighed, and sat, and trembled, and had a drink of rum.

PART THREE

The Abyss

Monday, November 23, 1733.

The first streak of dawn was still an hour away when Asari stealthily let into Sødtmann's house an awkward, elbowing, naked rabble of BUSSALS, led by a fully clothed Juni, the Indian Negro with the slanted, darting eyes.

In the forefront of Juni's followers were Sødtmann's Prince and Ginadi, the drummer, and the Company's Philip.

They all carried cane knives that glinted along the edges of the blades, honed like razors. The men breathed aloud, and the musk of their emotion, added to the unwashed sweat, made a stink that was like a weight on the clean air and moved with them and wafted ahead of them along the gentle breeze.

By the light of Asari's flickering candle they came to Sødtmann's door. Noiselessly they laid down their cane knives.

Asari knocked. "Master," he said.

Sødtmann must have been sitting awake, for instantly came his voice, sharply, "Yes?"

The bedroom door and windows were always barred inside at night. Body slaves had been banished from the room.

"There is an emergency," Asari said, in perfect Danish.

There came the sound of Sødtmann unsheathing his sword and hurrying.

He flung open the door, strode out toward Asari's candle, and was seized from behind and pinned upright by inexorable, sweating arms. The only sound he made was a tearing gasp.

Slowly, coldly, Juni wrenched the sword from his master's immobilized hand, and for the first time Sødtmann screamed in a shrill voice that must have surprised him.

There was no one who cared who could hear him but Helena, and she came running from his room in her nightgown, her golden hair streaming.

Without a sound from her mouth, she leapt upon the slaves, kicking their legs, biting their hands, clawing at their eyes as they moved along the hallway.

Asari set down his candle and followed the melée. He put his arms familiarly about Helena from behind and, with an effect almost of gentleness, pulled her away, speaking quietly, closely, beneath the hubbub, in her ear. She subsided, sobbing heavily.

Asari took his hands from her breasts and captured her wrists, holding them strongly, the left with his right hand, the right with his left, his elbows pressed tight against her sides. Holding her helpless, he propelled her in lock step, clutching her tight against his body, following the struggling huddle of BUSSALS into the high-ceilinged ballroom.

In the center of the room stood a table, made in KJØBENHAVN of sturdy St. Thomas mahogany, and above it hung a French crystal chandelier. The candles were already being lighted by quaking house slaves at Juni's command.

Onto this table the BUSSALS lifted Sødtmann. They stripped him naked and threw his nightclothes into a corner. His tousled black hair made a spiky silhouette against the candlelight.

One at a time the BUSSALS went to retrieve their cane knives, and the roused plantation slaves were brought, crowding, into the room.

Sødtmann stood before the chandelier. Sweat ran out of his dark hairline, sweat dripped off his chin, sprang from his armpits, ran down his arms, down the valley of his chest, the twin valleys of his groins, flowed down his trembling legs as he stood and panted. His face grimaced with rolling, unbelieving, unseeing eyes as if newly blinded.

Helena seemed unable to look at him. She stood slumped in Asari's grasp, her hair hanging like a tattered ensign.

The room was quiet now, with only the sound of breathing and of Sødtmann's gasps, like muted sobs. The odor of the aching crowd was a heavy, foul, acrid stench.

In the throbbing silence Juni's voice suddenly barked, "Dance! Sing and dance!"

A look almost of relief flashed across Sødtmann's tortured face.

"Oh," he faltered, "that! Oh!" He giggled hysterically. "Well, you see,"—the words started spewing rapidly "I can explain that, you see, it was expected of me, it was necessary, in the position I hold, it . . ."

"Dance!" Juni interrupted, and the flow of words ceased. Sødtmann opened his mouth and grimaced again.

"Dance and sing," Juni commanded once more, quietly this time.

"But I am not given to singing and dancing. I know not how." The BUSSALS clustered along the edge of the table began hacking lightly at his ankles with their long cane knives. The loyal slaves filled the room with a hushed gasping. Blood seeped red from the shallow cuts and formed drops at intervals. The drops broke and made irregular lines on Sødtmann's feet as he lifted them one at a time like a child being chastised with a GENIP switch.

"Sing! Dance! Sing! Dance!" Juni chanted, and the chant was taken up by the BUSSALS, and gradually by some of the loyal slaves whose eyes showed an unaccustomed daring.

Keeping time with the chant, the BUSSALS, almost absently, continued to hack at Sødtmann's ankles.

Sødtmann sang and danced. Quaveringly he sang a child's nonsense song, "MIN MO'R HAR DANS'T MED SKYERNE," and his feet shuffled awkwardly out of time with the syllables.

"Faster," Juni said, encouraging him with the point of the sword.

Sødtmann bounced higher and his genitals waggled like the pigtails of a rope-skipping girl.

He slid and fell heavily in the slippery blood on the table top. He retched, bent double. Saliva and green bile roped from his hanging, bawling mouth.

Asari released Helena and gestured angrily at Juni. Juni merely stood and watched, pleasure plucking at his eyes and lips.

Asari seized Sødtmann's sword from Juni's unresisting hand and quickly stabbed his master through the heart. Sødtmann sprawled heavily. His last breath rasped harshly "*Kah!*" in his throat and his gushing blood mingled with the bile upon the table.

"Oh!" his watching slaves cried. "Oh! Oh!"

Now for the first time Helena raised her head and looked. She screamed and her face twisted in trembling distortion. She scrambled upon the table to throw herself, sobbing wildly, upon Sødtmann's naked form.

The watching slaves let her suffer under the lights. Then she stood and stared down at Asari, her eyes deeply dilated.

"Asari!" she said in a hoarse whisper. "Me, too!"

He recoiled, almost threw the sword away but she held him with her eyes.

"Asari." She found her voice, and there was strong command in it, along with impassioned entreaty. "You know you must do it!"

And suddenly, with a look almost of compassion, he did, but his placing of the sword's point was an act of perversion, and she had to die too slowly, heaped shuddering, gasping in uttermost agony, upon her stepfather's body.

Asari dropped the sword with a clatter and walked away, his shoulders slumping.

II

AT the VÆRN the night had been a restless one.

It had all started with Høg, a solid stone gatepost of a corporal when he wanted to be—and he wanted to be now, with Governor Gardelin on his tail for having neglected his duty. Høg refused to let any of the garrison go out wenching among the Company's female slaves after technical lights-out.

"If I, a married man, cannot leave my post for the night with my wife," he shouted, mingling bluster with plaintiveness, "then a snot-nosed, drag-peckered rabble like you certainly cannot go whoring." He waved his hands as if annoyed by flies, and snorted. "I have enough to contend with."

Talencam snickered, and suddenly the whole drag-peckered rabble was laughing.

Høg was not amused.

"Lieutenant Frøling deliberately ignores the governor's orders and spends his time with his wife and plantation," he said angrily. "That only makes matters worse for me. It attracts the governor's attention, since someone,"—he glared suspiciously at Jan Gabriel—"someone,"—he repeated ominously, "apparently reports everything that goes on."

Jan Gabriel ignored the baiting, as usual, and even grinned tolerantly when Tiil demanded, "Say, what do you do, the nights you go down the hill? You go always alone. You must have something pretty special."

"You know I visit Bodger."

"But what do you do for a woman in this womanless waste?"

"I bide my time," Jan said. "What else is there?"

"Your fist," Tiil said, jeering.

"I wonder," Talencam said musingly, "if it isn't about time for that girl of Sødtmann's down there. . . . God, she is getting to be a morsel! And I have heard that she is already open to—suggestion, shall we say?"

He made the suggestion with a shoving motion of his body.

Jan hit the table with his hand. "You are making me sick! That child—just a child!"

"Yes, Tal," Høg said. "That is pretty disgusting. Stop it and get out the cards."

And so they had faced the task of whiling away another meaningless evening, had drunk too much, scuffled a little, caroused a little. They had even softened toward Jan, and he had had some drinks with them. Finally, hours after regulations required them to be asleep, they had draped themselves in a stupor on their bunks, leaving Jan, the only relatively sober one, on guard.

He had had to keep walking to stay awake. When the southernmost star of Charles's Wain, as seen when the eye was placed at a certain notch in the flambée post, touched the top of the wall of the western firing step, it was the accepted time for the change of guard. Jan had awakened Callundborg, apologizing and explaining that he knew it was not his turn, but he had drunk less than the others; he could get even some other night. Callundborg, moaning, had crawled out and taken his place on watch on the firing step above the værn's closed-and-barred door. The light of the flaming, smoking FLAMBÉE-STOK on its holder in the courtyard was hardly needed, for the moon hung bright and high, just two days past the full.

Jan had crawled into his bunk and gone off at once to sleep, but now, at what time he had no idea, he had awakened from a dream with a familiar pleasant discomfort in his genitals and found himself thinking warmly, wide awake, of the girls in town.

He tossed, and wished for a moment that he could be transferred back to Christiansfort.

He heard a knocking at the værn door, a soft pounding as with the heel of a hand.

He heard Callundborg scramble, and it flashed across his mind that he may have sat down and gone back to sleep. Oh, what if Governor Gardelin had arranged a surprise inspection!

Jan sat up on his bunk and leaned over to see out through the open door of the wattle hut. Callundborg was climbing to the firing step, bending, looking down at the outside of the door.

"WERDÆR?" he called in the CREOLE challenge.

"KOMPNI NEGA MI' HOOT," came the reply.

Callundborg seemed satisfied with what he saw, for he walked slowly down from the firing step, muttering about the slaves bringing firewood so early in the morning.

Jan was about to lie down again, when some misgiving made him watch Callundborg remove the heavy bar and open the door.

In through the doorway came, silhouetted, a file of mountainous bearers, each with a bundle of wood on his head. All but the first of them had to hold the wood on the ends with his hands and duck to get in the door.

Well, it was no surprise inspection.

Almost subconsciously it struck Jan that these were not accustomed bearers. A true bearer never touched the load once it was balanced on his head.

The bearers did not go to the cook shed. They dawdled about the entrance, about Callundborg, who was waiting for them to pass in.

Suddenly Callundborg simply disappeared in the crush. The

bearers' right hands held cane knives that they had pulled from the bundles. The wood was tossed aside and Callundborg, unable even to grunt before he died because held vise-like about the neck, had his throat cut.

It happened so suddenly that Jan Gabriel had no chance even to be frightened. With a rolling motion he scooped up his wheel-lock and kicked the nearest bunk, Knudsen's, hard.

Knudsen merely stirred, still drunk.

Jan Gabriel began to feel the ache of fear in his arms and the back of his head. He heard bare feet outside running to Corporal Høg's cubicle and the lieutenant's vacant quarters, and others stealthily surrounding the corps-de-garde. He heard Høg startled awake, heard his muffled shout, his massive grappling with assailants.

Frantically shaking Talencam and kicking the other bunks, Jan suddenly knew that it was too late, for streaming in through the moonlit doorway to the VÆRN came countless scurrying forms. They must have hidden themselves outside among the rocks and bush during the carousing last night.

Høg was still alive. It sounded like a running fight, up the steps to the west firing port. Then, from outside the wall, came Høg's scream of anguish and horrible burble of death.

Jan had now abandoned silence, had shaken and shouted Knudsen awake. The doorway was blackened with silhouettes. Jan shot the first one in the head, hurled the empty gun into the face of the second, and dived into the darkness. A torch was coming.

Knudsen died sitting up, starting to mouth a protest. The others died lying down, in their bunks. Jan Gabriel, before the torch was brought in, rolled under Tiil's bunk in the darkest corner. He flattened himself against the wattle wall. Tiil expired with a sigh just above him, and soon his blood was dripping on the floor in front of Jan's nose, splashing in his face, congealing there in little flecks of horror.

The dawn was mixing with the moonlight now. There was more light to see by. Jan could see feet scurrying, hear the low, intense muttering of African voices.

As the light grew it was evident to the BUSSALS that the VÆRN was taken, and as they realized it the voices came up out of muttering and into chattering. Suddenly everyone was shouting at once in a Babel of African tongues, and Tiil's drum began to roar with a beat the like of which its taut skin had never known.

Outside the corps-de-garde Jan Gabriel heard one of the excited voices pausing, stammering, "Mmmaaa," and starting again like the interrupted flight of a bumblebee. "Mmmaaa—mmmaaa." It was Odolo! Odolo, the bearer, the appealing one.

Scurrying, babbling BUSSALS ransacked the bunks, the lockers, the corners. Guns, powder horns, ball bags, pistols, clothing, letters, cards—everything the garrison possessed taken, pawed-over, broken, torn.

The ransacking spread through the whole VÆRN. Odolo was outside by the powder room. Jan could hear the door to it being opened. After a while he could smell spilled powder.

The greatest excitement was about the two landward guns. Odolo's bleating voice rose to a high pitch as he asserted his authority over them.

Jan could smell the stench of too much rum. Someone was bellowing for control, but the crowd was ignoring him. It was a mob now, a looting mob. Apinda's parrot voice shrilled in exultation.

As daylight came, the big seaward cannon boomed—too loud, too strong—it had too much powder in it, but it fired. Jan Gabriel heard Apinda's happy triumphant screech. Right after that the westward cannon roared. Then the bacchanal was a true uproar, with women's yelping, squealing voices now joining in, and the sounds of the drum climbing through an incredible crescendo.

In a little while the sixteen-pound cannon belched ineffectually, improperly loaded and wadded.

No longer was anyone running in and out of the corps-de-garde to see what he could find. Miraculously, no one had thought to look under the bunks, perhaps, Jan thought, because these men were not accustomed to bunks.

Jan began to feel that he might survive. But he could never get out of here now. He would simply have to lie still and wait, wait . . .

III

JENS ANDERSEN, Suhm's MESTERKNEGT with only house slaves now to drive, was dead as soon as he stepped out of his barred door into the bright pre-dawn moonlight to see what the trouble was. A cane bill, shaped like the profile of a turkey gobbler's head and wattles, pierced his skull from behind with its beak-like point and dropped him, with scarcely a chance to moan, on his stoop.

There was no one to scream for him, or mourn him, or fall in grief upon his prostrate form. His BUSSALS, all MARONS now, did not wait for his blood to stop coursing, but took his pistol and TSCHICKE-FELL, searched out his gun and powder and ball, and went swiftly on to Dr. Bodger's house.

MESTER Bodger, his stepsons, and slaves all slept behind unbarred doors and unprotected windows. Suhm's BUSSALS, and some of the Company's, led by heavy-browed Abedo, called Haly, came here without violence. Into the slaves' quarters one part of the force moved on whispering bare feet and immobilized them all. Others lifted MESTER Bodger from his bed. Still others went to the two boys' room, silencing the children with hard hands over their mouths.

Those with Bodger led him up the road past Sødtmann's, where the candles burned in the ballroom high above the road.

"But I have not my ÉTUI," he protested, assuming that he was on an errand of mercy. They ignored him.

Those with the boys carried them out the back way and headed eastward with them, but Bodger knew nothing of this. And westward another group herded his slaves, including Christian Sost; but Bodger could not know this.

At the Company PLANTAGE buildings on the hillock that rose above the valley floor, there was no special deputy designated to do the slaughtering. It had been intended that Kanta himself would provide the leadership here at the proper time, but Kanta had in full self-confidence given himself the task of being everywhere at once, and was not here.

The three MESTERKNEGTS had been up late, celebrating the sudden unexpected return of one of them, Dennis Sullivan, from Tortola. Svend Børgesen and Jan Frederik August had put Sullivan to bed in a spare room when he reached the point in his drinking where he stopped talking about young women and started talking about his mother, and had, themselves, rolled into bed.

Their concubines, Norche and Lisette, lying awake, awaiting the pre-dawn moment for the white men's death, felt at last, with their time sense, that the moment had come and gone, and yet no assassin had scratched at any bedroom door to be let in.

Norche was a woman of spirit. Svend Børgesen knew her for this in bed, and this was what he valued in her, for in him there was a need, not to seduce, but to subdue a woman by force, and each session with her was a ritual of physical battle and subdual.

Norche's flat face had eyes like torches, and her broad body had the strength of a tigress, but Børgesen's strength always won the battle.

Norche rose, softly unlocked the door, and then started feeling for Børgesen's sword.

He stirred, rolled over, and lay heavily on the sheathed blade, an outflung arm covering the haft. Norche knew that even in sleep he would know her hands, for often had she rolled him off her as he slept, and so he let her shove him off his sword and she took it and, holding it in both hands, chopped at him with all her strength in the darkness.

He came alive, bellowing like the wounded bull he was, and threw her with a crash against the wall. She crumpled, sliding down unconscious in a heap. Børgesen, bellowing still, groped in anguish for his sword. Blinded by blood and darkness, he was leaped upon from behind by Company BUSSALS who simply broke his neck and left him there helpless to die.

Lisette, with Jan Frederik August, was too fragile and timid to do anything but keep out of the way when her master came awake with the sound of Børgesen's bawling. He rushed with his sword, flung open his door and ran into the moonlight to be overwhelmed. Cut off from the house, he ran for the cookhouse. There he got his back to the wall and stood to fight off the seething assault of BUSSALS.

A slave named Claus had found Jan August's loaded gun where he had carelessly left it, and over the heads of the sweating attackers he leveled it and did not miss. Down slumped Jan August to be chopped by cutlasses and cane bills in the dim reflected light from outside.

Terrified children began to scream inside the house or burst out and ran off sobbing and gasping.

Dennis Sullivan lay drunk upon his bed, with no concubine to stab him or keep out of his way, and his door unbarred. The BUSSALS, coming in from the bush, did not know he was there; only the house slaves knew it, and they, excepting Norche and Lisette, had taken to their heels. Norche and Lisette forgot him completely in their preoccupation with the moment.

At the instant the killing began the loyal Company slaves, in their compound at the foot of the hill, had exploded off the PLANTAGE in all directions, frightened by the murderous BUSSALS. Now they were circling wide through the BARCADS in the moonlight to pick up the roads at a safe distance and flee to PLANTAGES where they had friends and might find protection.

IV

IN Brown's Bay, the sea was the ultimate curse to the Krøyers and van Stells, living so close to it. It did not roar, for this was not a roaring beach. It slupped and seethed and flopped and splashed, so that stealthy sounds were covered entirely, and many an overt noise could be disguised.

The BUSSALS from the point above knew which few of the loyal slaves were truly loyal, and where to find them. They would not hesitate to destroy them quickly and silently if they tried to give an alarm, but they knew that they had not dared warn their masters in advance, and so did them no harm.

It was Breffu, in the company of her husband, the now-sober drunkard, Christian, who came to the door of the MESTERKNEGT Charles Hill, and knocked. When he challenged, "WERDÆR?" she said simply, "Master, come." When he came out, bearing his gun, he stared in surprise at the splendor of the returned Breffu as she towered above him. Christian, from behind, quickly crushed his skull in what amounted to utter silence in the confusion of the sounds of the sea.

It was Breffu, armed with Charles Hill's loaded musket and holding it as if she knew exactly how to use it, who waited beneath the stone-and-brick exterior stairway leading from ground level to Krøyer's bedroom—waited, along with four male BUSSALS, for the opening of the door and the beginning of the day. Other knots of BUSSALS were concealed near the two other openings to the upper house, the living quarters atop the cistern, storerooms, and dungeon.

Christian, armed with Charles Hill's pistol, circled on the blind side of Gabriel van Stell's house and waited, with another handful of BUSSALS, in the shadows near the door.

The rest of the BUSSALS of the Gabriel van Stell's Point detachment stayed in the slave quarters to prevent any warnings by loyal slaves.

Peder Krøyer awoke at dawn. He sat upright in bed, startled, and shook Marianne.

"Marni! Did I sleep through the TUTU? Did you hear it?"

Marianne stirred, and stretched deliciously. "I heard nothing," she murmured. "Perhaps we both slept through it. We did have a waltz when you came to bed, didn't we?" She yawned. "I slept like a boulder after that—didn't you?"

Krøyer seemed not to hear. He leaped out of bed and ran to the window.

"Hill!" he shouted. "Charles Hill!"

When no answer came, he dressed hurriedly, muttering, "Accursed people who cannot be counted on . . ."

He unbarred the bedroom door, snatched up his unsheathed sword from the bedside, and strode out onto the landing.

"Marni, get up and bar that door," he called over his shoulder. Marianne padded quickly across the floor in her bare feet to obey.

As Krøyer started down the steps, peering, puzzled, in all directions for the expected signs of life, the first cannon shot sounded over the hill from Frederiksværn. He stopped, listening intently, until the second shot sounded. Then he ran the rest of the way down the steps, to be confronted by Breffu, who suddenly appeared, crouching.

She held the gun low, pointed upward at his throat.

She was silent as he gasped, "Breffu!" too taken aback to lunge at her with his sword.

Her eyes gleamed in a steady gaze. Her temples throbbed visibly.

The blood drained from Krøyer's face. Then suddenly he made his lunge, in the same motion moving to dodge the muzzle of the gun. But Breffu's muscles were quick, and she moved the gun exactly with him and fired upward through the base of his tongue and his brain. His sword caught her lightly on the side near her heart before it fell clattering.

Gabriel van Stell ran, partly clothed and fully armed, from his house two hundred feet away and was shot from behind by Christian. He fell, kicking madly, and stumbled to his feet in a whirl to face his adversary. His gun went off prematurely, the bullet ricocheting with a nasty whine from the stone of his house. While he still fumbled, bleeding, to unsheathe his sword, the tide of BUSSALS swept over him, and he died a writhing mass of cane-knife cuts.

Behind the BUSSALS, Neltje van Stell, with the animal instincts of a mother, scurried from where she had come to the doorway with little Gabriel, hurtled along the wall and up the slope of the hill into which the house was built. The noise of the sea, fifty feet away, made her effectively soundless as she plunged like a diver into the deep pool of fallen wind-blown leaves that had collected between the house and the slope.

The sea, which had helped destroy the men, was Neltje's ally, for when the child whimpered she did not have to smother him, but only to whisper passionately, sternly into his ear.

The BUSSALS running up the stairway at Krøyer's found the bedroom door closed and barred. Breffu reloaded and primed the gun.

The rest of the BUSSALS came now from the slave quarters, where silence no longer needed to be enforced. The loyal slaves scurried, bent over, into the cotton fields and away from there in terror.

Before anyone could come with a ladder to bridge the PINGUIN hedge, a BUSSAL lit a FLAMBÉE-STOK and threw it in through the open window of the room where Marianne was with her baby. She threw it back without showing herself at the window.

Breffu stood with the gun at the ready, ignoring the blood that streamed from her wounded side and down her leg to the ground. Christian came lumbering to join her; he had reloaded the pistol.

A group of BUSSALS arrived with a heavy stone slung between them, and labored up the steps with it. Two others came with a ladder and placed it on the windowsill. Another ran up the ladder without bending to touch the rungs with his hands, and fell sprawling into the PINGUIN when Marianne smashed his face with a hurled stool.

The BUSSALS with the boulder started swinging it ponderously against the door. The door began to splinter, but the bars inside held.

Another FLAMBÉE-STOK went in through the window and another BUSSAL ran up the ladder as the door bars gave and the door shattered open. BUSSALS hurtled in.

Breffu walked slowly up the steps and into the room, where the BUSSALS, with no cane knives to use, held the struggling Marianne immobile, soundless in her fury and fear.

Breffu came across the room. Her eyes showed more pity than anger. She held the reloaded gun and looked away as she pulled the trigger. Marianne's wild, cascading scream was silenced by the bullet tearing through her open mouth.

Christian came up and shot the squalling baby boy, Hans,

through the temple.

Neltje van Stell, breathing in terror underneath the covering of dried leaves, felt the pains of her labor begin and moaned to God.

Pierre Castan's slaves found when the moment came that they had no taste for blood, even the blood of the white man who had cruelly misused them. Not even King Clæs's wife, Judicia, wished to carry out the assignment to kill.

When the cannons fired and the first gunshots sounded down the bay, Castan roused himself told his wife to be on watch and prepare to hide herself and the children in case of need, took up his gun and sword, and started down the rocky GUT toward the bay. Long before he came to Krøyer's house he met a fleeing loyal slave who told him that death was in charge down there, and he turned back home.

Michel Hendrichsen was too old to go out to battle. His slaves, loyal and loving all, and knowing what was happening, hid him and his wife in the bush along the rocky part of the shore. There they suffered the punctures of a thousand cactus and sucker spines, but were not found.

William Eason, roused by the cannon and gunshots, knew that they were no signals, for the signal would be three shots regularly spaced. He dressed and took his gun and went down to the Stallart PLANTAGE to question the slaves in his charge.

They told him that the BUSSALS planned to murder him. He went to his boat, unchained it, and took to the sea, leaving the old people in his home to die when it should come to that. He rowed his boat across the strait to Tortola, and never came back to his PLANTAGE or Stallart's.

V

BODGER was herded in his rumpled nightclothes along the mile of road toward the Company PLANTAGE houses in the pre-dawn moonlight by BUSSALS unknown to him.

Arrival at the PLANTAGE showed him the bloody, hacked-up body of Jan Frederik August, which had been dragged into the open moonlight and breaking dawn. Bodger was confused and horrified. Was this a summons to treat wounds suffered in a fight here? He got no answer from the stolid BUSSALS.

He tried to go to the bloody heap that was the MESTERKNEGT to see if there might be life in him yet, but the BUSSALS restrained him.

Bodger was growing angry now.

"You will not touch me again," he said to his captors.

He started once more toward August's body, but was stopped.

Now he felt the anger spewing from his eyes, and the scar across his scalp and forehead ached as it always did when his blood was up.

He shook off the BUSSALS and stared at them one at a time.

"You—will—never—touch—me—again," he repeated. He took a step and raised his hands, palms outward, fingers spread. The BUSSALS fell back, made way for him.

He bent over the gory heap that was August, and knew that he was dead.

He heard a woman's moan coming from inside the house. He hurried toward the sound but came upon a wall of BUSSALS, one of whom, he saw, was Annassa, a burly, sullen female slave who belonged to the Company. The rest he did not know.

He felt not the slightest doubt of his mastery of them.

Slowly they opened a way for him.

He led them to the room where the woman moaned. It was Norche, regaining consciousness. He ordered a FLAMBÉE-STOK brought.

He saw the slaughtered Børgesen.

He turned to Norche. She held her head and moaned, but was not desperately hurt.

"Norche, what is this?" he demanded, but she could not stop moaning.

Lisette was huddled with her, pop-eyed with fright.

"Lisette," Bodger demanded then of her, "who are these, my captors?"

"Herre Governor Suhm's BUSSALS," she replied in a small voice.

"Ah!" he said. "No wonder I knew them not. But what do they here? What do they to me?"

Lisette looked about in fear and shook her head at Bodger, for she dared not speak.

Bodger gestured to the BUSSALS and they slowly, uncertainly, withdrew from the room. Bodger closed the door.

"Now, Lisette," he said, "you see how little there is to fear. Tell me what is happening. Why are these men murdered?"

Gradually, under his probing, she told him, sketchily, but so that he could put the pieces together, that when the guns of the fort should fire, every master on the island was to die at the hands of his slaves, but the masters in Coral Bay were to be killed before the taking of the fort.

"And why am I not murdered?" he asked.

"*Ju bin de dakta*," she said simply, as if anyone would know that. "You are the doctor."

"And my sons? Are they harmed?"

"They shall be servants. They are not for harm."

"Servants to whom?"

"To Bolombo, the king."

"Ah! And where is Bolombo, King Clæs?"

"He will come when the fort is taken."

They heard a shout, in English, from another room: "Ow! Here, now! Let me be!" It was Dennis Sullivan's voice.

Bodger ran out of the room. Daylight was overpowering the moonlight.

The BUSSALS were hauling Sullivan out into the open. They looked almost as puzzled as he. Apparently, it seemed to Bodger, there had been no orders concerning Sullivan, and no one quite knew what to do with him. Even Bodger had not known that he was here.

"Here, Doctor!" he cried, catching sight of Bodger. "What be this, know ye?"

"Rebellion it be."

The boom of the first cannon sounded at the VÆRN. Then the second.

"Oh, God!" Bodger cried, covering his eyes as if to blot out the vision of the knives of death flashing all over the island.

VI

The two tremendous booms of the cannons were heard throughout the island and faintly on the eastern end of St. Thomas. The third, the ineffectual belch, was not heard beyond Coral Bay. Had it been a full-fledged boom it would have completed what would have been taken as a signal for the planters to assemble at Coral Bay and Duurloo's prepared to deal with trouble.

In the rest of the island the planters, awake and starting their day, had no idea what to make of the sounds. They would hardly be a salute to a passing ship, for two shots did not constitute a salute. If the guns were fired in anger, with no chance to make a signal, the gunners would certainly not have stopped at two, but would have fired in sets of three, in order that the firing might constitute a signal.

So the planters were puzzled, but not fully alerted. Still, in an atmosphere where anything might happen at any time, no one was at ease, and all PLANTAGES went cautiously about their work. Only slaves knew what the noise was all about, and for a while no one thought to ask them.

Even though he heard only two cannon shots, Duurloo's sugar cooker, Samba, knew the sounds for what they were, an order for him to kill every holder of slaves in the west—masters, mistresses, and children, white and black. Samba walked numbly in circles, knowing that he could not do it, would not do it if he could. In any event, here in Klein Caneel Bay there was no one worth killing. The master was away on his ship, and the mistress and all her family were on St. Thomas. The master's house was empty save for house slaves. The thought of the rest of the west end filled him with

Frederiksværn, Coral Bay St. John, Marine and Craft Museum, Krønborg Castle, Elsinør, Denmark

helpless lassitude.

Susanna Runnels heard the shots and thought, "Oh, well, the men must know what they are doing."

Her slave Quassi heard them and knew that he was now under orders to kill Susanna and her children. Instead, he went and begged permission to see her, to tell her that she was in danger. It was too early; she was not dressed, and she sent word to put him off. Her house slaves, who had come with her from St. Thomas only two days before, had no knowledge of the danger.

But Quassi was not to be put off.

"It is important," he said. The nursemaid took the message to Susanna.

Susanna sighed and pulled her dressing gown tight about her. "Let him come in."

Quassi came and stood, bowing, in the doorway.

"Missie," he said, "I have heard shots from the fort."

"Yes," she said. "I heard them too. Are they truly important?"

"Yes, Missie. Trouble I do fear."

"Tell me, Quassi," she said.

"Trouble-trouble-trouble," he could only repeat, shaking his bowed head.

Susanna took the gun and the containers of powder and ball from behind her bed and handed them to him. "Fire the alarm," she said, "if such should be."

Quassi ran outside and fired, reloaded, fired, reloaded, fired, and returned to Susanna.

Susanna was calm. "Give me the gun and ammunition and run to call the field slaves together."

While he was gone, she dressed, with the aid of her body slave, and was ready to speak to the field slaves when they came trotting like obedient children.

"You know there is trouble?" she asked when she had silenced them.

"Yes, Missie," one of them said.

"What trouble?"

No one spoke.

"What trouble?"

No one spoke.

"Go, then," Susanna said, "and work in the BARCADS as usual. And see you behave yourselves!"

"Yes, Missie."

Susanna now busied herself getting the children ready for flight, and packing up her things.

Her father heard the cannon shots too. He saw to it that his slaves were calmed and sent to work as usual, and when he heard the shots from Susannaberg he was telling Daniel to get the family together and shepherd it down to father Duurloo's PLANTAGE for safety, just in case. He told Daniel to pass on the alarm and scrambled for his horse. He rode furiously to his daughter's house. Finding everything under control, he rode on, lathering his horse, toward Coral Bay.

The gunshot alarm was passed along only desultorily, for it was taken as a nervous reaction to the booms from the distant Værn; after all, there had been only two of them heard far away.

Quassi still felt uneasy. He traced his uneasiness to fear for the safety of Missie Maria, Captain van Bewerhoudt's wife, Quassi's former mistress. He left the BARCAD and went to see Missie Maria. He found her in tears, not knowing what might have happened, and worried about her husband. She squeezed his hands with real affection and told him not to worry about her, for she had plenty of help, but to go back and help Missie Susanna. And so, having a great feeling for Missie Susanna too, he went back to Susannaberg.

When Missie Sue was ready, Quassi hoisted the five-year-old Lambrecht to his shoulders, with the child's legs about his neck and its hands clutching his hair. Then he led a mule that led a mule that led a mule, each loaded with things for Missie Sue, who rode in a two-wheeled runabout cart. A slave nursemaid herded seven-year-old Janni. The MANQUERONS rode donkeys. Whatever slaves were frightened were welcome to come along, and they did, carrying bundles on their heads; the rest, more frightened of the unknown involved in going, remained behind, leaning on their hoes, not quite sure what to do next.

Soon behind them came the heart of Bewerhoudtsberg—Maria and eight of the offspring of Jannis, shepherded by the ninth, Daniel, with his new wife Adrianna, and Harry Hawkins, along with such slaves as cared enough to be frightened, and that was nearly all of them—a silent, disconsolate column, on foot and riding animals.

In Brown's Bay, Neltje van Stell lay in anguish under a pile of loose leaves and chewed her fists until they bled.

VII

At Frederiksværn the last of the revelling mob of BUSSALS roared out through the entrance to try to spread terror to every corner of the island, and Jan Gabriel was alone in the astounding silence with six dead soldiers. He would have to leave them there unburied and somehow find a way to get to Christiansfort on St. Thomas.

Cautiously he rolled from under the bunk. His uniform had been taken, as had those of the other men, along with everything else of any value including the oars to the soldiers' boat. He would have to go in the underclothes in which he had been sleeping.

He climbed over the loose stone barricade on the off side, carrying two sticks with which to plow his way through the cactus. He emerged from the cactus riddled with thorns and plunged into the third growth bush that covered the hillside. No one could see him now.

At the shore, he scrambled over the rocks around the edge of the hill toward where the soldiers' boat was chained at the edge of the mangrove swamp, praying that no one would see him.

The boat was undisturbed, but what could he use for oars?

He found a couple of pieces of rotting board.

The boat was chained, and the key to the padlock was gone along with everything else off Høg's body. Jan Gabriel took up a rock and, daring to make the loud noise, pounded at the stem's eye until he had smashed it and released the chain.

Using one of the rotting boards as a paddle, he would be able to get across the harbor to Høg's PLANTAGE, where there was no BUSSAL activity at all that he could see. He would have to inform Høg's wife that she had been doubly widowed and borrow Høg's small sailing KANO and some clothes. The widow would have to send slaves to spread the alarm, and Lambrecht DE COONING would have to bring the refugees from the few PLANTAGES over here down to TAPPUS in his BARQUE, for Jan Gabriel dared not wait that long to leave. Word had to be carried to the governor as fast as the KANO would sail down wind.

VIII

LIEUTENANT FRØLING, on his PLANTAGE, heard the boom of the VÆRN's guns and waited for the third shot that never came. Later he learned the news from a fleeing loyal slave and, having no wish to become involved in any trouble, prepared to leave the island with his wife and go to his friends, Vessuup, Robinson, and Dooris, on Tortola if it should become advisable.

The MESTERKNEGTS in the northeast at Waterlemon Bay and Annaberg, when the first trickle of fleeing slaves reached them, simply abandoned their posts and their employers' slaves and left the island, and such slaves as were afraid took to the bush.

The little poverty-stricken planters on the East End peninsula, similarly warned, took to their boats with their families, slaves, and other possessions as hastily as they could scramble away.

Those fleeing the south side almost swamped whatever boats they could come by with their belongings, including such family slaves as they could take along. The absentee-owned PLANTAGES were deserted by their MESTERKNEGTS. KIDDLE, at Concordia, simply sailed away in his KANO; none of the Coop slaves had the energy to try to kill him as they were supposed to do, and they dully watched him leave. Pietter even helped him load his boat and saw him off.

On the road, Jannis van Bewerhoudt met no one but a group of slaves from the absentee-owned Bredahl–Thonis PLANTAGE, L'Espérance, with their BOMBA on their way to the spot where they had left off road work the previous night, for it was the turn of L'Espérance to work on the roads. These were, like all of this PLANTAGE's absentee-owned slaves, trusties. They seemed in a state of unnatural excitement, but would admit to knowing nothing at all about what might be going on.

On every PLANTAGE the captain passed in his foam-flecked gallop the slaves were going about their work in nearly normal fashion, and Jannis began to wonder if he were not making a fool of himself.

He stopped on a shoulder of Mamey Peak, from where he could look out over Coral Bay and the East End, and he could see even with his naked eye that nothing was normal.

He saw dark figures erupting out of the portal of the VÆRN, in great excitement, figures disappearing again inside, the whole scene one of turmoil. As he watched, his mind in a whirl, a large, formless group started out from the VÆRN and down the swooping Værn Hill road through the bush. With his telescoping glass, which shook annoyingly with the thudding of his heart, he thought he could tell who some of them were. A number of them wore parts of soldiers' uniforms or underwear. Other slaves were racing up the Værn Hill road to meet them.

Jannis swung his telescope to explore the whole scene, out along the arms of the bay. Everywhere, on every PLANTAGE and every donkey trail and road, he could see the marks of confusion.

Near Dr. Bodger's house was a large group of slaves apparently composed entirely of women.

Flying from the flagpole at the VÆRN was, not the Danish flag, but what appeared to be a torn piece of a soldier's uniform.

The BUSSALS descending Værn Hill joined the group of women at the bottom.

The boiling mass of black men and women was stationary, as an anthill is stationary, but crowding, milling, and clamoring.

Through his telescope van Bewerhoudt watched. Fully half of the mob now appeared to be breaking off and heading west along the road skirting the bay, led by an exceptionally tall black man who could only be Kanta, walking backward, holding a flintlock high above his head and gesticulating with his left hand.

At the intersection behind them was the clot of women. Some burst from the group and ran after the men who were leaving. Some started, hesitated, went back, and of these a few thought again, turned again, ran to catch up with the raggedly departing group.

The splinter of rebels led by Kanta was now knotted near the sea, along the Bay Road, and another clot was heading eastward toward the North Side Road to Brown's Bay and Waterlemon.

Jannis felt he must not wait any longer, even to see what would happen next. He rode back westward as fast as his poor horse could go.

The loyal slaves were not so much fleeing toward the west, where they had no ties, as away from the danger in the east. The planter refugees in the east and south simply took to the sea, with no thought of the west.

Thus it was that news of what was happening was very slow to reach Great and Little Cruz Bay Quarter at the western end of St. Jan. No one thought to tell Preacher Grønnewald at all. He heard the cannon booms, and the flintlock shots from Susannaberg and Bewerhoudtsberg and, being neither militarily nor hatefully inclined, did not guess their significance.

Lieutenant Charles heard the shots and grumpily did his duty, heaving himself onto his horse and going down to Duurloo's to see what was to be found. The few planters and MESTERKNEGTS who were dutiful enough to respond to the alarm did so unwillingly, for to them the cannon shots signified Company, and the gunshots merely echoes of that. They did not feel threatened by their slaves, who were, ninety-nine out of a hundred, loyal, spiritless, resigned, or simply content to be members of the family. What was there to fear? Let the Company and its friends worry about their own troubles.

In Brown's Bay the rebel BUSSALS did not leave. They waited for

King Clæs and his fighting men to come over the hill from Coral Bay. They spent the time rummaging happily through the belongings of the Krøyers and van Stells, drinking the rum and eating the food from the storerooms, trying on clothes, hunting for guns and ammunition, and loading themselves down with whatever took their fancy. There were brawls over some of the items, but no one was seriously hurt. Breffu, the leader until Bolombo's return, regarded the scene with sardonic eyes, barking an impatient order from time to time to control the outbreaks of ebullience or greed.

In her hiding place, Neltje van Stell was immobilized in torment. She had been forced to knock her thirsty, hungry, frightened, uncomprehending three-year-old Gabriel senseless to save his life and hers.

The aged Hendrichsens huddled, hungry, thirsty, in the cactus-riddled bush along the shore.

Up the GUT Pierre Castan sat on guard with his gun, not knowing what else to do, while his wife and children crept out of hiding to be fed by the slaves.

IX

JAN GABRIEL ran down before a maddeningly listless wind at the tiller of Høg's KANO with a couple of borrowed slaves to help him hurry it along with oars. He fretted over whether he had done right not to wait for refugees to prepare themselves to come with him.

He wore some clothes of Høg's, oversized for him, to keep the blistering sun from cooking his body.

His mind was in sickening chaos. The bloody memories of early morning; the thought that those young men, for all their silly human faults, had not deserved to die like that with all their sins upon their heads and not even an instant in which to ready themselves for their God; the realization that he himself was a living miracle at this moment; the wondering what might have happened to MESTER Bodger, Sødtmann and his daughter—all these things tore at him, washed over him like remorseless waves.

That those soldiers should have been bloodied to death by slaves was a ghastly joke, for they themselves had been no less slaves in a different way. In bondage, paid less than it cost them to exist, sucked ever deeper into debt to the Company, their white skin, with its implied advantage for advancement, was their only real badge of separation from the BUSSALS who killed them; their uniforms and guns, the true symbols of tyranny that they bore—these were the curses for which they had had to pay with their lives.

Jan Gabriel thought again of Dr. Bodger, and tried to will the KANO to move faster.

Bodger, at the Company PLANTAGE, torn between the urge to find his boys and the need to stay with Dennis Sullivan and protect him, decided to stay. Lisette had seemed so sure the boys would not be harmed. She must have known the plan, to be able to tell it so simply. He would find the boys later, somewhere.

King Clæs was the key, and Lisette knew so well that he would come when the fort was taken.

He did come, wearing one of Lieutenant Frøling's military dress jackets with the symbols of rank on shoulders and breast. It was too small for him, would not fasten across his chest, and the sleeves came only to his upper wrists, but the garment was red and symbolic of power.

His first act was to order Dennis Sullivan killed. His BUSSALS seized the Irishman as Bodger took hold of King Clæs's arm and protested.

Sullivan's squeal was loudest.

"But King!" he cried, sniveling. "You know me! I am your friend. And I can help you. I can get guns and powder and lead for you!"

Bodger turned on the Irishman and shouted, "Sullivan!"

"Ah," Sullivan whimpered, "you save yourself as best you can, and I'll do likewise."

Bodger let him plead his case with an offer to go to Tortola and bring back not only guns and ammunition, but English slaves to help fight the Danes—for, make no mistake, he said, King Clæs was going to have to fight the Danes. Sullivan was an expert in the use of the CREOLE SLAVE TALK, and he even knew a great many words in African tongues. His plea must have been persuasive, for King Clæs hesitated.

Then his distrust of white men came to the fore, and again he gave the signal for Sullivan to be killed.

Bodger would not stand and see a man killed in cold blood. "Let him go," he said. "You know him for a friend to slaves as no other Company MESTERKNEGT is."

King Clæs relented, ordered Sullivan stripped of everything he owned, including his clothes. Telling him that if he ever showed his face upon these shores again he would be killed without mercy, he sent him scurrying naked down the road to get off the island as best he could.

Bodger wasted no time.

"King Clæs," he demanded, "where are my sons?"

"They are my servants," the king replied.

"At what place?"

"At a place I have chosen."

"Where is that?"

King Clæs turned his back on Bodger and walked away.

"Bolombo," Bodger said, deliberately using the African name for its effect, "you know that I can destroy you." He did not know any CREOLE word for "destroy," but he used the English word, which he knew would sound impressive.

King Clæs turned on him with a sardonic smile. "Whatever it is you say," he said, hampered by the SLAVE-TALK tongue, "you cannot harm a king."

Bodger narrowed his blue eyes at him.

"I can cure a king; you know that very well."

"You can cure a king," Bolombo said. "That is why you are alive."

"If I can cure a king," Bodger said levelly, "you know that I can make him sick as well, and make him die."

"I am king, you are my medicine man," Bolombo said, but there was a touch of uncertainty in his deep-set eyes as he turned again to walk away.

Suddenly Bodger said to him, "Your leg is weak, is stiff, it gives you pain! Careful! You will fall!"

The BUSSALS gasped at what they saw.

The tendons at the back of Bolombo's naked right knee stood out, taut, and his right leg stiffened and almost tripped him. He seized his knee with both hands and twisted his body around to Bodger, grimacing with pain.

Bodger had known that the African who could be made to believe was astoundingly suggestible, but he had never tried such MUMBLE-DJAMBI tricks before. He could scarcely believe that this had worked so well.

He was quick to follow up his momentary advantage. "Bring my sons to me, or take me to them."

"No," Bolombo said, "you have not made me sick."

"Your men," Bodger said, "can see you in your pain."

He turned away again, and Bodger overextended himself.

"You will not be able to walk!" he said.

Bolombo motioned to his BUSSALS to follow him, and led them down the road, heading for Brown's Bay and the north side. The women followed, and only Bodger still stood there. Bolombo limped heavily at first, but as he went, the cramp worked itself out of his leg and he walked properly.

He stopped and called back to Dr. Bodger, "You are free. Go or come or stay. You will never be harmed in this land."

Down the road the rebels went, and Bodger stood and watched them go, feeling empty and confused and filled with grief.

X

IN the far north of St. Jan all was still serene.

Seigneur Moth's new MESTERKNEGT at newly purchased Frederiksdal was a stranger to the island. No one had told him he had anything to fear, and no one warned him now that the booms from far away had any meaning for him.

Under the looming heights of Mary Point, young Didrik van Stell, living alone with his slaves, trying to develop his share of his father's PLANTAGE while his wife and children stayed in town, heard the distant sounds of the cannons. Being the new Civil Guard officer for Maho Bay Quarter, he felt duty-bound to report to Lieutenant Charles at Duurloo's PLANTAGE according to the latest general instructions to the Civil Guard, even though he had heard only two cannon shots. He did so, for there might have been a third shot that he did not hear at this distance. His slaves, who were supposed to kill him, went to work instead.

Didrik's brother, Lieven, on the other half of their father's PLANTAGE, was ill with West Indies fever. His wife and child and two stepchildren were with him. His slaves heard the booming order to kill, and ignored it.

The widow Jansen of Caneel Bay, the Cinnamon Bay of the north, feeling old now, had retired to town on St. Thomas for a comfortable old age. The slaves she had left with her sons were without exception loving old family slaves, many of them born and raised in Cinnamon Bay. They knew what the guns in the VÆRN were saying, and after keeping quiet until now, told their young masters that it might mean trouble. Everyone in the bay, master, mistress, or slave, got busy putting up a barricade for defense if it should become necessary, with boats ready at their backs in case the defense should fail.

There was no one else on the north shore but slaves, as far west as Klein Caneel, Duurloo's PLANTAGE, and even there only a couple of mulatto MESTERKNEGTS besides the slaves.

Jannis van Bewerhoudt reached Duurloo's on a near-spent horse soon after his and Susanna's households had arrived. Didrik van Stell was there, and Lieutenant Charles, along with a sprinkling of MESTERKNEGTS who had heeded the uncertain summons. Pietter Duurloo was away on a charter to 'STATIUS.

No one knew what should be done, for until Jannis arrived no one really knew what the danger was. Jannis destroyed the uncertain calm with his news of what he had seen.

Quickly he organized a troop to go with him to Coral Bay to reconnoiter. John Charles was to remain at Duurloo's; refugee women and children might keep coming and would have to be attended to, and male refugees would have to be pinned together into a fighting force if it should come to that.

Jannis took a fresh horse and the six white men available to him besides The Old Englishman, put the twenty-one extra guns available into the hands of twenty-one slaves of known loyalty. He put horses and mules under his men, doubling them up on the stronger mounts, and walked them up to Konge Vej. At Susannaberg, Bewerhoudtsberg, Adrian, Hammer, he acquired mounts for them all.

Then they galloped toward Coral Bay.

Bodger, left alone and disoriented with the bloody dead at the Company PLANTAGE, finally told himself to go home for his medicine bag and instruments, without which he felt lost. With them in his hands he could think what he should do next.

The sun was high enough to make him sweat as he walked. Far ahead of him down the valley King Clæs was gathering followers as he headed his procession toward the north side road.

Bodger saw the procession pause at Sødtmann's, where suddenly there was a burst of excitement; he could not tell what it was all about. As he drew near, the uproar became a din, and he saw Juni parading up and down in front of his audience with a bloody human head stuck up on a pole, which he jounced jubilantly up and down. It was Reimo Sødtmann's head.

Juni, in his triumph, was permitted to lead the procession for a little way, waving his trophy in the air, but before the dancing, howling mass reached Suhm's and the road to Brown's Bay, he was forced to fall back, give way to the majesty of the king. Under the GRIGRI tree Bolombo commanded the women to stop and wait, and sent a detachment of men back up VÆRN Hill to occupy the fortification.

Bodger pushed himself down the road to his house. More than

ever, he needed the stabilizing effect of having the tools of his trade in his hands.

He could not bear for long the depressing emptiness of his place and wondering where his sons and slaves might be. Before leaving, he remembered to dress himself in daytime clothing.

Back up the road to Sødtmann's he went, for now he felt that he had the strength to go inside and see if there might be anything he could do, to see—he knew in his heart that this was what drove him—whether Lena Hissing were present or absent, alive or dead, injured or miraculously whole.

He found the table, with Reimo's headless body, Helena's gored form with stiffened, gaping face, heaped upon it, and the room awash with their drying blood, with bare footprints and marks of sliding feet and knees and elbows in it.

He could no longer be anything but numb, and without any feeling but that someone ought to clean up the mess and see to the burials, he lumbered like a drunken ape out into the open sunshine.

There Jannis van Bewerhoudt and his posse found him.

When Jannis came from Sødtmann's house he was weeping. "Forgive me," he said illogically to Bodger. "I have never seen anything like this. I am not accustomed. . . ."

He put slaves to work, hurriedly scooping out shallow graves. Then, after speaking a few awkward words over each grave, he hastily collected his men and headed back toward Duurloo's, for Bodger had told him that two forces had headed west, one by the south and one by the north, with a third going toward East End.

At first Bodger would not go with him to Duurloo's. He wanted to find his sons.

"Nelli, come," Jannis said gently but urgently. "The best way to find the boys is to come with us. These savages have not a chance against us. We shall have all but the killers themselves back to work in a few days."

"How do you think that?" Bodger asked dully.

"They have shown themselves to be stupid. They had a good plan. They could have killed us all, every white man on the island, once they had the fort. When they fired the signal, they could have ambushed every last one of us on the roads as we came to report for duty."

Peder Sørensen, a member of the posse, interrupted bitterly: "Ha! They could not, for almost none of the Whites would have answered the signal, even if it had been unmistakable! Cowards, craven cowards they are!"

Jannis paused, tilted his head in half-agreement, then continued: "Anyhow, they could have ambushed all of the leaders, who would have responded and who did respond, and that would have placed the island at their mercy."

"I suppose so," Sørensen said angrily, "for you may be sure that the MESTERKNEGTS would mostly have deserted, as they have now done, and the women and children would have been easy prey. Only the small planters without MESTERKNEGTS would have been left to deal with, and since they have proved that they would not have sense enough to combine forces, they would have been easy to destroy one at a time, if they could have been prevented from leaving the island with their families."

"Yes," Jannis said, "and it would have been easy for intelligent rebels to break holes in all of the small boats in all of the bays at the given signal, so that no one might leave the island. The point is Bodger, I tell you we are dealing with a stupid rabble. They did not have the brains to work together, they do not know how to work together, but only how to dance and sing together when it suits their fancy—and so we shall destroy them!"

"And destroying them," Bodger said dully, "will of course solve everything. Things are never quite so simple as that, my friend."

"So what would you have us do?" Jannis cried. "Submit like cowards? We must kill the few leaders, and that will be the end of it. Our slaves are not rebels at heart—Negroes as a people are not rebels at heart."

"Nonsense," Bodger said quietly. "Turtle-doves are rebels at heart if you push them far enough. And killing will not be the end of it. Nothing bad ever gets better before it gets worse."

He did not know, at this dazed point, what to do but go with Jannis after all.

On the western wing of Coral Bay, Kanta and his little horde arrived at Lambrecht's anchorage of Ullik Burk's BARQUE in time to cut it off from the refugees. Mme. Høg was forced to jettison most of what she planned to take with her to town, including her slaves, and run wailing on her fat legs, with her children, to Martin Porter's BARQUE, taking pot luck with Porter and Lambrecht, who were getting out as fast as they could, with their barest belongings.

Thus, from Coral Bay to Rendezvous Bay there was no quarry for the BUSSALS, but only some paltry loot, which kept them longer than any quarry would have done.

XI

IN Brown's Bay, King Clæs's swelling force came over the saddle of the hill, with the drums of Frederik and Ginadi roaring in triumph.

The Hendrichsen home was found completely deserted, with little loot worth pawing over.

At Krøyer's, King Clæs found the Brown's Bay BUSSALS waiting. His force took the time to see the dead and complete the looting of the houses. Some BUSSALS had more than they could carry, and others picked up what these dropped.

Now they clambered up the GUT toward Castan's. Castan heard them in plenty of time and once more hid the weeping Elisabeth, who wished to know what had happened to her sister Marianne in the bay below. The slave women, Sara and Judicia, tucked Elisabeth and her children in among the cotton bales. The problem was to keep three-year-old Agethe and eight-month-old Jacob quiet.

Castan hid out in the cotton piece below the house. He hoped to decoy the marauders away from the hiding place and keep running ahead of them under cover, leading them away. The plants were higher than his head as he ran, crouching, and would serve as fair concealment.

Reefbay waterfall, *F. von Scholten, 1833*, Marine and Craft Museum, Krønborg Castle, Elsinør, Denmark

As the BUSSALS came up the GUT Castan fired at them, wounding one and reloading as quickly as he could. They paused, but then went on, for they were more interested in the house than in the cotton field.

Castan changed his vantage point and fired again. This time, when the BUSSALS paused, Bolombo sent three of his men to rout out the gunner. Castan, with no time to reload, had to take to his heels. He dodged from row to row, and up and down the BARCAD, thrashing about, decoying here, there, until the pursuers left him and went after Bolombo toward the house.

Castan never got off another shot, for in his haste he fell sprawling and broke the flash-pan off his gun against a stone. Moaning in despair, he tried to recapture the attention of the BUSSALS, but they ignored him and went on.

At the house, Judicia welcomed her husband, Bolombo, and went and stood by his side as Breffu turned away with slanting eyes. Bolombo ordered the place sacked while he told Judicia briefly what had happened that day.

Sara showed the BUSSALS where her mistress was hidden, and they pulled the cotton bales away and stabbed her to death. Agethe came at them, bawling and clawing like a tiger kitten, and they broke her head and threw her, quivering against the wall. One of them took up the baby and swung him by the heels as he squalled, then exploded his head against a stone pillar.

When the place had been sufficiently ransacked, Castan's two ox-like male slaves went along as Bolombo's slaves to carry loot. The female slaves who had not taken to the bush were permitted to follow the procession, also bearing loot.

Breffu, her eyes flashing fire, was obliged to give her gun and ammunition to a male, for fighting was not woman's work—it was reserved for privileged males.

When they had gone, the roar of their drums reverberating among the hills, hard-of-hearing Pierre Castan came in from the far cotton piece to take his wife and children out of hiding.

The rebels were not quite beyond earshot of the Krøyer place when the time came for Neltje to scream uncontrollably and give birth to her second child, a girl, who died with her mother before she even learned to breathe, chopped to twitching pieces by the cane-bills of the returning, panting rebels. Neltje had time and strength to roll protectively on top of her small son, Gabriel, who had regained consciousness. Smothering, too terrified to do more than moan, he somehow went unnoticed in the grunting confusion.

At Stallart's few slaves had vitality enough left to be caught up in the excitement of the occasion and of the drums and go along with Bolombo, armed with cane knives. One, Jacky, was not old enough to have lost his verve. Born on St. Jan, but taken at birth to St. Thomas to be raised in the slave-children compound, he was high-spirited and somewhat troublesome and, as punishment, was now newly returned to St. Jan to live and work with the slack-jawed, spiritless elder slaves. Any excitement was welcome to this lonely boy, and the noisy sweep of the rebels held irresistible glamor.

At Water Bay, Frøling hailed the fleeing Johan Minnebeck's boat and left the island with his wife and his few slaves.

At Waterlemon Bay, Bolombo paused. Here, where escape to the out-islands of the English would be possible in case of disaster, he would set up his royal establishment. Here Bodger's stepsons, Hans and Peter Minnebeck, in their nightclothes, waited uneasily under guard; in time they would be put to work as servants to the king and queen.

Bolombo sent a detachment of bearer slaves to Gabriel van Stell's Point above Brown's Bay to move his headquarters from there to Waterlemon Bay. He ordered all loot stored in the Water-lemon Bay warehouse and set a guard over it. He took over the MESTERKNEGT's hastily deserted house for himself and Judicia and installed her there, ordering all female followers, including the magnificent Breffu, to remain with her. Then he proceeded west-ward with his male followers and all of their bearer slaves.

A few of the Waterlemon Bay slaves were swept into the caval-cade, either as fighters or as bearers and servants, and at Annaberg a few more.

At Mary Point a slave of the sick Lieven van Stell met Bolombo outside the house and demanded, "WA WIL JU HEH?"

"We come to kill your master."

"But that was for me to do."

"It was."

"And so I have done it."

"Let us see the blood."

The slave let them look in the door of Lieven's bedroom. There in Lieven's bed in the semi-darkened room lay Lieven, ill, but not too ill to hold his breath in the welter of red bush juices his slaves had poured over his head, neck, and pillow.

Lieven's slaves showed the BUSSALS that there was nothing on this meager place to loot, and went along with the mob as it headed for Frederiksdal, but filtered themselves out and went back to bring Lieven's wife and children in from the bush where they had hidden them. Then they carried Lieven to a boat they had been preparing in Francis Bay with Lieven's most important belongings packed into it—there had not been time enough to get away ahead of the rebels.

It was Lieven's slaves, who had found out from the BUSSALS the whole story of Coral Bay and Brown's Bay, who reached St. Thomas island with the first news of the rebellion and its early results. Being the word of slaves, it was taken as an exaggeration; no one believed the VÆRN was taken or the soldiers dead, but only that a few BUSSAL MARONS had gone on a rampage in St. Jan's northeast and done some damage.

At Frederiksdal, Herre Moth's unsuspecting new MESTERKNEGT was dead of overwhelming assault by the time Bolombo reached there, for Moth's slaves were afraid, at the last moment, not to have carried out Bolombo's orders when he arrived.

Hours after silence descended on Brown's Bay, a Tortola slave fishing boat answered Castan's frantic yells and came into the bay to take him aboard, along with a grimy, sobbing little Gabriel van

Stell III. Aged Michel Hendrichsen and his wife crept out of the tangle along the far shore and begged to be taken off the island; their slaves remained behind, able to manage for themselves.

XII

CANEEL BAY was ready behind its little shoreside barricade of handmade mahogany furniture, a stove-in small boat hauled up for repair, with a downed silk-cotton tree for a central stay and body.

When the BUSSALS came, Jani Jansen and his younger brother, Lieven, with their slaves, put up a rousing fight. Jani's wife and baby were placed offshore, lying sweltering in the bottom of a boat.

The BUSSALS knew how to make satisfying noise with guns but by and large not how to shoot them properly, so none of the Jansens or their slaves was seriously wounded; a couple of them were nicked. The BUSSALS, leaping like crickets, were hard to hit squarely, but three of them died and several were hurt by the calm firing from behind the barricade.

Some of the Jansen slaves were actually Aminas, and the Aminas in King Clæs's force knew them, shouted at them, calling them traitors, only to receive from them the whine of lead in reply.

But King Clæs's swarming BUSSALS were too numerous, too wild for the small Jansen force. In the end, with slaves Thomas and Francis, who knew how to shoot, covering them, the Jansens and their house slaves got away in their boat, followed in the other boat by the rest of the slaves. Thomas and Francis, backing into the sea, keeping off the attackers to the very last, miraculously were not hurt.

It was noon, and the rebels were hot, tired, hungry, and thirsty, and Caneel, Cinnamon Bay was a good place to refresh themselves. There was plenty of food to be found, plenty of rum, and water for those whose thirst was too deep for rum alone. And there was looting to be done, with two houses, a sugar mill, and a rum distillery at hand.

King Clæs, aware of his royal role as general, was too canny now to be drunk. He had no idea where the next enemy might be. While his forces looted and caroused, or slept in the shade, he sent runners through all the bush paths that were known to them, to spot any surviving white or black masters and report their whereabouts to him. Within two hours he knew that Pietter Duurloo's PLANTAGE, which he had never seen, was where he had to go.

By now most of the BUSSALS, besides carrying quantities of loot, were at least partly clothed. They wore garments or pieces of garments gathered here and there, not for comfort, but for color, status, and the symbolic effect of wearing the clothes of the bested master or mistress. Mistresses' clothing was more popular with most of the BUSSALS than masters', for it tended to be more colorful and voluminous. If this had been a parade instead of a tide of vengeance and death, the masters and mistresses, artisan slaves and house slaves would have been watching, howling with delight at the sight and sounds of them.

Everywhere the BUSSALS passed, a few slaves were sucked along by the excitement and boldness of this effort, as bits of steel are drawn to follow a magnet, but most slaves either ran in fear when the rebels demanded their allegiance and help, or hid themselves away before the demands could be made.

It was past two o'clock in the afternoon by the sun pin on the cotton gin before the rebels started out again to the westward along St. Jan's north shore, with the great prize of Duurloo's Klein Caneel Bay ahead.

There was no road along the northwest shore, from Mme. Jansen's PLANTAGE to Duurloo's and Little Cruz Bay. All roads from the bays went up the GUTS to Konge Vej, but there were bush paths along the shore and over the low ridges from bay to bay. Through these paths the rebels made their way. They had with them some local slaves who were as willing to be enslaved by Africans as by Europeans and might, they thought, some day be better off this way.

On the East End peninsula Prince Aquashi, brooding over the assigned task of leading a force over the fiercely steep and rocky hills for almost no rewards at all, took his men to the bitter, cactus-studded end of the land. Nowhere did he find anything truly worth carrying away, for this was, of all the island, the poorest part.

And nowhere did he find anyone to kill. The little subsistence planters, with their families and few slaves, had left the island without looking back twice. Their possessions were so meager that it was easy to put them all in the family boats.

On the road along the south, Kanta and his ragtag mob found the pickings little better. The planters and MESTERKNEGTS, what few there were in residence, all got away, warned in plenty of time by fleeing loyal slaves, taking along everything that could be put in a boat and was worth carrying. Kanta's men soon bogged down in pawing over the leavings, and most of them forgot all about the rebellion. They ended up at Lieven Kierwing's shaded PLANTAGE, which was by now their home, and there they lay down and went to sleep, for they were tired, and drunk, and swamped by anticlimax.

With them they had Dr. Bodger's Christian Sost as their medicine man. He alone was sober, and he sat in the shade looking at the spent, puerile rabble, shaking his head, and watching over the only motherless child, little January.

Kanta and four of his more dedicated lieutenants had not been satisfied to be drunk and oblivious. They had gone on over the hills to the north side, hoping to find better pickings and some white men to kill.

The western end of the island, restless, uncertain after the two inexplicable booms from the east, finally began receiving news in garbled, varied form. Then came slave messengers from Duurloo's Bay with word from Lieutenant Charles of the story Captain van Bewerhoudt had to tell after returning from Coral Bay. Then the frenzy was on.

The first that Little Cruz Bay heard of the horror was when families from the hills to the east began arriving on the beach, begging Francis Gonsel to take them to St. Thomas.

Peder Sørensen had brought his Dina and her children down to Gonsel and demanded that he get them safely to town, since he,

Sørensen, had to report for duty with the Civil Guard.

Gonsel's fishing boat and Jannca Girard's, both small, were the only boats in the bay at that time. Gonsel was taken aback as more and more refugees crowded onto the beach and clamored at him. He sent for Jannca Girard, and the two of them conferred on what should be done.

The KILL-DEVIL Widows threw everything out of joint by arriving, in donkey carts, leading a caravan of carts and mules heaped with possessions hastily collected. With them they brought every last one of their non-field slaves, whom they proposed to keep with them whatever might happen; their field slaves they left to subsist on the PLANTAGES as best they might.

The widows, bearing parasols, furled them and started belaboring everyone within reach who might be able to carry out their peremptory orders to get them, their slaves, and other possessions off this island at once.

It was finally decided that, since it was impossible for Gonsel and Girard to transport everyone to St. Thomas in their two small boats quickly enough to satisfy anyone but the first boatloads, all would be taken as rapidly as possible out to Meeren Cay, outside the harbor, for temporary safety.

When the two boats were brought up to the beach, the two widows, wielding their parasols and their commanding voices, managed to beat off all competition and get their belongings and a few of their slaves loaded first.

The boats, using sails and oars to go out to the cay, and oars to come back, made three hasty, heavily laden trips before the widows were satisfied to go themselves and let others go. They had won their point: their slaves and other possessions were more important than those of anyone else. Their neighbors began fully to understand how the tax assessors and collectors managed to let themselves be browbeaten by these two women year after year.

XIII

IN mid-afternoon, at the moment when Bolombo paused on the ridge above Duurloo's Klein Caneel Bay to survey the prospects there, Jan Gabriel at long last, cursing the fitful November breeze, slid Høg's KANO in to the Company dock at TAPPUS and leapt ashore to run to the fort on legs that felt too weak to carry him.

Brusquely he pushed aside the protocol at the fort entrance and ran straight to the rooms of Governor Gardelin. He rushed past the governor's guard, who knew him, and burst in to find Gardelin looking startled and fingering his sword.

"Pardon, Excellency," he panted, "but I must tell you—Frederiksværn is overrun by rebel slaves, and all there but me are murdered. The slaves have gone on, I daresay to take the rest of the island."

The blood deserted Gardelin's face, and he sat down heavily in his chair.

"Then it is true," he whispered.

He slid from his chair to his knees beside the desk and prayed aloud for the mercy of God. Jan Gabriel stood weeping for the enormity of the news he brought.

In a few moments Gardelin resumed his chair. His desk vibrated with the pounding of his fists.

Jan Gabriel still stood at attention; his tears dripped from his cheeks and chin.

"My sons and their families," Gardelin asked, "what of them?"

"I know not, Excellency, but I fear . . ."

Gardelin shouted for the guard and sent soldiers scurrying for the other members of the Secret Council, Chief Merchant-and-Accountant Horn and Secretary-Treasurer-and-Magistrate SCHØNNE-MANN.

The little towns beside the bay, already buzzing with the rumors started by Lieven van Stell's slaves, now were beginning to feel the shock waves begun by Jan Gabriel's arrival. The sounds reached Herre Frederik Moth, titular head of the Civil Guard and the true power figure of the islands, at his manor house up the slope from the fort. He buckled on his sword and strode down the hill to join the Secret Council, uninvited.

He found Gardelin on his knees again.

"Get up, man!" he cried in anger. "The time for groveling is past. It's time for action!"

Gardelin stayed on his knees, looked up, and quavered, "Very well to shout for action. What would you have me do? We are faced with the wrath of God Himself!"

"First let us deal with my wrath," Moth said. "Get up, man, and tell me what you know of the facts."

While Gardelin calmed himself, Moth extracted from Jan Gabriel every word of information he could supply, and sent for Lieven van Stell's heroic slaves.

The slaves came and lay on the floor in the face of Moth's thundering demands.

Now they were believed. Judge Sødtmann was dead, and Helena his daughter and all of the MESTERKNEGTS in Coral Bay but one. MESTER Bodger was spared, but his sons were taken. All of Brown's Bay, babies, women, men, were either murdered or had disappeared, and the rebels were attacking everywhere, murdering and looting.

Moth turned to Gardelin. "You can see that you cannot abandon the interests of these the children of your government to the barbarity of their infidel slaves."

"But it is *God!*" Gardelin cried. "Do you not see that God is punishing us for our sins? Who are we to struggle against the Almighty Himself?"

"You, sir, are in the position of responsibility. If you do not act, you are responsible for anything that may happen."

"But what do you wish me to do? You know very well the impossibility of getting any cooperation from any planter! If you have in mind counter-measures, proceed with them. I give you my

Carolina Plantation, Coral Bay, St. John, *F. von Scholten, 1833*, Marine and Craft Museum, Krønborg Castle, Elsinør, Denmark

permission!"

"You," Moth said coldly, "will do your duty, I am sure."

"But what is my duty? What would you have me do?"

"I would have you pull yourself together," Moth said, as the rest of the Secret Council and some leading planters who happened to be in town crowded into the sweaty room. "I would have you send a force of men and destroy the thieving, murdering black bastards."

Jan Gabriel was possibly the only one present who noticed that the word "thieving" came first in Moth's fury.

The planters shouted at Gardelin in Dutch.

"Now," Moth said, "order the alarm fired, to summon the Civil Guard."

Gardelin bowed stiffly, and sent orders to the gun crew. The triple roar of the cannons went out over the island.

Gradually Gardelin was getting hold of himself and spoke in the LINGUA FRANCA of the planters.

"You will see," he said, hoarsely at first, "that no one but the poor and the FREE NEGROES will respond to that alarm. But you are here, you are part of the Civil Guard, and here is your captain"pointing a waggling finger in the direction of Moth "and where is the action you demand of me? You talk of leadership, but you are mostly pigs who will not be led. Because you have to pay taxes to a government
. . ."

He was interrupted by a roar, some of it mirthless laughter, some of it rage, and the words "Government! Hah! Tyranny! Thieving, self-serving business organization!"

". . . a government," Gardelin went on when he could, "that has to maintain armed forces and forts to protect you—I say protect you—no, not merely the Company and its warehouses—No! Listen to me! . . . protect you and your PLANTAGES, and maintain for you a harbor for ships to bring and take trade for your life blood, provide you with . . ."

He gave up trying to outshout them, and waited, like a tired bull, with lowered head, for them to finish berating him.

When the room was silent again except for the murmur of private conversation, he repeated: "You will see that there will be no proper response to the alarm, and the reason is that, because of your hatred of the Company, we are disunited, and until you decide that we are all human beings together, I can be of no help to you. If any of you has lost as much as I on St. Jan today. . .'." His voice broke. "I have lost both of my sons and most of their children. If any of you is able to feel deprived, perhaps you have some suggestions as to what should be done in the face of your determination to be of no assistance to this government. And when God has finished punishing you for your sins by raising your slaves against you as He is punishing St. Jan, I trust you will remember the names you called me today."

The planters who were able to hear him muttered and squirmed, and Moth said, "Enough of this, gentlemen. We have trouble to face. I suggest that the governor send the garrison of this fort to St. Jan to destroy the rebel bastards, and man this fort with the Civil Guard."

"Good," Gardelin said. "Sir, you have the power, perhaps, to find your Civil Guard wherever it is that it hides when it is needed. If you will do that, the garrison of this fort is on its way to St. Jan."

XIV

To Pietter Duurloo's PLANTAGE on St. Jan, planters were coming in with their wives and children and their most trustworthy slaves. Some unsupervised slaves were running in ahead of the rebels with tales of terror on their tongues.

Jannis van Bewerhoudt was back now, in charge.

He placed his wife, Maria, and all of their children and his but Daniel, who was old enough to stay and fight, his daughter, Susanna Runnels, and her children, in Duurloo's fishing boat. There was barely room left for the fishermen who would row it, but he crammed in John Charles's wife, Rachel. Fortunately, the sea was calm.

He and John Charles sent the boat off after affectionate and tearful goodbyes, to St. Thomas island across the sound, with orders for the boat to return as soon as possible.

The only other water transportation left, with trusted slaves to man it, was Tim Turner's rowboat; all others were off on sundry errands. The refugee women, children, and old men were under-foot, and there simply was not time to ferry them, few by few, to St. Thomas.

Jannis ordered MESTER Bodger to have them all, slave and free, white and black, rowed out to the largest of the Duurloo cays outside the bay, where they would be safe until they could be transported to St. Thomas.

Before complying, Bodger wrote a note to be sent to Gardelin. There were obviously going to be more people wounded by guns before this was over, and Bodger was not properly equipped to deal with gunshot wounds. He most urgently requested a probe, forceps, and any other like instruments that could be found for him.

Meanwhile, Jannis was setting up a defense based upon the two small cannons that he was now proud to have insisted upon installing here.

Duurloo's house, although unpretentious and a long step down from Magistrate Sødtmann's in Coral Bay, was the second best of the eighteen houses on St. Jan that were ever used by their owners. It was adequate to his and his family's needs, since they had a better one on the St. Thomas PLANTAGE and customarily came "up to the country," St. Jan, only for vacations and to escape the sultry heat of the hurricane season in the interior of St. Thomas.

Constructed like nearly all of the better houses on St. Jan, the one at Klein Caneel Bay was of wood on a high stone foundation that continued up to chair rail height on the superstructure. Unlike most, it was roofed with Dutch tiles.

All around the superstructure ran a brick paved, stone walled terrace enclosing also the open cookhouse and the household storehouse and tool shed. On this terrace were now collected piles of ball, grape, and chain, scrounged from every PLANTAGE within miles, with kegs of powder handy to each pile.

The two cannons, for four-pound ball, could be rolled on their wheels into position to cover any approach to the terrace.

The outlook to the west and slightly south was straight down the PLANTAGE road through cotton fields to the sugar works on a knoll a thousand English feet away, and the shipping storehouse on the beach another two hundred yards beyond.

To the northwest the view sloped gently down and across the flat land through cotton to the sea, disturbed only by two up-jutting clusters of huge boulders a hundred and fifty and two hundred yards away. The passages among the nearest group of towering boulders, providing privacy from any direction and, being down-wind from the house in normal weather, served as a privy for the lowly and an emptying place for the chamber pots of the master class.

Northeastward the land continued upward above the Hawksnest Point road, planted with cotton for a hundred yards or so, and then the bush began as the land rose steeply to the crest of the ridge.

To the east and south the vista was across rolling pastureland and up the sugar-terraced flanks of surrounding hills.

Thus the home terrace was well situated for defense, except for the nearness of the bush and ridge crest to the north; but bush does not provide good cover against cannons, and the ridge top would be useless as a protected firing step for muskets because of the thickness of the bush. For this reason Jannis resisted the temptation to set slaves to a hurried job of clearing the ridge.

The only other cover was provided by the privy boulders a hundred and fifty yards away, and the other pile of rocks a little farther down.

Everything else in all directions from the terrace that could obstruct the line of fire or serve as cover was torn down and burned, and the cotton stalks for several hundred yards all around were cut, stacked, and burned.

Captain van Bewerhoudt and Lieutenant Charles were well enough satisfied with the defense. As an afterthought they added clusters of huge hogsheads filled with sand hurriedly transported from the beach by slaves. Now the musketeers might sometimes fire standing up instead of always crouched behind the low stone wall.

"Well, Lieutenant," Captain van Bewerhoudt said to John Charles, "I have heard much—from you—of your prowess as a cannoneer. The guns are yours!"

The Old Englishman rose to the stimulus and shook out his creaking joints.

"See you give me two good men to serve me on each cannon," he said with the gleam of battle in his eyes, "and I'll shoot the bleary things 'til hell itself rise over the ridge!"

Before three o'clock the island's interior, and its fringes too, except for the Duurloo PLANTAGE, had been almost fully evacuated of its master class and its most trusted and essential slaves. Duurloo's was as ready for the coming assault as it would ever be.

Forty-and-a-few planters and MESTERKNEGTS stood ready, armed with flintlocks and wheel-locks. They were supported by some twenty-five trusty slaves bearing firearms, and an uncounted number of other slaves for whom there were no weapons available but cane knives and other tools of the field.

The house, storehouse, and cookhouse bulged with them, and there was a good deal of milling about to find food, which few had thought to bring along. Slaves were dispatched in all directions in a hasty effort to stockpile food.

Samba, who had not carried out his orders, was there, facing outward from his master's house, holding a gun. Quassi, too, was there, armed, uncertain, wishing he were on some other island, anywhere with no choices to be made.

Cornelius Bodger had busied himself with helping the women and children, and the male MANQUERONS, out to the largest of the cays off Hawksnest Point. He was seeing to it that they were supplied with food, water, wraps, and other comforts in case they should have to spend the night there. There were sick and hysterical among them, and he was so preoccupied with his mission that he had no time to think of what was happening elsewhere.

Cesar Singal was with the women on the cay because, hunchbacked, he was considered useless. He made himself as useful as he must, keeping his own counsel when he could. He was here and not with the rebels not because of any particular preference for the white man, but because he had assessed the situation and decided in advance that the BUSSALS were making a stupid overestimate of their brains and power and would be ground into the dust in the end.

That his woman, Martje, did not agree with him, had chosen to stay with the rebels as a camp follower, infuriated him. She was the only woman, white or black, who was not afraid of him. Even in his anger, he missed her more than he would have been able to say.

He was old and could perhaps afford to die with the rebels. Still, Bodger observed, the old man everywhere, with far less to lose than the prodigal young, calls precious the little time that is left to him, whatever sort of slave he may be.

Over the high hill to the southwest knelt another old man, the preacher, Grønnewald, the only white man on the island besides MESTER Bodger who was not afraid for himself. He had been told by now what was going on, but he did not believe it was irreversible. He had been begged to flee and save himself, but he preferred to remain, in case he could be helpful in his own way. He had sent his slaves down to Little Cruz Bay to try to get off the island.

The preacher prayed to God for the rebelling Africans and the souls of the Whites they had killed. He prayed for light. What might he do to stop the killing, and how might he best begin to try?

XV

The St. Thomas Civil Guard, as Gardelin had predicted, did not report in strength to the fort. Most of the planters who should have responded to the alarm preferred to remain on their PLANTAGES, fearing their slaves might get the word from St. Jan and themselves rebel. The planters who did come, bearing arms, found themselves excluded from the fort and told to assemble under the sea grape trees on the water side.

Without exception, they had relatives, friends, or possessions on St. Jan and came, not to fight the rebels, but to demand that the Company do so. Gardelin was afraid that if they were permitted in any numbers within the fort, they would try to take possession of not only it but the Company warehouses and other installations nearby.

Even Moth had to concede that this fear was not ill-founded. He called the noisy group of malcontents together under the sea grape trees and tried to reason with them. He explained that if they wished their St. Jan interests protected they must enlist their services and their arms and go there and fight the rebels, for the Company obviously had not the manpower both to man the fort on St. Thomas and to fight the planters' battles on St. Jan. His audience barely listened, spat angrily upon the ground in reply, and went home.

Through the late afternoon hours Gardelin and a somewhat chastened Moth tried to raise a substitute, trustworthy garrison for the fort. Finally, they had to ask Captain Holm, of DRONNING ANNA SOPHIA, in the harbor, for a detachment from his crew. In order to get what they wanted, they requested more than they expected; they asked him to send his men to St. Jan to round up the rebels. His polite reply was that he could not do that, since his men were not familiar with the island or the slaves, but he might possibly send a detachment ashore to man the fort while the garrison went to St. Jan. This was precisely what Gardelin and Moth wished him to do. In addition, they induced him to move his ship in close, to act as an auxiliary to the fort. This was safe enough for the sea was calm in the nearly unruffled November air.

Gardelin and Moth sent posses out over the island to bring in the key men of the Civil Guard, under arrest if necessary. And Gardelin, keeping from his mind the horror that had immobilized him, fired off written orders in all directions, with Moth as consultant.

At Duurloo's the lookout on the ridge came in to report the approach of apparent rebels along the north shore.

King Clæs led his loot-laden horde up the bush path from Hawksnest Bay and paused where it came out of the bush a little way up the road from Duurloo's house.

The defenders spotted him and, because he darted back out of sight, knew that he was no friend, and leapt to the ready.

King Clæs now knew that the reports of his runners were true. His orders had not been carried out. The white man in the west was very much alive. King Clæs had now to decide what to do.

The sensible thing would be to surround the bay and starve it out; but he would need hundreds of men for that, and he had at present only eighty-odd, including those he had enslaved to act as bearers, servants, and procurers of food and other necessities. Kanta's and Aquashi's forces, if they could be added to his, would perhaps double that number.

His warriors were not to be held with talk of a siege, in any case. They had shed, by now, so much of the white man's blood that they were as drunk with the thought of it as they were with his good rum.

All of King Clæs's warriors and some of his slaves had guns, some forty in all, and the rest were very proficient with knives and bills if they could get to close quarters.

King Clæs decided to attack.

The rebels left their loot on the Hawksnest side of the ridge, but kept their clothing for purposes of morale. Some wore into battle their masters' formal dress—a once-powdered wig, askew, a dress sash altered by sweat and dirt, with cane knife in place of sword, women's finery hanging in wild disarray on long, shining male flanks.

The warriors approached Duurloo's at its nearest point to the bush. The sweating bearers of lead and powder were commanded to be always closely available to the warriors.

Captain van Bewerhoudt knew that this onslaught could take the island completely if it were pushed straight through, with the warriors in the front willing to die for the success of those in the rear. The defenders could not reload fast enough to stem the tide, and could be overrun, put to rout, cornered one by one, and killed. But when the charge began, it was undisciplined, uncertain, and met a fusillade of fire that killed one of the noble warriors, Suhm's Aqua, and wounded several others. The assault broke and wavered; Bolombo found himself leading empty air, and ran in a curving, dodging course back into the bush, leaving Aqua lying lifeless in the road.

As it dawned on the defenders that the first assault had been repulsed so easily, a shout of joy went up.

Bolombo had to train his men while offering them in battle, shouting at them, threatening them. He found that they were willing to stand behind trees in the bush and fire from cover at any head or part of a body that showed itself at Duurloo's.

John Charles had the answer to this. His two small cannons, loaded with grape and fired alternately, tore at the bush with a thousand teeth and sent the warriors scampering, many of them bleeding.

Changing tactics, Bolombo's men popped out from the cover of the slope and fired, leaping again for safety. They had not yet learned how to use the guns for anything but noise, and their hasty, jerky efforts did no harm at all.

Now down the cane road from Konge Vej came Kanta and his four lieutenants to join the force behind the ridge.

Samba stood behind the hogsheads and fired his gun at the rebels, and suddenly wished he were on the other side. He did not wish to be here among Whites. It was not his fault that he had been unable to kill the planters in the west. Somehow he had to find a way to get away from here and go with the rebels.

He fired as rapidly as he could, raising his sights and wasting as much ammunition as possible. The white men, noticing his vigorous activity, glanced at each other and nodded approvingly.

Quassi was less sure what he wanted. He was confused. What he really wanted was for things to be as they had been, with Quassi beloved by the white mistress for his gentleness with the children and his kindness to all, and with freedom to go where he wished in his off time, to visit slave compounds anywhere and enjoy himself in the company of Africans he admired. It had not seemed too much like slavery, really.

But this, standing with the white man's gun in his hands, was slavery and worse, and he wanted to be away from here. Still he fired his gun because he did not wish to be caught not firing it.

When Preacher Grønnewald, over the hill from Duurloo's, heard the croomp of the little cannons and the crackle of musket fire, he got up off his knees and started walking toward the sounds. If only he could talk to the rebels, he was certain that he could somehow persuade them to stop murdering and look at God.

He descended into the GUT and crossed its rocky bed. He slowed down to hoist himself along the steep, winding path out of the GUT and up to Konge Vej. Turning east, he walked the twisting half-mile to where the Hawksnest Point cane road plunged off to the left. He paused to survey the scene a mile below, from the vantage point of a boulder.

He could see the mass of men at Duurloo's and, opposing them, figures darting out from the cover of the slope of the hill to fire at the house and running back in again to reload.

He started the thudding walk down the steep, switchbacked road toward them. His legs were old, and he fell often, hurrying; but he kept getting up and stumbling on.

When he reached the stretch of road that was no longer so steep but sloped gently down to Duurloo's, the rebels saw him coming, limping badly, calling out feebly, "Stop! Listen to me!"

The defenders at Duurloo's saw him too, and started yelling, "Go around, go far around and come in from the south!"—but he kept going toward the rebels, who stopped in their cover and silently watched him come.

The warriors from the eastern part of the island had never seen or heard of this man; he was white, and that was all. One of them raised his gun to shoot, but found his arm tugged by one of the bearers, who said, "That is a good man."

"There is no good white man."

"MESTER Bodger is a good white man. You let him live."

Other BUSSALS who knew this old man joined with the first in defending him. King Clæs and his noblemen listened in silence to the conversation as Grønnewald stumbled toward them and fell, exhausted.

The old man could not get up. Something was wrong with his legs. He lay for a few moments, panting, and then started to crawl toward the rebels.

The defenders at Duurloo's could see him plainly, but could not see the rebels, who were off the road. They fell silent, and watched in fascination as they saw him crawl out of their sight.

Grønnewald came close to King Clæs and his warriors, who looked down at him in silence.

"My children," he said, gasping for breath, "I speak for your Father, the Father of your spirits, the Father of all men." He was using the CREOLE tongue. "I love you. The Father on high, Father of all men, loves you so much that He gave His son to die for you. I can show you the way to peace, and happiness, and everlasting life in a Paradise to which all good men go!"

Somehow he tried too hard, failed to use the imagery with which he could unfailingly fascinate a slave when not so desperately moved as now.

He tried to stand, to gain dignity, but his legs gave way and he fell again.

"Cotje!" he cried to the simple, bumbling great son of Santje, now a bearer for King Clæs. "You know me, your mother knew me on St. Thomas. You know I love you and would not tell you wrong. Cotompa! Philipo! You know me. Beg these men to listen to me."

Cotje said to him gently, "Go, Master, go!" He pointed toward Duurloo's. He came to help the preacher to his feet.

King Clæs rushed up and knocked Cotje sprawling.

Grønnewald fell again and King Clæs bawled at him where he lay: "Die, you! Die!"

"Go, Master!" other slaves began urging the old man, and at last, convinced, he struggled up and turned toward Duurloo's, stumbling, crawling, bleeding from cuts.

The argument over him continued among the rebels, and when he had gone a hundred feet down the road toward Duurloo's, King Clæs shot him.

Grønnewald crawled a little more, then stopped, coughed up a bright fountain of blood that glinted in the sunlight, and died.

From Duurloo's came a fusillade of angry fire, but it merely rattled through the bush over the rebels' heads or zoinged in ricochet from rocks.

Some of the BUSSALS began making a crude cross out of two sticks lashed together with a piece of cloth. When King Clæs objected, they told him they did not dare fail to pay respect to the white man's god when they had killed his son, for fear of what might happen to them. King Clæs had to admit that he saw the sense in this, and his fellow noblemen agreed.

It was Cotompa who yelled, in the Amina tongue, to the defenders at Duurloo's, told them what he proposed to do, asked them not to shoot. Those who understood told Captain van Bewerhoudt what Cotompa said, and the captain agreed to hold his fire.

Cotompa, not wholly trusting the white man, ran out, zigzagging wildly across the line of fire, carrying his crude cross. He sprawled in the dirt beside the preacher's body and stuck the cross into the earth beside his head. The earth was too hard to receive it, and he propped it upright against Grønnewald's shoulder, using a stone to steady it. Then, without attracting a single shot, he ran back, zigzagging again, to cover.

"God!" Jannis van Bewerhoudt exclaimed grudgingly. "That is a brave BUSSAL."

Now a call in the Adampe tongue came from Duurloo's for King Clæs to permit the body to be picked up and buried, and King Clæs, looking at the unburied body of Aqua lying farther down the road, said yes; but Jannis van Bewerhoudt was lacking in faith, and would not permit anyone to take the risk.

XVI

AT Christiansfort, confusion, utter and complete; recriminations and counter-recriminations; advice received, advice accepted, advice thrown back in the adviser's teeth; hatred spoken, fear unspoken; bedlam, disorder, discord filled the afternoon.

Yet by evening, somehow, Rosetti's BARQUE, *The Sweet Tooth,* was almost ready to sail for St. Jan. *EENDRAGTEN* was off Great St. James, in full sight of St. Jan, its crew, unconcerned, picking coral to transport to town to be burned for mortar. Gardelin, who now had word of the refugees on Meeren Cay outside Little Cruz Bay, sent out orders to watch for *EENDRAGTEN* at St. Thomas's East End and send her to rescue them.

The Sweet Tooth had aboard sixteen apprehensive soldiers from Christiansfort, accustomed to nothing more dangerous than guard duty and the firing of salutes, led by Sergeant Øttingen, who saw at last a chance to regain a lieutenancy lost in a drunken moment; fifteen FREE NEGROES armed with guns; and a supply of ammunition, powder, and food for the soldiers and FREE NEGROES only. *The Sweet Tooth* was going to Coral Bay to retake the VÆRN.

The posse sent out by Gardelin had brought in William Barnds, an Anglophile Dane married to a Tortola Englishwoman. Barnds had a boat, was a vigorous member of the St. Thomas Civil Guard, and was known to be a man of direct action. Although he owned a large part of the huge valley behind and above Rif's Bay, St. Jan, he flatly refused to serve in this situation unless an armed guard were posted on his St. Thomas PLANTAGE day and night.

Gardelin commandeered eight men from ships in the harbor and put them to various guard duties.

He then commandeered Barnds's BARQUE, *The St. Jan.*

Also brought in under violent protest was Johan Jacob Creutzer, ship chandler and planter, who owned land on St. Jan. Creutzer was generally called unfeeling, but was no such thing; when affronted or thwarted in any way, he felt and displayed genuine rage.

Beetle-browed and barrel-chested, he shook Gardelin's solid desk with his hamlike fist.

"You—can—not—do this to me!" he shouted, showing almost all of his splendid teeth in his grimace. "Why, I can buy and sell you seventy-seven times over!"

Barnds was on hand at this moment to receive his orders, and his comment now was a mild "Harrumph." He had already spent his anger. He waited half-humorously for Gardelin's reaction to Creutzer's fury.

Gardelin glanced at Moth, who stood by, nodding almost imperceptibly.

"I believe I can do this to you," Gardelin said slowly. "Indeed, I can do even more, if you press me."

As Creutzer's wide mouth started to spit out more rage, it was Barnds who spoke sharply: "Namely?"

"I am empowered by His Majesty"—Gardelin glanced again at Moth, who nodded still—"to impound everything you own, here and on St. Jan, including your PLANTAGES, your boats, your slaves— your ship-chandler business, Herre Creutzer—everything but your wives and children—if need be for the common weal."

Both Creutzer and Barnds stared, incredulous, at Moth, who continued to nod his white-wigged head. Creutzer emitted a wheeze and thudded across to stare silently out at the harbor.

Barnds was placed in command of the ships of the expeditionary force that was to be sent to recapture Frederiksværn at Coral Bay, with orders to press into service any and all vessels he could find for the relief of St. Jan. This was a grandiose order that gave Gardelin, as supreme commander, a great deal of satisfaction; but even the forceful William Barnds was realistic enough to know that he had not the means of carrying it out, and he pressed no vessel at all into service.

Creutzer was ordered to take command of the Civil Guard and loyal slave forces to be sent from St. Thomas. The two men were to raise at least one BARQUE-load of fighters and transport them to Coral Bay. If they could not get planters or MESTERKNEGTS for this duty, they were to get deputies in the form of trusty slaves, and arm them, all at the expense of the planters whose deputies they were.

Not one planter would go to St. Jan as a guardsman or contribute a MESTERKNEGT or slave for the purpose. Gardelin refrained from exercising his power of impoundment lest he have two rebellions on his hands at once; he could never deal with the united wrath of the planters.

Time was wasting, so the Company, noting and storing up its grievances against the recalcitrant planters, had to contribute more of its own trusty slaves.

Skipper Jacob Seys was in harbor. Gardelin chartered his BARQUE *GEORG DE TWEEDE* by hasty verbal agreement and had it loaded with trusted Company slaves under arms and sent off into the night for Duurloo's. After delivering his passengers, the skipper was to cruise the waters between St. Jan and St. Thomas, watching for rebels who might try to carry the rebellion across the sound to the mother island. Skipper Jacob recognized this last order for the hysterical measure that it was, since any slaves who had boats with which to cross the sound could do so in darkness with an entire flotilla of BARQUES cruising on watch. The skipper was glad to be chartered for such safe and uncomplicated duty, and said nothing; he simply sailed on the fitful west wind that had now set in.

At The Bitch, Meeren Cay, outside Little Cruz Bay, the refugee women, children, MANQUERONS, and house slaves were unable to attract the attention of any distant sail. They demanded that Francis Gonsel and Jannca Girard ferry them a few at a time to the east end of St. Thomas, four-and-some miles away, in their little fishing boats. Of course the first trip transported The KILL-DEVIL Widows and as many of their chattels, human and otherwise, as could safely be carried.

When the boats returned for the second trip, the remaining refugees simply sank them by trying all to get aboard at the same time. A few of the more hysterical refugees drowned, but most made shore and tried to dry themselves as the afternoon sun began to fail.

On Duurloo's Cay the hysteria was under control, for MESTER Bodger was there. Two slave children from Duurloo's PLANTAGE were twitching and thrashing in delirium from identical fevers. Bodger could only bleed them and give them the only febrifuge he had—powdered Guinea pepper—which he reduced with sweetened water.

Elisabeth Delicat was undulating in convulsions that made her froth at the mouth, and Bodger, after bleeding her, coaxed down her, little by little, a draught of sugar water containing ten drops of vile tasting oil of amber as an antispasmodic, to calm her and reduce the hysteria she was causing in some of the other women.

At Duurloo's PLANTAGE house the sporadic forays by rebels from behind the shoulder of the hill continued all afternoon. A rebel was occasionally killed or wounded, but no one at the house was damaged by the rebels' disoriented firing.

When a letter from Jannis to Gardelin arrived by runner from St. Thomas's East End, bringing information as to what was happening, the decision was made at the last moment to send *The Sweet Tooth* as well as The St. Jan to the relief of Duurloo's and put off the recapture of the VÆRN.

The breeze was from the west, bringing the two BARQUES an unexpected fair wind for their sail. Before midnight they were finally off.

At Duurloo's the waning moon was up and bright, a blessed light by which the defenders might see movement on the field of battle. The desultory firing gradually died away in the night as the rebels fell asleep.

PART FOUR

A Writing of Worms

I

THIS rebellion was a prism with a thousand facets. Each person viewing it saw a different facet and was partially blinded by the reflection from it.

In one way it was almost uniform in its effect: with few exceptions it transformed men and women who had previously been inclined to compassion into bitter haters, capable of cruelties that would normally have appalled them. Jannis van Bewerhoudt was no longer a laughing man, but a relentless, glowering goad. In Governor Gardelin the venom of vengeance flowed under pressure from self-appointed advisers and ebbed when he felt fit to take his own counsel.

The Sweet Tooth, The St. Jan, and GEORG DE TWEEDE, on their way to Duurloo's, had not yet arrived when the dawn of Tuesday, the second day of the rebellion, came.

As the morning overpowered the light of the waning moon, the rebels resumed their pot-shooting at the defenders of Duurloo's house. During the night some of them had circled to take over the sugar mill, unopposed by the loyal slaves who were lodged there, armed only with cane knives. From here they could shoot over the brow of the knoll; but the range from this cover was too great, and they wasted all of their shots.

Others had hidden themselves much nearer the house among the two stinking groups of rocks that served as privies, but their shots from here were ineffective too. John Charles's accurate replies with four-pound cannonballs notched the edges of the brittle rocks and threw stone splinters ricocheting among the ordure. All this, added to the stink, made surviving snipers wish they were still safe with King Clæs over the brow of Hawksnest Ridge.

The three BARQUES, sailing into the bay in the broad morning light, put an end to this assault upon Duurloo's. Barnds's six cannons

aboard *The St. Jan,* responding to signals from Captain van Bewerhoudt, blasted terror into the rebels in the sugar mill and sent them
streaming for the hills. The group among the privy rocks, now
virtually surrounded, ran for the bush too, losing some blood to
John Charles's murderous grape.

After forcing the retreat of the rebels' main force from Hawksnest Ridge, the BARQUES landed their soldiers and FREE NEGRO
JÆGERS, supported by the loyal Company slaves, all armed with
muskets.

Creutzer's first words ashore were to Jannis van Bewerhoudt,
who came to meet him with relief and gratitude.

"Prepare your forces for inspection," he ordered without preamble.

Jannis's face flattened. After a moment's hesitation he said, "I
have already completed my inspection."

"I speak," Creutzer said sharply, "of an official inspection. I am
in command here."

"By whose authority?" Jannis demanded.

"By the authority of the governor of the Danish West Indies."

"I, sir," Jannis said stiffly, "am the governor of this Danish West
Indie, and you stand in my jurisdiction."

"Come, man," Creutzer barked impatiently. "Enough of such
nonsense. I have much to accomplish, and my time is limited."

In this manner Creutzer assumed command of all forces on St.
Jan, with Mingo Tamarin, under him, responsible for his FREE
NEGRO Corps and all loyal slaves pressed into service, and Sgt.
Øttingen for the military.

Vigorous to the point of riding roughshod, these three ignored
the nearly apoplectic Jannis. As John Charles pointed out, they had
enough to do being jealous of each other's authority and vigor
without bothering about the prerogatives of still another commandant.

The rebels were scattered in the bush behind the hills.

The defenders of Duurloo's were in a sorry state. The Old
Englishman was crumpled, impatiently conscious of his age. Only

Captain van Bewerhoudt, who had decided to bide his time, was still striding about trying to pump some spirit into his men. Some of them were sick with simple fear. None had slept. All were hungry and thirsty, for no one had been able to get together enough food for so many men, and the rebels had shot the water hogsheads full of holes. The night had been spent in a turmoil of fear, recriminations, and speculations.

The hero among the defenders was Samba. He was the only wounded one. He had exposed himself too freely and had been shot clean through the neck muscles. He sat bandaged with a bloodied rag and was treated with respect by all, affection by some. Now he would be taken to St. Thomas and, recuperating on Duurloo's St. Thomas PLANTAGE, could forget for a while about this miserable mess in which he had been entrapped.

The body of Preacher Grønnewald was brought in and buried in the coconut grove behind the bay, where the digging was easy. So was Aqua buried, for fear of plague if he were left to rot. Water casks indoors, not damaged by the rebels, were filled by bearer slaves bringing water from the sugar mill cistern behind the distant knoll; and Quassi, sent with a large group of bearers, simply faded away and in the confusion was not at first missed.

Before midday *The Sweet Tooth* and *The St. Jan* were unloaded and ready to sail. They took aboard Samba and the sick from the defenders' compound, but would not bother with Bodger's charges on "the women's cay" except the few "white" ones of whatever skin color.

At the last moment, in a fit of anger at the high-handed actions of Creutzer, Jannis van Bewerhoudt went aboard *The St. Jan*. He meant to have it out with Gardelin, this matter of command of the civil and military forces on St. Jan.

The ships headed back for TAPPUS against the fitful west wind.

Bodger came in to the bay and commandeered as much food for his charges as he could lay his hands on without committing mayhem, but before he could return to the cays he was stopped by John Charles and told that he would be relieved by Cesar Singal.

Now that only slaves remained on the cays, Cesar was, Charles said, perfectly capable of caring for them in spite of his infirmities, and Bodger might be needed ashore. Bodger sent the boat back with supplies and a message to Cesar.

While Creutzer blustered off to inspect the slaves who waited about in the sugar mill, Bodger set out to find his stepsons. When he called for his horse, Lieutenant Charles demanded: "Where go you?"

"I go to seek my sons."

"I forbid it!"

"Oh, come, now!"

"I forbid you to expose yourself alone to those heathens, and I cannot spare a force of men to accompany you. They are all needed to chase the rebel bastards when the number one force tires. When this campaign is done, the rebels will be finished and your sons found."

Bodger sighed. "John Charles, you know you cannot stop me without putting me in irons. You know no one will harm me. You know there are no rebel bastards, but only people trying for no good reason to kill each other—this does not concern me unless someone is hurt. Are you putting me in irons or not?"

Charles sighed wearily. "Of course not—albeit I shall probably end in irons myself for failing to do so. But I plead with you not to go out alone. I know how you must feel, but it is best to depend upon the concerted effort and join in it. Your sons, alive or dead, will be no more alive or dead in such case."

"Thank you for your concern, but I will not join in any force of any kind. I simply do not believe in the ultimate wisdom of the use of force, even against force. I will find my sons in my own way."

Charles shook his massive head. "I am not equipped to understand your meaning. Go, then, and take your consequences, and I pray God to help you."

"Thank you," Bodger said.

On this second day of rebellion, Skipper Jacob took up his patrol duty with a reach along the West End toward the point beyond Little

Cruz Bay.

It was not long before he noted the unusual appearance of Meeren Cay. From a distance it looked like a massive sore aboil with maggots at the nearer end.

The boil of maggots turned out to be people virtually climbing upon each other trying to attract Skipper Jacob's attention.

The refugees had spent an angry, hungry, thirsty, and apprehensive night. *EENDRAGTEN* had never been intercepted, her skipper had never received the order to pick up the fugitives.

Skipper Jacob loaded them on board and returned to St. Thomas. With Meeren Gay finally evacuated, the parts of the West End of St. Jan that related to Little Cruz Bay were cleared of every person who wished to leave. The planters or MESTERKNEGTS of the plantations to the east of Little Cruz Bay along the southwest and south, all warned of danger by loyal slaves, had salvaged themselves and their more privileged slaves in their own boats.

St. Janians scattered themselves over the island of St. Thomas among relatives and friends, and overtaxed the capacity of the six villages beside TAPPUS harbor. Most of them were dependent on others for their food and drink, as well as shelter, and resentment against the refugees soon boiled over.

As Bodger rode away from Duurloo's he asked himself what his plan was. He had no idea where to begin looking for his sons. The only rebel encampment he had ever visited was high up at the top of Vessuup's PLANTAGE. He could go there first, working out from there after questioning anyone he found.

Yet the force that attacked Duurloo's had not come down the mountain on the visible road, but apparently by the bush trail along the north shore, and had evidently scattered in that general direction when fired on by the ships.

He would start along the shore.

He had barely crossed the ridge and headed down the bush path into Hawksnest Bay when he began to see plenty of evidence of the rebels—discarded minor loot, disturbed ground and foliage, and blood on the path. He followed the trail of blood until, after a couple of miles, it gradually stopped.

Nowhere was there a living human being visible, but from above Trunk Bay he heard the drum announcing his presence—although he could not read the sounds, he knew what they meant; they were passed into a distance beyond his hearing, and as he advanced, the nearest vantage point above announced his progress.

He followed the signs of rebellion all along the north shore. Trunk Bay was empty and silent. In Caneel Bay the signatures of the Jansens' resistance and the rebels' looting were scrawled everywhere, underlined by the three dead rebels whom no one had buried. Vessuup's lower PLANTAGE, and Moth's newly purchased Frederiksdal, where its MESTERKNEGT lay slaughtered, drawing flies, birds, and crabs; Annaberg, perched high above the road—all were silent, but with eyes, eyes, and eyes surely watching.

He approached Waterlemon Bay. The rebel coming to meet him was Asari. Bodger was astonished to find him here.

"Asari!" he cried, actually glad to see him.

"MESTER Bodger," Asari said composedly. "We were expecting you."

"I know," Bodger said. "Where is King Clæs?"

"It is well you have come. Bolombo has need of you."

Bodger noted the correction.

"Come, please," Asari said.

He led the way into the main house.

There on the floor in the hallway, where the slight breeze could reach him, lay Bolombo on a KABÆN. Chanting over him were two medicine men, Asa and Kompa, both Company KAMINA slaves known by Bodger to be witch doctors, who were forbidden by law to practice their craft. They fingered their crude amulets and charms while Breffu and Bolombo's wife, Judicia, kept the air stirring and the insects away with leafy GENIP branches.

Bolombo was dreadfully wounded, moaning rhythmically, with three gaping holes in his body, congealed blood wrinkling with each rapid breath.

Bodger's first impulse, which he stifled, was to rush to him, brushing aside the witch doctors who glowered when they saw him.

He believed deeply in the power of the witch doctor if the sick one had faith.

The medicine men wore no masks, but Asa had smeared red earth on his face to signify that in his present role he was not Asa, but a being possessing the power to heal.

Bodger was startled to note that Kompa wore on his head a shredded piece of white cloth in an apparent attempt to create the effect of straight white hair. He wondered whether it could possibly be intended as an impersonation of him, MESTER Bodger.

Bodger did not flicker so much as an eyelash or speak a word of question.

He turned away, and Asari gave him precisely the opening he was hoping for: "MESTER, please help him."

Unfortunately, Asari spoke in Danish, but Bodger made the best of it and replied in SLAVE TALK: "I am not needed here. Asa and Kompa make good medicine."

He did not even glance at the witch doctors' faces to see the effect of what he said. Asa and Kompa increased the intensity of their chanting; they sounded like water gurgling into a quiet pool in a cave—it was an impressive sound, accompanied by rhythmic motions, shaking of fringe-decorated batons, and a muted drumming from Thoma in a corner.

Bodger signaled to Asari with his eyes and went outside. Asari followed.

"Truly," Bodger said, "I am not needed unless either Bolombo or the medicine men think I am needed. In that case I am badly needed, and please see that I am notified without delay. I must not interfere, but you must try to make it clear that if there are grapeshot in those holes in Bolombo's body, they must be removed, or he will die of the poisoning of them. They must be tweezed out, no matter what the pain. I am not properly equipped, but I do have tweezers of a sort. I dare not leave my ÉTUI with you. If the witch doctors be persuaded of a need for me, you must send quickly, wherever I may be."

"Yes," Asari said. "The drums can tell us where you are."

"Yes. And now—where are my sons?"

"Ah. They were here. But they spoke most earnestly to the queen and Breffu, and they set them free."

"Queen? A monarchy has been set up here?"

"Yes, MESTER. The island is to be a kingdom. Your sons were to have been the highest court retainers."

"But slaves?"

"Slaves, yes, but highly honored because of their beauty and who they are."

"I see. But they have been released. Know you where they went?"

"Back home, I believe, to Coral Bay."

"Alone?"

"Alone. They wished it so."

"Afoot?"

"Afoot, MESTER. We ride no horses as yet."

"They should not have been sent alone. They are in awful danger."

"No, MESTER. They are under constant care."

"Care? What care, if they are alone?"

"The drums, MESTER, speaking to all who may not know the children or who might wish them harm. The drums speak ahead of them wherever they go, clearing the way."

"Of course!" Bodger almost whispered. "Of course. I go, then, to Coral Bay."

"Speed and joy, MESTER," Asari said, touching his forehead politely in salute.

Bodger spurred his horse, then stopped, turned back.

"There are bodies lying unburied, all over the island. Are your people aware of the danger of these bodies?"

"No, MESTER, I believe they are not."

"They create the danger of great sickness on the island. I know not why, but I have heard that they can cause a plague that can kill you all. Are you in charge here?"

"I have assumed charge, in the absence of orders."

"Then you have an obligation to see to the burial of all bodies. I have seen several already, but I am unable to do so much digging, even if I had the tools. Of course, if you have boats, which I doubt, you can bury at sea; but remember that you must not cast the bodies into the edge of the sea."

"It shall all be done, MESTER, to the best of my ability. But you well know the difficulties. It will require force to persuade any of our people to touch the dead, particularly if they be white."

"Do what you must," Bodger said crisply. "There is no one here to protect you from these dead."

Asari lowered his eyes in the old household servant way, and bowed slightly. Bodger felt an impulse to apologize for his peremptory tone, but suppressed it because of the importance of being obeyed in this.

He spurred his horse away again without looking back.

He heard the drums on the commanding heights speaking of his presence and found himself actually saluting the familiar hilltops that were now suddenly such secret places.

At Brown's Bay he went off the road at Krøyer's estate to water the horse. At the well, inland from the house, in the shadow of the uncompleted HORSE MILL, he drew water and poured it into the masonry trough that encircled the well.

The sickening odor of putrefaction came down the gentle breeze to him. He tied his horse and forced his feet to carry him toward the house.

The carrion birds and crabs were at work, each species of bird fighting off the others between greedy pecks and gulps. The silence, accentuated by the sounds they made, and by the idle lapping of the wavelets on the nearby rubble beach, was dreadful.

Bodger rushed at the creatures and chased them away from the sprawled corpse of Peder Krøyer at the foot of the outside steps. They were reluctant to go, and the crabs sidling off took a circuitous route, not to be forced too far away. The birds too stayed nearby, glaring.

Even as he shouted furiously at the scavengers, Bodger's mind was telling him that they, more honestly than he ever had done or would do, were only carrying out their mission in life.

Other birds were upstairs. Bodger forced himself up to find

Marianne and her baby, eyeless, cheekless, maggoted, covered with ants, their pools of blood almost fully cleaned away from the floor by the hordes of ants.

Bodger retched uncontrollably and ran out, gasping for air.

He ran on wobbly legs to the tool house to find pick and shovel. He sought out the nearest soft, sandy ground and started digging, panting, sweating, weeping, finding relief in the effort.

He could not dig proper graves for all these people—he had not the strength or endurance, and he must be off to find his boys.

He managed a large but shallow hole; went, chasing away the contentious scavengers each time, and dragged what was left of Charles Hill and Peder and Marianne to the hole. He could not control or change their grotesque shapes.

He carried little Hans, wetting him with his tears, and placed him between the parents, trudged wearily to the van Stell house and found Gabriel by the wall. He had to trace Neltje and her newborn baby by the flapping of wings behind the house. He looked in vain for little Gabriel—called, shouted, hunted, and gave up.

As he heaved the loose earth into the shallow grave, he heard himself whimper and moan in his continuing horror.

II

On St. Thomas, at Tappus and Christiansfort, this Tuesday, November 24, 1733, was another day of anguish, anger, frustration, and almost total confusion. Representatives of every possible point of view, all of them selfish, pulled and screamed at Governor Gardelin.

There were four main, partially overlapping, areas of interest involved in the scuffling: the Company, which was Gardelin's primary concern; the local business interests; the St. Thomas planters; and the St. Jan planters.

The Company's job was to avoid blame and expense, and if possible to emerge from any situation with a profit.

The local businessmen, many of them also owners of PLANTAGES on St. Thomas or St. Jan, or both, were concerned with making a profit out of whatever was happening; with avoiding losses on St. Jan by making the Company pay all St. Jan costs and reimburse PLANTAGE owners for losses; and with fear that the rebellion might spread to St. Thomas, damaging their businesses, their PLANTAGES, their lives.

The St. Thomians who were St. Thomas planters and nothing else were largely preoccupied with the fear of a spreading rebellion. Refugee St. Jan planters and the families or other representatives of the beleaguered planters at Duurloo's PLANTAGE, as well as St. Thomas planters who also owned St. Jan PLANTAGES, vividly saw their whole world collapsing, their earthly goods taken away, their futures blighted, their lives endangered.

Gardelin was the only person of any stature in this whole structure who was pure Company, with no property, even slaves, of his own. Still, he was not free of confusion in his outlook, because of the people he loved and called his close relatives who were still alive. He wanted to help them, and yet he had to be even more concerned for the Company's point of view.

He saved his sanity by asking former Governor Moth to continue to stand by as adviser and mentor. Moth, as a heavy property owner, would have to take the consequences, along with everyone else, of necessary measures against the people's interests; and he would be obliged to temper any actions against the Company's interests. He was Gardelin's consummate insurance policy.

At the same time, as additional insurance, Gardelin insisted that SCHØNNEMANN and Horn, his fellow members of the Secret Council, be consulted in all decisions. Never before had he shown any need for their advice, and being consulted now was a pleasing change for them.

Almost at once, as though instinctively, each of the four decision-makers adopted the ancient "I'll-have-to-speak-to-my-partners dodge when confronted by a planter with irate demands.

Process servers were sent out with orders to all persons owning property on St. Jan to deliver to Christiansfort manpower, either white or trusted black, under arms and supplied with ammunition and provender, in numbers and amounts specified in the individual assessments carried by the process servers. Notices were published promising that any slave bringing in a rebel, dead or alive, would receive ten PIASTRES for a dead, twenty for a live one; any slave distinguishing himself in any action against the rebels to receive either his liberty or his value in cash.

For Prince Aquashi and his fellow Aquambos at their vantage point at Vessuup's PLANTAGE, this day following the beginning of the rebellion was puzzling and frustrating.

The bitter disappointment over the miserable results of their foray onto the East End peninsula the day before had made it necessary for them to get uncommonly drunk when they had come "home." This morning the taste in the mouth was more vile when they began to discuss the situation. It appeared to them that Bolombo had deliberately sent the prince and his men into that wasted day in order to reap all the benefits of the first day for himself; and Prince Aquashi called for runners to go and find out how badly he had been bilked.

Early he sent Johannes Runnels's Andre to find Bolombo and learn what he had been doing.

After the runners had left, the Aquambos heard the early morning firing at Duurloo's, John Charles's little cannons, and Prince Aquashi and his warriors took up their arms and started in that direction along Konge Vej. On the way, they looked down and saw the three ships arriving at Duurloo's and heard the ships' cannons roar. Then from high above they watched the retreat of Bolombo's forces along the north shore. They cut down the GUT from Rustenburg, ignoring the winding sugar road and plunging straight to Caneel Bay to intercept Bolombo, only to find him being carried, almost unconscious and horribly wounded. His warriors turned Prince Aquashi rudely away, refusing to talk to him of their defeat, but Aquashi could see the blood and the dejection.

He spoke to some of his men who had been caught up in the excitement of Bolombo's Coral Bay adventures and had followed him instead of their Aquambo prince. The Aquambos now split off from Bolombo's group and went with Aquashi back up the mountain. The Aminas, Kanta nursing a shoulder through which a bullet had passed clean, accompanied them.

At Mamey Peak the Aminas turned off on the Bourdeaux road to go to Kierwing's. There were no words of parting, for all these men were confused, and in doubt about the future, and wanting now only to be with their own tribal kind.

Abedo, Prince Aquashi's right-hand man, urged him to take up the attack where Bolombo had left off, but Aquashi felt that he was not strong enough. His fighting force, not counting the worn out men who had just returned to him, was less than a third of Bolombo's—he actually had had for a while more women than men in his encampment.

Café was now Aquashi's head woman; Aquashiba, a true Aquambo princess who was born on the same day of the week as he, and so had the feminine equivalent of his name, was his second woman; and there were twenty-four other women besides, and a number of children.

From the warriors newly returned to the fold Aquashi learned of Bolombo's intention to rule single-handed over the island, which was to be his personal kingdom.

Prince Aquashi could well remember that he had been Bolombo's conqueror in Africa. Furthermore, he, Prince Aquashi, was the only man on this island who could boast of actually taking part in an attack on the white man's fort at Accra. Therefore, he was the rebels' natural leader.

In Kob Flat, a shallow, fertile bowl high up between the peak behind Concordia estate and the heights of Bourdeaux's Mountain, were gathered most of the women who had wished to follow the warriors but had been turned back. They were here because there was plenty of food in the well-filled, deserted gardens of several absentee-owned PLANTAGES. With them were some of the slaves of those PLANTAGES, male and female, almost all of them trusted OLD-LINE SLAVES who had no interest in the rebellion, and who simply waited, keeping themselves fed, and carrying on with whatever work was necessary to assure a decent harvest of their masters' and mistresses' crops at the proper time. Cotton-picking time was now, and here and there some cotton was actually being picked and ginned.

When he had finished covering the mass grave in Brown's Bay, MESTER Bodger was so exhausted that he fell flat upon the ground and lay there dully until disturbed by fire-ants that found him too near their nest. Their bites brought him to his feet, stamping and slapping.

What was he to do? Must he now, because he had stopped here, stop also at every other PLANTAGE?

He simply could not. He had not the strength, physical or emotional, to stand it. And he must find his sons.

Methodically he replaced the digging tools where he had found them. He went to the well, untied his horse, and mounted. He turned the horse's head toward the steep trail over the saddle of Buscagie Hill. Making his heart stone, he resolutely refused to turn aside to visit Castan's PLANTAGE, and Hendrichsen's, hoping that there was no need for him to go there.

As he crested the saddle to the west of Buscagie Hill the day was far gone. The shadows of Bourdeaux's Mountain and the other heights lay long on the valleys, on the water of the hurricane hole below him, and on the outer reaches of huge Coral Bay.

Outside the shadow of Bourdeaux's Mountain and casting a shadow of its own on the water, a small sloop cruised slowly in the weakening wind. Bodger could tell by its long boom and short mast, and its sturdy, no-nonsense shape, that it was of Tortola construction. It was heading on a beam wind southward out of the bay.

Just inside the mountain's shadow, casting out of Groot Bay which was out of sight behind the bulk of VÆRN Hill peninsula, came what looked like Ullik Burk's little BARQUE, apparently in pursuit of the Tortola sloop. As Bodger paused to watch, the BARQUE was knocked flat by one of the capricious swooping gusts off the mountains. Bodger fancied he could see the splashing of the crew in the gentle swells. He knew that by the time he could get there, all the way around the bay, the seamen would be ashore in darkness, or dead of sharks, or drowned, for the Tortola sloop was not jibbing to come to the rescue, but was sailing on, heeling with full skirts in the gusts.

By the light of the setting sun, Bodger left it to his horse's sense to pick his jolting way down to Konge Vej at Suhm's PLANTAGE. There, in the failing light, he saw from the road the telltale signs of carrion. He encouraged the horse into a lope and rode on to his own house.

The silence was there, too; but at least there was not death. He called out hopefully for the boys. There was no reply. He searched the buildings and found no one.

In the gathering darkness there was little point in trying to go anywhere, do anything, find anyone. The moon would not be up for hours—it was halfway to its third quarter.

He could only stay, and try to rest, waiting for the dawn, and wonder where the boys might be.

After some sleep, Kanta found that the use of his left arm was partially impaired by the flesh wound in the shoulder; but although painful and annoying, the wound was not fully debilitating, and Christian Sost had taken proper care of it.

Kanta listened intently for any sound that might give a clue to how things now stood on St. Jan. He summoned the four best and most trusted runners among the true Aminas. He could not send out any of the camp's best runners, for they were all newly taken, unwilling slaves of the Aminas and might not return in spite of threats or inducements.

He chose Sødtmann's Adu, Bodil Friis's Abram, Krøyer's Accra, and Suhm's Autria, and ordered them in four different directions to learn what was happening.

Autria was back almost at once, accompanied by the Company's Comanche, the runner sent by Aquashi from the Aquambo camp. Comanche was a North American Indian purchased long ago from a skipper who was having trouble with him at sea. He was willing to be even a slave's slave in order to be a rebel.

Comanche had been dawdling all day on the fringes of Kanta's camp, afraid of being shot as an alien if he approached. Having left the Aquambo camp at dawn, he was able to tell only what Kanta already knew from Aquashi himself: that the Aquambos felt very much passed-over by events.

Before long, Sødtmann's Adu was back with Vantje from Estate L'Espérance, a deserter from the defense of Duurloo's who brought news and a gun and was a good runner.

Next to return was Abram, with a gaggle of women and their children. At Coral Bay he had found not a living soul anywhere. He had gone up to the VÆRN and found no one alive; the white men, and Atra, who had been shot in the head in the taking of the VÆRN, were stinking now, and he had hurried away. Then, because he had reason to know where they were, he had gone up the Company GUT on the side of Bourdeaux's Mountain where the spring was, and found the women.

Last of the runners to return was Accra, who had had the longest way to go and come. He brought the missing news that Vantje had not known.

Kanta's face was expressionless as he learned that Bolombo had proclaimed himself king. He made an impatient gesture.

"Who are the other noble ones in the kingdom?"

Accra, using the African names unknown to white men, indicated that Krøyer's Christian had high station because he had killed many Whites in Brown's Bay. Breffu stood as high as Bolombo's wife because she killed Krøyer. SCHØNNEMANN's Pieter, Suhm's Adamo, Moth's Don Juan, the Company's Bootsman and Asa, SCHØNNE-MANN's Christian, Runnels' Cupido—everyone who killed, captured the fort, fought well at Duurloo's was honored—Odolo, already a prince of his tribe, Apinda . . .

Kanta interrupted impatiently. "I killed. I too took the fort."

"Yes, master."

The day was far gone by now, but Kanta was impatient. He chose a retinue from among his fighters to accompany him. He armed

RACCOLTA DEL COTONE

1. Albero di Cotone   5. Negro che lo Imballa
2. Negro che lo raccoglie   6. Negro che bagna la Balla al difuori
3. Negro che lo netta   7. Barche per caricarlo
4. Negro che lo passa al Mulino per   8. Parte di una piantazione del cotone
   cavarne i Semi   9. Capanna

COTTON HARVEST
1-Cotton Tree, 2-Cotton Picking Slave, 3-Slave Cleaning the Cotton, 4-Slave Ginning the Cotton, 5-Slave Baling the Cotton, 6-Slave Wetting the Bale, 7-View of Cotton Plantation in distance, 8-Workshed. Geografia Americana, Livorno, 1763, MAPes MONDe Collection

himself and his fighters with the only guns he had, and the party prepared to go to Coral Bay.

The boy January, who had been listening intently, begged to be taken along and permitted to find MESTER Bodger and stay with him. Bodger's Goliath and Magerman, who, like January, were also now Kanta's slaves, dared to speak up too, and begged to be allowed to go and take care of MESTER Bodger, who would be needing them if he returned to Coral Bay. Kanta angrily struck all three of the suppliants, making no other reply.

He set out with his retinue along the cane road toward Konge Hill and Coral Bay.

On a shoulder of Konge Hill overlooking the whole sweep of Coral Bay, he stopped. A tiny Tortola sloop was approaching the Company dock in the inner harbor, nearly three English miles by road from where he stood.

He grunted. "Get them!" As he started off again at a lope, the sloop dropped her sails and nudged in to the dock, where two figures dressed in white waited. Before he and his party reached the bottom of Konge Hill, the sloop took the two figures aboard, pushed off from the dock, hoisted sails, limply filled its jib to turn abeam of the breeze, and was away. With a mile yet to go, Kanta and his men ran at a steady pace, breathing easily and deeply.

By the time they reached the dock, the sloop was too far off to be reached by musket fire, and Kanta ran south along the shore road parallel to the path of the sloop. He easily outran the sloop, which did not have a happy wind. He had perhaps a mile to run, to the place from which Lambrecht DE COONING had fled, leaving Ullik Burk's little BARQUE at its mooring beyond the shallows.

The sun was low now, and the shadow of the mountain lay across the shore road and out upon the water, almost to where the Tortola sloop went heading to round the point outside Groot Bay.

No one had taken Ullik Burk's BARQUE and left the island. If Kanta felt surprise at finding it still there, he did not pause to show it. He and his men found its longboat pulled up on the dirty beach where it was padlocked to a tree, and the chain was stoutly fitted into an iron eyelet set in the wood of the boat's bow.

Kanta ordered a stone brought and the tip of the forepeak smashed to free the chain. He ordered the boat hauled into the water, even lending a hand himself in his frenzy, despite his wound.

Now there were no oars and no pieces of wood to serve as oars. Kanta ordered all of his men to run to Lambrecht's house and search out the oars, which would be locked up somewhere. He stayed and held the boat as it rocked in the lapping water. The Tortola sloop was browsing along on whatever breeze it could get, and had not yet come abreast of Kanta. By the time it was abreast, Kanta felt sure he knew the three white passengers aboard it.

His men had found the oars and a good haul of rum from Lambrecht's locker, and all seven of the warriors swarmed with their guns into the boat, almost swamping it. One of them, Kob, knew something about boats. Facing forward and pushing on the oars in the island way, looking like a praying mantis, he rowed the men out to the BARQUE.

Aboard the BARQUE, Kanta took charge with authority. He had seen people sailing ships, and he knew exactly how to command as captain. His men got the sails up, but loosely and the rigging not tightly belayed. The mainsail was not properly set, but in such a mild breeze the BARQUE did not object. It moved, with Kob at the tiller, in the intended direction, but with too much sail too broadly exposed to the breeze.

The Tortola sloop had drawn away toward the point. Kanta brought the BARQUE out to the edge of the shadow of the mountain and, as Bodger was seeing from the crest of Buscagie Hill, a sudden gust from the heights knocked the ship flat on the sea before anyone could do more than gasp. The sails filled with water, and soon the top of the mast rested on the bottom of the bay. Kanta and his men splashed and coughed and managed to get handholds on the exposed parts of the BARQUE as it floated, nearly upside down.

The current, the breeze, and the choppy waves pushed the prostrate BARQUE onto the reef outside Groot Bay. Kanta and his men were able to go to work salvaging what they could. They could not swim. They pulled themselves under the water and searched, and pulled themselves up again to breathe. They found three of the guns, a bag of ball, but no rum, caught in a companionway. Everything else had gone to the bottom of the bay. All of the powder they found was ruined.

They waded ashore on the black coral tops that sometimes cut even their horny feet, and raided every PLANTAGE on the way to Coral Bay for whatever food, guns, ammunition, and powder they could find locked up. The pickings were poor.

In darkness they headed for VÆRN Hill.

When Kanta's men went hunting for oars to Ullik Burk's long-boat at Lambrecht DE COONING's PLANTAGE, four of Lambrecht's seven slaves were there, unseen. Three of the seven had joined the rebels, but the remaining four had listened to Lambrecht's parting words as he fled: "Remain here in peace. You have a good garden, and the animals. I will come for you when I can."

All four of them were BUSSALS, but did not wish to rebel. They had been slaves all their lives in Africa. Jacquo was one. Pieter and gentle, simple, frightened Susanna and their little son, Pierre, were the others. They were waiting patiently for the master to return. When Kanta's men approached, they hid, and watched as the Aminas broke into the locker and took the oars—and the master's rum.

At Duurloo's a new worry was plaguing the encampment by evening: how do you tell a loyal slave from a disloyal one by looking at him? This camp was full of black slaves, many of them armed with guns; how was one to know to which of them one could turn one's back? And all over the island there were slaves left on the PLANTAGES to shift for themselves. Most of these were surely loyal, and ought to be rescued and either put to work as fighters or bearers or servants, or sent down to St. Thomas to be put to useful work there—yet how was one to know for sure which ones were truly loyal? Also, slaves of unquestionable loyalty who were willing and smart enough ought to be found who would join the rebels as spies, and others simply to sneak around and keep an eye on the rebels without being seen or sensed by them, for obviously there could be no spy work done at all except by Negroes.

Late in the evening a lopsided moon peered over the ridge to the east to pick out the dirty sails of a Tortola sloop lazing into the bight below the sugar mill. The watch sounded the alarm, which was passed to Duurloo's master house on Hawksnest Ridge where Creutzer and Lieutenant Charles and their men were asleep inside their ring of Free Negroes and loyal slaves. They came awake at the shouts of their own sentries, and Creutzer, sword and pistol at hand, mounted the nearest horse to gallop down to the bay to investigate.

A figure in the sloop identified itself as Lieutenant Frøling, commandant of Frederiksværn at Coral Bay. Creutzer invited him ashore, a disheveled and crestfallen Dane, and with withering scorn exceeded his authority by placing him under arrest for criminal dereliction of duty. Frøling, yellow-haired even in the weak moonlight, offered no resistance or word of defense, and Creutzer barely managed to extend him the courtesy of not clapping him in irons.

Ashore with Frøling came two young boys, Bodger's sons, whom he had picked up on the dock in Coral Bay. He had ventured in to survey the situation and the two boys had sadly assured him that the place was completely deserted, with only dead bodies at the værn and the Company plantage. He had thought for a moment to take possession of the fort by himself, since he knew perfectly well how to man the guns, sending the boys on with the sloop's Tortola trusty-slave crew to summon help for him. But they had told him that there was no powder left in the værn, so he had come on down to Duurloo's.

By the time the lieutenant had finished his report, a tousle-headed John Charles had managed to join the group on the beach, and he exclaimed with some awe, "I do not fully take your Danish language, but I believe you can understand my English well enough. Are you saying to us that you came down from Tortola and landed alone in rebel territory, not knowing what you might expect?"

"Yes, Lieutenant," Frøling said modestly.

"Well, sir, that took some courage, I must say!"

"Thank you, sir."

At this point Bodger's stepsons looked at each other in the moonlight, grinning, and Peter turned to Lieutenant Charles and said, in Dutch, "Sir, will you be so kind as to tell us what you have been saying? We think we understand, but are not sure."

John Charles explained to them in Dutch what a remarkably courageous thing Lieutenant Frøling had done and had been about to do, in order to make up for his dereliction of duty.

Peter laughed. "But, sir, with Hans and me standing on the shore, how much courage would it take for him to land?"

Lieutenant Charles clapped his hands to his head. "Oh, oh, oh! How right you do be! Herre Creutzer, I leave your prisoner to such mercies as you can spare!"

He clumped back up the hill to bed, beckoning to the boys, who were still clad in their nightclothes, to come with him.

III

THE dawn of the third day of the rebellion, Wednesday, November 25, 1733, in the Danish West Indies began with the look of chocolate syrup splashed above the eastern horizon. As it grew to near-full light, it turned the whole sky a flaming red. The sea took on the color by reflection, so that the islands seemed to sit in a sea of fire. It was a sight to fill some men with fear.

Fright did indeed run through the Adampe encampment at Water-lemon Bay on St. Jan, where Bolombo lay apparently dying of his wounds; on VÆRN Hill in Coral Bay, where Kanta and his best warriors and his bearers had taken possession of the vacant VÆRN the night before; and at Vessuup's upper PLANTAGE, where Prince Aquashi still sat in indecision.

The women in Kob Flat were frightened, cut off from their men, and the camp at Kierwing's, without Kanta and the leading warriors, was fearful. The loyal slaves on PLANTAGES deserted by their masters everywhere on St. Jan were filled with unease.

All of them had seen this phenomenon before, or approximations of it, and always they had taken it as an omen of evil. It had always been easy, later, to say, "Aha! You see?" for in the life of a slave every day had in it obvious consequences of an evil omen.

At Bodger's house in Coral Bay, the doctor was stirring at first light, looking for food, realizing that he had not eaten since early the day before. In Finkil's empty kitchen he found the stinking leftovers from that last normal day that was only an incredible two days and a night gone. As sea and sky turned to flame he paused to marvel at the beauty of the sight.

Surprised to notice sounds of human life at the vÆrn, where he had seen or heard nothing the evening before, Bodger rode his horse up to see if his sons were there.

Kanta and his men saw him and without rancor let him come. They gave him food and told him that his sons had gone down last evening with Lieutenant Frøling aboard the little Tortola sloop that Kanta had tried to intercept. He sighed with relief and did not regret the wasted search. He would go back now to Duurloo's and his duties.

At Duurloo's, little opportunity was given for anyone to notice the colors of sea and sky, for Jannis van Bewerhoudt was back, armed with a diplomatically worded note to Creutzer and Mingo Tamarin. It said that in all Civil Guard actions on St. Jan, van Bewerhoudt must be regarded as commandant, and in all military operations, Sergeant Øttingen in the absence of a higher military officer. In the case of concerted action, command was to rest with van Bewerhoudt, who would consult in advance with Creutzer and, when the Free Negro Corps was involved, Mingo Tamarin.

Jannis van Bewerhoudt was preparing to lead sixty CHASSEURS white and black, in search of the rebels. He got off in good time. Creutzer went with him as goad and adviser.

Lieutenant Frøling tagged along without rank, wanting badly to retrieve at least a touch of his reputation. The crowning blow to his pride was the fact that as a soldier, even though in disgrace, he was consigned to the military contingent, and there he found himself under the command of a sergeant. Sergeant Øttingen was torn between pride and embarrassment at finding a lieutenant under his command.

John Charles remained at Duurloo's with twenty-five men armed with guns and an uncounted number of slaves armed with steel in various sharpened forms.

On St. Thomas, Jan Gabriel was judged fit for duty, but was spared being sent to St. Jan. He was placed on guard in Christiansfort. Reminiscing, he was heard to say that he was saddened by the knowledge that two slaves of whom he had been fond—Apinda, for one, and Odolo, called Abraham, for another—had been among the leaders of the massacre at the VÆRN Monday morning; he had recognized their voices as he lay hidden under his bunk.

Jannis van Bewerhoudt with his sixty men, augmented at the last minute by a half-dozen mercenaries from the British Virgin Islands, scoured the north side of St. Jan all day. He found nothing but debris.

Prince Aquashi was surprised to find the VÆRN in the hands of the Aminas when he had thought it was vacant. Kanta was not unhappy to have more men and weapons there, since he had lost most of his guns and ball, and all of his powder, in the sea. There was no powder left in the VÆRN, and Aquashi's relatively meager supply was all they had with which to defend the position in case of attack by either the white man or the forces of the wounded Bolombo, self-proclaimed king of St. Jan.

As night fell, Prince Aquashi, when he thought about it, was not sorry to have Kanta's support.

It was in the middle of this night at Duurloo's that Bodger was touched on the shoulder by one of the well-known camp slaves. Bodger was wanted in the bush. An emissary from Bolombo waited outside the outer ring of night guards.

Bodger knew at once that it had been decided that the witch

Coral Bay, St. John, *A.C.R. Carstensen*, Denmark, MAPes MONDe Collection

doctors could not save Bolombo. He was not in the least surprised that the message had penetrated to him without causing any alarm. All that was necessary was for Bolombo's emissary to imitate, say, the sound of a tree-frog and speak softly from the edge of the bush.

No KAMINA slave would hesitate to deceive the sentries in order to deliver the message; indeed, they would all be afraid not to do so. They would merely choose a slave well known to the sentries, he would think up a plausible story to get him into the house, and the message would be delivered.

Bodger thanked the messenger and got dressed. He took his medicine bag and the newly acquired instruments and went out into the night, which by now was decently lit by the late moon. The sentries knew him, and merely saluted as he passed. The messenger pointed to the edge of the bush, but dared not accompany him.

The emissary spoke at Bodger's approach. It was Apinda, called Emanuel, no BUSSAL, Bodger knew, but an ACCUSTOMED SLAVE.

"King Bolombo say come," Apinda said in SLAVE TALK, without greeting.

"Witch doctors too?" Bodger replied.

"Witch doctors too."

"You are sure? This is important."

"I am sure."

"I will come."

Apinda had brought a horse for him. It was down by the sea, in Hawksnest Bay, where it would not attract attention.

Apinda had not brought a horse for himself. Bodger offered him a ride behind him, but Apinda was embarrassed and preferred to walk and run in the accustomed fashion.

"As you will."

It was a long, slow ride in the moonlight. The bush trail was fearfully rocky where it lifted over the ridges reaching down to the sea on either side of each idyllic little bay. Daylight had come before Bodger reached Waterlemon Bay.

Bolombo was rolling his head in delirium.

Bodger greeted the two tired-eyed witch doctors, Asa and Kompa, with a deference that was not feigned.

"Think you he will die?" he asked, in SLAVE TALK. They nodded solemnly.

"Think you then that this is not a usual sickness? Think you that a bullet in a man's flesh must be taken out?"

They nodded again, emphatically; they were being consulted, and that was what counted.

"We have here the means,"—he showed them the probe and a pair of sharp-nosed forceps—"but it will hurt him terribly when we do it. Are you willing to hurt him so, in order to save his life?"

They nodded again, but he asked them if they were sure they had understood him.

"Yes, he must be hurt to save his life. We have talked of this with Asari," Kompa assured him.

Bodger began by painting the wounds with oil of anise, in an attempt to reduce the coming pain with this poor excuse for a local anesthetic, the only one he had.

"Much rum would help."

"Much rum he has already," Asa said.

"Can you give him more?"

"We can try," and they did manage to get some more down him in spite of his thrashing.

Even so, the operation was a dreadful affair. Bodger had to probe for each piece of metal in flesh so sore it was near to mortification. When the probe located metal, and a tap-tap proved it, he had to replace the probe with the bulkier forceps and drag forth the piece of metal. He did this for each hole in the flesh, with Asa and Kompa holding their king down. He screamed in his delirium and the sounds of his anguish tore at the ears of the whole encampment until he finally, blessedly, fainted.

When the job was done, Bodger washed the wounds with rum, heavily powdered them with a styptic he had made from PULVIS TORMENTILLÆ reduced with a milder carrier of BOLUS ARMENIAC. Then he bound them with some of his boiled bandages.

He was limp, and soaked with sweat.

He took a stiff drink of KILL-DEVIL, for there was no good KJELTUM left in the camp. Requesting that a pot of water be put on to boil, then cooled, he lay down to sleep for an hour.

When he awoke he removed the bandages and examined the wounds again. Bolombo was conscious now, and watched him silently with eyes partly closed.

Bodger called for the boiled water, noting that it was cool enough to use. Pouring it from some height, he rinsed away what he could of the styptic powder while Bolombo shuddered with pain but made not a sound.

Now Bolombo was moved from the wet KABÆN on which he lay to a clean, dry one, and Bodger packed the wounds with a mixture of species CONTRA-GANGRÆNAM and healing MALAGUETTE, rebound them, and gave the patient a delicious drink of thirty drops of sweet spirits of nitre in sugar water to make him feel that he was getting better while nature worked at curing him.

He sat and watched over Bolombo all day. The women brought food and drink when needed. Bolombo dozed, and whenever he came awake again, Bodger gave him another draught of the sweet spirits of nitre. Whenever Bolombo fouled his KABÆN, he was cleaned up and moved to a fresh one. Twice during the day Bodger took off the bandages, washed away the medication, replaced it with fresh, and rebound the wounds.

To promote healing, he repeatedly used his hands—sometimes wet, on Bolombo's forehead, for cooling effect, sometimes dry and warm under the back of his neck or pressed lightly against both sides of his rib cage; and softly he sang his little Danish *lykkesange,* "happy-songs," whether Bolombo were awake and listening silently or deep in unconsciousness.

He heard the distant drums from time to time, but no one translated their messages for him and he did not think to ask.

When night came and the evening grew late, he slept. The women, captained by the apparently tireless Breffu, took over his vigil and regimen, which they had learned perfectly, and sat out the night. The difference was that the songs they sang were not Danish tunes but rhythmic, nearly tuneless African chants out of some deep well of tradition.

On this same day at Duurloo's, Thursday, November 26, the recapture of the VÆRN was the chief objective, and the encampment was roused long before dawn.

The absence of MESTER Bodger was noticed at once, but no one seemed to know where he had gone. It had been planned that he would go on the expedition to treat the wounded. Another mark was placed against his name, yet no one cared to send a formal complaint to Governor Gardelin.

It was decided that, in view of the message from Gardelin offering such tempting rewards to slaves bringing in rebels, dead or alive, with no rewards offered to white men or FREE NEGROES, it should be the loyal slaves who would have the opportunity to retake the VÆRN as well as to capture as many rebels as they might encounter.

Very early in the morning, before dawn, thirty-three loyal slaves newly arrived from St. Thomas, plus such armed loyal slaves as had not been involved in the previous day's fruitless chase, were herded ahead of the Civil Guard and military Whites up to Konge Vej and along toward Coral Bay.

When both your enemy and many of your friends are black, some of the friends who look so loyally into your eyes may be spies reporting to your enemy. Thus, a full report soon somehow reached the nearest hilltop drummer, who passed it along addressed to whoever might be in the VÆRN at Coral Bay, and Kanta and Prince Aquashi and their men knew in advance every move that was made. Some of the loyal slaves could understand the drums, and they were treated to detailed descriptions of their own movements and intentions. Word was eventually passed back to the white men that there was to be no surprise attack, but the white men, although embarrassed, ignored the fears of the loyal slaves.

The white men followed the slaves at a safe distance, pointing their guns at them. With death from the front somehow preferable to death from the rear, and in view of possible rewards, the loyal slaves charged a fully alerted VÆRN, moving uphill against whatever fire Kanta and Aquashi could muster, shooting as they went, and killing and wounding some of the rebels. The rebels quickly ran out of powder and jumped over the walls to make for the bush.

One of the loyal slaves was killed, and one was wounded, to die later. Of all those who showed outstanding bravery in this assault, the only ones who ever received their freedom as promised were the two who got it naturally and completely by being killed.

The white men, who had remained out of range, climbed the hill to the VÆRN, found the bodies of the original defenders and Atra, who was killed by Jan Gabriel, thrown down the slope for the scavengers. Slaves were put to the fearful job of burying the remains of the white dead, and the white men mumbled a few words over the soldiers' graves for the good of their souls.

It was decided that it was useless to reactivate the VÆRN. It would be impossible to man it sufficiently and still have enough man-power to keep hunting and killing rebels, and so it was left vacant, but with its cannons spiked so that the rebels could never use them even if they obtained enough powder.

Rather than dig graves for mere slaves in VÆRN Hill's stubborn soil, the commanders ordered the remains of Atra and the newly killed to be burned, when someone insisted that they be disposed of to prevent plague.

IV

ON Friday, November 27, the rebellion was four days old and still essentially in a state of suspension.

At Waterlemon Bay, Bolombo was much improved, and the thanksgiving began with OBI celebrations. Bodger was not particularly interested; insofar as they were mere MUMBLE-DJAMBI and had nothing to do with healing, OBI ceremonies were a waste of time and ingenuity.

The dancing later, however, he could appreciate. Although the women were not included in it, they were permitted to chant and sway and smile and clap their hands in time with the drums. The men who were privileged to dance in public, noblemen all, tall and beautifully made in body, were so powerful in their foot and leg muscles that they seemed to levitate, expending little visible effort, reaching great heights without seeming to leap, and keeping perfect time with the beat of the drums and hands.

This was very different from, and far more exciting than, the usual slave dances, which consisted of shuffling and turning about, locked to the ground—inadequate, somehow, as a response to the beat of the GOMBEE DRUM.

Bodger knew that the dancing at Waterlemon Bay would go on until the noblemen were insensible, and he felt that he should not remain so long as that, because he might be needed elsewhere, but he wished to leave instructions here, and he could get no one's attention.

He gave in and spent the day and night attending to Bolombo.

At Christiansfort, Gardelin heard, at long last, that Lieutenant Frøling was on St. Jan, tagging along with the JÆGERS. He ordered him sent down at once, under arrest, and had him dumped unceremoniously into jail.

Odolo, finding himself belittled after his contribution to the rebellion, had decided to forget about it. He had made his way to Duurloo's, easily able to arrive from the bush unnoticed by anyone he needed to fear. He had presented himself, smiling and ingratiating, saying that he had been hiding out in the bush for fear of the rebels because he knew too much.

What, for instance? Jannis had wanted to know.

Well—maaa—he could tell where the loot was hidden on the Company's PLANTAGE. He could tell a lot of things. Would Master please take him to TAPPUS, away from these terrible BUSSALS?

Jannis had taken him to town and put him in the charge of the FISCAL.

At Waterlemon Bay, all was calm on Saturday, November 28, and MESTER Bodger prepared to leave. He instructed the women in what they should do for Bolombo, and told them that he would come whenever he might be needed.

Before he could get his horse saddled and away, he was summoned by Bolombo.

"Doctor will stay, be king's doctor," Bolombo said in the SLAVE TALK that was so unbecoming to him.

"I am no man's doctor," Bodger replied, "but every man's."

"I wish you to stay with me," Bolombo repeated firmly, but in a weakened voice.

"I will not do it," Bodger said flatly. "I will come to you, if I can, when you truly need me; but you do not need me now, and you have Asa and Kompa. They are excellent medicine men. You are a strong man and will soon be well. I go now."

He bent to touch Bolombo in the island way, to show that he was not angry, but only determined, then turned with a farewell gesture and left the house.

No one made a motion to stop him, and he mounted his horse and rode away.

When he reached Duurloo's he found that John Charles was the only white man there, and it was a bit of a relief, for he had expected an explosive encounter.

John Charles merely said, "Ah! The prodigal son!"

"Where, then, are the fine robes and the fatted calf?" Bodger asked, smiling.

They sat under the thatched outdoor roof near the cooking area.

John Charles called for a bowl of food for de dakta, but it was already on the way, in the hands of a pouting kitchen slave girl who almost smiled when Bodger thanked her.

Bodger sat and began silently to eat, and the girl brought him the tiny pewter tankard of rum that was customary with meals for upper-class men.

A slave woman, one of those detailed to grow garden food or find it wherever possible on other PLANTAGES, was walking past, bearing upon her head a basket of TANIAS destined for the kitchen. She walked stately like a queen, and the lines of her body, naked but for a breechclout, all culminated in her richly steatopygous buttocks.

Lieutenant Charles's gaze was following her as she moved, and when she passed on he murmured appreciatively, "ARSE GRATIA ARTIS!"

For the first time since he could remember, it almost seemed, Bodger burst into laughter, and it felt so good to laugh that he put off stopping for a little while.

"Ah, Nelli," John Charles cried, "you have no idea how good it is to be in the presence of an educated man, a man who can understand what I say! I forgive you everything that is unforgivable about you, and if necessary I will stand and fight for your right to be unforgivable! Now, see who comes there."

Old Cesar Singal had come scuttling like a crab up the road from the bay.

"Cesar! You wear a cloud upon your face!"

"Well, it rains in my heart," Cesar said without subservience.

"What's wrong?" Bodger asked.

"No one has yet come for my people on the cay," Cesar said angrily, "and I have not been able to wheedle enough decent food for them out of anyone. My people are starving and sick."

"Oh, God!" Bodger turned wrathfully on Charles.

"I knew nothing of this," Charles protested. "No one has asked me for food or ships or anything else for those creatures on the cay. I assumed that they were by now safe on St. Thomas."

Wearily, Bodger found food and took it, his ÉTUI, and medicines, with Cesar Singal to the cay, rowed by slaves who had somehow learned to obey not only Cesar's words but his slightest hand signal. Cesar, who had been an object of fear and contempt among the KAMINA slaves, was here a master, and Bodger guessed that with his keen mind and knowledge of bush medicine and human nature he had done some wonders on the cay in the past few days.

He had indeed, for with some food and a little medicine Bodger was able quickly to restore the spirits of the black refugees and return ashore to write to Gardelin a blistering demand that a ship be sent to rescue them.

At Waterlemon Bay that evening there was a confrontation.

Prince Aquashi and Kanta came to demand of Bolombo their share of both his power and his powder.

Bolombo was improving rapidly, but was still weak. His royal retainers stood stolidly by, fully armed. The guns of Kanta and Prince Aquashi and their warriors were empty. In any case, their intent was not to fight, but to palaver in the ancient African way, with danger lurking behind every word and nuance.

The palaver began with the proper ceremonies, and it was some time before Kanta said to Bolombo in a noisy lingua franca that all West Africans could understand, "I have heard that you proclaim yourself the supreme monarch of St. Jan, owner of all slaves left on the island, all PLANTAGES, cotton gins, sugar works, to profit from trade with the English islands."

Bolombo waited a moment, then spoke cautiously, slowly. "It is my plan, as you know from our earliest palavers in the bush, to make use of the PLANTAGES. That is why I have damaged none of them wherever I have been, and that is why I have issued orders that no more crops are to be burned in the BARCADS."

"All for yourself alone," Aquashi said bluntly.

Bolombo's voice was weakening, but his tone was positive. "Of course not. You know that I intend to divide all but the royal PLANTAGE among my noblemen as soon as the white man is pushed off the island and provisions are set up to keep him off forever."

"But who are your noblemen?" Kanta blurted. "Adampes all? Adampes only?"

Bolombo was tiring visibly, and he signaled his retainers to prop him more comfortably.

"See you, both. I was born a king. I am the only born king on this island. Therefore I am the monarch of this kingdom."

Kanta started to speak, but Bolombo held up his hand and continued. "Aquashi was born a prince in Africa—an Aquambo prince, but a prince. He is the only prince on this island who has acted as a leader in this fight against the white man. He is the prince of this kingdom."

Bolombo pointed his finger at Kanta. "You," he said sonorously, almost accusingly, "were not born a prince in Africa. You are no

William Blake, ca 1790, from a painting by Stedman, ca 1775, Busy slave spinning cotton as she goes about her business, MAPes MONDe Collection

prince here. But you are a leader in this fight, so you are the highest nobleman in this kingdom, second only to Prince Aquashi."

"The division," Kanta began with an impatient gesture.

"The biggest and best PLANTAGE," Bolombo interrupted, "belongs to the king. The next best to the Prince. The next best to the chief nobleman. The lesser ones go to the other noblemen."

He leaned back and closed his eyes, speaking with an air of finality. "All of these things will be determined at the proper time, when the white man is wiped out. Meanwhile, you will remain with me, and we shall have councils of war to find ways to free this land of white men once and for always."

In the face of Bolombo's regal manner and simple logic, both Aquashi and Kanta were like ships in a battle at sea with their sails emptied of wind by the clever maneuvers of a rival ship.

They stayed to wait for Bolombo to gain strength. They would confer on what was best to do next.

V

On Sunday, the sixth day of the St. Jan uprising, Pietter Duurloo arrived back at TAPPUS from his charter to 'STATIUS and was astounded to learn of what had been happening.

At his St. Jan PLANTAGE it was a day of rest, with only a watch on duty to look for signs of rebels approaching. Jannis van Bewerhoudt was in TAPPUS badgering Gardelin for more help. John Charles was still in sole command.

In the middle of the day the sails of *The St. Jan* appeared, emerging from behind Hawksnest Point, sweeping along the swift current and hustling breeze from Tortola.

The ship came down and swung in a stunning maneuver—"Gad," John Charles said to Bodger, "that Barnds is a seaman!"—to come up into the wind and anchor in the bight off Duurloo's sugar mill.

The longboat came ashore, bearing Barnds and as scurvy-looking a collection of white renegades as Bodger had ever seen.

John Charles beckoned Barnds aside while the newcomers stood shuffling like a gang of bad boys only momentarily nonplussed.

"What have we here?" John Charles asked.

"A group of wandering adventurers I found on Tortola," Barnds said, "looking for whatever devilment they can get into."

"English all?"

"Mostly Cockneys, I should say, judging from the odor of their conversations. Perhaps a few Irish. They were recruited by Annaberg's MESTERKNEGT Will Narkit—he's Cockney enough, God knows!"

"Why bring you them here?"

"Narkit proposed that they come and help put down your rebellion."

"Promising them what?"

"All the slaves they can capture."

"On whose authority?"

"Mine."

"Hmph. I once heard the keeper of the deadhouse in London give the answer to that."

"When he said?" Barnds prompted cooperatively.

"Remains to be seen."

"Hmph," Barnds said in his turn.

Lieutenant Charles cocked his head. "Let the proper authorities decide. We had six mercenaries here, but they soon disappeared. Actually, I should be glad to have such ruffians as these to chase the rebels—they would stop at nothing, once the quarry were in sight, but I doubt that they would last long at the hard work of getting the quarry in view. Meanwhile they would have to be fed."

"That," Barnds said, "can be managed, I should think."

Lieutenant Charles walked over to the randy-looking adventurers.

"Gentlemen," he said in Shakespearean tones, "I was not expecting you, and I have not enough food for you."

The group stirred, and one, Will Narkit, red-headed, toothless as an old crone while still surely only in his early thirties, slid forward as spokesman and snarled, "Aye?"

"Aye," John Charles intoned smoothly, "and so if you propose to remain, I suggest that you follow a group of slaves I shall lend you and go to some of the deserted plantations over the hill and find cattle to drive back here to slaughter."

This brought a roar of derisive laughter. Will Narkit let loose an imaginative string of oaths and shouted happily, "Just tyke ya friggin' slyves and walk 'em up ya fuckin' arse, an' 'ere they coom aht ya mahth ye sh'd be bloody well fed!"

Even Lieutenant Charles had to suppress a chuckle as the visitors wallowed in mirth.

"Well." He turned to Bodger. "It's still a good idea to round up some stray cattle," and he sent a party of armed trusty slaves to do it without the help of the Cockneys. Then he broke out some KILL-DEVIL for the renegades to keep them entertained meanwhile.

Bodger begged Barnds to take along to TAPPUS as many as he could of the black women and MANQUERON male refugees on the cays, but he refused, saying that he had not been commissioned to do so and therefore would never be paid for his trouble.

Bodger, because he wanted his letter delivered to Gardelin, refrained from saying that he hoped Barnds would never need to be rescued from a desert isle, and the ship weighed anchor for TAPPUS in mid-afternoon.

In TAPPUS, the following day began with Gardelin taking note of Bodger's outraged plea on behalf of the Duurloo Cay refugees and dispatching Rosetti with *The Sweet Tooth*.

The time had come to start sifting through the captives from St. Jan who lay in The Trunk.

Judge Hendrichsen and FISCAL Friis both being desperately ill with fevers, written orders were issued to Chief Clerk Gregers Høg Nissen to examine the captives in open court and prosecute those suspected of being rebels. In particular, he was directed to arrest the Company's Abraham, known among the Blacks as Odolo, and bring him to trial as a rebel.

Gardelin remembered hearing someone say, quoting Jan Gabriel, that Abraham had been among those attacking the VÆRN on November twenty-third.

Abraham was plucked from the household of the Fiscal, where he was enjoying the relative freedom of the slave compound, and shackled, much to his astonishment.

Jan Gabriel was ordered to the courtroom.

The hearing began innocuously, with Abraham permitted to talk, encouraged to tell whatever he knew. His voice rose in his excitement, and he bleated almost uncontrollably at times.

He said that he knew where the loot from the Company PLANTAGE was hidden.

"Where?"

"At the upper PLANTAGE, the portion of it up the valley toward Konge Hill, in the house on a little hill that's being built for a MESTERKNEGT under a pile of building materials."

"Of what does it consist?"

"Rum, mostly; but other things too—trinkets, clothing, carrying cases . . ."

"Why did you come to town?"

"To work—maaa-aa, to go to work for master."

"Why were you so late in coming to your masters?"

"Fear, Master. Afraid to leave the hiding place, for fear of the rebels."

"What do you know about the attack on the VÆRN?"

"Everything, Master."

"Can you name the rebels who were there?"

"Some, Master. Maaa, not all. I know not all the names."

"Name them."

"Apinda, maaaa—Apinda was there—he fired the big cannon."

"Who else?"

"Maaa, the drummer called Frederik, he beat, maaa, the drum."

Suddenly a look of terror came into Abraham's eyes. It was as if for the first time, he realized what he was doing.

"Who else?"

"Maaa. Maaaa. I know not."

"You know. Speak."

Silence. Abraham's head was lowered.

"How know you what you have told?"

"I listen, Master. I hear."

"You know these things because you were there."

"No, Master, maaaa, no, oh Master!"

Jan Gabriel was summoned to confront him. Abraham was glad.

"Master, tell them. Maaa-aaa, you know me well. You know me a good man."

"Odolo," Jan Gabriel said, his voice shaking. "A man must be punished for murder. You killed at the værn, and you fired the cannon as a signal."

"Master, you saw me not. You were not—maaaa—there!"

"I was there. I saw you not, but I heard you. No man can mistake your voice, Odolo."

"Oh, Master—maaaaaa—Master, kill me not. I am your friend! Let me work for you!"

Jan Gabriel was unable to speak. He turned away numbly and left the court without permission.

"Abraham," Nissen said in Danish, for the record, as the scribe wrote down the words, "property of the honorable Danish West India and Guinea Company, you are judged guilty of rebellion and murder, and for this the penalty is death, preceded by the proper punishment."

Abraham did not understand the words, and was taken, in shackles, back to The Trunk, unsure of his fate.

There was some talk in the courtroom about the ownership of Abraham. Someone insisted that he had recently been purchased from the Company by Governor Moth. This was important, for if he were owned by a private planter, the planter would have to be reimbursed by the Company for his value. The matter was left for later determination.

Nissen was enjoying himself in his unaccustomed authority and power as both prosecutor and judge. He went to speak to Governor Gardelin.

Mester Bodger's sons, Hans and Peter Minnebeck, Nissen pointed out, had spent time among the rebels. Would it not be well to make a practice of showing each captured Negro from St. Jan to them for possible identification?

"That," Gardelin answered, "is an excellent idea."

"Well, your Excellency, why not bring the Minnebeck boys to court right now and let them see the prisoners?"

"If it is to be done," Gardelin said, "let it be done. I am busy. I leave it to you."

The two Minnebeck boys were now living with their Aunt Margaritha on St. Thomas. When they were sent for, she accompanied them fearfully to the fort. Nissen came out of the courtroom to them.

"We are told," he said, "that you have many friends among the slaves on St. Jan."

"Yes, sir," Peter, the elder of the two boys, replied. "We do."

"We have some St. Jan Negroes here," Nissen said smoothly. "Would you like to tell us which ones you know?"

"Well, yes, sir," Peter said, a bit uncertainly. "But, why? What difference does it make?"

"Merely that it is difficult for a white man to tell one Negro from another unless he knows them personally, and when they do not wish to talk, one needs someone who knows them to identify them."

"You are speaking now of rebels?" Peter asked.

"I am. You would agree, would you not, that the rebels must be identified and punished, and that the innocent must be protected?"

Ten-year-old Hans was listening with a reddening face. His blue eyes darkened as he heard his brother say, "Yes, Sir, I should think so."

"He means," Hans put in rapidly, "that the innocent must be protected."

"I mean also," Peter said gravely, "that the guilty should be identified and punished."

The boys were led into the courtroom. Hans held back, but was firmly propelled by hands that were stronger than he.

Seated in the room, facing the light, were the St. Jan slaves who were being held in The Trunk, all save Abraham.

Peter looked at the prisoners and said, in CREOLE, "*Morruk,* Aera.

Christian, MORRUK, MI VRIEN."

The two named Aera and Christian smiled uncertainly at the boys, ducking their heads respectfully.

Hans kept his eyes lowered. His face flooded deeper red and he said softly, angrily, in Dutch, "Peter, how could you?"

"But they have done wrong," Peter said defensively.

"What have they done wrong?" Nissen asked, nodding to the scribe.

"They lifted us from our beds and took us to King Clæs to be his servants," Peter said.

Now Hans lifted his chin and glared at his brother.

"But they were kind to us!" he shouted.

"Then," Nissen turned to Hans, "you agree that they abducted you."

Hans's eyes darkened even more. "No! Oh, no!" he cried. "Oh, Peter! What have you done?"

"He has done his duty," Nissen said, motioning for the boys to be removed from the courtroom. They went, both pale under the suntan on their faces, to rejoin their aunt in the fort yard.

There was no trial. Judgment was simply pronounced, as soon as the ownership of the two slaves was established.

"Aera, property of the honorable former Governor Moth, and Christian, property of His Honor, Secretary SCHØNNEMANN, you are judged guilty of rebellion, and the penalty is death."

The sentences would be carried out later at the slave gallows at the far end of the savannah, on the Sugar Estate, before an audience of slaves, as examples of what happened to rebels. No two rebels would be executed on the same day, in order that the lesson might be spread over a larger audience and a longer time.

At Waterlemon Bay, the day had begun in some anger.

King Bolombo continued to improve, but was still unable to lead his men.

Kanta and Prince Aquashi had grown more and more restless and dissatisfied. They had acquired a little of Bolombo's stock of powder, but not by any means enough to satisfy them. Bolombo kept insisting that he himself would have to find a cache of powder and ball somewhere on the PLANTAGES before he felt properly equipped to attack the white man again. The harvest of such things up to now had been far less than he had expected.

Kanta and Prince Aquashi were growing testy with each other and they agreed to return, each to his own precinct, searching every PLANTAGE in his area that had not previously been exhausted, for powder and ball.

At all times both Kanta and Prince Aquashi, along with Bolombo at Waterlemon Bay, were kept informed, by the drums, of the movements of the FREE NEGRO Corps and the military troop from Coral Bay.

When the drums made it clear that the FREE NEGRO Corps had joined Øttingen and his soldiers on the warpath and that both forces were heading for Waterlemon Bay, Bolombo reacted. That bay would not be easy to defend, so Bolombo had his men move him and all his dependents to the top of the headland above. There, Lieutenant Frøling's PLANTAGE offered a position easily defended from three directions. Once there, he could see that from the fourth direction, the southwest, the approach of attackers was easy, up a gentle slope. He decided to have himself and his royal entourage moved back to the original Adampe hideout at Mme. van Stell's summer place on the point above Brown's Bay. Here was a spot that would be easy to defend because of the steep approaches and the thick undergrowth that would make ambushes easy and complete.

He left a small band of men at Frøling's to keep watch for the white man's forces and throw them off the track if possible, and retired to the blessed safety of Gabriel van Stell's Point, to keep on regaining his health and strength.

At Waterlemon Bay the two JÆGER forces from Duurloo's found the place deserted, but showing recent occupancy.

There were signs of life on Frøling's PLANTAGE on the headland above, to the northeast. The combined forces charged up the hill.

On the path up the hill a rebel ball caught one of the men in the head and killed him.

Now, for the first time in this little war, rage swept through the ranks of the soldiers. They roared up the rest of the slope with only the thought of revenge, and reached the open eminence above just in time to see a band of rebels disappearing on the run over the brow of the hill to the southeast.

Sergeant Øttingen paused long enough to ask the FREE NEGRO Corps to bring the dead soldier to Coral Bay; then he ran to catch up with his troops.

No one in the troop knew where the rebels had gone. Not one of the men had ever been exposed to the bush before this expedition, and none knew how to read the clues along the path. They could only keep going and see what happened.

At long last the weary soldiers came down the path over the saddle from Brown's Bay to Suhm's PLANTAGE, their camping place, and there they met a fusillade from a band of rebels who ran away so soon and so unnecessarily that Øttingen could only conclude that they were out of ammunition. There seemed to be about twenty-five of them, some armed with guns, some with machetes and cane knives.

The soldiers knelt, took careful aim, and fired. Three of the fleeing rebels fell dead.

One was wounded in a leg enough to slow him down. The soldiers ran after him and took him captive.

The rebels had fled eastward, out the peninsula toward Creutzer's Point, and Øttingen sent a troop of soldiers to try to round them up.

The rebels' castoff, useless guns were gathered up and smashed to pieces before anyone realized that they ought to be kept for use by the Civil Guard and loyal slaves.

William Blake, ca 1790, from a painting by Stedman, ca 1775, A freed armed African on the Colony's Force, MAPes MONDe Collection

VI

THE first of December, 1733, began at TAPPUS with the methodical destruction of Odolo at the slave gallows on the Sugar Estate.

The Company slaves were permitted to delay the start of work that morning so that they might gather to see the show. Slaves from private PLANTAGES were brought by their MESTERKNEGTS to add to the audience.

Tight armed supervision of the throng was provided, for the gathering together of so many slaves, even unarmed, in one place was thought to be potentially dangerous.

The executioner, a giant slave with a massive, expressionless face, stood in front of the gallows, feet apart, arms crossed.

The audience crowded in a circle around the place of execution, according to the custom.

The newly constructed wheel stood on its support, elevated for best visibility. Coils of tarred line and a rack of stone-mason's hammers of three varying weights lay handy.

The JUSTICE POST was supplied with new skeins of sail-yarn that would cut deep into a man's musculature and hold him tight, hurting more the more he struggled. Buckets of water were on hand to throw on the prisoner in case he should faint, and to wet the cords after they were tied, to make them shrink and add to the torture.

The fire was burning, and in it the pincers of three sets of iron tongs were heating red.

Odolo was taken from The Trunk. As soon as the savannah came into view he knew his fate. He gasped as if doused with ice water, and struggled with his escort, the fort slaves. He was delivered, moaning, head hanging, to the executioner.

The crowd babbled like children at a birthday party.

Nissen, the condemning judge, jury, and prosecutor, arrived in a Company carriage. He mounted the stone JUSTICE POST platform and read out the record of Abraham's crimes and condemnation.

He nodded to the executioner and took the front row seat that was provided for him.

The executioner, with no words but only imperious gestures, supervised the lashing of Odolo to the JUSTICE POST, seeing that the stout cords were pulled tight. Then he saw to the wetting of them, slowly and deliberately, while Odolo moaned in pain and terror.

Now the executioner took a pair of tongs that glowed at the pincers end. Beginning at Odolo's fingers and toes, he pinched the flesh with the red-hot tongs. Odolo's screams flew out across the savannah. The crowd laughed a little, and sobbed a little, and showed in its faces every expression from pleasure to pain.

The experienced executioner does not proceed too rapidly with his tortures. If the condemned one is pushed too fast, he may faint and rob himself of some of the pains of justice. Therefore the executioner waited a while after each searing pinch of the tongs before applying the next.

He advanced slowly up Odolo's arms and legs, taking turns, motioning for a fresh pair of tongs as each one cooled. The smoky-sweet odor of burning flesh drifted across the savannah, and Odolo's screams settled down to a steady moaning, intensified spasmodically with each hissing pinch.

Methodically the executioner proceeded from the extremities to the trunk, working more slowly as the danger of oblivion for Odolo grew. All over the quivering body, front and back, he proceeded, ending, by design, with penis and then testicles. At this point it was permissible for Odolo to faint.

Act one was a seemingly endless performance, enjoyed all the way by some. To a few it was unbearable; not permitted to leave, they turned their backs and stopped their ears. Nissen ended by staring at the ground.

When Odolo had been revived by being doused with water, the second act began.

Odolo was lashed, spread-eagled, on the wheel, with the tarred line. By now he was so helpless that there was no need for tight or careful knots, but they were tightly and carefully tied.

Now the executioner took up the smallest hammer and began crushing Odolo's smallest bones and joints against the wooden wheel.

Odolo quivered at each blow, but no longer screamed. Each exhalation of breath was a low moan, punctuated at each blow by a grunt. His eyelids were partly open, his eyes rolled up beneath them as if he sought to faint again.

The executioner did not propose to give him a chance to faint. He proceeded very slowly. He tried not to draw blood, but to crush only the bones, leaving the skin merely bruised, for blood is slippery and made his work more difficult. Some of the fractures were unavoidably so compounded as to break through the skin, and Odolo's blood ran down the boards of the wheel in little dark streaks.

When the small bones had been broken, the executioner took up a larger hammer and went to work on the larger bones, starting with the bases of the hands and working up the wrists and arms and ankles, then the ribs and collarbones.

By the time he reached for the largest hammer there was not much life left in the victim, and not many in the crowd were still watching. The show was palling. The executioner abandoned deliberateness, and smashed the large bones and joints of the upper legs, the hips, the shoulders, regardless of blood. Then he crushed in the chest and, last of all, the skull.

The mangled, scorched corpse was now strung up by the neck on the gallows to hang throughout the day as an exhibit for all to see, and in the evening to be burned because unworthy of burial.

The assembled slaves were sent back to work. Nissen returned to his duties showing no expression on his face. The soldiers on guard marched to the fort, a few of them retching shamefacedly.

That night the MARON drums in the mountains of St. Thomas announced the execution. O — DO — LO, they said in their hollow, wooden voices, and even a white man might catch that much. The drums' sounds could not carry upwind to St. Jan, and Odolo was unknown on St. Thomas except to a few St. Jan slave refugees.

Nevertheless, word would find its way to the rebels, who would not care, for Odolo was a deserter and a traitor.

William Vessuup, the refugee murderer, was square of face, with a straight mouth paralleling the square chin. His hair was dark. His blue eyes had highlights that were often interpreted as glints of cleverness, and he would have supported that thesis if asked.

Curiosity brought him to the beach off Freshwater Pond, Tortola, when he saw a strange schooner put in. Then when he saw Frederik Moth and learned of the plan he had devised with Gardelin, the straight line of his mouth turned up at the corners.

The plan had originated in the fact that the rebels knew Vessuup and Robinson to be out of favor with the Danes. These two would attempt to capture the rebel leaders, not by force but by trickery.

Robinson arrived empty-handed from a boar hunt in the hills. He was gaunt of face and dark, with a petulant mouth that was a bit too feminine for the comfort of a man like Moth; and Moth, who had known him for many years, had little patience with him. The excellent Madeira he now offered, though, he could tolerate.

The plans for the morrow were rehearsed and ready.

At Duurloo's on December first, with Creutzer in Coral Bay, Jannis van Bewerhoudt was in sole command, and liking it.

At breakfast at dawn, in which he joined John Charles, he was expansive and good-humored. He had slept well. The rebels were on the run, without weapons, he believed, and the uprising was nearing its end.

He noticed that Cornelius Bodger was absent.

"Has he gone off into the bush again, to doctor some wretched Black?"

"No," John Charles said. "He sleeps."

"Tell me, Lieutenant," Jannis said, spearing a boiled TANIA with his knife, "why do we tolerate Nelli Bodger's behavior in this rebellion? Above all, why do we protect him as best we can from himself—that is, from the wrath of the people who do not understand him?"

"You have just said it, Captain," Charles answered. "We understand him."

"Do we really, though? We like him. Let me say it: we love him in spite of ourselves. Yet is he not actually working against us when he serves our enemies precisely as he serves us and our friends?"

"I have asked myself that a thousand times of late. And yet I cannot honestly say that I believe he makes our battle any more difficult by doctoring our enemies."

"Perhaps not. Still, he might just heal the very man among them who can lead them more effectively than might another."

"True. Do you, then, agree with the MESTERKNEGTS here, and the ruffians who are currently with us, that if we insist on letting him have his way in the matter of going among the rebels, we ought to squeeze his balls until he tells us what he knows about their number and disposition?"

"Yes, I agree with them perfectly," Jannis said, "but I will never do it, nor will you."

"We are not alone. Governor Gardelin should have thrown him into the fort cell long ago, but every time Bodger arrives in his presence he winds him around his finger."

"Precisely. Gardelin cannot help it, either. Like so many of us, he is cursed with a touch of logic and conscience. That is all Bodger is—logic and conscience. He is like a child finding out about things—asking, asking. But it is generally himself he asks, and like a child he pursues his own mind in the light of what he sees. He is interested in everything, leaving nothing out. When his moment comes to die, his last words will be, 'Aha! So this is what it is like!'"

In Coral Bay, the military, seeking vengeance and loot, and the FREE NEGRO Corps, seeking loot and reward, kept up the pressure against the rebels in all directions. The rebels fought back and ambushed them wherever possible. Bolombo's men, from Gabriel van Stell's Point; Kanta's from Bourdeaux's, where the Aminas were living now; and Aquashi's from Vessuup's prodded in, without ammunition, from all three land directions, creating the impression of a large coordinated force of unarmed men. Actually there was no coordination save the hate and the yearning for freedom that was common to them all.

William Blake, ca 1790, from a painting by Stedman, ca 1775, Breaking on the Rack, MAPes MONDe Collection

VII

Aт Fat Hog Bay, Tortola, this December second was the day that Vessuup and Robinson were to put an effective end to the ten-day-old St. Jan rebellion. They would capture its leaders, as known to the authorities from the many questionings at Christiansfort; at the same time they would regain for themselves their good names, their properties, and any slaves they could manage to appropriate.

Moth's ship, coyly named *Den Elskelige Jomfru*, suited today's uses very well by being unknown in these waters.

She set sail with Vessuup and Robinson aboard and a St. Thomas slave who was an expert African drummer familiar with the tribal languages that would be known to most of the rebels.

Vessuup told the skipper to head for Waterlemon Bay, where, he had been informed, the leaders of the rebellion were located.

Approaching the bay, he ordered the drummer to announce his approach and say that he came unarmed, to palaver. Vessuup felt sure that every slave on the island was aware that he was persona non grata on St. Thomas, so it would not be surprising to them that he should wish to harm the Danes.

He listened to the message being sent.

"I hear nothing that I can recognize," he said. "I often wonder how they name a white man with their drums. I am sure that no white person is known among them in private by his true name, but by some heathen appellation that no white man would recognize. Now, how do I know that this drummer is sending the message I gave him? How do I know that he is not saying, 'I have white men here, and a ship. Kill the white men, and spare me, and you have a ship at your disposal'?"

"You do not know, nor do I," Robinson said. "We shall have to take our chances."

Vessuup spoke to the drummer in SLAVE TALK. "How do you name me with the drum?"

The slave smiled and made some irregular beats on the drum.

"What does it mean?" Vessuup demanded.

The drummer merely repeated the sounds.

"With your mouth, say it."

The drummer shook his head and repeated on the drum.

"Very well," Vessuup said. "At least, now I know how I am described by drum, for I would be known the same on both islands. Now repeat the message," he said to the drummer.

There came from the heights the sound of drumming.

"What do they reply?"

"They reply not," the drummer said.

"What say they, then?"

"They pass on the message."

The ship came to anchor shoreward from Waterlemon Cay. The hills reverberated with drumming sounds, but no message came back to the ship.

"What say they?"

"They speak to each other," the drummer said.

"But what say they?"

"They speak to each other, not to me."

"Must I have you beaten now? What say they?"

"They speak not to me."

"What say they to me, then?"

"They speak not to you."

"Must I then kill you?"

The slave was silent, and Vessuup glared indignantly, not at him, but at Robinson.

"We need him," Robinson said, in English. "Best let him be. You can punish him later, after he has done what needs doing."

"Tell them reply," Vessuup said to the drummer. Still no reply came, yet still there was a clamor of drums. "Dare we go ashore?"

"I believe so," Robinson said. "We are well known here, but they are surprised. That is how I judge it. They will be glad of our mission."

"Let us go, then. I fear them not in such circumstances."

"No more I."

They took to the longboat, the two white men and the drummer, and were rowed ashore by the slave crew.

No one was there to greet them. The PLANTAGE was deserted.

The drum spoke from the heights.

"What say they?" Vessuup demanded.

"Start to walk," the drummer said.

"But whither?"

"They will tell us where to turn, when to stop."

"I am not sure I like this."

"Depends how far," Robinson said.

"Shall we obey?"

"It seems we must, or go away."

They walked, and the drummer, following the directions of the other drum, whose drummer was watching them from above, led them up the slanting road eastward, inland, over the ridge.

It was hot walking in the sun, and the white men grumbled. They rested wherever there was shade, but they continued to follow the orders of the distant drummers.

Over the ridge and down the other side toward Brown's Bay, it was a long slow walk for the white men, accustomed to ride over such distances.

It was an hour and more before a voice from the bush outside Krøyer's PLANTAGE in Brown's Bay brought them to a halt.

Since they were plainly unarmed, the speaker stepped forth, armed with Peder Krøyer's sword. It was the Company's Thoma, and he was backed by a dozen warriors carrying machetes and cane bills.

"What do you here?" Thoma demanded.

"You have not been told?"

"You tell again."

"We come to palaver—to trade."

"You have what to trade?"

"Your name is Thoma?"

"So I was called by the white man."

"You are a great drummer," Vessuup said, deliberately flattering.

"I know you."

Thoma said nothing.

"I know you," Vessuup said, "but you are not the leader here. I do not palaver with you. Where is your king?"

"You will wait," Thoma replied.

"Take us to King Clæs."

"You will wait."

"How long?"

"You will wait."

"We shall go to the well. We thirst."

Thoma nodded. He took the drum from Vessuup's drummer, and with a marvelous flourish beat out a quick message, which was instantly repeated in the east, in the south, and in the west.

Vessuup and Robinson went into the PLANTAGE and sat on the curb of the well. No one drew them water until they ordered their drummer to do it.

They took mouthfuls of the water and spat it out. It was brackish enough to be hateful to the taste, but their thirst forced them at last to drink it.

They could hear the sea lapping on the sandless beach a hundred yards away; they could see its bright glint through the trees in the morning sunlight.

"These bastards," Robinson grumbled, in English, so as not to be understood.

"May their souls be blasted to hell," Vessuup said. "They might have told our drummer where they were. We could have sailed around here to Brown's Bay. But they preferred to make us walk over that Godforsaken, hell-hot ridge."

"Dare we send our drummer back to tell the skipper to sail around and be prepared to pick us all up?"

"I think we must bide our time," Vessuup said.

They waited impatiently, but nothing was explained to them. There was only silence when Vessuup made demands.

At last there were footsteps, and Prince Aquashi appeared on the PLANTAGE road, accompanied by a band of warriors. All were armed with cutting weapons.

"You are Madame Runnels's Prince!" Robinson exclaimed. "I know you well!"

Aquashi said not a word, made no gesture of greeting or sign of hearing. He took a drink of water, and then permitted his men to drink. He sat on the well curb and waited, staring impassively into the distance. Neither Vessuup nor Robinson could provoke a word from him.

In about a half-hour Kanta, with his retinue, arrived from the southeast. Neither Vessuup nor Robinson knew him and he would not introduce himself.

Now that both Kanta and Prince Aquashi were here, Thoma made an African sound, and soon slant-eyed Juni and Asari the eunuch appeared as if from nowhere.

Both Vessuup and Robinson knew Asari well. He could speak to them in their own tongues, with such dignity that they were embarrassed into trying to emulate him.

He would not tell them where King Clæs was. They told him that they knew he was wounded. Was he dead?

"He is not dead."

"Then he can speak with us. Take us to him."

"Juni and I shall speak for him. What do you wish?"

"The question is: what do you wish?"

"What have you?"

"What wish you?"

"In general," Asari said, switching to Danish, "we wish the means to kill the white men who remain on the island, and to keep their like forever from our shores unless they come unarmed, to trade."

"That is what we have to offer."

"You have it on board the ship?"

"No. We have there other things that you may need or wish, such as excellent food and drink, and fine clothing. Such powder and ball, and even guns, as you might wish to order we can obtain for you in any quantity you may desire."

"At what price?"

"It depends on what you offer in trade. What, then, do you offer?"

"Cotton we have. The English are always wanting cotton. When the present crop is harvested we shall have a great deal more."

"There are many ways of paying," Vessuup continued. "We can palaver. If you care to come to the ship, we can show you what we have with us, and have a treat while we talk terms."

Kanta and Aquashi were growing restless. They spoke abruptly to Asari. Juni, too, had not understood most of what was said.

The four of them had a spirited conversation. Asari was obviously explaining to them what had been said.

"They say they will go and look at the ship," Asari said, eventually.

"May we not send a runner to have the ship sailed here?" Vessuup asked.

Asari spoke again to the others. They shook their heads. "It is well," Asari said to Vessuup, "to keep the ship a distance from here. We will go to it."

Vessuup and Robinson sighed and shuffled their aching, hot feet. "Have you no horses for us?"

"We have no horses for you," Asari said, with obvious pleasure.

"Let us go, then. The day advances." Asari spoke to Juni, who remained behind.

Vessuup turned to Robinson. "You notice that they do not signal to King Clæs what is said among us here, lest we note from the sound of the answering drum where he lies. Certainly he is somewhere here in Brown's Bay. That one—Juni, the Indian, is it not?—will report to him, and when we are far enough away, the drums will speak again. It is a wondrous thing, you know, whether you like it or not."

The long, hot trudge back was exhausting to the white men, and when at last they reached Waterlemon Bay they were perishing for food and drink.

"Come aboard the ship," Vessuup said casually to Kanta, Aquashi, and Asari. "We shall have some treats for us all, and some rest, while we palaver."

The three conferred, then agreed to come. They spoke to their followers, who remained behind on the shore.

As the three leaders climbed into the longboat to go out to the ship, Vessuup and Robinson managed to exchange looks, but were unable to communicate their thoughts.

Aboard the ship, they still had no chance of discussing the turn events had taken. They apparently had at least two of the true leaders aboard, but their king, the important one, was still outside their grasp. There was no way of discussing what should be done.

Vessuup paid the three rebel guests the unprecedented compliment of seating them, with himself and Robinson, at the table in the captain's cabin and taking food and drink with them as equals. This gesture was not lost on Kanta and Prince Aquashi, to whose minds it was only their due, but who were nevertheless surprised and suspicious. Asari gave no sign of being either impressed or suspicious.

With the good food and excellent rum, palaver was easy and bold.

Vessuup showed the men rich raiment they might have, and bright trinkets of real value, pretending not to know what it was that they were really there to talk about. Prince Aquashi and Kanta were attracted by the beautiful things, but Asari spoke gruffly to them and brought them back to practicality.

What the rebels wanted of Vessuup and Robinson was the means of carrying on the war against the Whites—powder, ball, and of course more guns. For these they were willing to give Vessuup such gold and silver objects as they had found in their looting, all of the cotton that remained on the island, and such slaves as were not needed to work the PLANTAGES.

"We shall talk about gold and silver and cotton in future transactions," Vessuup said smoothly, "but for the present, the simplest payment would be slaves."

The rebels conferred and Asari answered, "Very well, but there is a limit to the number of slaves we will part with. We shall need them all in the future, and more as well."

"I can understand that, but for the present we need slaves more than anything else."

It was agreed that the first delivery should consist of ten kegs of powder and the weight of two men in ball. The ball presented less of a problem than the powder, for there was still a supply in the rebels' hands—what was needed was the powder with which to propel them. Payment for the powder would be at the rate of one able-bodied slave for each keg of powder, and for the ball, or bulk lead, slaves by equal weight.

"How soon comes this powder, this lead?" Asari demanded. "I will obtain whatever I am able on Tortola and at Spanish town," Vessuup said, "but, being a foreigner there, and having no credit, I shall have to deliver slaves in advance in order to obtain anything at all. For the long run, I shall have to obtain my supplies from the island of Montserrat, where I now live and have both standing and credit. Montserrat, as you know well, is the enemy of the Danes of St. Thomas, and will be happy to supply what is needed."

The rebels knew no such thing, never having heard of Montserrat, but they nodded in tipsy agreement. Even Asari had no way of knowing that Vessuup was lying, and nodded.

For the first quick order, then, the rebels offered a down payment of two slaves, with the balance on delivery.

Vessuup balked at that. He wanted at least ten of them in advance. But the rebels were firm, and Vessuup finally agreed to two—and to his astonishment found that Juni had brought two slaves to the beach and was waiting with them there.

Vessuup put Prince Aquashi, Kanta, and Asari ashore, with gifts of trinkets and rum and words of friendship, and his guests departed with an air of good will only slightly restrained.

At the last moment, Vessuup ventured a hint that he would expect eventually the return to him of his PLANTAGE on St. Jan and the rebels' fealty to him as ruler of the island. Asari laughed aloud, for he understood what Vessuup said; but Aquashi and Kanta nodded and smiled in perfect agreement, and almost fell into the sea.

Only after the longboat had departed from the ship could Vessuup and Robinson talk. Vessuup explained that he had let the rebels go for the present in order to make a better coup later because of the confidence it would inspire. King Clæs was not yet in their grasp.

When the longboat had returned with the slave pawns, the ship weighed anchor and sailed for Tortola, with Vessuup and Robinson waving goodby to the rebels on the shore.

Vessuup had the slaves and the drummer placed in irons and thrown into the hold.

VIII

THE expeditionary forces, both FREE NEGRO Corps and military, returned to Duurloo's from Coral Bay on December third, leaving the VÆRN untended. The military was tired and having difficulty getting enough food, and the FREE NEGRO Corps was surfeited with loot and rum.

Juni, the Indian Negro, soon tired of being considered inferior to Asari and unworthy of nobility and property in the new kingdom, and went up into the mountains to join Prince Aquashi, whom he admired for having been the original captor of King Bolombo.

At Vessuup's he got busy making bows and arrows and teaching Aquashi and his men how to make and shoot them. The hard woods growing in the St. Jan bush, their growth laid down in thin, dense rings between the dry seasons that came more frequently than winter, made rigid, steel-like arrows and formidable bows requiring powerful arms to bend them.

It was a restless night at Duurloo's, with an unaccustomed sultriness in the air. Tree frogs, crickets, GECKOS chirruped and shrieked while the huge tropical bats made the night seem silent with their endless winging, wheeling close overhead, like shadows of shadows, blind and soundless in the moonless dark.

Two of the men who were free of duty were unable to sleep. As if prodded by the same stick, Bodger and John Charles rolled out of their hammocks and emerged in their nightshirts into the thatched outdoor living area, encountering each other in the uncer-

A Rebel Slave armed and on his guard, *Bartolozzi, from a painting by Stedman, ca 1775,* MAPes MONDe Collection

tain light cast by the smoky CRESSET LAMPS that ringed the camp. A few watchmen wandered back and forth, silhouetted against the lights, and in the dimness under the thatch lay huddles of mercenaries and loyal slaves, rigidly segregated while breathing the same air and making the same sounds in their uneasy sleep.

"Ah, there, Nelli," John Charles said softly. "A bit smothery tonight, what?"

"Aye."

Silently they took chairs from a table and sat out-of-doors at some distance from the sleepers, looking at the murky sky.

"Bit of a westerly rain brewing, eh?" Charles said. "Aye."

"You are troubled?"

"Aye," Bodger replied. "Inside my head. I cannot stop thinking about the future of all the black people we have dragged here to the New World."

"The future is the same as the present. Slavery, with some of them achieving freedom and gradually joining the civilized community."

"No," Bodger said. "I speak of the more distant future. Men cannot forever continue to degrade themselves by holding other men in slavery. The burden of guilt is too heavy and sooner or later will have to be cast off. Then what happens to the people who, through countless generations, have been accustomed to be slaves?"

"I know not," Charles said, somewhat distant and bored.

"Education. That is the great need."

"Oh, come, now. You know they cannot be educated."

"Who?"

"The Blacks, of course," Charles said crossly. "Of whom then are we talking?"

"I speak of the Whites. It is the Whites, first of all, who have to be educated—and you may be right, perhaps they are incapable of it."

"Gibberish, Nelli Bodger!" John Charles was no longer bored. "Nonsense, utter and complete. You are merely trying to unsettle me."

"Not at all. The modern history of this end of the world is both white and black. The black part is almost entirely ignored by Whites, but the black man is fully aware of both parts. Who, then, is lacking in education? The White, obviously!"

"Oh, you are making game of me—you are straining to make a point."

"You know as well as I do that those Blacks who wish it and are given the chance to learn, can and do learn with blinding speed—including every last ugly, bitter evil that the white man perpetrates and perpetuates. So I would say the education of the Black in the white man's ways will take care of itself."

"Am I presumed to be CHAWING THE CUD OF GRIEFE AND INWARD PAINE?"

"If you are quoting, you quote above my head," Bodger said. "But look about you. You are by no means a wealthy man, yet if you can see, in a whole day's looking on this island, one black man—I am not speaking of dark people who are really in this connection white, enslavers rather than enslaved—if you can find one black man in comparison to whom you are not wealthy beyond all possibility . . ."

"But the black man demands enslavement by being inferior—and besides, he invented the institution of slavery."

"I would change that slightly," Bodger said. "He demands enslavement by submitting to it, since it is apparently the white man's nature to exploit the institution that he found among the Blacks—whose ruling classes did not invent it, but learned it, apparently, from Arabs—which is all beside the point. The point is that there is a flaw in the enslaved black man, as in the white men who throughout history have been enslaved. The flaw is a willingness on the part of the enslaved to go along with the idea of his essential inferiority—otherwise he would not submit to enslavement."

"In general, what could he do about it?"

"He could die," Bodger said. "He could fight and die, as you and I would do, rather than submit."

"Would we?" Charles said softly, looking at the ground. "I wonder."

"We shall never know, but I like to fancy we would."

John Charles sighed, raised one eyebrow and lowered the other, glaring quizzically at Bodger.

"You are forever tricking me into corners of solemnity where I, a player of comedies by preference, feel not at home. But a goodly number of our St. Jan slaves appear to be willing to risk the death you speak of, rather than submit."

"Precisely," Bodger said. "And when the whole truth is known it will be seen that the ones who are truly ready to die rather than submit are accustomed to be slaveholders, not slaves. They have a clear notion of themselves as superior beings—and they truly are superior to those who go along with them merely, like small boys, to follow the leader, or because forced to go as slaves. But what I really started out to say was that the white man here has to learn that the source of his wealth is the bodies and the brains of his slaves. Next he has to learn that a body and a brain add up to a man, and that one man has sooner or later to make room for another man. And when all men have learned this, they will at last know what happiness is. And thus I believe I have proven to you that I can dream as well sitting on a chair as lying asleep in a hammock!"

"Indeed you have," Charles said good-naturedly.

The two men replaced their chairs under the thatch and returned to their hammocks to stare at the ceiling and listen to the sleeping sounds about them.

IX

Dawn of December fourth found an Englishman, Captain Doudas, sent by Vessuup, sailing from Fat Hog Bay, Tortola.

The ship sailed, not to Waterlemon Bay, but to Brown's Bay. The bay was shallow, and the ship had to anchor far out.

When the captain and his men, all strangers to the rebels, reached the rubble beach in their longboat they were met by angry Adampe noblemen led by Thoma, armed with sharp steel. They would not permit them ashore.

Captain Doudas ran his boat onto the sandy bottom just offshore to steady it, and stood in its bow to talk to the rebels.

"Asari," he said, as he had been instructed, for he needed someone to whom he could talk.

"Asari ka kom."

The MALAGASY had indeed come. He stepped from behind the sea grape trees.

"You speak English," the Englishman said.

"Well enough for trade," Asari said.

The captain explained that Vessuup was trying his best to find powder and ball in the nearby islands, but had sent word that it was impossible.

The rebels were not interested in the message; what they wanted to know was why the ship had come here to this bay.

"Because this is where you are," Doudas said in some surprise.

"How knew you we were here?"

"Oh," Doudas said, faltering. "Ah—I was told."

"By your Vessuup," Asari said, speaking slowly. "You tell Vessuup never to come here or send you without powder and lead. Never come or we kill."

"Mr. Vessuup sends word that it will take a long time for powder and ball to be obtained from Nevis or Montserrat. You are understanding me?"

"I understand," Asari said.

"It takes much time. You are not safe to wait here so long. You and all your men come aboard. I will take you to a safe place. Take you to Montserrat where Danes are not liked. You have freedom there, and land for good crops."

"We have land for good crops here, we have freedom here. We need only powder. You go away. You never come back without powder. We kill."

Captain Doudas sent slave crewmen overboard to lift and push the keel off the sand bottom, returned to his ship, and sailed away.

Doudas knew an opportunity when he saw it. He never reported back to Vessuup, but made straight for Nevis and sources of powder and ball to which he had access.

Vessuup saw him go and guessed what his errand was, for he knew, perhaps better than most, how little trust a man could put in another in such a situation.

It was necessary to do something drastic about the apparent presence of spies at Duurloo's, and Planter Barnds was sent back from TAPPUS to do it.

The loyal slave CHASSEURS had brought in some prisoners—the CREOLE slave boy, Jacky, belonging to the Stallart estate, whom they remembered seeing only yesterday at the Duurloo encampment; an Aquambo warrior named Quassi, belonging to Mme. Gottschalck's Annaberg, and Susanna Runnels's Cupido, an Adampe drummer who had a charming way with the girls.

Barnds set himself to examine them.

Jacky was first.

"Jacky," Barnds shouted at the trussed-up, frightened youngster, "you are a spy."

Jacky did not know the word. Still, Barnds did not deign to use SLAVE TALK.

"You came and stayed here to find out our force and report to the thieving murderers."

Still Jacky did not understand.

William Zytzema signed to Barnds and painstakingly, in SLAVE TALK, tried to get at the truth of the matter.

Jacky knew nothing.

Jacky was wearing clothing—in itself one sign of a rebel—of torn OSNABURG. Barnds had his captors strip him naked and squeeze his testicles, gently at first, between two flat pieces of wood.

Jacky grunted and struggled, tossing his captors almost into the air.

Barnds then suggested to him that he had been sent to see if the St. Thomas people were here, or if only the St. Jan Civil Guard were holding Duurloo's. Zytzema repeated the suggestion as Barnds signed to the loyal slave torturers to tighten the squeeze; they did so, and Jacky screamed, "Yes. Yes, Master!"

Next it was suggested, first by Barnds, then by Zytzema, with the pressure greatly increased, that he had been sent to see whether Captain Vessuup were there.

When Jacky shrilled, "Yes, Master. Yes!" Barnds ordered him hanged as a spy, with the concurrence of the majority of the Civil Guard.

When Bodger came to Jannis van Bewerhoudt to protest, Jannis said to him, "Nelli, this is war"; and Jacky was hanged from a wide-spreading limb of a saman tree that Pietter Duurloo had brought from St. Eustatius many years before.

This was enough for one day, and Jannis insisted that the other two captives be sent to TAPPUS for judgment, even though Cupido was declared by one of the FREE SLAVES to have been the rebel drummer at the time of the attack on Duurloo's two weeks earlier.

On St. Thomas, before a huge involuntary audience of slaves, Moth's Aera went to an elaborate death in a Sunday day-off spectacle for his part in the abduction of Hans and Peter Minnebeck.

On Monday, December seventh, Fuli, Thora, and Cupido were placed on trial at Christiansfort. FISCAL Friis and Interim Judge Nissen were both ill, and Secretary SCHØNNEMANN acted as prosecutor, judge, and jury. Two hired soldiers sat as witnesses, deputies for two planters.

Fuli and Thora, husband and wife, after a thorough, insistent examination, emerged as hapless victims, enslaved against their will by the rebellion. They were exonerated, held to testify against Cupido, and then turned over to the Company MESTERKNEGT of the St. Thomas Sugar Estate to be put to work pending further trials at which they could testify.

Cupido exerted his charm in nervous smiles that turned to tears when he saw his mistress stand up to defend him on grounds that he had been a good, pleasant slave in her service. He was shown by the testimony of Fuli and Thora to have been an enthusiastic rebel drummer before his disaffection with Bolombo's royal attitude toward him. His mistress, pretty Susanna Runnels, daughter of Jannis van Bewerhoudt, wept with him and left the court when she could not save him.

He was put to death without an invited audience because the day was growing late and everyone was busy.

Captain Toller—Tallard to the Danes, spelling by ear—of the Royal Navy of His Majesty of England, had put in to Tortola Old Road with his ship of the line, H.M.S. *Pearl,* newly built and commissioned at Woolwich in the early summer. The ship had a complement of two hundred and fifty men and an armament of fifty guns—a magnificent ship.

Captain Toller, asked if he would be willing to come with his ship and help put down the rebellion, replied that he would be glad to do whatever he could to help if he received an official request.

Gardelin winced when he learned of the presence of Toller's ship at Tortola. He was torn. Such a splendid ship could perhaps put an immediate stop to the uprising. On the other hand, such a splendid ship could easily capture the island for the British flag, and if Gardelin requested Toller's intervention on St. Jan the British would have written proof to show protesting Danish officialdom, of his error in inviting them in. He put off making a decision.

Bodger had his hands full with sickness at Duurloo's. To no one did it seem remarkable that he himself did not fall ill. Even though he pointed out that they should be as careful as was he what they put into their stomachs, everyone but Jannis van Bewerhoudt and John Charles assumed that merely being a doctor was all he needed to assure him good health.

The women in all three of the rebel camps were beginning to stir. They were tired of stalemate. They were tired of the creeping hopelessness. Now they heard that Santje, having been driven insane by the hurricane and having tried to run off into the night with the Krøyers' baby Hans, had been sentenced at Christiansfort to lose a leg. That was enough to make them push against the bounds within which they were confined by the male leaders. They began to complain, and then to rail against the inactivity of the males. No man struck them in the mouth, yet neither did any seem to listen.

Cornelius Bodger was urgently summoned by the drums in broad daylight to come along the north shore until met by a guide. The message of the drums was imparted to him openly by Pontier, a Company slave among the CHASSEURS. Pontier's loyalty was so completely unquestioned that not even the English mercenaries accused him of being a spy.

The mercenaries did, however, loudly object to Bodger's going on this errand without leading them to the rebel camp. When he tried to mount his horse, they seized him and took him to Captain van Bewerhoudt, demanding that he either be put in chains to prevent his going or ordered to lead a posse to the rebels.

Jannis van Bewerhoudt scratched his head and told the mercenaries, "We have been over this ground before. This is not an ordinary man. Unhand him, and let him be."

The mercenaries, led by Will Narkit, refused to back down. They sent one of their number for a rope with which to hang Bodger on the spot, while the rest of them stood facing van Bewerhoudt with their guns ready. Their backs were to the terrace of the master house. John Charles, sitting on the terrace at his ease, rose and manned one of the cannons, which was loaded with grape. He poured powder into the pan. He took the slow match in his hand. The cannon was pointed at the backs of the mercenaries—but also at Bodger, and at Jannis van Bewerhoudt, who faced them.

Jannis told the mercenaries, calmly, gesturing to Thrane to translate, "You are near to mutiny."

"We are not required to be here. Ye cannot call us mutinous."

"Kindly look behind you," Jannis said.

When Thrane translated, Narkit snorted. "That be a dirty nigger trick: 'Wa da behine yo, mon?' Expect us to fall into that old nigger joke?"

Behind them John Charles spoke coldly: "This be no nigger joke."

The mercenaries turned stupidly, as one head, and saw the threat.

"Ah!" Narkit exclaimed, "but you too, Captain, are in the line of fire."

"There are enough of you in front of me to absorb the grape."

They tensed as if to scatter, and John Charles barked in English, "Move not!" bringing the slow match close to the pan.

No one moved. Narkit said to Jannis, "But you endanger Bodger as well as yourself. You dare not!"

"You will not know until you try me," Jannis replied. "Now, unhand MESTER Bodger." He paused longer than it took for the translation.

John Charles shouted, "Unhand him, he said!"

They let him go, and scattered.

Bodger looked at Jannis van Bewerhoudt for a long moment, then said in Dutch, "Captain, I stand speechless in admiration. Thank you."

"Nonsense, man," Jannis said. "Can't have mutiny, you know. Go, then, if you must, and do your nefarious duty."

When Bodger returned it was evening. He had removed a bullet from the leg of one of Prince Aquashi's noblemen.

John Charles greeted him and ordered a drink brought.

Jens Thrane approached.

"Good evening, MESTER," he said. "Saw you Monsieur Castan in your travels—know you of his whereabouts?"

"No. Why?"

"A messenger has arrived regarding his sister on St. Thomas."

John Charles threw back his head in a gesture of mirth. "Ah! I know her. Ugly as sin, but a delight in bed. My Lord Hamlet must surely have known her too, for he spoke of a Castan more honoured in the breech than in th' observance!"

He was so delighted with himself that Bodger and Thrane smiled. Then Thrane said bluntly, "She is dead."

"Oh," John Charles breathed, subdued. "Sorry—I'm so sorry. How did it happen?"

"Out in her carriage, in a hurry, she came to a place on a mountain road where it was necessary for her footman to sound the horn to warn any oncoming vehicle to stop and wait. The footman could not get a hoot out of the horn. She ordered the driver on, full speed, anyhow. An oncoming carriage had sounded no horn either, and Madame's carriage went over the cliff at the narrow ledge."

"Gad! How awful!"

"The footman survived. The strange thing is that, as was later discovered, there was a spider in his horn that caused it to fail."

X

BOLOMBO, in his enforced idleness, had at least had time to think and to be aware of the need to plan ahead.

It was necessary to see to the cultivation of the PLANTAGES, and he had been on the island long enough to know that before the end of December, before the Christmas breeze should start to blow, the planting of new cane rattoons and the topping of old cotton and planting of new should be completed. In view of the stalemate while he waited for powder and lead, he ought to be putting the slaves and sugar mills to work all over the island in order to be sure to have trade goods with which to acquire the things his kingdom would need.

He knew by now roughly how he would divide the land under the new regime. All of the PLANTAGES in the northwest, from Little Cruz Bay to Mary Point—the richest in soil and the best-watered, as well as requiring the strongest defense from attack across the sound—he would combine into one enormous PLANTAGE for himself. Prince Aquashi would have the entire south side, including the Company's huge Coral Bay and extending all the way to the edge of Little Cruz Bay in the west. The top of the central ridge would roughly separate the two domains, and that would give to Aquashi the desirable PLANTAGES of the high central valley and Yoshi and L'Espérance GUTS to placate him for being given the relatively unproductive south side. Kanta, no prince, but artificially one for his leadership of the Aminas, would have to be satisfied with the arid East End peninsula; the rest of the north side, from Brown's Bay on around to Mary Point, progressively more productive, would be thrown in to make him feel better.

The lesser noblemen would be accommodated according to tribe by the three masters. Bolombo sent runners to call Aquashi and Kanta in for a meeting. He told them of his decision, and made them like it, at least for the present, because of his kingship and his aura of command. He told them that it would be wise to put their slaves to work in their respective areas, and to commandeer all slaves now living on the former masters' PLANTAGES or hiding in the bush.

This ukase made Kanta a double rebel in his heart, but uncharacteristically he held his tongue and temper for the time being, until he could gather strength about him and assess better his chances of improving his lot.

Aquashi was not sure whether or not or how much he had been wronged, and he too bided his time, watchfully and contemplatively. He knew the value of the high central valley where his home PLANTAGE was located, and he knew something of Coral Bay, but he did not know what he might expect of the south side.

Both Kanta and Aquashi obeyed the instructions to gather up as many slaves, male and female, as possible. They even made efforts to put the slaves to work, but this kind of activity was foreign to them, and they soon lost interest. Excepting Bolombo himself, who had been a BOMBA but now was royalty again, there was not a black man on the island experienced enough in responsibility to be put to it, for every other BOMBA had fled for his life to the Whites.

Bolombo had Breffu, who was energetic and willing, and she did get a modicum of productive labor going at Waterlemon Bay, but she knew few of the secrets of management and enjoyed only the contempt of the OLD-LINE SLAVES, who were not accustomed to being bossed by women, and simply failed to work except when Breffu showed up in person at different locations to threaten them.

Weeds, grass, TAN-TAN, CATCH-AND-KEEP, KASHA, MARAN had sprouted and were busily putting down deep roots in the BARCADS everywhere on St. Jan.

A group of Loango noblemen who were attached to Bolombo grew tired of their inferior position as compared to the Aquambos, and left the Waterlemon Bay encampment. Having no guns of their own, and feeling too weak to set up an independent Loango force, they decided to go to Coral Bay and join Kanta and his Aminas. They liked Kanta and his unruly ways. At Coral Bay on their way to the VÆRN, where Kanta was, they were caught by a detachment of Adampes sent by Bolombo to emphasize his supremacy, and shot. The Adampes, in order to underline their point, then hanged the dead men, with liana vines, from the lowest limbs of the huge GRIGRI tree near the Company's waterfront.

With the new feeling of disunity among the rebels had come a breakdown in the drum communications on St. Jan. None of the leaders was now quite sure what the other two or the white men were doing.

When a series of fires broke out, one after another, all over the island, there was no certainty outside of Kanta's Amina camp as to what the sudden flare-up meant.

To the white men, seeing the smoke, it appeared to be a concerted effort on the part of all the rebels to destroy the property of their hated oppressors.

To both Bolombo and Prince Aquashi it seemed possible that the white man was sending loyal slaves in to burn the PLANTAGES to prevent their use by the rebels for the furthering of their independence.

Only Kanta and his men knew the truth for sure; and Kanta alone knew the whole truth. His warriors may have thought that they were simply seeking excitement after weeks of dull inactivity; they may even have agreed with the white man's guess that they were taking vengeance on their former oppressors. These were parts of the truth for Kanta too, but he alone knew how it happened that the PLANTAGES affected were all in the areas assigned by Bolombo to himself and Prince Aquashi. It was not vengeance precisely; more like a comment which it was a real pleasure to make.

The loyal slave CHASSEURS who were now going into the bush every day without leadership from outside their own ranks to look for rebels and other loot knew that there were three rebel centers, not including the women's encampment, and they dared not attack any of them, for they were ignorant of their size and strength. They contented themselves with prowling through the bush to pick up whatever errant slaves they could find, and visiting all PLANTAGES not occupied by rebels, for looting purposes.

The slaves they caught in the bush were almost all women, some of them loyal and going about their confused lives while waiting out the rebellion, some of them rebel hangers-on who were disaffected with the males and heading for the rapidly expanding women's encampment in Kob Flat. Males in the bush were generally too fleet-footed to be caught on the run and too cunning to be trapped. Only the women could be run down or trapped, some of them willingly because tired of fear and uncertainty and ready to go back to the relative security of the white community and take their chances on being able to prove their innocence. From the CHASSEURS' point of view, the promised reward for bringing in a female rebel was just as great as for a male, and the catching of her was much easier.

The very few males who were now being caught by the CHASSEURS were old or unwary enough to be surrounded on their masters' PLANTAGES, and to some of them it was a relief when it finally happened, come what might as a result.

The women's encampment, because of the recognized need a man had on occasion for female companionship, was in a sense neutral ground. The CHASSEURS were neither welcomed nor fought off by the women, who had no effective means of fighting them off and had, after all, no great physical aversion to them in any case. Thus it was that CHASSEURS came, in effect, unarmed to the women and such rebel men as were there at the time faded away unmolested so long as they were wise enough not to raise a hand.

In the stalemate things were beginning to ease for Dr. Bodger. The official grumpiness over his apparent disloyalty was falling away. As the sight of him going and coming on his self-appointed errands grew more common, it grew less noticeable, and he could move more and more at will without attracting comment.

Sooner or later it had to happen that Bodger would be called to all three of the rebel camps. He alone, of all white persons, knew of the disunity among the rebels. He neither reproved the rebels for their debilitating disunity nor reported this weakness to anyone. The entire upheaval was essentially outside the bounds of his responsibility, except as it affected the health and welfare of everyone concerned in it, and he felt that he must not play God with any of his special knowledge.

When he learned that most of his slaves were being held as slaves by Kanta, and—excepting Christian Sost—ill-treated, he requested their release to him, particularly the young boy, January, but was peremptorily refused.

When eventually he was called to the women's camp it was to help a girl who was dying because she was trying to give birth to a child rump first, and no one would or could help her. The midwives and witch doctors would not touch her because of the evil of the omen that confronted them. They glimpsed the helpless little rump and ran away.

Christian Sost was at the women's camp, with Kanta's consent, to act as doctor, for many of the women were ill. This was an "illness" with which he had no idea how to deal, and so it was he who had sent for the doctor.

Bodger toiled, sweating, over the long, tortuous path through the mountains to Kob Flat, southeast of Bourdeaux peak. He had to ride a stubborn, plodding donkey, for the footing was much too dangerous for a horse, or even a mule.

He had had almost no experience with childbirth. Like pregnancy, it was not deemed an illness, but a natural phenomenon, and men, doctors included, were generally unwelcome in its presence. This was the province of women.

He did know that babies were properly born head first, and he was not afraid to use his hands to turn the dead child and pull it out. The mother herself was so near death after the daylong agony that she was limp in unconsciousness. This was probably fortunate, for he soon realized that the taut muscles of a conscious, terrified girl would have made his task impossible. He finally had to hook his fingers into the child's mouth to get a purchase, and this seemed to him a dreadful thing to have to do. In spite of the fearful mixture of blood, fluid, and afterbirth with which he had to deal, he saved the life of the mother.

This was the first time since the eve of the rebellion that Bodger and Christian Sost had seen each other. As soon as Bodger had done all he could for the girl, he cleaned his hands with the earth of the vegetable garden and spider-grass and the two men sat down.

"You knew that this was going to happen, this rebellion," Bodger said.

"I knew that it was planned, sir, but not the exact day upon which it was to begin."

"And why did you not warn me?"

"I believe, sir, that you can imagine my reasons."

"Let us say," Bodger said humorlessly, "that I now wish to test the accuracy of my imagination."

"Sir, if I had warned you, you would have had to make some painful decisions."

"That is true, but perhaps I had a right to a chance to try and stop the rebels."

"Sir, you could not have stopped them. You could only have endangered yourself."

"Perhaps I had the right to decide whether or not to endanger myself."

"Perhaps, sir. But I too had a right, the right to spare you if I could."

"And what of the people who were murdered? I might have saved them by warning them, even though I might not have stopped the rebellion from taking place."

"Sir, forgive me, please. I knew that you and your sons would not be harmed . . ."

"That my sons would be taken captive as servants—knew you that?"

"No, sir. That I did not know. That was a decision of caprice,

William Blake, ca 1790, from a painting by Stedman, ca 1775. Each side piked heads to intimidate the other, MAPes MONDe Collection

regrettable. But I knew that neither they nor you would be killed, or even hurt. And I confess that to me the lives of the others were no more important than the lives of the rebels. Indeed, if I had to choose on pain of death for making the wrong choice, I would choose that the man enslaved against his will should live rather than the man who enslaved him."

"The choice was not between death for the masters and death for the slaves. The slaves were threatened only with punishment for going MARON, not with death."

"Sir," Christian Sost said gently, "they were already suffering a thing worse than death."

Bodger got up and walked away. He sighed and sat on a stone with his head in his hands.

XI

IT was on the seventeenth of December that the first hint of friction among the rebels began trickling through the veil that separated them from their common enemy.

The trouble started at the Jansens' Caneel Bay. None of the Jansen slaves remained there, but some refugee Company slaves, and one of Bodger's, named Pietter, who were not eager to go to St. Thomas and be put to work, were living there furtively because it was a good place to live. There was food growing in various spots, and some animals and fowl still hung about the fringes.

Kanta came first with a group of his marauders. They came down the bush trail from Konge Vej, having gingerly skirted Prince Aquashi's strong point on the heights of Vessuup's PLANTAGE. They were bent on looting and doing some damage, for this was part of Bolombo's proposed domain.

It happened that it was the king's favorite part, and a group of his warriors was on its way there along the shore road from Waterlemon Bay, leaderless because Bolombo was not yet well enough to lead an expedition. The intention was to check on the

William Blake, ca 1790, from a painting by Stedman, ca 1775, Maroon Hunt, MAPes
MONDe Collection

place with the idea of putting it to work, preferably with its own slaves if any could be caught there. The warriors wished also to do some hunting of stray animals for meat. The only reason Bolombo did not move his camp here was the need he still felt to be near the English islands, for possible escape as well as possible bargaining.

A troop of loyal-slave CHASSEURS from Duurloo's came stealthily along the north shore bush trail from the west.

Kanta and his men swooped exuberantly down the GUT like an Indian raiding party. The huddle of refugee Company slaves and Bodger's Pietter scurried away to westward and stopped to watch from the nearest heights. They saw food and some KILL-DEVIL gulped happily by the raiders, who then searched for whatever they might find. The loot was negligible, for the place had already been plundered many times, but the coals were hot, and Kanta and his men began transporting them to the wooden parts of the various buildings.

At this point Bolombo's men arrived, and a fracas developed when they saw what Kanta was about to do.

Bolombo, alone among the rebel chiefs, still had some ammunition for his guns, and his party of warriors was well armed. When Kanta's men took to their heels at the sight of such force, four of the warriors shot at them, killing three and wounding one in the shoulder.

The watching refugees scampered away in terror and ran straight into the arms of the CHASSEURS who were by now just beyond the brow of the hill.

Bolombo's men melted away to eastward at sight of the CHASSEURS and the CHASSEURS settled down for the rest of the day and the night with the ten refugees as captives. Kanta and his men, on their way home over the mountains, had a holiday of burning in the domains of Bolombo and Aquashi.

Jannis van Bewerhoudt, suffering from dysentery, was in an uncharacteristic abyss of despair, near the end of his hope for St. Jan.

So deep was his despair that the next day, December eighteenth, when the CHASSEURS returned with the ten captives and he questioned them and half-listened to their frightened replies, he actually did not realize that he was hearing of rebel disunity, even though he had seen the dead Loangos in Coral Bay.

On this day the process of emptying The Trunk to make room for new captives continued with the trial of six prisoners, three male and three female: Bodger's Pietter, newly arrived without Bodger's knowledge, and the Company's Bootsman and Domingo; and Judge Hendrichsen's Santje and Eva and Secretary SCHØNNEMANN's Eva.

Pietter was quickly acquitted, for he was an obviously gentle little being. Domingo too was judged guiltless. All three of the women were flogged for having been, at some point, apparently camp-followers, willing or unwilling, of the rebels, and for being too frightened to divulge any information about them. They were released to their owners pending further evidence.

The Company's Bootsman was found guilty of rebellion because, when asked, Pietter quite simply told the truth: Bootsman had been one of those who, along with Aera and SCHØNNEMANN's Christian, had lifted Doctor Bodger's sons out of their beds and taken them away.

Now the witnesses had to watch Bootsman's brutal execution, preceded by the grisly use of glowing pincers and then, slowly and deliberately, hammers on the wheel.

On Sunday, December twentieth, a storm was building in the Danish West Indies. A heavy weather disturbance was drifting in from the southeast. The sky and sea, in preparation for it, were calm, leaden, and forbidding, with a strange sheen that made the neighboring cays and islands, near and distant, appear like mirages in a dark desert. Gusts of easterly wind pushed boats and ships spasmodically on their way and ruffled the sea like fur on a cat's neck.

During the night the storm of December 21, 1733, began with the usual preamble, "the warning shower" in local parlance.

By morning it was a roaring, lashing tropical storm that washed out terraced crops, inundated those in the level lands behind the bays, ripped out moorings and anchorages and ran boats and ships onto rocks, reefs, and beaches. There was no hiding in the night from its driving drenching, and everyone was miserable.

By the time it ended in the afternoon, with the sun suddenly shining gratuitous and clean, the water in a previously empty tub under the open sky at Duurloo's measured nearly twenty English inches, mighty boulders were tumbling with thundering roars in every big GUT on St. Jan, and *EENDRAGTEN* was aground in Current Hole, between Great St. James and St. Thomas, having been blown across the sound and sucked into The Hole by the hurrying sea and a southern tide.

The food crops on both islands were virtually destroyed, and ahead loomed weeks and weeks of waiting for fresh food to grow.

This storm altered the history of St. Jan in one way that would never be measurable. It caught the Englishman, Doudas, too near to Anegada Reef on his way back from Nevis with guns and ammunition. It brushed him against some coral prongs, and forced him to beach his BARQUE on the sands of Anegada Island. There he had to remain for nearly a month, repairing his hull and fighting the pirates who subsisted there by reaping the harvest of the deadly reef.

After the storm, Vessuup, having abandoned the plot to capture the rebel leaders and now thinking only of profit, came prowling about St. Jan in an English sloop. At Coral Bay he sent runners inland to find any one of the leaders.

They found Kanta at the Company master house, and summoned him to palaver. He had been afraid to approach the shore, for lack of arms, but when he learned who was there, he came, with his warriors pressing impotently behind him.

Vessuup, for revenge on the Danes, traded him all but bare necessities of the arms and ammunition he had aboard for four of Krøyer's slaves whom Kanta had captured from Bolombo. Kanta was willing to part with them because, of all his slaves, they were the most likely to give him trouble.

Vessuup went on his way, leaving Kanta with an expanding horizon and a mind that suddenly saw a possibility of conquering first Bolombo, then Aquashi, then Duurloo's Bay and St. Jan.

The Christmas–New Year's season in the Danish West Indies in the 1730s was far more than a merely religious occasion. To almost everyone but a BUSSAL straight from Africa, to whom he could mean nothing at all, the Christ child was a superb reason for surcease from work and care. The surcease expanded normally into communion, in the form of rum and other delights, with one's fellow man and woman. From this came a continuous din of music, drumming, dancing, singing, or simply shouting or screaming if one could not sing, along with fireworks, flag-waving and, at special points, the firing of cannons and handguns as fast as they could be loaded and exposed to the slow match or flint-steel spark.

All of that was changed, this year, Gardelin announced from his sickbed, to which he more and more frequently retreated. Because of the rebellion on St. Jan and the unrest among the slaves of St. Thomas, all would remain quiet. No guns would be fired. Everyone, slave and free, would remain in his home except for the necessary excursions of everyday life. There would be no carousing; no fireworks; no visible or audible celebration of any kind, save the solemn religious rites of the season.

The result was that no cannons were fired from the fort, no flags waved, and no fireworks were set off. The fort was quiet. The rest of the island of St. Thomas was drunk and noisy, as always starting the weekend before Christmas and ending when exhaustion set in, in early January.

On St. Jan the atmosphere was totally different. Duurloo's was quiet and glum. Womanless, deprived of family altogether, eating bad food, with only rum for consolation, the men of all stations thought of the good old days and quietly got drunk. Creutzer had left early in the holiday season; on Christmas Eve the Civil Guard members from St. Thomas who were doing their particular tour of duty simply deserted; and before Christmas the Cockney and Irish mercenaries had melted away into other fortune-hunting pursuits—

they had got no rewards, and although the rum was tolerable, the food was dreadful, and serious action against the rebels had appeared about to be demanded of them.

Some of Duurloo's force, such as Peder Sørensen, left for the holidays with dignity, as a matter of right, and with Captain van Bewerhoudt's permission. Sørensen, before leaving St. Jan, went home, over the ridge from Duurloo's, for the first time since the beginning of the rebellion.

There he found his secret cache of rum. Excellent KJELTUM it was, and he had always kept it hidden well. He took all but three flasks along for his Christmas pleasure. Into those three, being careful that none of the black men saw him—lest word somehow, in that magic African way, should reach the rebels—he poured white-arsenic rat poison. He left the flasks where they could be found and went away to his Christmas vacation in TAPPUS with his wife.

Doctor Bodger had a peaceful Christmas time. Ordered to remain on duty, he was no longer an outrage to anyone, and he was hardly noticed, save by those to whom he ministered.

The CHASSEURS all came in from the bush on Christmas Eve, bringing four female captives, and settled down to their KILL-DEVIL. Øttingen and his men, having no families and nowhere to go, holed in to get drunk and stay that way.

It struck Doctor Bodger that this, of all times, was the perfect moment for the rebels to strike and destroy the last vestiges of the white man on the island of St. Jan. But they were unaware of the open invitation that Duurloo's represented; they were more concerned with each other. In any case, no one among them but Christian Sost kept a calendar in his head.

Kanta, with his new-found wealth of guns and ammunition, was in a state of euphoria, but something made him hesitate to rush to wipe out Bolombo, who was now inferior in armed strength. Bolombo, hearing of Kanta's windfall, sent word ordering him to turn in the arms and ammunition and join with him in attacking the Whites. Kanta's answer was to run the ridges and heights overlooking Bolombo's strong point at night in the moonlight, stirring the horizon with flaring, sparkling FLAMBÉE-STOKS, threatening to set fire to the entire countryside. Still he drew back from outright confrontation.

Aquashi sat on his heights and watched, brooding, without arms with which either to assert himself or to take sides.

XII

THE rebel women were getting to be a problem to the males. Tired of sitting, waiting, with no betterment of their condition in sight and nothing happening to indicate any plan of action whatsoever, they were growing difficult to handle. Not only had most of them left the men's camps and joined together at Kob Flat, but the men who came to visit them now had to face a barrage of invective so withering that it put them on the defensive. Since no male warrior ever stooped to explain anything to a woman, nothing was clarified, and a man often had to end by beating his woman into submission. Tenderness, not a battle, was what one made the long, tedious journey there for, and so the visits grew less and less satisfactory to all concerned, and "The Women," as Kob Flat was now called, had begun to resemble a fortress under attack.

By now even Breffu was there, as well as Café, the sullen, burning Spanish-African; and Bolombo and Aquashi, respectively, were so attached to these two women that they found themselves coming at last to speak to them as equals.

Even Kanta, with his sweeping sense of his own infallibility, was not proof against the women's scorn. He was solving the problem by staying away from them these days, preferring deprivation to degradation.

The loyal slave CHASSEURS on St. Jan were restless and irritable. Those who were Company Negroes from St. Thomas felt superior to the rest, and even to the St. Jan white men, who, in their eyes, were after all merely country farmers on what they regarded as a backward island.

The CHASSEURS did not like their treatment and food, and threatened not to cooperate any further. They had to be placated somehow, for they represented the greater portion of Jannis's strength. He gave them extra rations of food and rum, the best he could lay his hands on; he even gave them KJELTUM instead of KILL-DEVIL, and ordered some of his White contingent to drink KILL-DEVIL to compensate, explaining that this was war and one could not be particular, but not explaining that he had given the KJELTUM to the Blacks.

On St. Thomas someone mentioned the fact that old Cesar Singal, the hunchback, was again living on the Magenses' St. Thomas PLANTAGE. Gardelin knew him well, and was fond of him. In the days before Cesar was sent to St. Jan, Gardelin had heard governors actually ask his advice on dealing with Company slaves in certain situations.

Gardelin now sent for Cesar, who came scuttling, crablike, into his presence, head down and neck twisted, cringing in exaggerated respect and wringing his cap as if laundering it. He all but fell face down, as would a Siamese minion in the presence of his king, but his face wore a covert grin that cancelled all of his obsequiousness.

Gardelin chuckled in pleasure at the sight of him. "Pay me all respect to which I am entitled, Cesar, but spare me your theatricals. I am sincerely glad to see you after all this time."

Cesar nodded his thanks in quick, birdish bobs, but said nothing.

"I trust that you are hale," Gardelin said. Cesar bobbed again.

"Good, for you are now, and shall be until further notice, in the service of the Company. Your master will be paid a reasonable rental, and you yourself, if you prove worthy, shall have rewards suitable to your deserts."

Cesar still spoke not a word, and his face said even less. "I am sending a new expedition to St. Jan to capture the rebels. You shall serve it as guide, and adviser on how and where to find them."

Cesar twisted his trunk as if testing a sore shoulder muscle, and very slowly shook his bent head from side to side, as if in pain, still staring at the floor.

"What are you doing?" Gardelin exclaimed. "Are you saying no to me? To me you are saying no?"

MAPes MONDe Collection

Cesar Singal spoke for the first time. "I am old," he said.

"You are spry as a mountain goat."

"I am crippled."

"You are sound as a household lizard."

"I am unwilling," Cesar said boldly, knowing that in this room he could say that and survive.

"You are willing," Gardelin said abruptly but not angrily, "or you shall be sold cheap to the next passing troupe of black entertainers to serve as their trained monkey on a tether."

Cesar winced as if struck by a TSCHICKEFELL, for he knew the full meaning of the threat.

"You will report to Herre Creutzer and be told when and where to be ready to go to St. Jan. You may go now," Gardelin continued wryly, "and I thank you very much for your kindness. I shall look forward to the reports on your helpfulness on St. Jan."

Cesar Singal bowed and left, seeming slightly more crippled than when he had entered.

"The Women" on St. Jan was now a more rebellious camp than was any of the three rebel encampments. In the nighttimes there were singing and dancing, deliberately staged to work up a martial fever in the stagnant males, who, when they came to visit now, were likely to meet with not only the usual barrage of abuse, but the wild, flame-like dancing of Café.

Café was not permitted to dance. It was against all tribal rules; but Café danced, and none could stop her. Indeed, none could for long resist the savage rhythm of her body, accentuated by the chanting and clapping of the others. Little by little a tapping of drums was added, and then a roar of drums, and male warriors demeaning themselves by joining a woman in a dance that became, in the end, a war ritual.

This ritual crossed tribal lines and little by little succeeded, where talk and taunts had failed, in bringing a touch of cooperation into the relationship between the male rebels.

It was after sleeping off the exhaustion of such a dancing, drinking night that Aquashi and Bolombo, at the insistence of the female leaders, began to speak quietly together. Aquashi had found a source of ammunition for his few weapons, as well as some guns, from CHASSEURS decamping from Duurloo's. Instead of threatening Bolombo, he chose to palaver, for he was running out of treasure to offer the JÆGERS and he wished to make a bargain with Bolombo.

The palaver ended in an agreement for a cautious collaboration between Bolombo and Prince Aquashi for the good of the rebellion. Bolombo would provide trinkets, some clothing, and a little gold for the JÆGERS Aquashi would contribute the ammunition to the common stock, and the two rebel camps would renew communication by messenger and drums, and try to strike as one, when the time came, against the white man.

Breffu and Café were exultant. They took their royal masters into their beds happily, and the lesser warriors found similar welcomes.

EENDRAGTEN was now on expedition to Coral Bay, with Johan Jacob Creutzer bearing special orders to assume command at Frederiksværn, and with Cesar Singal safely on board. The ship stood outside Coral Harbor all night, and at dawn, Sunday, January seventeenth, Creutzer had the cook serve a banquet of food and good rum to everyone on board, to fortify the men for whatever was to come of their attempt to round up the rebels.

At SIX-GLASS, SLAVE TIME, two hours after dawn, armed Blacks were seen coming over the pass from Brown's Bay and down the shallow GUT toward Suhm's.

Hastily Creutzer led ashore all his men who had guns.

The first sight that assaulted their eyes was the macabre collection of clean, white Loango bones beneath the GRIGRI tree near the shore. Some were in grotesquely haphazard heaps upon the ground where they had fallen, and some still dangled like rigid wind chimes from the crude coils of liana vine, turning slowly back and forth in the wind. The ants and crabs and carrion birds had long since moved on.

The oncoming Blacks had disappeared behind stone fences and walls, but as Creutzer's men fearfully approached, keeping as much cover as possible, there was enough shouting back and forth to establish that the strangers were a party of CHASSEURS four days out of Duurloo's on a hunting foray.

They were welcomed into the expedition with a good treat of rum, and then the enhanced force pushed up VÆRN Hill from both front and back to discover that the VÆRN was deserted.

As the day grew older and warmer, unknown Blacks were spied from above coming out of the Company bush at the foot of Bourdeaux's Mountain. Creutzer sent half his armed men to chase them if they turned out to be rebels; the men stayed away all the rest of the day, avoiding work, and came back in the evening in time for supper to report that the rebels had fled.

Monday, the eighteenth of January, was reconnoitering day, and Creutzer set out, with half his men, to inspect the nearby PLANTAGES. He sent some of his men on over the ridge toward Brown's Bay and Waterlemon Bay to see what they could find; they returned after a reasonable time and reported that they had found nothing.

Creutzer also found nothing, and led his men back up to the VÆRN by the back side of the hill, only to meet a report at the top that a large group of Blacks had come out of the Company bush and was advancing on the VÆRN from the front. Creutzer sent a patrol to intercept. The new arrivals turned out to be reinforcements sent by Captain van Bewerhoudt, in reluctant response to an order from Gardelin. A very tired John Charles shepherded them to make sure they did not desert.

Captain van Bewerhoudt was on the point of leaving St. Jan in the hands of Creutzer, and Øttingen with his soldiers, and letting the island, in his opinion, go to hell. He was sending Creutzer all of his black armed men. The Whites—all sixty of them—were informing Gardelin categorically that they were through with St. Jan and would retire to St. Thomas.

On Tuesday, the nineteenth of January, Creutzer's command in Coral Bay started to crumble when the CHASSEURS grew bored and deserted for the day, ignoring all orders, preferring to hunt wild pigs for fun and have a feast in the bush. But life in Duurloo's Bay took on some excitement that gave pause to the planters who were preparing to depart. The English Captain Toller suddenly sailed his majestic *Pearl* into the outer waters of Duurloo's and dropped anchor.

Creutzer's troubles with the CHASSEURS came to a head when they returned to quarters after shooting and eating eight pigs. They were contemptuous of Creutzer. When he gave them a lecture about the pigs, they ignored him. When he shouted at them and threatened them, they turned on him. Through their leader, the Company's Prince, a true prince of the Loango tribe, who felt at ease here in Coral Bay because this was his home PLANTAGE, they told him flatly that they would take no orders from him that did not please them.

Creutzer, beside himself with rage, felt helpless in this situation. John Charles, departing for Duurloo's by boat, went on his way, shaking his head.

Creutzer then called Cesar, whom almost all slaves feared, put a gun in his hands, chose twelve CHASSEURS including the Loango prince, and told Cesar to lead them on a rebel hunt from which they must not return empty-handed. They were to stay out until the evening of the next day.

Cesar led them into the bush. They circled around the PLANTAGE of the deceased Corporal Høg, where Cesar happened to know of a secret cache of excellent KJELTUM. The next day, the Loango prince decided that he did not wish to be under Cesar's command, and left for Duurloo's Bay, followed by two of his tribesmen. Cesar returned with his residue of nine, reported the defection of the Loangos, and told Creutzer that in his opinion there were no rebels in the bush, only some MARONS.

Creutzer noted that, oddly enough, the nine CHASSEURS under Cesar's command were no longer afraid of him. He chose to take this as a good sign: Cesar was a born leader.

Creutzer forgave him for returning empty-handed and sent him out again with his nine, plus three new CHASSEURS ordered not to return without a captive, even if it took a number of days.

Cesar led his patrol eastward this time, and they crossed the ridge to a tiny bay east of Brown's Bay where an isolated cottage stood right by the beach, and the bush there, Cesar knew, was usually crawling with wild pigs because of the good, soft rooting.

Next morning, Creutzer's own BARQUE came from TAPPUS and anchored in the harbor, bringing additional supplies and men.

Creutzer organized another party of CHASSEURS from among the newcomers, led by FREE NEGRO Emanuel Christian, and sent it eastward.

A fearful and beautiful English warship, which Creutzer thought he recognized as the one called *De Spargement,* but actually HMS *Pearl,* put into the outer bay that day, luffing grandly. Creutzer had the Danish flag run up on the pole at the VÆRN and manned the guns, from which the spikes had been removed with great labor. The ship turned her cluster of marvelous white sails to catch the wind and sailed away around East End.

The next day, Friday, January twenty-second, Creutzer decided that it was safe to put the Company work force to cleaning up the BARCADS and gathering food crops. He informed Gardelin that he might as well put the PLANTAGE back into full production, since there were no rebels to be found, and the VÆRN was now strong enough to keep watch and repel attack from the land side. He did this, not out of regard for the Company, but to encourage his fellow planters to return and put the island back into production, so he could leave.

Cesar Singal brought his detachment back to the VÆRN because the rebels had cleaned out the pigs he had expected to find. He reported no rebels seen or heard, and Creutzer seemed not displeased despite his previous orders.

FREE NEGRO Emanuel brought his party of CHASSEURS back, and likewise had seen no rebels.

At about noon on this day, HMS *Pearl* reappeared outside the harbor. This time, instead of hesitating, she sailed right in, in all her majesty.

As she approached the inner harbor, the VÆRN became an agitated anthill. Creutzer ordered the guns manned and the drums and trumpets sounded. He broke out powder and ball for the small arms and ordered the men to be ready for action.

The ship swung her sloop out on her davits and dropped it alongside. It filled with a landing party, visible from the VÆRN, and sailed smartly to the Company dock.

Captain van Bewerhoudt and William Barnds came ashore and up to the VÆRN, escorted by an armed English guard consisting of a midshipman, a quartermaster, and four sailors.

Creutzer and van Bewerhoudt greeted each other with pro forma cordialities spoken with hostility.

"Sir," Creutzer then said coldly, "it is out of order for you to bring armed forces from another nation here into this fortification. I authorized no such thing."

"This is not the time for such niceties," Jannis replied. "Captain Toller is here by special arrangement with Governor Gardelin. He picked us up at Duurloo's and explained Gardelin's plot to put an end to this rebellion. Gardelin is smart enough not to wish a written record of this."

Creutzer scowled but held his tongue for the moment.

"The rebels," Jannis continued, "have seen the great English warship with its many guns and its two hundred and fifty men sail into this harbor and send armed men up here to the VÆRN. You will run up this white flag as a signal to the ship that you are convinced you cannot fight against such power and that you will surrender. Then thirty armed men from the ship will come up and strike the Danish flag and hoist the English flag as a sign that the English have captured the island."

"You are insane, sir!"

"Oh, come, man," Jannis said sharply. "Be not a fool. It is but a deception. Early tomorrow morning when you hoist the white flag I shall send the thirty men from the ship and they will make a show of taking all of the armed Negroes from here and marching them as apparent captives down to the ship. Word will be passed to the rebels that the English have conquered the Danes here and will give freedom to all St. Jan slaves to celebrate the event. All will be invited to a great party, with much rum and roast pig and beef and goat, and music and dancing, and all will then be easily taken!"

Creutzer burst out, "You may do what you will, but I will not give over this fortification! Never!"

Jannis van Bewerhoudt circulated throughout the VÆRN, searching out his thirteen CHASSEURS from Duurloo's. He lined them up and ordered them to come down to the bay the following morning at dawn, with their hands on their heads as if surrendering.

He and Barnds returned once more to shout at Creutzer, trying to persuade him to help them in their plot. He adamantly refused.

They tried to bribe him with promises of gifts. He disdained them.

Finally they left the VÆRN, shaking their heads elaborately at each other in frustration.

Creutzer spoke, in what English he could muster, to the midshipman in charge of the detail of English sailors. He requested the sailors to leave the VÆRN at once, report to their captain and inform him that if he wished a fight, he had one, for if he chose to fire upon the VÆRN, the VÆRN was prepared to give him shot for shot.

The sailors saluted and departed.

Creutzer sat down and had a drink, plainly feeling that he had acquitted himself rather well.

At Anegada, the earth's-end, nearly inundated sand-covered reef easternmost of the Virgin Islands, the Englishman, Doudas, had at last got his ship repaired and off the beach, and he sailed into Waterlemon Bay, St. Jan, near midnight by the light of a half moon.

King Clæs was again using Gabriel van Stell's Point above Brown's Bay as his camp because the heights around Waterlemon Bay made him too vulnerable, but he had a watch posted at all strategic points, night and day. Doudas was quickly observed, and King Clæs was awakened. He went in the night with his warriors to Waterlemon Bay to palaver with the white man, and by dawn he was the owner of seven good new flintlock rifles—all that had survived the pirate raids on Anegada—the weight of two slaves in ball, and three kegs of dry gunpowder, and Doudas, richer by four able-bodied male slaves and one female, was sailing into Tortola Old Road with his legitimate cargo of English trade goods to sell to the planters of the British Virgin Islands.

XIII

A ship out of Amsterdam for the Dutch colonies in the Caribbean went out of her way, for a price, to drop at St. Thomas some important mail from Kjøbenhavn, along with a stout box, padlocked, sealed, and chained.

The box contained an infusion of life blood to the islands: cash money, enough, almost, to put an end for a time to the cumbersome trading in promises and credit slips.

The ship brought also word of rumors circulating in Europe of a treaty, so far kept secret, between Denmark and France, calling for the sale of the island of Ste. Croix to the Danish West India and Guinea Company.

Everyone knew that France and Denmark were not friends, but the rumor had it that King Louis XV wished to restore his father-in-law, Stanislas Leszczynski, to the Polish throne. In such an undertaking, it would be useful to have, if not the help, at least the neutrality of Denmark, a traditional friend of Poland.

Since Ste. Croix was known to be a far better agricultural island than both St. Thomas and St. Jan together, the Danish West India and Guinea Company badly needed it for business reasons. The Company, the rumor said, had therefore prevailed upon King Frederik, the chief stockholder in the Company, to promise neutrality during the war that would have to precede Louis's retaking the Polish throne for Stanislas.

"This is news indeed!" Gardelin exclaimed when he heard of it in his sickroom.

If true, it would give him good reason to envision a doubling, at least, of his importance in the Indies.

While the Dutch ship was in port, members of her crew spent a great deal of time in the TAPHOUSE of Mme. Oligh talking to the

Dutch-speakers among her regular customers. They heard all about the rebellion on St. Jan and the fact that it was precipitated by high-spirited, powerful-bodied African nobility. They applied their minds, with the help of rum, first to the problem of putting down this rebellion, and then to the matter of preventing such a thing from happening again.

One of them observed that a slave had to be, first of all, docile. Now, he had heard it said that eunuchs were docile. Why should it not be common policy simply to castrate high-spirited male slaves as soon as they showed their high spirits?

The question was heard and nodded over, and in passing from mouth to ear it spread everywhere as a statement instead of a question, and by the time it reached the slave compounds it was told as official government policy.

All male slaves showing any spirit would henceforth be castrated, and any captured St. Jan rebels would be castrated, whether any other punishment were given them or not; every slave who heard this believed it implicitly, and there was no slave on St. Thomas, and eventually on St. Jan, who did not hear it.

There was a war dance at The Women, in the northerly shadow of the peak that was beginning to be called Amina Hill; but very little rum was drunk, for important matters hung in the air.

Kanta had heard in advance of this war dance and was irresistibly drawn to it. For the first time in many weeks the three leaders were dancing together, and then talking, and Kanta's favorite woman, Bomboe, was there to make it all seem right to him at last.

Talking with the men was Breffu. She could not be denied. Then Café sat in. The male was being subtly undermined—yet not one of the males, once he grew accustomed to this new development, seemed to feel degraded; and the time soon came when free discussion, punctuated by violent arguments, took place at Kob Flat without regard to sex. If the males had examined the results closely, they would have found that it was the female advice that was being followed; but they did not care to look too closely.

"Attack the white man without further delay. He is gaining

Picart, 1723, MAPes MONDe Collection

strength."

"The time is not yet. We are not strong enough."

"Trick him, then. He is forever sending word that all who surrender peacefully will be pardoned. Send him word that we wish to palaver, we are ready to talk of surrender, if we be assured of pardon. When his leaders come into the bush to palaver, ambush them, kill them."

At Coral Bay when dawn of Saturday the twenty-third came and Jannis's thirteen CHASSEURS did not descend VÆRN Hill in an attitude of surrender as they had been ordered to do, Jannis and Barnds cursed Creutzer's pigheadedness and prepared to march after the rebels.

To build excitement, as was customary, the morning began aboard ship with the hoisting and waving of flags, a gradual crescendo of rolls on the drums, changing to a deafening march tempo beat, with a screaming of trumpets joining in. To this accompaniment, the expedition from the ship started going ashore in the ship's sloop, ten at a time.

Barnds, following an order from Gardelin, insisted on limiting the British participation to thirty of Toller's sailors. Creutzer had spent the night reconsidering his own attitude, in view of official reports that would be made accusing him of refusing to help in the fight against whatever rebels there might be. As the forces from the ship were being ferried ashore, he sent out a detachment to join them in the hunt. Cesar Singal, curled up in a corner with his arms clasped tightly about his abdomen, managed to be too ill to serve as guide and adviser.

The combined forces of more than a hundred men, well-armed, well-fed and -rummed, emboldened by martial noises and stream-ing flags, marched smartly up the floor of the valley of the Company estate. Someone had seen human forms high in the Company GUT near the spring, and so the little army headed in that direction.

After a sweaty climb to the spring, they found some frightened Negro women who started timidly toward them, then lost their nerve and ran like gazelles. Someone fired at them and brought down one, kicking in the dirt. The others got away into the bush.

A detachment of JÆGERS was dispatched to carry the wounded woman down to the bay. Bodger had been transferred to Coral Bay because now the greatest concentration of people was to be there and he might be needed in case of fighting. He removed the bullet from the woman's back and tried to make her comfortable.

Kanta's Amina warriors watched from hiding as the expeditionary forces spent the day lunging ineffectually about the edges of the bush. The black JÆGERS, not permitted to do anything in their own way, performed lethargically and cynically according to orders, knowing that they were wasting their time. One of them limped in with one of Kanta's bullets in his buttocks, and Bodger had to use his probe once more.

At the end of the day the expedition, exhausted, split into its component parts. Creutzer's contingent went up to the VÆRN, and the sailors and Jannis's men returned to the ship.

Word somehow trickled through, by artful design, from the St. Jan bush to Christiansfort, St. Thomas, that King Clæs, being guiltless in the rebellion, would, if encouraged, come in with his men, lay down his arms, and take up his PLANTAGE duties once more.

Gardelin called the Secret Council into bedside session. This was the beginning of the end of the rebellion. Plans had to be made.

Toller's seamen on St. Jan were painfully aware of their uselessness in the bush, but still, on Sunday the twenty-fourth, they went out once more. They found no rebels. Now they had had enough. The process of giving and getting was out of balance, so far as they were concerned, and they persuaded Captain Toller to give up the St. Jan project.

With St. Jan sinking into hopelessness, and people with cynical second thoughts all around Gardelin insisting on discounting King Clæs's message, Gardelin relieved Creutzer and his ship and men of their special duty, and left Øttingen in command of the VÆRN, with Bodger in attendance. Jannis and his men returned to Duurloo's Bay.

The Secret Council now opened its ears to all ideas.

Bodger was regaining his spirits, watching in fascination as a nervous, thirsty young pearly-eyed thrasher, called t'rushie in the CREOLE dialect, tried to get a drink of water.

A barrel, standing under the open sky inside the VÆRN, had been filled to the brim by bearers for the use of everyone. The t'rushie was attracted to it at once; but as it flew in to alight on the rim of the barrel, it was frightened away by its own reflection.

Bodger realized that it had never had a drink of water out of anything larger than a crevice in a rock or an upturned blossom containing drops of rainwater or dew.

The bird came back again to the rim of the barrel, trusting that its adversary might have gone away; but each time as it alighted, the enemy came up from below to attack it, and it leaped into the air with violent defensive motions and fled to the nearest perch.

Finally it decided to approach from the ground, perhaps to surprise the enemy. Flying up to the barrel's rim and looking over the edge into the water, it was promptly menaced by the head and walled eyes of its enemy, and fled again in fear.

Bodger realized that even if he should put out a small amount of water in a dish for the unhappy bird, the problem would remain the same. It was best to stand back, let the bird learn by experience so that it would never again be afraid of its own reflection.

It took a long time, lengthened by the comings and goings of people about their affairs, but at last the bird, in desperation, attacked its adversary and was not harmed by it. Instead, it got a taste of water and, as Bodger smiled in satisfaction, took not only a good drink, but a luxurious bath as well.

The weight of the dry season was pressing on St. Jan's earth. The island was turning brown. Gardens dried up. The few coconuts within the rebel sphere were all consumed. Excepting soursop and the skimpy fruit of a few imported tamarind trees, neither very nourishing, the year's other fruits were all gone.

There was a small militant faction at Duurloo's, headed by Jan DE WINDT, that was certain there were spies among the JÆGERS who were responsible for the disappearance of arms and ammunition. They agitated constantly for drastic measures. They wished to execute one of the JÆGERS, any one at all, in the expectation that the guilty ones would betray themselves by trying to leave. Captain van Bewerhoudt would not hear of it, and John Charles backed him up.

When the captain went to TAPPUS, Jan DE WINDT and his fellows prepared to carry out their scheme in his absence. John Charles stopped them, threatening to throw them into the dungeon if he had to go so far as that to keep them under control.

The malcontents got off a fast message to Gardelin saying that John Charles was obstructing justice against rebels and demanding that he be removed as lieutenant.

Gardelin, feeling confused and tired, accommodated them and ordered Jan DE WINDT installed as the new lieutenant in command in Captain van Bewerhoudt's absences.

The moment he received this appointment, Jan DE WINDT picked out the first JÆGER who came along, Bombo, belonging to SCHØNNE-MANN, and ordered FREE NEGRO Captain Mingo to behead him on the spot. He called the JÆGERS to watch and told them that the same thing was going to happen to all spies and purloiners of arms and ammunition, one after another.

Captain Mingo carried out his orders in spite of John Charles's yells of outrage. He hefted every KAPMESSER he could find, chose the heaviest one, and sharpened it deliberately, seeming to savor the ringing, singing sound the metal made as the stone left the steel at the end of each stroke. He tested the blade, finally, on a thick banana stalk, and when the tree was nearly severed with one blow under the strength of his right arm, he was satisfied.

He motioned vigorously for Bombo to lie on the ground to receive his coup. Bombo refused, struggled to get free, gasping and rolling his whitened eyes.

Finally, impatiently, Mingo had him bound to a tree in a sitting position, and then, holding the KAPMESSER in both hands and striking as if chopping the tree, severed Bombo's head with one powerful blow.

The head bounced grotesquely on the ground and was pounced upon by some St. Thomas Free Negro jægers, who piked it on a sharpened stick and played games with it.

The Company owed Schønnemann a hundred and twenty rigsdalers for Bombo's death, and none of the slave jægers played into Jan De Windt's hands by deserting at this time.

When Jannis van Bewerhoudt returned to duty he angrily reinstalled John Charles as lieutenant, and Gardelin, explaining that he had nothing against The Old Englishman but had only been trying to calm the malcontents, made it official.

For the first time in weeks Gardelin was once more out of bed. He turned his mind wearily to Duurloo's defenders' latest threat to leave St. Jan to the rebels. His reply, couched in vigorous Dutch, employed the full force of the authority that was available to him.

NOTICE

To the Citizenry of St. Jan.

I, Ph. Gardelin, hereby make known that if any person of the citizenry of St. Jan, contrary to all his duties of faithfulness to his Government, pledged by his sacred oath to sacrifice his blood and property for the country, should dare to plan to desert the country and leave it in the hands of such barbaric heathens as we are engaged in fighting, then such a Citizen shall be regarded as a perjurer who has falsely sworn an oath; he shall also be considered a deserter whose goods and property and all he possesses here and on St. Jan shall be confiscated, according to the most gracious Law and Ordinances of His Royal Majesty. Each person must regulate his acts according to the said Laws in order to protect himself against dishonor and loss.

Given at Christiansfort on the Island of St. Thomas under the

Royal Company's Seal and my hand on this 12th of February, 1734.

Ph. Gardelin

XIV

AN English privateer named John Maddox, from St. Kitts, had sailed his ship Diamond in to Tappus and offered to make a contract to clean up the rebels on St. Jan with his own manpower.

The contract Gardelin signed was a measure of the Danish desperation. Maddox was to keep all rebels he could capture, except the ten "most criminal," for which he would be paid at the rate of twenty pieces of eight each. In addition, any rebels who might surrender to the authorities in hope of pardon, during the two weeks covered by the contract, would be turned over to Maddox.

Maddox signed and sailed away to St. Kitts to raise his manpower.

Everyone owning slaves on St. Jan was required to send in a notarized list of the slaves he had at that moment on that island, listing them as either rebel or nonrebel. People not owning slaves there were asked to make lists, too, according to their knowledge. These lists would prevent Maddox from capturing nonrebel slaves and claiming them as bounty. When all lists had been collated and tallied, the total number of slaves presumed to be with the rebels, either as rebels or as their slaves, came to one hundred and forty-six.

A list of the twenty presumed leaders of the rebellion was prepared for the use of whoever turned out to be the representative of Company and planters stationed with Maddox to see that he abided by his contract. Of the twenty, ten had to be delivered for public punishment; if fewer than ten of them should remain alive after Maddox's campaign, then the number of ten had to be made up out of captives, and an effort would be made to choose known active rebels to make up the balance.

Among the rebels the process of fermentation was working slowly. The Women had become the capital of the insurrection. Both Bolombo and Prince Aquashi with their men were there in force, relaxing after the minor victorious forays of the previous weeks, and the women were, at first, congratulating and rewarding them, and then working them up to a new pitch with tonguelashings in the daytime and the nightly excitement of war dances in the light of the TORCHWOOD flares.

Kanta had a great desire to stay with them, sharing the excitement, but he still had the matter of his pride to work out.

Meanwhile, he made a foray westward along the south shore and into the west end of the island, south of Duurloo's Bay, where no rebel had bothered to go since before Christmas. He found very little worth looking for in the southwest—a few sodden loyal slaves who were living in solitude and poverty, waiting for their masters or MESTERKNEGTS to return.

Going up the GUT from Little Cruz Bay he found, at Sørensen's, the elderly couple, Abraham and Martha, who rated as MANQUERONS. They had come back to live at the PLANTAGE, with their master's permission, in view of the peacefulness of the landscape.

Abraham and Martha knew about the poisoned rum that Sørensen had left there in case any rebels might wish to celebrate the holidays, and they had instructions to pretend to be trying to hide it if any rebels came by. The old people would be in no danger, for the rebels would not care to take them as slaves and would not fear them as enemies.

When Kanta and his men came, Abraham and Martha were too frightened to do anything but disappear into the GUT. They watched from cover while the Aminas found the poisoned rum and settled down to drink it.

Then the old couple crept down to Little Cruz Bay, where they took refuge in Jean Papillaut's empty house.

By the time the Aminas had drunk two of the three flasks of rum they were feeling sick. For one whole week they were so desperately ill that they could not move from Sørensen's.

After three days an Amina who had not joined the expedition came searching to see what had happened, and tracked them to Sørensen's. He ran back to fetch Christian Sost.

Christian came and used herbal remedies that he had learned from Cesar Singal to counteract the effects of the poison, the nature of which he could only guess. Whether because of his herbs or because of the passage of time, Kanta and his men were on their feet in four more days. After taking another day to gain strength, they left without burning the place down, to the astonishment of Christian Sost.

On this day Abraham finally sent word over John Solomon's Hill to his master at Duurloo's that the rebels had drunk the poisoned drum.

The message created a sensation such as had not been felt at Duurloo's in weeks. Could it be that the rebel leaders now lay dead at Sørensen's?

Captain van Bewerhoudt sent Sørensen with an armed party to see if the poisoned rum had really been drunk. Sørensen found the two empty flasks and, hearing shooting at The KILL-DEVIL Widows', advanced cautiously as soon as he heard the rebels move on toward Susannaberg. He found two dead slaves and their hysterical family. Then he returned to Duurloo's to report.

Jannis van Bewerhoudt sent Mingo Tamarin and his FREE NEGRO Corps in pursuit of the Aminas. They found them at Bewerhoudtsberg, scraping the bottom of the looting barrel, and chased them down the GUT.

Kanta and his warriors were still weakened from the effects of the poison and a week's illness, and the FREE NEGRO Corps had no trouble catching up to them below the old waterfall above Fish Bay.

The Aminas had to turn and fight. They fired from behind rocks and trees, and the Corpsmen took similar cover.

The batterie, as the CREOLE fighters called a battle, lasted until both sides had used up all their ammunition, and then both sides retired quietly, carrying some dead and wounded. Of the FREE NEGRO Corps only one was wounded, none killed.

That "batterie" and GUT were from that moment famous among the fighters, for this was the only protracted battle between the opposing forces that ever took place outside of Duurloo's Bay.

The third of March, Ash Wednesday, was the day upon or before which Maddox had contracted to arrive.

He did not arrive.

Water became a problem at the VÆRN, so supplies of it were requisitioned in hogsheads from TAPPUS to be taken up the harbor side of VÆRN Hill under the watchful eyes of the garrison.

The Company slaves at Christiansfort, St. Thomas, were ordered to fill the hogsheads and load them on the Company BARQUE. Ceremoniously they took turns urinating into the water as they worked.

The crowded VÆRN was distracted by a cry from the sentry on the north firing step. Two ships and a sloop could be seen coming to anchorages outside distant Waterlemon Bay. It was now the fourth day of Lent, Sunday, March 7, 1734.

Maddox had chosen to put in to Waterlemon Bay instead of Coral Bay because when he had left it was common knowledge that the rebels were concentrated between those two areas of St. Jan. It seemed to him that it would be wise to have the men of the VÆRN ahead of him while he and his men swept the rebels toward them from the north, with Duurloo's to watch over the west. He was due to receive at least ten live slaves, no matter who killed or captured whom.

Jan DE WINDT was ordered to Waterlemon Bay as representative of the Company and the planters, and he took along another man to keep an eye open while he slept.

There were no rebels between Maddox and the VÆRN. They were all in the central south, either at The Women or in the little forest behind Ram's Head; somehow they managed to live without betraying their location.

John Maddox, with his seventy men, in forces never greater than fifty at a time, scoured St. Jan for one week from Little Cruz Bay all the way around the south and east sides to Mary Point. His guides led him without fail to every unoccupied PLANTAGE. Nowhere was there a sign that anyone had been there within at least the past few weeks.

Kob Flat, in full knowledge, kept itself totally quiet and smoke-less.

Maddox moved his haze of operations to Duurloo's Bay. His conclusion, which he faithfully reported to Øttingen, Captain van Bewerhoudt, and Gardelin, was that the rebels had left the island— or that perhaps Vessuup had won the race for slaves.

Jannis van Bewerhoudt knew better.

The rebels at Kob Flat were by now nearly worked up by the women to the fever pitch that was needed for an assault. But the VÆRN, peered at constantly over the rim of the bowl, looked entirely too strong at the moment, and it was decided that the first thrust of the combined forces should be at Duurloo's; when the white man was cleared out of Duurloo's, Breffu explained, the white man at Coral Bay would weaken himself by splitting up to come to the rescue, and could be ambushed. Then the debilitated "fort" would fall.

Preparations were under way for a full assault on Duurloo's.

Jannis van Bewerhoudt was careful to conceal his contempt for Maddox and his men, but he wrote to Gardelin about it, saying that they were doing more harm than good, and requesting that old Cesar Singal be sent up once more to help them track rebels when they next set out into the bush.

Cesar was sent up by express boat. With him went a letter saying that if anything happened to him, Maddox would be held strictly responsible.

On Sunday the fourteenth of March, Maddox set out to scour the north and northwest of St. Jan, guided by Cesar Singal. The rebels' drums suddenly started working again, and Captain van Bewerhoudt's loyal slave spies reported to him that the rebels were aware of Maddox's plan. Jannis did not warn Maddox, for fear of frightening him off, earning more of Gardelin's wrath.

A full two-day storm blew in. It was so violent that a ship at sea near St. Thomas ran in to TAPPUS harbor for protection. She was French—*La Chasseuse*.

The French captain sat sipping wine at one of Gardelin's excellent meals, prepared by the famous black chef, Paris. The necessary interpreter happily received the same honor. The captain had heard from Gardelin all about the miserable situation on St. Jan. Gardelin now asked him whether, in his opinion, it would be a waste of time to send to Martinique asking for help against the rebels, in case the Englishman should fail.

"Not at all!" the captain said. "Have you not heard?"

"Heard what?" Gardelin said anxiously. "We have had no ships. One is long overdue."

"France and Denmark are now friends!"

"God be praised! We have had only rumors."

"I myself have heard, some time ago, Governor General de Champigny at Martinique say that he would gladly send six hundred men to help the Danes if they should ask."

By the sixteenth the storm cleared, and William Barnds, sent by Gardelin to look into the possibility of spies, came to Duurloo's. He simply rounded up every JÆGER who had come from Africa. There were thirty-one of them. One was Moth's Ambrosius, known by all to be as gentle and guileless a man as ever stumbled into slavery.

Without a hearing, Barnds summarily hanged the thirty-one to save ammunition, buried them in a mass grave in the coconut grove seaward from the sugar works, and that was the end of the matter.

The Englishman, Maddox, was an intolerable burden on Jannis van Bewerhoudt.

Duurloo's ran out of food. There was ill feeling between the regulars and the English forces, a large number of whom took the opportunity to leave for Tortola aboard a passing sloop.

Old Cesar Singal guided Maddox and the remnants of his men through the bush paths of St. Jan. In the afternoon of March eighteenth they were ambushed in Bourdeaux's GUT by the rebels, who, with arrows and some guns, killed three of them, including Maddox's own son, and wounded five, but somehow missed Cesar Singal. The Englishmen gave a good account of themselves in their first fusillade, killing six rebels, but then broke and ran.

The rebels, instead of pursuing them, stayed to lick their wounds. Cotompa chose to celebrate, mounting two of the English heads— Maddox's son's and another—on poles and exhausting himself in a savage war dance with a high-riding pole in each hand.

By evening, Maddox, mourning his son, had taken his shaken men aboard the ship. He hesitated overnight in case massive avenging reinforcements should arrive. Then, without bounty or booty, he sailed straight from Duurloo's Bay over the horizon to the British Leeward Islands and did not return.

Before sending Cesar Singal back to St. Thomas, Jannis van Bewerhoudt had a talk with him.

"Cesar, you are aware that you are under suspicion?"

"Of what, Master?"

"Of misleading instead of leading."

"But, Master, this island is a wilderness in many of its parts. It is the ideal hiding place for rebels—who, by the way, are extremely clever at covering their signs."

"Cesar, you are a well-educated person. Are you so well-educated that you would venture to lie to me?"

"Master! You know me—these how many years!" Cesar's face was such a picture of shock and hurt that Jannis actually apologized to him.

"I am sorry. See you, now—I hear that there are dogs on Tortola, some hounds from England, that are capable of tracking a man. If as you say, the rebels are so damned clever at covering their tracks, would not such dogs easily find them?"

"Yes, Master," Cesar said. "I know these English hounds very well. Not these at Tortola, but the breed."

"Now, I know nothing of English hounds. If you were shown these, would you be able to choose the ones that could track rebels?"

"Assuredly, Master," Cesar said.

"Then you will accompany me to Tortola when I send for you. Meanwhile, I shall make arrangements."

"Very well, Master."

Jannis van Bewerhoudt was jubilant.

Seeing Maddox sail away indicated a victory to the rebels, and that night, in spite of the scorn heaped on them by Breffu and Café for not having followed up with the projected attack on Duurloo's, which surely would have fallen, they celebrated in the usual way.

Breffu and Café subsided gradually, and before morning were dancing with the men.

Breffu knew now that these noblemen were capable only of sporadic warfare, incapable of pursuing a sustained campaign. Their upbringing had made it necessary for them to celebrate every victory before going on to the next. This, she knew all too well, was because in their homeland warfare was a pastime in the nature of an athletic contest, indulged in primarily for pleasure. True, of late it had come to be practiced for profit, but always on a sporadic pattern, with victory revels when indicated, and recovery periods when contests were lost.

As soon as he received the news of the Maddox fiasco, Gardelin called an emergency joint meeting of the Secret Council and the Committee for St. Jan Planters and got their agreement to his plan to send Chief Merchant Horn to Martinique by the French ship, to ask for help. The next resolution was to ask the French for one hundred men.

Horn was uneasy.

"We have only a tippling sea captain's word that France and Denmark are friends," he said. "The last dependable news we had from Europe was that King Louis was threatening Poland, our ancient friend. For all we know, Denmark and France may be at war at this very moment, and I shall be imprisoned the moment I appear in Martinique."

"We shall have to take that chance," Gardelin said. "There is no one else in the Indies to whom we can turn."

"You mean I shall have to take that chance, while you sit here safe behind the guns of Christiansfort."

"Hah! Safe I would not say, for if we are at war with France, Louis's naval power can blow this island off the map!"

La Chasseuse was sailready for the following dawn, and Horn was aboard.

The English ship *Maria,* out of Boston, Thomas Taché, skipper, was in port. As supercargo she carried a minor French diplomat on his way to a new post. This gentleman paid a courtesy call upon Gardelin, and in the course of the conversation let fall that he knew for certain that France and Denmark were now good friends and, technically, allies in a war against Poland.

After the diplomat's departure, Gardelin summoned Horn and told him of what he had learned. He then dictated to a linguist scribe, in Danish while the scribe wrote in French, letters to General de Champigny and the Intendant, the Marquis d'Orgeville, at Martinique asking for their help in putting an end to the rebellion on St. Jan.

The next morning, March twenty-second, *La Chasseuse* set sail, with Commander Horn as supercargo, bearing the letters to the two Marquis in charge of the French Windward Islands and six hundred RIGSDALERS in cash, a sum so enormous that it had made the bookkeeper in Gardelin shudder as he handed it over.

Jannis van Bewerhoudt and Cesar Singal took their trip to Tortola, where Jannis had made financial arrangements to borrow some bloodhounds, unofficially.

Cesar chose three of the finest specimens.

Back at Duurloo's, Cesar put in a strenuous night. He managed to drift away from the CRESSET lights and fade into the bush. Before morning he had made a wide circle over unimportant bush paths, beginning at Denis' Bay and ending at Duurloo's. The guard paid no attention to him when he returned, for they knew him well.

At dawn, when awakened for the hunt, he was sleeping deeply, and all day he seemed to Jannis and his men unnaturally old.

He led the dogs and men to Denis' Bay. He searched elaborately along the fringes of the trail, then introduced the dogs to his own scent along the bush path.

The dogs looked puzzled and fawned upon him. He urged them on, and finally—at first returning frequently to Cesar, wagging their tails—they went ahead and followed the trace. Behind them gingerly trudged half the manpower of Duurloo's armed to the teeth.

When they arrived back at Duurloo's, Jannis threw up his hands in disgust.

"*English* dogs!" he cried. "What would you expect? Still, just in case, we shall try again tomorrow!"

"But," Cesar said gently, "we must return the dogs at once to Tortola, or their owner will be very angry."

"Why is that?"

"Because the dogs cannot eat our salt pork or fish. They are very hungry, and by tomorrow will be half-starved."

"I have a mind to feed them you!" Jannis stormed. "Why in God's name did you not remind me to bring meat for them from Tortola? I have no experience with dogs that have to be *fed*."

He sent off a hunting party of loyal slaves, but strangely it could find not so much as a rat to shoot; and in frustration Jannis returned the highbred dogs to Tortola, and Cesar Singal to TAPPUS.

The rebels spent an entire month, first celebrating their victory over Maddox, then recovering from the celebration, and then being worked up by the women with tongue-lashings and war dances to the pitch necessary for another assault. As part of the ritual, they burned the whole Vessuup PLANTAGE, buildings, fields, and forest, deserted now by the Aquambos; the boiling-house and two fields at Magens's Rustenburg and Adventure estates; and the residence, storehouse, and a cane field at Hammer Farm.

XV

MARCH ran out. The days were blistering hot in the sun, cool in the shade, too cool with the breeze blowing, so that a naked, sweating man shivered. Evenings called for a wrap, in spite of the warmth of the earth so hotly baked all day by the sun.

St. Jan was dried brown, not only by the sun but by February's and March's immoderate winds. Yet somehow the plants sensed that it was spring. The MAMPOO trees, the MANJACK, the West Indies dogwood were blooming. Their blossoms looked like leaf buds; still, to the nectar-hunting birds and insects they were more beautiful than hibiscus.

The cacti were living now, shrinking slightly, on their stored up juices. Spider grass appeared dead, and GUINEA GRASS rolled its blades into spikes to avoid the sun while waiting for rain. The deciduous plants made their incredible effort to put out leaves, but got along on the minimum of moisture for purposes of transpiration.

Food crops were nonexistent on St. Jan, and the rebels were hard put to keep their bellies satisfied and their strength at the ready for reveling or fighting.

Masters and slaves alike waited for rain, to make it possible to plant Indian and GUINEA CORN and IGNAMES. Cotton topping should all have been finished by now, preparatory for new sprouting. Banana slips were waiting, withdrawing their juices underground until rain should make transplanting possible.

At Christiansfort, St. Thomas, Commander Frøling was going to be needed and knew that he was a fit subject for leniency after the healing passage of time.

St. Thomas, in spite of the influx from St. Jan, was no longer short of housing. Hordes of people had by now managed in one way or another to leave the island, legally or illegally, because of hurricane, famine, rebellion, and plagues of insects and sickness.

The Company ship EENIGHEDEN, by estimate of those who had come ahead of her on Dutch ships, was now at least two months overdue from KJØBENHAVN, and desperately needed.

From Maundy Thursday until the Tuesday after Easter nothing stirred but lizards unless by absolute necessity, and the new moon, tilted so as to hold water in its bowl of light, kept the rain from falling.

A supply of whale oil had been bought from a Dutchman, and the VÆRN at Coral Bay could now light its CRESSET LAMPS and stop sending men into the bush for TORCHWOOD.

The stump of Peder Krøyer's Santje's chopped-off leg was deemed sufficiently healed, and she was put to light work.

As April came, the possible time of arrival of Frenchmen approached. Cesar Singal was sent to Coral Bay to act as their guide in case they should sail straight there and get to work without wasting time coming to St. Thomas.

Half of April inched away. The islands seemed to hold their breath, watching, waiting.

Jannis van Bewerhoudt went to Coral Bay to scout the possibility and advisability of moving. Being there, he took command of all forces as a matter of course.

The rebels knew that Jannis van Bewerhoudt was away from Duurloo's. They knew also that more foreigners had been sent for, and at dawn of April nineteenth they made the all-out assault upon Duurloo's that had been so long planned.

Breffu, bearing a gun and fighting like a man, was among the leaders of the attack, which struck first at the protective ring of Blacks that surrounded the inner core of Whites. The Blacks fought back mightily, to save not the Whites, but themselves. The Whites, roused violently from their slumbers, knotted together behind their barricades and waited, reaping the benefit of the Blacks' self-defense.

The rebels had brought fire with them, and every building they could reach was put to the torch, along with every field and forest in the area.

The battle raged until full daylight made the visibility too good for the rebels' comfort. The attackers never penetrated to the white core of Duurloo's, but some of their bullets and arrows did, wounding a newly hired MESTERKNEGT called Frank Spaniard, young Jacob Stallart, and a slave guard, Andries. The black defenders, fighting from behind their barricades, lost not so many at first, but then the rebels surrounded and set fire to a warehouse where at least forty loyal slaves were hiding, armed only with bows and arrows which they had made for lack of guns. Many of them were burned to death; those who escaped the flames fought the rebels with arrows but ended up either killed or dragged away to be enslaved or, if recalcitrant, killed later.

The rebels began to pull back in the morning light, dragging their dead and wounded. The white inner core, unable to fire without endangering their FREE NEGRO and loyal slave JÆGERS in front of them, now followed John Charles in a charge after those bedeviling the burning storehouse. Charles and his men chased them up the bush path that led over the notch between Duurloo's Hill and Margret's, until The Old Englishman ran out of strength and sent his forces on ahead to salvage as many slaves as possible and kill the rebels. They did neither.

The failure to take Duurloo's despite their combined forces and the absence of Captain van Bewerhoudt was dispiriting to the rebels. In the recovery period that followed, not even Breffu was able, in the absence of sufficient food, to pump up their fighting power. She herself had been one of the leaders, and she had now lost face.

The Women reverted to its former state as an inter-tribal brothel and as a place where the women would raise vegetables for all the next time it rained.

Prince Aquashi and his Aquambos, their old headquarters at Vessuup's destroyed, took up residence at Aquashi's home PLAN-TAGE, Adrian Runnels's widow's estate, from which it was only a short distance to a vantage point for watching Duurloo's.

Kanta and his men drifted back to Ram's Head, then moved to

Jochum Stolley's, one of the poor PLANTAGES of the south, in Rif's Bay Quarter. That was not satisfactory for long; Kanta wished to be nearer to Duurloo's and in a position to keep an eye on Aquashi. Katrinaberg, anciently called Hammer Farm, was just up the valley from Aquashi, and Kanta decided to try that for a while.

King Clæs still liked Gabriel van Stell's point above Brown's Bay, even though the wooden parts of its buildings had been burned out and had to be crudely reconstructed. From there he could watch the English.

Drum communication continued for the time being, and the slaves assigned to make rum for the rebels in the still above Rif's Bay continued to work as usual.

Danish use of Native Troops (East Indies), MAPes MONDe Collection.

PART FIVE

Spider in the Horn

I

FOUR days and five hours after the end of the rebel attack on Duurloo's, two French ships sailed into TAPPUS harbor, signaling friendly intent. They saluted Christiansfort with their cannons and were thunderously saluted in return.

The ships anchored, and Chief Merchant Horn came ashore at Christiansfort to prepare the way for the French commander.

Gardelin met him at the dock.

"Never has any sight been more welcome to these eyes!" he cried. "But details, man! Details!"

"Ah," Horn sighed happily, raising his gaze to the distant skies, and spreading his arms in a French gesture of bliss as if he had been doing it all his life. "The French, they are a wondrous race!"

Walking rapidly with Gardelin to the fort, he told of his adventures in words that tumbled over each other in impatience.

"They welcomed me like royalty! France and Denmark are truly friends! Sainte Croix is ours—has been since August last, when the treaty was ratified—I have a copy of it and the purchase agreement here for you, with the compliments of General de Champigny."

"And eight months later we still have not been notified by KJØBENHAVN!" Gardelin cried, stopping and stamping his foot in annoyance.

"At any rate," Horn continued, "they treated me like a king. Wined and dined and womened me half to death—and what women!"

"Our little contract and haggling over terms amused the French—they tossed them into the wastebasket. 'Contracts!' they shouted at me. 'Who ever heard of contracts between friends? We shall simply help a friend!'

"So swiftly it made me dizzy, they raised a force of men—not only Blacks, but a detachment of their own citizens! Two hundred and twenty men, with arms and ammunition. They offered many more, but I feared we could not support so many. They outfitted two ships before I could bat my eyes."

"And what sort of man is the French commander?"

"A man of no nonsense—Longueville is his name—he wears the Order of the Star. And by the way, you had best send straightway for Pierre Castan to act as interpreter, for Longueville speaks nothing but French, and mine is not good enough."

"Now," Gardelin said, "let us prepare to welcome and provision these French avenging angels who fly to us so mercifully. I trust they will get to work quickly, without wasting too much of our food and wine. I trust also that you, being Vice-Commandant, and Commandant of Saint Jan, will accompany them to Coral Bay and see them ashore and properly treated."

"I suppose I must."

Commander Longueville got started at once; he was impatient to have done with the job and be away for home. There was barely time for Gardelin to send notifications up to St. Jan ahead of him.

II

Longueville was not long in writing to Gardelin of his progress.

Monsieur—

I entered the bush Thursday before daybreak, as I have had the honor of informing you that I would do. The Negro Cesar guided our march. We arrived by different routes at the habitation of Monsr. Bourdeaux. There I again dispersed the detachments, Cesar led the Free Negro one, and I scouted a nearby ravine and had the good luck to encounter the rebels. We killed four of them and wounded several; in pursuing them vigorously we arrived at their dwellings—I counted 25; after setting them afire, I sent the Free Negroes, who had rejoined me, to pursue them, and I took a road that to us appeared newly made by this rabble, who have not fought back one moment against us. I believe them to be at present completely dispersed in the bush, but I suspect Cesar of treachery. It is practically certain that he knows where they were, and he has not been willing to lead us there directly. He hesitated a long time, and when he saw that he could not delay any longer, he separated the FREE NEGRO Corps in two, which is the reason why we did not surprise the Aminas. Yesterday we beat the bush without encountering anything but a Negress whose head someone had cut off perhaps 2 hours before . . . Today I came to see Monsr. Bewerhoudt to ask him for some guides and a party of his men who can lead us in the area where the rebels are hiding. That is all we need, but I do not believe that he is able to do it. He, along with Monsr. Castan and Monsr. Froeling, feels that you should have the kindness to send 100 CREOLE Negroes, most trustworthy, armed with sabres, lances or bayonets, to bestow in several detachments suitable for running in the bush after these unfortunates. I think that this is the shortest means to end this affair, which could go on and on if we did not take all precautions necessary. It is impossible for my men to go through country that they do not know at all if they are not led by well versed people. That is what has been lacking up to now, Cesar being a traitor (or I am badly mistaken). . . .

I forgot to tell you that we have had one man slightly wounded in the arm. Thirty resolute men are more than enough to put an end to those rascals.

I have the honor to be very perfectly, Monsieur,

> Your very humble
> and very obedient servant,
> Longueville

* * *

Monsieur!

My men are extraordinarily fatigued. Yesterday I led them all to the camp with the intention of letting them rest, but Monsr. Barnds,

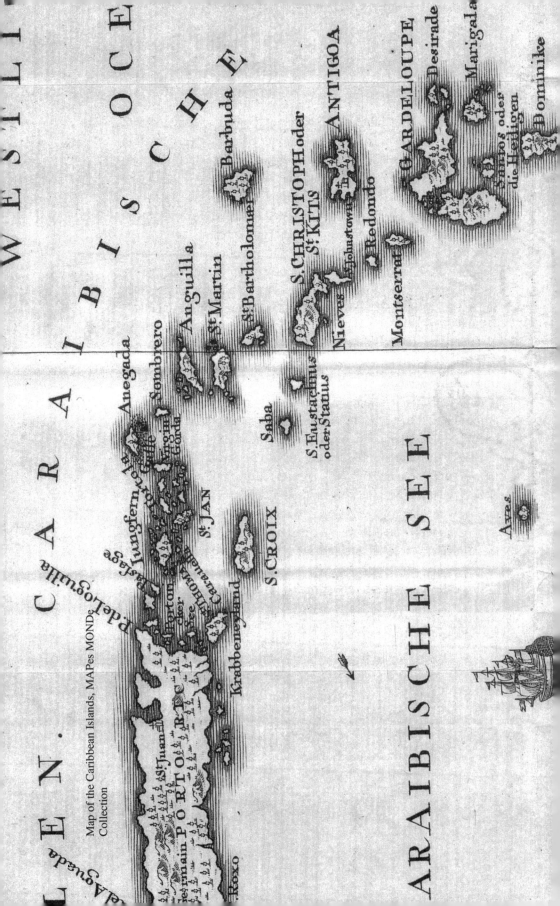

WESTLI... OCE...

CARAIBISCHE...

ARAIBISCHE SEE

Map of the Caribbean Islands, MAPes MONDe Collection

Barbuda

Anguilla

St Martin

St Bartholomew

Sombrero

Anegada

Jungfern Inseln

Porto Rico oder S. Juan

Virgin Gorda

Anegada

St JAN

Tortola

St THOMAS

Crabbeneyland

S. CROIX

Saba

S. Eustachius oder Statius

S. CHRISTOPH oder St KITS

ANTIGOA

Nieves

Redondo

Johnstown

Montserrat

GARDELOUPE

Desirade

Marigala...

Santos oder die Heiligen

Dominike

Aves

Roxo

St Juan

germain PORTO RICO

Krabbeneyland

Passage

P. de Loguilla

la Gueda

Santa Lucia
Alusia
S. Vincent
Bridgeto
Bekia
Granadinen
GRANADA
Gr. Boca
S. Iosepho
S. Ioseph
Testigos
Cola
Blanco
die 7 Tage
Margarita
Cona
S. Jago
Gudapitd
Golf von Curiaco
Verima
Comana
Tortuga
Perlen bank
Cona hagotta
Orchilla
White Klip
P. Caracolus
Of cheeradoti
Roca
Guiara
DER KRAAL
C. Blanco

who came to see me on your account, having seen smoke on a point when entering the port, caused me to judge that this could be the hideout of the rebels with the Negresses. I ordered formation of 3 forty-man detachments, each containing FREE NEGROES, to set out 2 hours before dawn. This was done. Monsr. Barnds had assured me that it would take only an hour on the road—and it took THREE—which caused the detachments to arrive after sunrise; furthermore, the guides did not know the first thing about the terrain. We missed all of those miserables with their women who had holed up there according to the conclusion drawn from Monsr. Barnds's having seen the smoke. That is the second time we have missed them because of not having been well led; it is astonishing that the Whites and Negroes that have been given us are so little acquainted with a little island which they have lived on for several years! The rebels are not more than 25 or 30, according to the report of several detachments who counted them from a distance as they got away. On top of a hill we found one who had just hanged himself, and another that they had killed the day before. The two heads were brought to me, and I exposed them on this savannah. We burned their habitations, numbering ten; one thing is certain: they are furiously disorganized and fleeing like sheep. Your Negroes, having been witnesses, have asked of me by Monsr. Castan to let them go after them. I let them. They ought to depart tonight. When my men are a little rested I shall send them hunting again, but it will be difficult to find the rebels assembled as they were. They have only four muskets of which not one is any good, if one can judge from the gun the one of them who was killed on Thursday had—which I intended for you to see, but the Negro in whose charge Monsr. Castan placed it, left it in the bush. You must have patience with my men, who are not too happy about being away from home so long. You may be sure that I will do all that I am supposed to do to succeed in the destruction of these miserable rebels who all deserve to suffer the most violent torment. I remain, Monsieur,

Your most humble and
obedient servant,
Longueville

At the camp on St. Jan,
the 3 May 1734

* * *

Monsieur!

I wish the party of CREOLE Negroes you have just sent might be of some use to us. These are not the people I need to reduce the rebels if we can find them. Twice we have missed them because of lack of good guides. Today the difficulty will be to find them. We suffer more from fatigue than from risk, running with these wretches, who think only of fleeing when we propose to pin them down. . . .

I have not mentioned the refreshments you sent. You know what you can afford. If the horned beasts you sent had been bigger they would have lasted longer. However, I still have three, but two of them are so little that they will not last a day at half a pound per man, as I am serving today.

Cesar, with 91 Negroes, was yesterday in the bush. Twenty-four of them were armed with muskets. I permitted them this on the assurance of Monsr. Castan that I could trust them. They returned yesterday evening without having seen anything from which we may draw any surmise as to where the rebels are. If they ask to go out again, I shall let them, although I doubt that they would dare to attack the rebels.

I remain, Monsieur,

> Your most humble and
> obedient servant,
> Longueville

Camp on St. Jan,
5 May 1734

* * *

Monsieur!

. . . Monsr. Bewerhoudt came to join me today with 18 Whites and 38 Negroes; this will help multiply the detachments which in the future will number no more than 1518 men; that is more than necessary to deal with the rebels be they all together, which unhappily they are not today—they are dispersed in all directions. Yesterday evening six of them were seen without the possibility of joining them; day before yesterday we took a youngster whom I am sending you—I am not sure he has the strength to get to St. Thomas. Monsr. Castan has questioned him on all particulars that might give us some clarification; he told us that the rebels were wanting to kill him when we found him on the point (the wounds he had were sufficient proof of that); that there were 13 of them who killed themselves not far from there; that they had no ammunition and had broken several of their guns; I had them threaten him that if he did not tell the truth I would hang him; he replied that if I wished he would take me to the spot; this morning I had him carried in a hammock to the place, to find out etc., and had him escorted by a detachment led by an officer, who reported having counted 11 cadavers, among which there were only two women; he found 4 smashed guns and one that was in perfect condition, along with a cutlass which he had caused to be brought along, and which I returned to Monsr. Castan. If all the others wished to destroy themselves likewise, you would soon be relieved of them, and they would save us a lot of pain and fatigue.

. . . Cesar is charmed to find his woman among the dead—at least that is what he says; as for his great fidelity, I do not know—the maneuver which he executed renders him suspect either of treachery or of the panic of terror. . . .

I have commanded the skipper of the BARQUE to take good care of the little Negro I put in his charge so that you may have the satisfaction of questioning him yourself.

I have the honor forever very perfectly to remain, Monsieur,

> Your very humble and
> very obedient servant,
> Longueville

At Camp, St. Jan
8 May 1734

P.S. I forgot, Monsieur, to tell you that I promised the Negroes you sent me four PIASTRES for each rebel head they bring me, and six PIASTRES for each live rebel. I trust you will not disapprove. They told me that they have had many promises made them that were not kept. I replied that I would pay them with my own money as fast as they bring me the heads, and they need not worry about me. They all seemed pleased. I wish I might find that way the means of finishing this whole affair. I believe this will be the only means left to you when I am gone—putting a price on heads—but you will have to be strict about paying what you have promised, otherwise you will never get the rebels completely destroyed. We used that method in Grenada. . . .

When Jannis van Bewerhoudt went to Coral Bay to join Longueville, he left a small force of loyal slaves to keep an eye on Duurloo's, old John Charles to keep an eye on them, and Bodger there for a rest suggested by Gardelin.

Gardelin considered his suggestion diabolically clever, for he had to worry about the wrath of Doctor Bodger if word got to him of the finding of the near-dead little January and the merciless use of him to identify rebels and implicate those concerning whom there might otherwise have been some doubt.

Anno 1734, 9 May, on orders from Governor Gardelin, an extra session of court was held at Christiansfort by Interim Judge Nissen in the presence of the Pedersen brothers, as official observers, to hear what the Negro boy January, belonging to Cornelius Frandsen BØDKER, had to say, who was captured along with the rebels on St. Jan, with whom he had lived from the very first, and as he had been perhaps mortally wounded by the Aminas, it was all the more important to question him. . . . He declared that the Company's Kanta, Suhm's Autria, Runnels's Coffie, Horn's Tjamba, Krøyer's Acra and another, Soetman's Sépuse, and three females, the Com-

pany's Bragatu and two others named Acubo and Bomboe, belonging to he-knew-not-whom, committed suicide at Ram's Head. They had six guns to kill themselves with; the last to kill himself broke up five of the guns and shot himself with the sixth; Kanta, the last one, first stabbed him (January) with a knife to kill him, but he fled and hid in the bush; also they sought to murder a Negress belonging to Castan who escaped from them. He enumerated 13 to 14 guns which the Aminas must still have, and a total of 25 guns which he knew they did have originally. Of powder he said they had only enough left to shoot themselves with, but cutlasses and bows-and-arrows they still have plenty of. They also murdered a Levango Negro belonging to Castan, at the Company PLANTAGE under the GRI-GRI tree.
. . .

—G. H. Nissen, Town Clerk

III

MONSIEUR!

This evening all detachments that I sent out to hunt the rebels returned. They neither met nor saw anything. I do not think it is possible to put an end to these unfortunates before my departure, which I cannot put off more than eight days longer, and that against the orders I have, but that you may witness the desire I have to be useful to you, I take it upon myself to remain the coming week, not that I persuade myself that I shall succeed with the rebels, being dispersed as they are, but for your satisfaction, and to give time to your inhabitants to return and take possession of their property, being convinced that the rebels are no longer in a position to harm them. Four men suffice to control them, you may be sure. This week I am going to send out small detachments to different habitations to keep these unfortunates always in check and in fear. All of my officers and even your people tell me that the bush is infested with bad odors, which makes us believe that more of them have killed themselves, without its being possible to find them, for we have searched diligently.

Mingo, though, has found a newborn baby, hanged.

Neither the Negroes nor Monsr. Bewerhoudt's crowd have done either their duty or their best by me. Particularly the Whites, who have amused themselves shooting at goats and at a young cow that they killed and ate along the seashore. These shots disturbed my men, who ran toward them, thinking it was the Negroes for whom they were hunting, but not at all! I swear to you, Monsieur, that things like that, committed by a people who have reason to be interested in our hunting with exactitude, disgust my men no end, who see people, who ought to be going through fire to help put an end to this unfortunate affair, appearing to care no more than if this matter did not concern them at all. . . .

I want nothing more than to be useful to you; I have not been as useful as I might have wished, but as useful as possible, please be sure of that and that I have the honor to be very perfectly,

> Monsieur,
> > Your most humble and
> > obedient servant,
> > Longueville

In camp on St. Jan,
The 14 May 1734

P.S. Cesar comes to me to ask permission to go to St. Thomas; as he is not at present of much use to us and as you will perhaps be glad to see him, I have permitted him to go; you will return him if you think it fitting. . . .

* * *

Monsieur!

I take this occasion, one of your settlers having asked permission to go to St. Thomas on personal business, to tell you that I have six Negroes and two Negresses in irons, by means of Monsr. Lambrecht DE COONING, who Saturday paid a visit to his plantation, and according to what he told me, he found his Negress with two of his Negroes, who indicated that they would like to surrender, if they would be pardoned. He promised them everything they wanted and had me notified yesterday afternoon through Monsr. Castan, on the field of battle. I sent to find them. He brought six of them, four Negroes and 2 Negresses. I had them questioned and I could see that Monsr. Lambrecht wanted them found innocent, but as they obstinately insisted that they had not seen the Minas or heard the gun shots on Ram's Head point when we found the rebels there, which could be heard all the way to the camp, then I concluded that these Negroes were guilty and had them put in irons. This morning I was told that they said there was still one Negro who had heard shots in the night and that he would tell many things if he were here. At once I summoned Lambrecht, whom I gave to understand that he must not for a moment think of saving his Negroes. If they were rebels, as they gave every appearance of being, this was a crime too black to let them off, and I ordered him to return to the spot where yesterday he found his Negroes. With this in mind, I had his Negress released so that he could take her with him, in order not to make those he found suspicious. He carried out the order very well, and returned with two Negroes, who will soon be put through the mill, because they were recognized, by several of the Negroes you sent me, as being rebels; so I count on burning the two miserables within a very few days, after having nevertheless extracted from them the greatest amount of elucidation possible. The better to succeed at this, if you, Monsieur, will kindly send me back the little Negro I sent you some time ago, he will serve us very well to discover the truth in the confrontation I shall make with those I hold in irons.

The great rainfall we have had has prevented my sending out the detachments which I had the honor of mentioning in my last letter. I have that same honor to be very perfectly,

Monsieur,
　　Your very humble and
　　obedient servant,
　　Longueville

At the Camp on St. Jan,
The 17 May 1734

* * *

Monsieur!

We have little news to impart to you. Yesterday we killed a Negro and a Negress whom we knew, from our prisoners, to have separated themselves from the rebels because of the decision to commit suicide, in which they did not have the courage to join. Unfortunately, they were killed very quickly and with one single coup. If we had been able to have just one wish, we might have had some enlightenment, of which we had great need, to know whether there remain still other rebels, of whom we find no further trace. Our detachments returned yesterday without having caught sight of a single one; which made us conjecture that perhaps they had destroyed themselves completely, as our prisoners assured us in their depositions.

Monsr. Bewerhoudt, who commanded the detachment of Danes, found two of them who appeared to have killed themselves about ten or twelve days previously, and another one, buried, of whom there was no way of telling how long ago he died. We knew from our prisoners that the women begged the men to kill them because they could no longer stand the fatigue, and that since the rout at Ram's Head point, the rebels searched for one of their principal leaders not knowing what they should do if they found him dead. They were supposed to kill themselves in that place, they told the Negroes we have in irons. . . .

> Monsieur,
>> Your very humble and
>> very obedient servant,
>> Longueville

At Camp, St. Jan,
20 May 1734

* * *

Monsieur!

You shall learn from Monsr. Horn of the executions we carried out yesterday. He brings with him 5 Negroes who do not deserve a lesser fate, nor do the 4 you doubtless had arrested, who seemed to me to be as guilty as those whom we burned. It is an accursed race, of which it is necessary to rid oneself totally of vigorous examples, if you wish to be safe.

There are two Negresses who accompany the four Negroes who are being returned to you, and the little wounded Negro whom I am sending back to you.

I beg you, Monsieur, to defer the execution of these unfortunates until I am in St. Thomas, that my men may witness the good and severe justice which you will mete out to the rebels, who not only do not deserve the least bit of mercy, but for whom it is impossible to imagine a torment sufficiently great to be proportionate to their crimes. . . .

> Your very humble and
> very obedient servant,
> Longueville

At camp on St. Jan
The 23 May 1734

* * *

To the Well-Born Heer Governor, Philip Gardelin:
Myn Heer!
   Since the departure of Herre Horn our chasseur Negroes have been out and found 20 Negro men dead on the point at Gabriel van Stell's, and 4 Negresses, who have been dead some eight days. Among them are King Clæs, Soedmann's Juni, Adrian Runnels's widow's Prins, Scipio and Sublica. Their guns were found smashed and brought in by our Negroes. We will inspect further.

J. van Bewerhoudt

St. Jan
23 May 1734

* * *

To Commander Sergeant Øttingen:
   We learn with surprise that one of the leaders of the rebellion, Breffu, whom none of us knew, and whom we assumed to be a man, having murdered my son Peder Krøyer and his beloved wife according to slave witnesses, is a woman! In case she be not among the suicides and come into your hands at any time, I pray you be in no way sparing of her because she is a woman. You will kindly make this order known to all and sundry.

Ph. Gardelin

Christiansfort, 24 May 1734

* * *

To Commander Sergeant Øttingen:

Since the sending off of my previous letter of this date, it has come to my attention that a loyal slave JÆGER who knew Breffu well and was with the party that discovered the suicides on Gabriel van Stell's Point, states that Breffu was among the dead. It is a pity that she is let off so easy.

Ph. Gardelin

Christiansfort, 24 May 1734

* * *

FISCAL Friis is hereby ordered without delay to take the following Negroes under examination:

The Negress Norche, belonging to
the glorious Company.
Friderich, belonging to Henningsen.
Pieter and Jacob and a Negress Susanna
with a little boy Pierre, belonging
to Lambrecht de Kooning

who have been in hiding since the revolt began until now on the seacoast they have surrendered.

Also three Negroes:

Vantje, belonging to Governor Moth,
Coffi, belonging to Willum Behrensen, and
Quassi, belonging to Isacq Runnels's widow,

who have admitted and previously been accused of having been with the rebels at the start.

And whereas justice must be appeased by making an example, without mercy, of all who have been accomplices in the execrable deed, although they may not have had a hand in the shedding of Christian blood, they must, however, be painfully examined until the truth come out, if there be room for the slightest suspicion in the matter.

And thereafter sentence is demanded according to the deserts of each, with the hardest death that can be thought up.

Ph. Gardelin

Christiansfort, 24 May 1734

* * *

Herre Jasper Jansen is hereby ordered to cause to be captured and brought to the fort the Negro Samba belonging to Pietter duer Loo.

And whereas he is accused of being one of the instigators of the revolt, therefore all the more care is to be taken that he shall not escape justice.

Ph. Gardelin

Christiansfort, 24 May 1734

* * *

For my own protection, in case of later questions as to my actions, I hereby privately file with you, Hr. FISCAL Friis, the following statement, to the effect that the Negro Samba, belonging to Sr. Pietter Duurloo, being taken by force on the St. Thomas PLANTAGE of the said Sr. Duurloo, was brought before me for questioning in regard to his activities as a rebel, but I received privately verbal instructions from Governor Gardelin to forget about any accusations against the said Samba, in view of the lack of good evidence against him, and it was stated in deference to the said Sr. Duurloo, in words to be unrecorded, that the said Samba was far too valuable a property, being the best sugar cooker in the land, to be endangered with destruction.

26 May 1734, by the hand of Gregers Nissen, Town Clerk, Interim Judge in place of Judge Hendrichsen, recently deceased.

IV

A show had to be arranged, according to Longueville's request, for the French, and it would be useful at the same time for making one more emphatic point with St. Thomas slaves who might have rebellion in the backs of their heads.

The selection of the victims took several days. The trials were long and strident. Confessions and betrayals were extracted by torture.

Doctor Bodger was still in Duurloo's Bay. This made it possible for the court to use little wounded January mercilessly for identification and exposure.

At last, five tormented creatures were selected from those sent down by Longueville after he had summarily burned alive his half of the captives adjudged by him culpable, as he had demanded the right to do. These five were put aside for the Roman spectacle set for Thursday, the twenty-seventh. The rest were either released, with a flogging on general principles, or sentenced to be worked to death, in chains, on the new fortifications being planned for Ste. Croix.

Gardelin issued orders to the Civil Guard to be on hand in full dress for the executions, and to round up a large audience of citizens and slaves.

On the twenty-seventh the French sailed down from St. Jan to

William Blake, ca 1790, from a painting by Stedman, ca 1775. A slave hung alive by the ribs to the gallows, MAPes MONDe Collection

TAPPUS. From the moment their sails appeared outside the harbor, the island of St. Thomas went thunderously wild, starting with the big guns of the fort, which fired so many salutes in such rapid succession that they finally had to be stilled for cooling. The outpourings of music, dancing, rum, flag waving, fireworks, and the firing into the air of small arms and cannons that greeted and surrounded the disembarking Frenchmen was so overwhelming, and for two days so impossible to interrupt, that the public executions of condemned rebels could not take place as scheduled. The Frenchmen, black and white, were taken into homes, hearts, and beds.

Commandant Longueville, coldly practical, held himself above the Saturnalia, only acknowledging the public acclaim with a bow and a wave from the elevated JUSTICE POST outside the fort.

In the evening, with the roar of the celebration going on outside, Gardelin banqueted Longueville and his officers in the fort, and for the night they were supplied with every delectation a Frenchman could desire.

By the evening of the twenty-eighth the celebration was beginning to slack as mass exhaustion set in. Gardelin ordered the execution of the condemned rebels for seven o'clock the following morning, Saturday, the twenty-ninth of May.

A great throng was present at the place of execution on the savannah of the Company's Sugar Estate. In the forefront, along with Gardelin, Horn, and SCHØNNEMANN, were placed the French guests, the officers seated, the men in ranks. Behind them on one side of the circle politely stood Company officialdom, business and civic, and on the other side the Civil Guard, properly accoutred; behind these were the lesser men, and in the rear of all, the least.

Never having fully understood their sentences, which had been read to them in official Danish, the five condemned ones were brought out to their execution.

They were three men and two women.

The men's sentences were identical: to be pinched in the customary way with red-hot tongs, then have their arms and legs smashed, stretched on the wheels, then be left there in the sun to die.

The women's sentences were merciful: to have their heads chopped off with an ax, the heads to be stuck up on poles.

One by one the men died on their three wheels. The onlookers endured the stench of burning flesh and the desperate, diminishing sounds of their screams.

The two women, not tortured, were too numb to scream. They shook uncontrollably until the last moment of their lives. Then their heads rolled on the ground as blood fountained from their neck arteries in the hearts' last convulsive beats.

Gardelin sat and watched the ground. What were the crimes for which these wretched ones died in such a spectacle?

Frederik, belonging to Andreas Henningsen, and so trusted that he and his wife had been the only inhabitants of Henningsen's Coral Bay PLANTAGE, illegally without supervision, died for having been an excellent African drummer at times and places adjudged wrong by his accusers.

The three hapless slaves of the orphaned Lambrecht DE COONING, Pieter and his wife Susanna—mercifully deprived of their child, Pierre—and Jacquo; their young master in the early morning of November twenty-third had told them to stay on the PLANTAGE and wait for him to come for them. They died for having told the Frenchman that they had not heard the suicide shots from Ram's Head when it seemed to the Frenchman impossible that they should not have heard.

And Norche—the Company's torch-eyed Norche, battling mistress of her bludgeoning MESTERKNEGT Svend Børgesen, until the very moment of his death. Norche's bloodied head, with its eyes peacefully closed, astonishing everyone, but its massive mouth hanging open in red horror, found its way atop a sharpened pole, paraded among the poor and the slaves, then set out on exhibition until it should become a skull along with Susanna's. She had tried to chop Svend Børgesen to death in that dawn of November twenty-third, but had failed; and then had gone on to be a camp-following convenience for the rebel males.

The guns of the fort began to roar in a salute to an arriving ship. It was the slave ship *GREVINDEN AF LAURVIGEN*, arriving from Africa.

She had lost much of her cargo to disease on a disastrous crossing. Her bill of lading, altered to less than half by circumstances and presented to Gardelin, read:

Good and healthy male slaves	60
Old and/or sick ditto	22
Good and healthy boys	7
Sick ditto	7
Good and healthy women	31
Old and/or sick ditto	43
Good and healthy girls	5
Sick ditto	5
	180

Even as he read it, one of the old and/or sick women died on the dock while being brought ashore; and soon thereafter two more women and one boy died ashore.

V

Dr. BODGER stayed in the haven of Duurloo's because no one indicated that he was needed at Coral Bay, and he was emotionally exhausted. The French had brought along their own medicine men, and Castan was with the Danish forces.

Bodger had received roundabout word from Christian Sost that all of his surviving slaves had managed to disengage themselves from the dispirited rebels and had returned to the home PLANTAGE in Coral Bay.

By the time Christian located Bodger at Duurloo's and told him of little January's plight, the holocaust at TAPPUS had ended. The French had started home.

So out-of-the-mainstream was Duurloo's by now that Bodger had difficulty getting transportation to town, but he finally clambered aboard a KANO that had brought supplies, and at last found himself in TAPPUS, where there was great excitement.

The day before, *EENIGHEDEN* had arrived at long last. Gardelin would be difficult to see.

In the matter of the little boy January, Bodger found himself faced with a fait accompli. Since ranting would now achieve nothing, he simply lifted January from the shelf on which he lay in Doctor Liebig's stinking sickhouse and took him to his temporary lodgings in the back room of Madame Stage's rooming house.

The child was unaware that, by being as truthful as he knew how, he had made certainties of uncertainties and sent a horrifying list of slaves to death. Bodger resolved never to spell it out to him; but he knew that the knowledge of it among the slaves would dog January throughout his life.

That life apparently was assured, for the present. With remarkable stubbornness the child was fighting off the near-fatal effects of the multiple stabbings the frantic Kanta had inflicted on him.

Bodger made him comfortable, put him to sleep with one of Christian Sost's bush potions, and went in search of an interview with Gardelin. To his surprise, he was admitted at once.

"Come, Nelli BØDKER!" Gardelin barked the instant he set eyes on him. "An end now, once and for all, to your treasonable—what can I call it, never having seen its like?"

"Tell me about it in your own words," Bodger said, "and I will try to put a name to it for you."

"It has come to our attention that there were three factions, groups, whatever, of rebels. Two of them, the Aminas and the Adampes, have been destroyed, or have destroyed themselves. But of the third, the Aquambos, there is not, has not been, the slightest sign anywhere. We know now that their leader, Madame Runnels's Prince, originally reported among the dead at Gabriel van Stell's point, was wrongly identified because of decomposition and the action of scavengers, and is presumably still alive and at large.

"Were it not for these Aquambos it would now be completely safe for all planters to return to St. Jan and resume their normal lives. It is important that they do so, for we must have the crops they could raise and the purchases they would make."

"Are they holding back?" Bodger asked.

"They will return—perhaps not the ones who have been so badly frightened as to desert the islands and their property, but in their places others will take over the Saint Jan PLANTAGES because of the tax freedom we have granted, placing the island once more virtually in its original category of colonization, but with most of the work already done.

"But some of the better planters are holding back, particularly those with Aquambo rebels, unaccounted for, among their slave holdings. Madame Runnels, for example, refuses to put Estate Adrian back to work because of the danger to her loyal slaves and her equipment and crops, so long as Prince what's-his-name— Aquashi?—Aquashi and his followers are at large. Now, I know perfectly well that you know where this Aquashi is hiding, and how many followers he has."

"Then you know more than I do," Bodger said. "I have lost all contact with the rebels. Since the moment I was assigned to the VÆRN, where they had no access to me, I have not, to my knowledge, seen a rebel, alive, except from a distance. I have not seen Prince Aquashi or any of his men, even from a distance, so far as I know."

"A likely story!" Gardelin protested. "What have you been doing all this time at Duurloo's?"

"Stealing your money."

"What do you mean, stealing my money?"

"Being—I trust!—paid by you for sitting there, doing next to nothing, resting, thinking, trying to rescue my soul from the pit of fire."

"Oh, bilgewater!" Gardelin exclaimed. "Speak comprehensible Danish, and tell me where the Aquambos are hiding!"

"I sincerely hope," Bodger said, "that they have found a way to get to Puerto Rico, and are now free men and women, even at the price of learning to be good Catholics!"

"This is precisely what I might expect from you!"

"You might expect a great deal more, after obviously tricking me into leaving you with a free hand to torture my little boy January, of whose desperate troubles I had no knowledge, thanks to you!"

"Oh, that. Well, a man must do what he must do—and you know very well you would have been insufferable."

"You may guess how insufferable. But now you must suffer me."

"Oh, come, you can change nothing now. And I have plenty to suffer. But how can I complain, really? I mean, with the French angels of mercy having come out of the blue to save us . . ."

Bodger nodded. "I am minded of Castan's sister, destroyed by a spider that just by chance hid in the horn of her carriage slave. These French, moved by the whim of their king a myriad miles away, wanting the Polish throne in the family—equally unpredictably they come and smash the rebel Africans on Saint Jan . . ."

"Yes," Gardelin said absently, not even hearing what Bodger said, "and *EENIGHEDEN* finally arrived. She had to winter over in Norway because of troubles with ship and weather, and then she had a dreadful crossing, with everyone sick and near to dying. She brings the long-delayed notification of the acquisition of Sainte Croix."

Shuddering visibly, he pointed to the envelope in which the copy of the treaty was enclosed. Beneath the address there was a note: "In case Herre Gardelin is dead, this is to be opened by the Governor pro tem on St. Thomas."

Bodger could not help chuckling.

"You fooled them, eh?" he said.

"Barely," Gardelin said. "At least I had time to open it, but I may not last much longer." He paused. "I have no pleasure in informing you, what I was about to have to write you, that you are appointed official physician to the new project on Sainte Croix. This is, of course, because in Kjøbenhavn they have not yet heard of your perfidy—and because everyone here knows that you will be badly needed on Sainte Croix. You will receive an augmented salary, which is fixed in the official papers I shall hand you when the time comes."

"Well!" Bodger exclaimed softly. "That is a piece of news! I admit that it is not unwelcome, for our bloodied little isle of Saint Jan is, for the present, a place of heartbreak to me."

He saw that once more Gardelin was not listening. After a few moments, Gardelin said, "I presume that even from the loftiness of my position I can still reach down and call you my friend."

"I daresay you can manage it," Bodger said.

"Well, *EENIGHEDEN* struck me a blow across the face. The ship and all its contents are for the benefit, not of Saint Thomas and Saint Jan, but of Sainte Croix. It brought no manpower for my use, to replace those who have died or served their time and choose to go home."

"What do you mean, for your use? You will have use of them on Sainte Croix."

"Well, ah . . . it seems I shall have no say on Sainte Croix. His Majesty himself has ordained that that rich isle shall be separately governed by Seigneur Moth, with responsibility directly to KJØBEN-HAVN. It will shortly become my duty to swear Moth in as governor."

Bodger watched Gardelin's Adam's apple go up and down in an effort to swallow saliva that was not flowing.

"Oh," Bodger said, subdued. "It pays, then, to have a father who is an intimate of the King."

"I know not what it pays. I doubt that Herre Moth is desirous of the job. I think rather that he is commanded to it in order to see that it be done right."

"Come, now. I am not here to listen to you run yourself down. You must have other troubles."

"Indeed!" Gardelin walked toward the window. "Øttingen is about to scour Saint Jan for missing rebels.

"Aha!" Bodger interrupted. "I wager he goes accompanied by a heavily armed guard and that he travels in the very center of his escort!"

Gardelin smiled fleetingly. "Be not unkind to a coward," he said, "lest cowardice come upon you in the night. But the worry I have is that innocent slaves, working their masters' PLANTAGES, will become frightened at sight of the armed white men. If they run, Øttingen will shoot or capture them as rebels. How do I prevent that?"

"Put it up to each master to explain to his workers, and make them understand, that the armed men will come and that they must stand stock still when they see them."

"Good! It is done. Perhaps you had better sit here and deal with these matters."

"Gladly. I hereby cancel Øttingen's orders to find and kill or capture any remaining rebels."

"Get out of here!"

VI

ØTTINGEN, with his bodyguard, was making his rounds on St. Jan, under orders to look for rebel remnants and check on PLANTAGES restored to cultivation. Cesar Singal had been sent once more by Gardelin to serve as guide.

Bypassing Øttingen, Cesar made his way back to Gardelin with the word that Prince Aquashi and his shrunken band of followers hiding in the bush had at last lost heart and were willing to return to work, if they could do so with impunity.

Gardelin was so overjoyed by this news, so relieved to learn of it, that he was sincerely ready to welcome Prince Aquashi back into the fold, all forgiven, with no penalties. He sent Cesar Singal straight back to St. Jan with specific instructions to Øttingen: let Cesar take word to Prince Aquashi that he and his followers, unarmed, should meet Øttingen at Aquashi's vacant home PLANTAGE at high noon on a given day, and Øttingen would then and there certify him and his people as once more respectable members of the St. Jan slave force. If their owners no longer wished their services, then the Company would purchase them and install them at the Coral Bay PLANTAGE.

At high noon on the appointed day, Prince Aquashi came, betraying a deep respect for the white man's honor, to Estate Adrian, his home PLANTAGE, leading his fourteen scraggy, dispirited, frightened followers. He walked erect, slowly, unarmed, through the arched gateway to the main compound, looking neither to right nor to left, but in an intently listening attitude.

Sergeant Øttingen, taking careful aim from behind a barricaded window, shot him dead at quarters so close that it was impossible to miss, and his bodyguard rushed out of hiding to surround the hapless followers before they could flee.

Øttingen cut off Aquashi's head and packed it, bloody and wadded with rags, in a leather porter-bag, as Jannis van Bewerhoudt arrived on horseback from his PLANTAGE down the GUT to investigate the sound of the shot.

Jannis was overjoyed at this development—for now he could bring his family back home—but he did not propose to let Gardelin set any of these Aquambos free.

He sent runners to gather a committee of planters at Duurloo's Bay, and he and this delegation escorted Øttingen to Christiansfort with his grisly luggage and fourteen captives.

Gardelin had to give in to the overwhelming pressure of planters of both St. Jan and St. Thomas. Of the fourteen Aquambo followers, six were tortured to death and four were sentenced to be worked to death on the Ste. Croix fortifications; the other four died in The Trunk before being put to trial.

Øttingen was paid the reward previously offered for a rebel leader, dead or alive, and for his bravery when attacked by Aquashi was promoted to Lieutenant. The men of his platoon were honored and rewarded.

The rebellion was now ended, at a cash cost to the Company finally reckoned at 6,884 RIGSDALERS, 3 kroner, 13 stivers.

VII

BODGER was ready to make his leisurely way to Ste. Croix.

He chartered the sloop *La Puisante,* because her skipper, Pierre Leon Puisant, was familiar with the Ste. Croix reefs and waters—and was furthermore an interesting, spirited traveling companion, with enough compassion and understanding in his flashing French-mulatto eyes to help lift Bodger's spirits, and Bodger was in need of any pleasure he could find.

Bodger felt a great affection for this lighthearted, book-loving man, partly because of a conversation he had once had with him. "I treasure every bit of my black blood," Puisant had said in the course of it. "I must, because of the high value the white man puts upon it. It appears to be very powerful blood indeed."

"You mean . . ."

"If a white man have a single drop of so-called black blood, he is forever black; but even if a black man have a great deal of so-called white blood, he is still forever black."

"I take your meaning. Greatest joke the white race ever played upon itself!"

"It is no joke," Puisant had said, laughing heartily as if to belie himself. "It is simple modesty!"

Saying goodby to Gardelin and the few others on St. Thomas who were interested in bidding him godspeed was easy enough for Bodger, but his stepsons, Hans and Peter, were another matter. They frantically wanted to go to Ste. Croix with him.

"But," he told them patiently, "you will be much better off here with your Aunt Margaritha, for the present. I know not what the conditions on Sainte Croix may be—but most of all, you can get your education here. The English schoolmaster Kemp can teach you in Danish, Dutch, and English, according to your needs and my wishes."

It was so settled, with little satisfaction on either side, and Bodger went aboard *La Puisante* to set sail first for Duurloo's Bay. He could not go away without a last farewell to The Old Englishman and the rest of St. Jan.

He found that John Charles had returned to his own PLANTAGE, and Duurloo's was being put back to work, with slaves cleaning out the weeds and bushlings that had accumulated in the BARCADS.

He borrowed a horse, promising to send it back, asked Puisant to sail around to Coral Bay and wait for him, and set out to ride overland.

Throughout the West End area, everywhere Bodger went or

looked, the PLANTAGES were coming back to life.

Riding up the GUT from Little Cruz Bay, he gave close attention to the deserted little PLANTAGE of the Boufferons children, for he had some plans involving it. It was overgrown, but the rebels had not harmed it.

Higher up, Peder Sørensen was back in residence with his Dina, the children, and slaves. Bodger shouted his goodby across the narrow GUT.

The KILL-DEVIL Widows at the top of the GUT were making rum again, but for lack of cane the production was limited.

Nearby, John Charles had his wife back with him from Jost van Dyke, and Bodger stopped for a quick visit. As Bodger left, Charles seemed depressed, and as he said goodby his farewell was oddly sentimental and earnestly cordial.

Susannaberg was being manned by slaves, but Susanna was not there.

Bewerhoudtsberg had Jannis and Maria and the children, and many slaves. The sounds of it were not the old happy ones, and Jannis was not his old laughing, high-riding self but deeply, perhaps permanently embittered—changed in other ways too, perhaps, for Maria now seemed strangely happy.

On Bodger rode, and on, glad to be alone, with only a horse for breathing company.

At Magens' Rustenburg, high at the top of the island, he stopped, for there, suddenly beside him, was old Cesar Singal, wanting to talk.

"Cesar!" Bodger cried, dismounting and clapping him on the back.

"MESTER Bodger. I am glad to see you."

Bodger looked into Cesar's hooded eyes. "It has been a strange, sad time, has it not?"

"Indeed it has," Cesar said. "You leave the island now, I hear? You go away from here?"

"Yes."

"But why? This land has need of you."

"Perhaps it does. I know not how much good I can truly do. At any rate, I feel a need to go to something else, for a while, at least, until my spirits are restored."

"My spirits," Cesar said, looking at the ground, "will never be restored."

"Come," Bodger said, gesturing to a low terrace edge, "let us sit and talk a bit. Now, what is this about the spirits?"

"I am tired of being a slave. I must have my freedom."

"That is good, but can you sustain it, without slaves of your own?"

"No," Cesar said bitterly.

"I will help you as I can, and I know some others will, to purchase your freedom whenever you see your way clear ahead. Meanwhile, what can I do?"

"You can abolish slavery!" Cesar burst out angrily.

"You speak in general terms, of course. I wish I had it in my power to abolish slavery, and I shall always speak against it."

"While practicing it!" Cesar said.

"While practicing it," Bodger said calmly. "It is the system under which we all survive, at present, and meanwhile we can work against it little by little, as we may. What more can I do?"

"You can lie awake nights feeling guilt for the hundred years, the two hundred, three hundred—how many years?—of enslavement of the black man by the white!"

"Oh, shit!" Bodger exclaimed. "Where does it all end? I bear a heavy burden as a white man, a burden of guilt. But so do you, as a Negro."

"How is this?"

"I am willing to feel guilty, night and day, for the enslavement of Negroes, and for this enslavement you are entitled to the same number of hundreds of years of bigotry, if you truly wish to poison yourself so. But I insist that you in turn, while balancing the books of bigotry, feel guilt for your part in the enslavement of the Black by the White. The master part of you must feel guilty for selling black bodies for profit to the white man; but the slave part of you must feel even more guilty for being so lacking in self-respect as to stand for being sold. Do you not see how ridiculous it is, demanding bookkeeping for all the rights and wrongs of the past? Can we not get on with the truly important work of changing all these idiocies—the custom of the White, of whatever skin color, to be master, and the unworthy custom of the Black to be slave? The way is through the building of your totally unassailable feeling of respect for yourself and the self-respect of every other enslaved man in the world, white, black, red, yellow, or brown. Do you honestly think that the Negro is the one man on earth who has within him the capability of being enslaved? Do you know that men of all colors, in many parts of the world, are similarly lacking in pride and are therefore similarly enslaved? No, you would perhaps not know, not having been there. Well, I have been there, and I know, for I have seen it. Such men have always been slaves since time, or the keeping of it, began, and doubtless longer. How many years is it now—perhaps three hundred—since the white man, encouraged by your sales of your own kind to Arabs, began to buy you from your rulers along the African west coast? For those, let us say three hundred years, I am willing to feel guilty. Feel you guilty for your craven part in it!

"I confuse you, do I not?" he said, more gently. "I am myself confused."

Cesar, anger still in his eyes, turned away. "You confuse me, yes."

"I am sorry. Let us be mere men together and go on from here."

"Go from here? To what? To more slavery!"

"Why? Must you be slaves?"

"But what is the—ah, the . . .?"

"What is the alternative?"

"Yes, what is the alternative?"

"You know very well what it is. You fight against enslavement. You die, if necessary . . ."

"But we are—you know that—we are—in spite of what you have seen these past months, we are by nature a gentle people."

Bodger looked at him with compassion and frustration.

"Well," he said softly, "you will eventually have to make up your minds what kind of people you are."

With his hand on Cesar's shoulder for goodby, he turned away.

He walked to his horse, mounted slowly, and rode at a walk for Coral Bay, head bowed, looking back once and waving at the still, twisted figure.

He had gone perhaps a quarter-mile when he had to turn back, kicking his horse into a gallop, for he heard a shot ring out behind him and knew instantly, with sinking heart and a sudden anguished scream, what it meant.

Cesar Singal had gone straight to his hut, and taken up the gun that no one knew he had, and shot himself through the open mouth.

VIII

At Coral Bay the next day Bodger spent the morning with his remaining slaves, packing his few possessions aboard the boat. Then he took all of his slaves and their belongings on board Puisant's sloop, without explanation.

The little ship ran easily down the bay, rounded the rearing monument to rebel blood, Ram's Head, on great lifting and swooping swells, and ballooned along the wind past the disconsolate south shore of St. Jan to Little Cruz Bay at the west end. On the way, Bodger rehearsed with Christian Sost the various bush medicines with which he wished to be as familiar as possible.

At Little Cruz Bay he asked Skipper Puisant to wait out the afternoon for him, and shepherded his slaves ashore and up Margret Gut to the Boufferons plantage.

Here he stopped. The moment had come when he must make his speech.

First, he presented Christian Sost with a document that set him free. Christian said nothing, for the moment, but lifted his head to stare at the peak of Margret Hill above the plantage.

Then Bodger spoke, as simply as he could, to all his slaves together. He told them that he had leased this plantage for the use of Christian Sost. He hoped that Christian would care to operate it for his own benefit and theirs. Some day the Boufferons family might wish to return, and if that happened, there would always be another suitable PLANTAGE made available.

He told them that when any one of them felt completely sure that he wished his freedom he might have it.

"I am convinced that Christian Sost is now capable of sustaining himself and all of you, as master of this PLANTAGE. As a physician he can earn extra funds, food, other supplies, or services. He is able to bleed patients, draw teeth, weigh out medicines according to prescription, apply plasters and poultices—I suggest that, until you feel sure of sustaining freedom in safety, you trust yourselves to him as slaves—except January, who is automatically free, never having been purchased as a slave. Christian will of course free all of you when the proper time comes. If I have not made myself fully understood, Christian will help me to do so."

It was a long speech, and Bodger wished that to be the end of it. He did not wish the protestations of gratitude that followed when all was made clear to everyone, with Christian's help.

Little January was the only silent one. He simply clung to Bodger.

Christian Sost sought Bodger's right hand and pressed it. "I believe you know, sir, what I cannot adequately say." Bodger could only clap Christian on the shoulder affectionately.

"What not one of you seems to understand," he finally said, "is that I owe you inexpressible gratitude for having been, of all unimaginable things, my slaves. Good God, how can you bring yourselves to thank me for anything?

"Damn it, my eyes run over! I must go. The day is waning and the boat waits. Make what you can of the little PLANTAGE, and go on from here as far as you can. I shall come and see you whenever I am able, wherever you are. Please, come not with me to the shore."

He took his left hand gently away from January and pressed the child's head against his side.

January wept without cries or words as Bodger walked away.

Anchor up, *La Puisante* fell off before the breeze to push out of the bay. Well beyond the reef the skipper hauled her mainsheet through croaking blocks to quarter the wind, tightened her jib, and headed her, nodding, nodding, southward.

Bodger looked back, now, at the lovely hills of St. Jan and the incredible beauty of its shoreline. In the light that was beginning to fail, the pelicans were busily at work stocking up for the long night. They dove like bullets through the air, but struck the water all aclutter to stun their prey.

As they came up, tossing their catch in their pouches with a gobbling motion, the little white citizens of summer here, the terns—"half-half birds"—came fluttering to perch atop their heads, demanding, in plain English, "Half! Half!" and helping themselves to supper out of the permissive pelicans' pouches.

There was at least that to smile about, and Cornelius Frandsen Bodger smiled.

auf der See zur linken ein Stück von St Thomas
Westende zur rechten Keyen. Betha

The first Protestant Mission to the Slaves in the New World came to St. Thomas in 1...
the year before the St. John rebellion. This is the view of the fields being clea...
overlooking the Bethanian Mission, St. John and beyond to Pillsbury Sound and...
Thomas. *C.G.A. Oldendorp, 1767*, MAPes MONDe Collection

Jan. } In St. Jan zur rechten hinten eine Kleine Plantage, weiter forn die reformirte Kirche, in der Mitte Bethanien

GLOSSARY

LIST OF PRINCIPAL CHARACTERS

Glossary

Accustomed slave. A slave born in slavery and knowing no other kind of life.

Agave. Century plant.

Anole. A type of lizard; it likes to live in human habitations, where it does its best to keep the place insect-free.

Arse gratia artis. A play on the Latin "Ars gratia artis" (Art for art's sake).

Barcad (Dutch **Creole**). Field. Actually it means "barricade." A field, on this rocky island, was created by removing the stones from the soil and piling them along the boundaries, automatically forming a barricade around the field.

Barque. In those days and in that part of the world, the barque was not necessarily a three- or four-masted vessel. The local version was likely to have a single short mast and an unusually long boom.

Binne (Dutch **Creole**). Inside. When approaching a house, it was customary, for politeness' sake, to stop at some distance away and call out, "Binne." If no one answered, one was to turn and go away without approaching closer. The custom is observed to this day, but using the English word.

Bødker (Danish). Barrel-maker (cooper).

Bolus armeniac. A powdery red soil from Armenia that was actually used as medicine.

Bomba (**Creole**). Slave-driver (foreman of a slave crew, himself a slave).

Buite (Dutch **Creole**). Outside.

Bullet-tree. A tropical timber and shade tree (*combretum* family), whose wood is so dense and heavy that it was often used in the absence of lead to make bullets.

Bussal. A slave newly or recently—within one year—imported from Africa.

Café con leche (Spanish). Coffee with milk.

Calabash-gourd. Gourd-like fruit of the calabash tree.

Calelu (variously spelled c[k]allaloo, kaleloo, etc.). A ground-vine with edible (delicious) leaves somewhat like spinach, but milder. *(Ed.). The original leaf used by the Amerindians, from whom the word derives, was a wild Amaranth with a high protein content; its use spread to Africa in the earliest colonial period, where various leaves were used, especially Taro leaf or Elephant Ear, introduced late from the Pacific and reintroduced into the Caribbean. The vine is an even later Asian introduction, but Amaranth is still used.*

Catch-and-keep. An entangling briar plant with hooked thorns that catch and keep the passer-by.

Charata. **Agave,** century plant.

Chasseur (French). Literally, "chaser"; hunter.

Chawing the cud, etc. Edmund Spenser, *The Faerie Queene*, V, vi.

Chirurgeon. Surgeon.

Contra-gangrænam (Latin). Against gangrene.

Creole (Ed.): European stock native in the New World.

Cresset lamp. An iron bowl, hanging by chains or, as in this case, elevated on an iron post, containing oil or pitch, for outdoor illumination.

Dannebrog (Danish). Literally "Danish breeches." It got its name during a sea battle when the Danish flag was shot away by the enemy and was immediately and defiantly replaced by a pair of red breeches; from that time onward, the Danish sea flag was shaped, more and more vaguely, like a pair of trousers.

De Cooning, De Windt, etc. The Dutch "De" means "The" and is capitalized in names, unlike the French "de" which means "of."

Den Elskelige Jomfru (Danish). The Lovable Virgin.

Djambi. In the Africa of that day, a serious term for the spirit world. In the Virgin Islands it was transmuted to "**jumbie**," and lost much of its seriousness, becoming something like the mischievous poltergeist, but still, to this day, to be feared by a few, half-feared by many.

Dronning(en) (Danish). (The) Queen.

Eendragten (Danish). The One Suit.

Eenigheden (Danish). The Unity.

Ell. A unit of measurement that has varied from time to time and place to place. I believe that at that time and place it was equivalent to about sixty-eight centimeters.

Ellubè. I don't know what herb this is.

Etui (French). A small carrying case; at that time and place, a doctor's handbag for medicines and instruments.

Factory. An establishment for factors and merchants carrying on business in a foreign country. *(Ed.). A fortified trading post.*

Firkin. Originally a quarter-barrel, it was at this time a measure not consistently determinable today. The amount varied with the nature of the commodity and with local custom.

Fiscal. A government attorney.

Fishpot (Ed.). A fish trap.

Flambée-stok (**Creole**). A torch, of **torchwood**, a pitch-rich jungle wood.

Flux. Dysentery.

Free Man. A landless black man who came, not as a slave, from elsewhere, but who had not yet achieved status enough in the community to make it unnecessary to call attention to the fact that he was free.

Free Negro. An ex-slave in these islands who possessed a piece of paper on which it was officially stated that he was now free. Either he had been given his freedom as a gift or he had earned the money with which to purchase himself.

Free Slave. A black man of local origin not in possession of a certificate of freedom, but still belonging officially to no one, even himself. I do not know how a man might have arrived in this state of suspension.

Galliot. An inter-island sailing vessel of the day, with a long-footed, short-gaffed mainsail.

Gecko. A nocturnal lizard.

Gemütlichkeit (German). A word ranging in meaning all the way from cheerfulness through friendliness to coziness; there is no one word in English that defines it.

Genip. A fruit and shade tree (*Melicocca bijuga*) of the Caribbean.

Georg De Tweede (Dutch). George II.

Gjambo (African). Okra (gumbo).

Gombee drum. A small African hand-drum held between the knees or under an arm. It was made by stretching a goatskin over the open end of a short piece of hollowed log.

Grevinden af Laurvigen (Danish). The Countess of Laurwig.

Grigri. A superb timber and shade tree of the family *combretum*

Guinea corn. A kind of millet. *(Ed.). Sorghum.*

Guinea grass. A coarse, very tall grass that grows in individual clumps; imported, early on, from the Guinea coast of Africa.

Gut (Dutch **Creole**). Ranges in meaning from "gully" to "ravine," like the arroyo of the American southwest and the wadi of North Africa.

Haab(et) (Danish). (The) Hope.

Half-slave. A slave aged between twelve and sixteen, taxed to the master at half the adult rate. Above sixteen everyone, slave and free, was an adult, fully taxable at 2 ½ **rigsdalers** per head. Children under twelve were not counted in the census because not taxable.

Hem le slæp (Dutch **Creole**). He's asleep.

Hem sa rie (Dutch **Creole**). He shall ride.

Horse latitudes. A region in the Atlantic Ocean normally at about 30 North, in which the winds are fickle, weak, or totally lacking. Sailing ships often were stuck there for long periods, resorting sometimes to oars. Dead horses that had died of starvation when food ran out, floating in the sea here, gave the area its name.

Horse mill. A platform and machine using horse (or mule) power to press the juice from sugar cane.

Hystera (Greek). Womb.

Ignames (French). Now pronounced "yams," in the islands as well as in the U.S.

Indian corn. The ancestor of present-day American corn. *(Ed.). Maize.*

Jack-spaniard wasp. Similar to the American yellowjacket, and just as irascible.

Jæger. In eighteenth-century Danish, this word had its original meaning, "pursuer," **chasseur**.

Jeat (**Slave talk**). Eat.

Jeg lugter fisk (Danish). I smell fish.

Ju da ken mi (**Slave talk**). So you know me.

Jumbie. Local spelling of the African "djambi."

Ju sa kom (**Slave talk**). You shall come.

Ju slaaf sa rie? (**Slave talk**). Your slave shall *ride?*

Justice post. A post to which a person was bound for punishment by whipping or other tortures.

Kabæn (eighteenth-century "island Danish"). Crude pallet for sleeping on the floor.

Kakkatess (Dutch **Creole**). Lizard.

Kamina (**Slave talk**). A local colloquialism applied to a field slave.

Kano. Not really a canoe, because heavier, but in general inspired by the American canoe.

Kapmesser (German). Literally "top knife," it was a cane-topping cutlass.

Kasha. A pestiferous shrub. *(Ed.) a wickedly thorny* Acacia.

Kiddle. A weirlike, netted arrangement for catching fish.

Kill-devil. The product of the first distillation on the way to producing rum. **Kjeltum** was the product of the second distillation. **Kill-devil** was so raw and strong that it could obviously kill the devil himself. For the use of the thirsty masses, one distillation was considered sufficient.

Kjæreste (Danish). Darling (literally "dearest")

Kjeltum (Latinized Danish). The high quality rum of the clay in the Danish West Indies.

Kjøbenhavn (Modern spelling, "København"). Now colloquially called "Copenhagen," even, frequently, in København. The "ø" in Danish gives the same sound as the German "ö".

Koffardimand (Danish). Literally "merchant shipping man," it was a heavily armed merchant ship.

Kompni nega mi' hoot (**Slave talk**). Company Negroes with wood.

Lignum vitæ (Latin). Wood of life. *Lignum vitæ* is one of the hardest, most dense of all woods.

Lingua franca (Latin). Common tongue (i.e., common language).

Lussing (Danish). Whipping. Far more serious than the modern meaning of the word: a box on the ear.

Maby. A local beer made (at that time) from the inner bark of various trees. To this day *maby* is made in rural areas of the Virgin Islands, but it does not resemble the eighteenth-century *maby.*

Makombi. Now called Camelberg.

Malagasy. Native of Madagascar.

Malaguette. An antiscorbutic that was thought to have other beneficial qualities.

Mampi (Dutch **Creole**). The midge, or sand fly, a tiny insect with biting propensities out of all proportion to its size.

Mampoo (also spelled mampu). A member of the four-o'clock family of trees, of the genus *mirabilis.*

Manjack. A member of the borage family of trees.

Manqueron. From the French "manquer," meaning "to be lacking." It meant a mutilated or otherwise damaged slave who could do only light work in kitchen, garden, or barnyard. Planters were not taxed for **manquerons**.

Maran. A pestiferous shrub of the islands; but its extremely coarse and tough leaves were very useful in scrubbing pots and pans.

Maron. Originally "cimarron," a Spanish-American word meaning "wild, unruly." Most people in the West Indies thought of it as meaning "ape." A runaway slave. *(Ed.). Maroon. The first black non-Moorish slaves common in Spain were called Camaroons, after their country. Runaways to the "Cima," or mountain peaks, were called Cimaroons from which cimarron and maroon derive.*

Mester. In Danish it means "master." In the eighteenth century, in connection with Dr. Bodger, it signified that he was a "master barber." Barbering was, in effect, the origin of the medical profession; barbers developed the art or science of bleeding patients to relieve (it was thought) various illnesses. This was done with suction cups (small cups that were heated before application to the skin; as they cooled, a vacuum was created inside them which sucked blood through the skin), or by surgically opening blood vessels and allowing blood to flow. In 1733, the word "mester" before his name entitled Bodger to be thought of as a doctor.

Mesterknegt (Danish). Overseer.

Mestizo. A person of mixed blood.

Middag (Danish). Lunch (noon).

Min mo'r har dans't med skyerne (Danish). My mother has danced with clouds.

Missie sa jeat (**Slave talk**). Mistress shall eat.

Molle-molle. An East Indian cotton muslin.

Monkey-pod gutters. The monkey-pod tree is hollow, and when split can be—was, in those days, in the absence of aluminum and galvanized iron—used as gutters to catch the rain coming off a roof and convey it to rain barrels or cisterns.

Morruk, cabé (Dutch **Creole**). Good morning, friend, but somewhat more familiar than "friend," more like "pal."

Morruk, mesta (Dutch **Creole**). Good morning, Master.

Morruk, mi vrien (Dutch **Creole**). Good morning, my friend.

Mumble-djambi. Mumbo-jumbo.

Muscovado (from vulgar Latin via Portuguese; has nothing to do with Moscow, in spite of appearances). The first coarse sugar precipitated in the sugar-boiling pots. The *muscovado* was shipped, wet, to Denmark for refining into the various household and industrial forms of sugar.

Obi. Known in the United States as obeah; an African form of sorcery and witchcraft.

Old-line slave. Same as **accustomed slave**, but with an implication of many generations of slave ancestry.

Osnaburg. A coarse cotton fabric, like gunny-sacking, made at Osnabruck, in northern Germany.

Outside. Illegitimate, when applied to offspring.

Pekelvlees (Dutch). Pickled (salted) meat.

Penistone. A coarse woolen cloth, often blue, from England—used only for slaves, as a rule.

Piastre. The same as a **piece of eight** at that time.

Pièce des Indes (French). Literally, "coin of the Indies." A slave as a commodity of trade.

Piece of eight. The Spanish eight-real coin of the day—the Spanish dollar.

Pinguin. A spiny bromiliacious plant that makes a very effective hedge against intruders.

Plantage (French). Meaning "a patch of ground under cultivation"—for some reason the Danes used this word, or a variation of it (*plantagie*) to mean "plantation."

Poorjack. A dried and salted fish, generally hake or cod, virtually inedible; the word was applied also as an adjective to the poor people who had to eat it.

Potfish. Small frying fish caught in a fish pot, or trap.

Pulvis tormentillæ (Latin). The powdered root of the Spanish tormentil plant; a powerful astringent used medically at that time.

Rigsdaler. The Danish dollar.

Rus en vre (**Slave talk**). Keep quiet (rest—i.e., remain—at peace).

Sa (**Slave talk**). Shall.

Salop (Dutch **Creole**). A large leafed vegetable.

Schijtkop (Dutch and Dutch **Creole**). Shithead.

Schønnemann (German). Beautiful man.

Servinger (Danish). Plural of "serving."

Six-glass. Six o'clock by the hourglass.

Slave talk. A bastardized Dutch **Creole**. (Ed.): Technically a pidgin language is made up of words and grammar of two or more languages spoken by persons who need a means of communication other than their native language. A **Creole** language evolves when subsequent generations grow up speaking this as their native tongue.

Slave time. Dawn was arbitrarily four o'clock, the beginning of a slave's day. Sundown was arbitrarily six o'clock, the end of the field slave's working day. The hours in between were marked sometimes by a "sun pin" (a perpendicular spike in a board, which acted as a crude sundial), an hourglass, if anyone took the trouble to turn it over every hour, or, most commonly, a sense of what time it was as a result of the position of the sun and observing the shadows it cast.

Sno de mun (**Slave talk**). Shut up. (Close the mouth.)

'Statius. St. Eustatius (Eustachius), a Dutch Caribbean island.

Suckerdons. An East Indian muslin.

Tania. Like the taro; a mildly sweet root vegetable.

Tan-tan. Wild tamarind, a pestiferous shrub that can survive almost anything, and spreads "like wildfire" when there is any moisture at all in the soil.

Taphouse. (Ed.) Tavern.

Tappus. A group of six villages—Charlotte Amalia North and South, Christianstad North and South, The Brandenburgerie, and the **Free Negro** village—called collectively "Tappus" because of the **taphouse**, known to sailors everywhere, near Christiansfort. The six have long since merged into the capital city Charlotte Amalie, unofficially and incorrectly called "St. Thomas." (Ed.): also Taphus. The combined town was named after the Danish Queen Charlotte Amalia in 1690, but acquired its present spelling in 1936 after the United States postal service issued a commemorative stamp with the misspelling.

Torchwood. A tropical tree, and the wood from it, which is very rich in pitch, like pitch pine; used, of course, for torches.

Tre kabaj (Dutch **Creole**, but of Spanish origin: *tres caballos*). Three horses.

Tschickefell (Ed.). Whip.

Turpentine tree (Bursera simaruba). No relative of the pine tree of the North; it merely smells like turpentine when cut.

Tutu. A conch shell made into a horn by cutting off the tip end; the name is from the sound it makes when properly blown.

Værn (Ed.). Fort.

Vier a di, etc. (**Slave talk**) Four of them; they jumped out of the bush, grabbed the breakfast and water the children brought.

Wahtah fo trik (**Slave talk**). Water to drink. There were two kinds of water—drinking (fresh) and washing (brackish).

Wa ka ha plats? (**Slave talk**). What happened? (What has taken place?)

Wa wil ju heh? (**Slave talk**). What do you want here?

Werdær? (Dutch **Creole**). Who's there?

Woman's-tongue tree. One of the mimosas. The everlasting rattling of its dry seed pods caused by the slightest breeze gave it, obviously with masculine help, its name.

List of Principal Characters

ABEDO (called Haly; also called Maby, for the local beer he loved). Slave of the Suhm **plantage** and Aquambo nobleman.

ABRAHAM. See Odolo; not to be confused with Sødtmann's or Sørensen's Abraham.

ANDERSEN, Jens. Mesterknegt on the Suhm **plantage**, Coral Bay, St. Jan.

APINDA. Male Company slave, a **bussal** nobleman called Emanuel, assigned to Frederiksværn as a special bearer.

AQUASHI, Prince. A prince of the Aquambo tribe in Africa, enslaved on Estate Adrian, St. Jan.

ASARI. The eunuch, majordomo of Magistrate Sødtmann's household on St. Jan.

BARNDS, WILLIAM (Danish name Berents, also spelled Behrensen). Anglophile Danish planter and sailor.

BODGER, CORNELIUS FRANDSEN (Danish name Bødker). The Company **chirurgeon** and physician on St. Jan.

BOLOMBO (also called King Clæs). A king of the Adampe tribe in Africa, under-**bomba** on Suhm **plantage**, Coral Bay.

BØRGESEN, SVEND. Head **mesterknegt** on the Company's Coral Bay, St. Jan, **plantage**.

BREFFU. Female slave of Peder Krøyer, wife of the drunkard, Christian.

CAFÉ. Female slave at Bewerhoudtsberg **plantage**.

CASTAN, PIERRE. French Huguenot leech, planter on St. Jan, neighbor of Peder Krøyer; husband of Elisabeth.

CESAR. Trusted slave at Bewerhoudtsberg **plantage**; not to be confused with Cesar Singal.

CHARLES, JOHN. The Old Englishman. Former actor, now a small planter on St. Jan.

CHRISTIAN. Drunkard slave of Peder Krøyer, husband of Krøyer's Breffu; not to be confused with **Schønnemann**'s Christian, who attached himself to Bolombo, or with **Free Negro** Emanuel Christian.

CREUTZER, JOHAN JACOB. Ship chandler and planter on St. Thomas, owner of a **plantage** on St. Jan's East End peninsula.

DE COONING, LAMBRECHT. Teen-age proprietor of a small **plantage** on the south shore of Coral Bay, St. Jan.

FRØLING, LIEUTENANT PEDER. Commandant, mostly in absentia of Frederiksværn, Coral Bay, St. Jan.

GABRIEL, JAN. Soldier of the garrison of Christiansfort, St. Thomas, then transferred to St. Jan shortly before the rebellion.

GARDELIN, PHILIP. Governor of the Danish West Indies and head of the Danish West India and Guinea Company operations in the Danish West Indies.

GRØNNEWALD, ISACK. Dutch Reformed minister resident of St. Jan.

HISSING, HELENA. Stepdaughter and ward of Magistrate Johannes Reimert Sødtmann on St. Jan.

HORN, JOHAN. Chief Merchant and Chief Bookkeeper of the Danish West India and Guinea Company on St. Thomas, second in command under Governor Gardelin.

JANUARY. Eight-year-old orphaned African child, taken home and cured by Dr. Bodger.

JUDICIA. Female slave of Pierre Castan; number two wife of Bolombo (King Clæs).

JUNI. Indian-Negro-White **bomba** on Magistrate Sødtmann's **plantage** in Coral Bay, St. Jan.

KANTA. A lesser nobleman of the Amina tribe in Africa, an assistant **bomba** on the Company **plantage** on St. Jan.

KING CLÆS. See Bolombo.

KRØYER, MARIANNE. Wife of Peder Krøyer and sister of planter Pierre Castan's wife Elisabeth.

KRØYER, PEDER. A stepson of the deceased **Creole** wife of Governor Gardelin, claimed as a son by Gardelin for sentimental reasons.

LONGUEVILLE. Commander of the French forces sent from Martinique to put an end to the rebellion on St. Jan.

MINNEBECK, HANS and PETER. Stepsons of Dr. Bodger.

MOTH, FREDERIK. Danish nobleman, former governor of the Danish West Indies, the true power figure of the islands.

NORCHE. Slave concubine of Svend Børgesen.

ODOLO. An **accustomed** male **slave** called Abraham by the Whites, of Amina origin.

ØTTINGEN, SERGEANT. Demoted lieutenant at Christiansfort, St. Thomas; sent to St. Jan as head of military forces at the start of the rebellion.

QUASSI. Male slave of Susannaberg, St. Jan; not to be confused with Quassi of Estate Annaberg.

RUNNELS, SUSANNA. Young widowed proprietor of Susannaberg **plantage**, St. Jan; daughter of Jannis van Bewerhoudt.

SAMBA. Male slave of Duurloo **plantage**, St. Jan; the finest sugar cooker on the island.

SANTJE. Household slave of Peder Krøyer; not to be confused with Hendrichsen's Santje.

SINGAL, CESAR. Brilliant but physically deformed slave of the Magens family on St. Thomas, serving on their St. Jan **plantages** Rustenberg and Adventure. Wife Martje.

SØDTMANN, BIRGITTA SWAIN. Wife of Magistrate Johannes Reimert Sødtmann of St. Jan. Mother of Helena Hissing by an earlier marriage.

SØDTMANN, JOHANNES REIMERT (called Reimo by intimates). Magistrate of the island of St. Jan, living in Coral Bay. Son-in-law of the deceased **Creole** wife of Governor Gardelin—claimed as a son by Gardelin for sentimental reasons.

SØRENSEN, PEDER. Owner of a small **plantage** behind Little Cruz Bay, St. Jan. Husband of Dina.

SOST, CHRISTIAN. Highly educated slave of Congo origin belonging to Dr. Bodger and acting as his assistant.

SULLIVAN, DENNIS (Denis Sylvan to the Danes, spelling by ear). **Mesterknegt** in charge of sugar operations on the Company **plantage** at Coral Bay, St. Jan.

TAMARIN, MINGO (also Mingo Sobe). **Free Negro** organizer and captain of the **Free Negro** Corps of St. Thomas.

VAN BEWERHOUDT, ELISABETH. One of The "**Kill-devil** Widows," with her sister Anna Matheusen.

VAN BEWERHOUDT, JOHANNES (called Jannis). Proprietor of Bewerhoudtsberg **plantage**.

VAN BEWERHOUDT, MARIA. Wife of Johannes van Bewerhoudt and daughter of Pietter Duurloo.

VAN STELL, DIDRIK AND LIEVEN. Brothers. Owners of a **plantage** at Mary Point.

VAN STELL, GABRIEL. Close neighbor, with his wife Neltje, and friend of Peder and Marianne Krøyer, in Brown's Bay, St. Jan.

VAN STELL, NELTJE. Wife of Gabriel van Stell.

VESSUUP, WILLIAM. A St. Thomas Dane who owned a huge **plantage** on St. Jan's north side. Had fled to Tortola to avoid prosecution for murder.

William Blake, ca 1790, Allegory of Europe supported by Africa and America, MAPes
MONDe Collection

Hilly Part, St. John, *A.C.R. Carstensen*, Denmark, MAPes MONDe Collection

Printed in Italy
by Marchesi Grafiche Editoriali - Rome
on acid free Carta Palatina Fabriano

MAPes MONDe Editore